I0564033

Make Nice

Make Nice

Mark Pritchard

HEAT SEEKING PUBLISHING
SAN FRANCISCO

This book is a work of fiction. Aside from the obvious celebrities, politicians and other historical figures named herein—the statements and actions of whom are entirely fictional as depicted and of the author's invention—any resemblance to real persons, living or dead, or to actual events, is entirely coincidental.

MAKE NICE. Copyright © 2003 by Mark Pritchard. All rights reserved. Printed in the United States of America. No part of this book may be used or reproduced in any manner whatsoever without written permission except in the case of brief quotations embodied in critical comments, articles or reviews. For information, write the publisher, Heat Seeking Publishing, 1516 Alabama Street, San Francisco, Calif. 94110.

www.toobeautiful.org/makenice.html

ISBN: 978-0-615-34838-4

First edition.

2 4 6 8 9 7 5 3 1

for Cris

Chapter 1

1

We're shooting interiors for *Ocean's 11* in Hollywood, having wrapped up the Vegas scenes a couple weeks before. It's Monday morning, and I'm dead tired. Inbetween shots I try to get some sleep off to the side, but fat chance of that. When you're working for Frank Sinatra, there are no breaks.

While I'm sleeping, Frank and Dean put a dress on me—not on me, but around me—and a bonnet on my head, and they stick a baby bottle in my hand. And then they start singing a lullaby. I am so dead that I don't wake up for this even. They go on singing, they sing louder and louder, the crew is standing there laughing their asses off. Finally I wake up and realize what's going on. I look around and get the picture: the dress, the baby bottle—and I throw the bottle and hit Frank smack on the forehead.

Well, he doesn't get sore. It's still part of his big joke. But then he acts like a baby fighting with another baby in kindergarten. He starts yelling baby talk and swinging at me, slapping me. Imagine Sinatra, at the top of his career—movie star, TV star, recording artist, famous leader of the Rat Pack—yelling "Goo goo goo goo, you hit me! Bad baby, nasty baby, I fwight you!"

I have to go along with it. This is key. If you don't play along with Frank, that's when he gets sore. Look at it this way—I'd rather have Frank play tricks on me than ignore me completely.

So I put up my dukes, and Dean is making like a fight announcer now—"It's the Fighting Dago versus the Battling Jew, the Dago throws a right, another right, now a left—the Jew is slipping the punches, he's circling..."

I'm thinking, if I had my own dressing room, this wouldn't happen.

When we were in Vegas earlier in the month, we would shoot this picture all day, play the Sands until past midnight, then stay up til almost dawn playing cards. Shoot, eat, perform, then drink and play cards, night after night. Maybe getting a couple of hours of sleep a night.

At the end of those four weeks, I got what I thought was a big break—five consecutive weekends headlining the Riviera in Vegas. The biggest gig of my life.

Then filming on *Ocean's 11* resumed in L.A., with a makeup call on Monday morning just nine hours after I walk off the stage in Vegas. So I drove all night to get here. When you look at *Ocean's 11* now, you can tell the scenes I shot on Mondays. Some of those scenes where we're all standing around, planning the heist, all of us squeezing into the shot at once? I look dead on my feet. This casino heist that's supposed to make us all millionaires, and I look like I think it's the most boring shit ever.

Well, the boxing match woke me up and we did the shot. One take—that's the thing about Frank, he wants to get things done in one take—then it's on to another setup. They need to take out a wall and shoot from the other side of the set, and that takes a half hour. I pick up a chair and look for some dark corner, telling an A.D. to come find me when it's time for the shot, but not to tell anybody where I am no matter what they say.

I find a hiding place and close my eyes. After a minute and a half, no more, there's Frank again. "Hey! You're sleepin' on the job."

I cover my face with my hands. "Frank, for God's sake—I did a show in Vegas last night, then I drove all night to get here. I've worked all day, and now all I want to do is go home to bed. Have mercy for God's sake!"

"Driving all night, what kind of movie actor does that? You're a star now, get a plane."

"Frank, not everybody's a big shot like you. Where should I get a plane?"

He sits down in a chair next to me. "Okay, cheapskate. So get a driver."

"Sure, why don't you ask—" I was about to say "Why don't you ask one of your Mafia pals?" but I stopped myself.

"You don't need some big bruiser like Ed"—that was Frank's driver at the time. "Some kid'll do it for fifty bucks a week."

I agree, closing my eyes again. Maybe if I can just get twenty minutes, I can make it through the rest of the day.

Oblivious, Frank lights a cigarette and starts talking about his next project, a war picture. "Or more precisely, it's set during the war. About the only American soldier who was executed for desertion in World War II. *The Execution of Private Slovik.*"

"What—it's about an execution?" I ask around a yawn.

"It's really a courtroom drama, like *The Caine Mutiny,* you know? The guy is a conscientious objector, only he doesn't figure it out until he's in the Army and over in Europe. When the time comes to pull the trigger, he can't do it. He deserts. He gets picked up, and there's a court martial. That's the heart of it, where the guy has a chance to speak his mind about his beliefs."

"Sounds controversial."

"You don't know the half of it."

Now I remember hearing about this project. A blacklisted screenwriter named Albert Maltz—one of the Hollywood Ten who wouldn't knuckle under to McCarthy—wrote the script. The John Birch types are screaming because they think his script is somehow anti-American. But Frank likes the guy. They worked together in the past.

That's not why Frank wants to do it, though. Ever since he resurrected his career in *From Here to Eternity,* where he played an Army deserter who gets the crap beaten out of him by Ernest Borgnine, Frank's loved playing martyrs. Now with this *Slovik* picture, he gets a chance not only to play another martyr—who gets executed, no less—but one who has noble values. He gets, I'm guessing, a big showy courtroom speech.

Better yet, not only is the main character an underdog, but so is the writer. So Frank can play the martyr in the movie, while in real life playing the hero by resurrecting this poor loser's career.

Of course, that's not exactly the way Frank puts it. All he says is, "I want to do something about this blacklist hooey. Take a stand. See?"

"Sounds wonderful, Frank," I say. "Controversial, as you said. But a great role for you." If I can only get ten minutes of sleep before the next shot...

"And for you, Bobby. Guess what I got in mind for you. You're gonna be the lawyer. A smart Jewish lawyer who takes the kid's case because he believes in the American right to be a conscientious objector. The guy is fair, objective. And complex—he doesn't like the fact that Slovik deserted, especially because it's just come out what the Nazis are doing to the Jews over there. And yet he believes in the kid's right to a fair trial. You'd have a lot of scenes—big scenes. How's that sound?"

Now I wake up. "Frank— what a part. You kidding? It sounds great!"

"It's not a sure thing yet, Bobby, so don't get too excited. I'm getting pressure from some people not to do the picture at all."

"Yeah, I heard about that."

"But I think I can stand up to it." He slaps me on the knee, stands up, and goes off toward the set. I hear his voice saying to somebody, "Whattaya say we blow this joint and get some drinks?"

2

Thrown with imperfect spiral, a football looms against an overcast sky— larger and larger as Gene runs under it, his hands reaching out awkwardly. He skids to a stop right before he runs into a yellow Cadillac. The ball bounces off the Caddy's roof with a thud.

The passer is another parking valet, dressed like Gene in a dark yellow jacket with black lapels and collar. When the ball hits the Caddy, he flinches and looks around for the boss. Gene trots between cars and locates the ball underneath a pink-and-cream Bonneville convertible.

Trotting back across the parking lot, Gene says, "Geez, Kenny, you tryin' to kill me?"

"Kinda took off on me."

"Me versus a Cadillac. Some odds."

"Didn't dent the car, did it?"

"Dent the car—I'll dent the car." Gene flips the ball to Kenny, who fakes a passing motion.

"Because if it did, I'm blaming you." Kenny hesitates as Gene takes off again, cutting across the gravelly asphalt, where the odds are even between slipping on the gravel or twisting an ankle in a pothole. Kenny throws and the ball sails over Gene's head again.

A black Lincoln turns into the lot, driven by a third valet. "White New Yorker!" he calls out. Kenny sprints off across the parking lot, looking back to see if Gene is going to try a pass. But Gene is leaning on the Lincoln, catching his breath. After a second he reaches into his pocket and pulls out a paperback.

"Hey, don't read. Park the car," says the other valet, Tom. He's older than Gene and Kenny and considers it his prerogative to order them around.

"'*Paak* the *caa*,'" Gene repeats, attempting to imitate the voice of the presidential candidate from Massachusetts. "If I yam elected President, everyone will have a *caa* to *paak*."

"Keep readin' and you *won't* have a car to park," Tom says. "What the heck is so interesting?"

"*On the Road*," Gene says. "Hey, did I tell you I met Kennedy?"

"Oh yeah, when?"

"He was in town earlier this year. Campaigning," Gene says, his face neutral, his voice as casual as he can make it.

"I never heard about it."

"Well, that's how he talks: 'We need to address our problems with *vigga*.'"

"'Vigga?'"

"Vigor. But he says *vigga*."

Tom shakes his head, walking away. No sense of humor. He keeps himself aloof from Gene and Kenny, as if their juvenile antics couldn't possibly amuse him.

Kenny fetches the ghost-white Chrysler and Gene gets in. They drive around the corner to Chasen's Restaurant. A tuxedoed man is waiting deferentially next to a knockout blond. The blond comes around to the driver's side—it's obviously her car, only a woman or a fairy would own a white New Yorker with gold trim—and Kenny holds the door open for her as Gene does the same for the anonymous man. The woman is glowing, warm, and she gives Kenny a complicit smile for less than a second while simultaneously pressing a bill into his hand. She sits and swivels her legs into position as Kenny thanks her and shuts the door.

She pulls away, and a big, black Cadillac pulls up. Kenny opens its door and a tall man with a pompadour unfolds himself from the driver's seat. "Good evening, Mr. Martin."

The famous singer and actor mumbles, "'Bout an hour" without looking back. He passes into the restaurant, barely nodding at the doorman.

Kenny pulls away in Dean Martin's Cadillac as another, even larger, car arrives. Its doors fly open on their own before Gene can get to them. An enormous bodyguard emerges, brushing Gene out of the way and walking around to hold the passenger door open.

Passersby on the sidewalk stop and whisper frantically to each other; a flashbulb goes off. A small, lithe black man—Sammy Davis Jr.—emerges from the shotgun seat, lights a cigarette, and laughs at something a short, dapper man has said. Between them, straightening up and briefly looking around, is Frank Sinatra. He takes a cigarette out of his mouth and tosses it into the gutter as he steps forward and accepts the doorman's greeting. Sinatra is warm with the doorman, calls him by name, makes a joke, slips him a bill as the party disappears inside.

"What the fuck are you lookin' at?" the doorman yells at Gene. "Go park the fucking car! And have it ready in an instant when it's needed!"

Gene leaps into the car and slams the door, but still takes a moment to assess the vehicle. The driver has left it running, and there's freezing air pouring out of the A.C., battling the cigarette smoke and the smell of whiskey. On the seat rests a matchbook from the Santa Ana racetrack. Then the doorman leans down to look menacingly into the passenger window, and Gene pulls away.

Frank Sinatra's car! Gene reaches up to adjust the rearview mirror, but then remembering the palooka who had emerged from the driver's seat, thinks better of it. He switches on the radio fully expecting Sinatra's voice to come flowing forth, singing "One of Those Things" or "Luck Be a Lady." What he gets is a Chrysler commercial. "The man on the move knows what he wants!"

Rounding the block, he passes the car dealerships and appliance repair shops and beauty salons that look the same all across the country. Nothing to tell him he's driving in Hollywood, nothing to announce that just around the corner is Chasen's, packed with movie stars and singers and important people. Gene's three months as a parking valet have made him realize that, threaded among the regular working stiffs, the way gold dust is mixed with common soil, are the stars. They motor between movie studios and restaurants, recording studios and bars, racetracks and glamorous mansions—the stars and directors, and the behind-the-scenes people who are just as important. They're there, down on the streets, all the time; you just have to be aware of them.

He turns into the lot, does a big U-turn, and points Frank Sinatra's car right back out toward the street. He jumps smiling from behind the wheel, takes a rag from his pocket, and starts wiping down the door handles and the chrome.

The boss has arrived, a fat man named Irv who favors green shirts and yellow ties. Standing near the tiny office shack, he spits toward the gutter and asks, "Just what do you think you're doin'?"

"Gotta have this ready at a moment's notice."

"Oh really? Whose car is it, hot shot?"

"This is Frank Sinatra's car."

Irv sighs, pursing out his lips. He turns his head and sees Kenny walking back from the rear of the parking lot, where he's parked a shiny black Cadillac. "Hey, you. Whose car is that Cadillac?"

"Dean Martin's."

Irv turns back to Gene. "What's good enough for one dago is good enough for another," Irv says. "Take the fucking car back into the lot."

"I wanna wash the windows," Gene says, filling up a bucket.

"What are you, his butler? Who pays your salary around here, hot shot? Why don't you wash *my* windows?"

"Are you gonna tip me a hundred bucks?"

"I'm gonna kick your ass a hundred bucks."

Gene ignores him, going over the windows like he's prepping the car for a prom date. Then he hangs the doors open to air the car out while he removes any water drips.

Kenny returns from the restaurant with another car, but can't get into the lot because the Lincoln's in the way. Cursing, Irv walks over and slams the doors, startling Gene, who is cleaning out the ashtrays. "This is a parking lot, not a car wash! Get your nose out of that
fucking car before I kill you." Gene obliges him, getting out of the car, but then starts trotting back toward Chasen's. Irv shouts, "Hey, don't leave it here. Hey!"

* * *

Frank likes telling everybody what to order, and he makes a big joke out of whether or not I'm going to eat the antipasti. "Are you sure you want to eat that? I think that came from something with a cloven hoof!"

"Frank, I'm so hungry I don't care if it came from a unicorn, I'm going to eat it."

Sammy sings, "The unicorn / was never born / with more than one protrusion." He grabs a lit candle out of the holder on the table and holds it to his forehead, "It saw a wildebeest one day / And cried, 'What an illusion!'"

Dean says, "What the fuck is that, Alice in Wonderland?"

"It's a kid's thing I did a few years ago," Sammy explains.

"A kid's thing! When are you gonna grow up, junior?"

"I dunno, daddy, somebody told me this is as big as I get."

It's like we're always on. Everyone always kidding, always topping everybody else. We keep it up until something interrupts.

While we're eating, the maitre d' comes into the private room — there are a couple of fairly big bouncers at the door, and Frank's factotum Hank is eating with us, on a corner of the table — and mumbles something in Frank's ear. I see him frown, but he says "Sure."

Enter Maltz, the blacklisted writer, in a five-year-old brown suit. German, maybe, with a sharp, hungry face. He has the look of a guy who used to be in good shape but has lost weight.

"Hello, Albert," Frank greets him, no longer scowling but being polite. "Sit down, have something to eat."

"Thanks, Frank—no," he waves a waiter away. "I don't want to intrude."

This is ridiculous since obviously he is already intruding. But fine, the quicker the better. Frank pours him some wine at least. "Your health."

"And to you," Maltz replies.

"How are things?" Frank says politely, as if they're just running into each other at the gas station.

"Frank, you know. The *Herald-Examiner* today said—did you see it? No?—they published an editorial about our picture, *Private Slovik.*"

"Oh yeah?"

"Nothing direct, of course. They didn't even mention you or me. They just said that when the entertainment world tries to get into politics, a higher standard applies."

Frank sits back, wipes his mouth. "A higher standard!"

"That's a good one," Sammy says.

"A higher payola," Dean says.

"You got it with you? One of you guys," Frank says to the bouncers, "Go get me a *Herald-Examiner.*"

"There's more, but that's the gist of it," Maltz says. "Frank, I know you're getting a lot of pressure on this."

Frank shrugs. He doesn't mind if people think he's on the hot seat, but this transparent attempt to butter him up is getting nowhere.

Maltz goes on, "And I think what we should do is make an announcement."

At this Frank turns back to his plate. Just this physical movement, I can see, is something that should tell Maltz to back off, but he doesn't know Frank like I do.

"If you meet the press," Maltz goes on, "hold a news conference, tell them that you won't succumb to pressure—that this is a worthy story and you're going to make the movie. That's what we need."

Frank has been shoveling food in during this speech and there is a pause while he chews. He puts his fork down, takes a mouthful of wine, and swallows. "Maybe what you need." He lifts his napkin and wipes his mouth again. He doesn't look as enthusiastic about the picture as he did just an hour ago, that's for sure. I break out into a quiet sweat.

"The project needs it," Maltz persists.

"Albert," Frank says, taking on his fatherly voice, a voice which mixes a gentle tone with an aloof, somewhat judicial distance—"You know who I got a call from this afternoon? After we wrapped? Who called me in my dressing room?"

"I give up, who?"

"Cardinal Cushing."

"No kidding."

"Hey, I thought the Cardinals traded him to the Giants," Sammy pipes up.

"The Roman Catholic Cardinal, ya dope," says Dino. "The Archbishop-and-then-some."

"He called me personally," Frank goes on. "And told me how important it was for John Kennedy to get elected."

"Sure," Maltz says, uncertainly.

"He knows I'm backing Kennedy, and he wanted me to do everything in my power to help him. This man is a prince of the church," Frank says reverently.

"A man for all seasons," Dean says in the same tone, though he gives me a merry look.

"A chip off the ol' block," I chime in.

Frank holds up a hand to still us. "I cannot ignore the call of my church."

Maltz looks around the table. "Frank, this is not a religious issue! This is just a movie about some poor shmoe. It's *anti-capital punishment*, for Chri—for cryin' out loud. It's moral." Frank seems to consider this. For a moment I think the tension will pass.

But Maltz goes too far. "Compared to some of the movies you make—I mean, that are made—"

We all wince simultaneously, except Frank, who is jumping to his feet. He reaches down and tugs on Maltz's tie and shirt and, more through force of will than anything else, lifts him out of his chair.

"You two-bit pinko," Frank snarls. "What the fuck do you know about morality?"

We all jump up. Hank is the slowest to rise; he does so wiping his mouth.

"I try to pull you up out of the trash heap, and this is what I get? Ungrateful louse!" Frank gives Maltz a shake and propels him toward the door. Hank takes him by the arm, almost charitably, preventing him from hitting the door frame. At this moment a waiter appears with a copy of the *Herald-Examiner*, and seeing the commotion, steps back, wide-eyed.

Frank shakes his finger under Maltz' nose. "Do you realize any other respectable person would not get within ten miles of you? That I am the only one, out of respect for the work we've done together, who'll touch you with a ten-foot pole? And you try to tell me what's moral? You fucking atheist!"

"Frank, for God's sake," Maltz whines, trying to straighten himself. "It's just a movie. It's not even a movie yet—it's just a development project."

"There is no more project!" Frank screams. He takes the newspaper from the cringing waiter and whacks Maltz over the head with it. Maltz flings up his hands to protect himself, turns to flee, and receives a kick in the ass. "You can take your commie script, and your fucking army deserter, and go to hell!" Throws the newspaper after the escaping writer.

Dean is already going back to his place and sitting down. His face is cool, ironic. He lifts another bite of lasagna to his mouth. "Let's get some more drinks in here," he proposes. Sammy goes back to the table too but doesn't have a chance to sit.

"Let's blow," Frank orders. "I'm going to the head. I'll see you bastards outside." He exits, followed by Ed, who has managed to grab one last bite before he goes to ask for the car.

I sit down for a second, light Sammy a cigarette and another for me. The three of us sigh.

Then Dean says, in mock scandal, "An *atheist.*"

4

At the parking lot, Sinatra's Lincoln is still poised for launch in the driveway. Kenny pulls up in a big Chrysler and says out the window, "Brown Impala."

Gene fetches the beater and drives it to Chasen's; the interior reeks of cigarettes and failure. He opens the windows but the fetid Los Angeles air is no help and he cranks them up again. He had been tipped a single dollar when the car's owner arrived fifteen minutes ago, and he'll be lucky if he gets another one.

When he pulls up he sees the Impala's owner looking as if he'd just been kicked out of class and sent to the principal's office. The man looks over his shoulder at the restaurant as if someone's chasing him, jumps into his car, and putts away.

Then a flurry of activity. The maitre d' leans out the door and signals to the doorman, who turns to Gene. "Okay, hot shot, get Sinatra's car. And the Cadillac too!"

Gene sprints up the empty sidewalk like a purse snatcher and rounds the corner with a skid. He runs down to the lot and pulls up to the Lincoln in horror: Tom, the older valet, is sitting in the driver's seat, smoking. With the door closed.

Gene pulls it open. "Get out!" he cries.

"I'm sitting here."

Gene reaches his hands out and makes a vague grabbing motion, without touching Tom. He wants to pull him out of the car like John Wayne might pull a guy up from his chair in a western saloon. But Tom outweighs Gene by twenty pounds. "Please, they need the car now!" he pleads.

Tom spits between Gene's feet, who steps back. Tom reaches out and shuts the door, rolls down the window and flicks his cigarette at Gene. He starts the car and drives off toward the club.

Enraged, Gene sprints over to the black Cadillac and peels rubber out of the lot. He turns into the street and heads toward the intersection, when he sees the unthinkable.

Ahead in Sinatra's car, Tom does a California stop at the corner and swings into a right turn just as a little Thunderbird comes swooping across the twilight intersection like a swallow across a backyard. The T-bird honks, brakes, swerves, and kisses the Lincoln's rear fender. What with the blaring horn and screaming brakes, there is no sound of impact, just the T-Bird—light pink, practically beige in the lights of the intersection—spinning out. Both cars disappear out of Gene's view.

Gene has stopped several yards short of the intersection, aghast. It's his nightmare: a fender bender in a VIP's car. He sits there looking at the empty intersection for a minute, then slowly eases the Cadillac up the street and around the corner.

The Lincoln is sitting in the right lane, idling, the tail lights bright red. Gene stops behind it and steps out. On the sidewalk, here comes Sinatra, hatted, striding toward them. His famous blue eyes are flashing, bulging; his fists are clenched. Behind him trots his entourage, the famous and not-so-famous, with the big bruiser of a driver.

Tom has just eased his door open, in that extra-careful way one has after an accident, and put one foot on the ground. Sinatra, scurrying to the driver's side, yanks the door open and pulls Tom out of the car by his lapels, shaking him, screaming "What the fuck did you do to my car?"

Tom has his arms out to the sides, hands open—like he wants to make clear to everybody that he's not about to do anything to this maniac, not with that big bodyguard hovering—and says mildly, "Lemme go, lemme go."

The other men bend to inspect the damage. Dean Martin announces in a boozy voice, "Ain't nothing that a little patch won't fix."

"Hardly more than a scratch," concurs Sammy Davis Jr. "Hey Frank, you've done worse than this coming home drunk—let the guy alone."

The other man, the short one with a deadpan expression, says, "Frank, Dean's got bigger scratches on his back than this."

"She was a tiger, a tiger," Martin nods. "Frank, come on, let's go."

"Nobody fucks up my car," Sinatra shouts. He looks around wildly, twisting his neck to see the damage while still hanging on to Tom.

"Hey, what about the other driver?" wonders the other man. Gene's trying to remember his name. "Oh, shit, it's a T-Bird."

"Ooo, little filly," Martin drawls, seeing that the T-Bird's driver is a young woman. He lopes across the street to check her condition.

"Bobby, say something, get him off the guy," Davis says to the other man, who steps forward. That's who it is, Gene realizes, Bobby Blaine, a comedian.

"Frank," Bobby says, "you heard this one? This dame is driving and she's lost. And she gets out a map and she's trying to read it while she's driving, right, and she hits a big black car. Slam—she really creams it—but because it's such a big car, you know, nobody is hurt—she just fucked up the fender real bad. *Much* worse than this. And all these mobsters get out, she's hit the car of some big capo—they're all in black suits and they look plenty pissed off. She says—" and here Bobby raises his voice, "'Oh gracious me, I've hit the Supreme Court!'"

Still holding Tom by his lapels, Sinatra pauses for a second to wait for the follow-up.

"And they've got a colored driver—so she goes up to him and says, 'Adam Clayton Powell! I'm a big fan of yours.'"

Sinatra is starting to chuckle, despite himself.

Gene has drifted forward, along with Davis, so they're all more or less standing with the bodyguards in a circle around the combatants.

"'She says, 'Can I have your autograph?' And the driver says to her, 'Miss, it's not my car!'"

Sinatra laughs, and so does everybody else. Even Tom is smiling, hoping that in the hilarity he'll be forgotten. "What—what the fuck—is that it?" Sinatra says. "That is the stupidest punch line I ever heard."

Bobby opens his mouth, and Gene blurts out, pointing to Davis, "And the whole time, Adam Clayton Powell was right here."

They all look at Gene, surprised, and then Davis throws back his head and laughs, and so does Sinatra, and Bobby, and then they're all laughing. Sinatra lets go of Tom and doubles over, pointing at Sammy Davis Jr. "Adam Clayton Powell! Haw haw haw!"

"Okay," Bobby says. He looks across the street to the T-Bird. "Hey Dean! Zip up your pants and come on."

Davis steps up to Tom, who is trying to sidle away. "I sentence you to—" he laughs again to fill time, trying to think of a funny sentence.

"A year parking cars," Gene suggests.

Everybody thinks that's hilarious, too. They're already piling into the Lincoln. "Not bad, kid," Bobby says, pitching his cigarette away and climbing in. Tom finally gets to step away, just so the driver can open the door again.

Dean Martin trots over and leaps into the back seat, then springs out again. "He's got my fucking car back here," he exclaims happily. Tossing a twenty to Gene, he climbs into the Cadillac.

The Lincoln's rear window rolls down and Sinatra sticks his head out. "Hey buddy," he beckons Tom over. When he bends down next to the car, the rear door suddenly explodes open, slamming against his knees; Tom collapses with a squawk.

"Aw Frank..." Gene hears Sammy Davis say in a chiding tone. The door slams shut and the Lincoln pulls away.

Gene bends down to assist Tom, who's rolling on the ground, grimacing in pain, when he hears a loud honking. Gene looks up. They're in the Cadillac's way.

"Tom," Gene says, "you have to get out of the street."

"My fucking legs are broken," Tom cries. "I can't walk."

"That's what she said!" Gene shouts. Tom only groans.

Gene makes a big shrugging motion toward Dean Martin, who shakes his head in disgust, pulls around the yellow-jacketed figures and roars away to catch up to the Lincoln.

5

"Did you see Dago with that chicky?" Frank says, so we'll know he didn't miss a thing. "Make sure he's still behind us. I think he went back for a blowjob."

"He didn't go back, she's ridin' with him. Not that you can see her," I say, pretending to look out the back window. "Oh wait—I think I saw the back of her head. No, it's gone again."

"So what's your next project now?" Sammy asks Frank innocently. This risks bringing up the unpleasant incident with Maltz, but Sammy turns it into a gag. "I kind of like the Supreme Court idea—me as Powell, Bobby as Brandeis—I see you as maybe Brennan."

"You should be Black," Frank retorts.

"But Black isn't black."

Frank lights a cigarette. "Listen, Bobby, I know you were counting on this *Slovik* picture."

"I didn't assume, Frank." Sammy and I light up too.

"Great role, that Jewish lawyer: He detests the kid's cowardice but he'll do his damnedest to get the kid off. He's got some tricks up his sleeve, you know. And there's a scene in the movie where he talks with Slovik about the war and the Nazis, and what they're doing to the Jews. And you come off as sympathetic, principled, dedicated."

"That's wonderful, Frank," I say of the movie that will never be made. "Thanks."

Frank smokes. "Then these shits in Washington have to screw it up." It's not clear if he's still talking about the plot of the movie, or about the Red-hunters who got Maltz blacklisted, or about the politicians putting pressure on him to kill the project. Sammy and I simply nod.

"No, the next project," Frank goes on, waving his cigarette grandly, "is this Norman Krasna script. I want to do it with Marilyn."

This is news to me. "I heard she was doing some kind of Western."

"Yeah," Hank puts in. "They're shooting this summer."

"We're gonna squeeze it in before that," Frank says. "Get this: I play her boss, she's the lady businesswoman whose father owns the firm. Typical stuff. But I figure with her and me: dynamite! Listen to the title: *Make Nice for Daddy.*"

Sammy guffaws.

"I figure Edward G. Robinson as the father," Frank goes on.

"Robinson as Marilyn Monroe's father!" Sammy cackles. "Oh man."

I ask, "Who's doing it?"

"I'll produce it independently, just like *Ocean's.* It doesn't matter where we shoot. Hey, get this," he says, suddenly changing topics. "Speaking of Marilyn. I was in New York last month playing the Copa, guess who shows up. Peter and Pat and Bobby Kennedy. And Bobby's wife."

He means Peter Lawford and his wife, Pat—who is Jack and Bobby Kennedy's sister.

"Bobby's married? Who to?"

Frank blows smoke toward the roof of the car. "Phw! You'd never know it—not with him, not with his brother. He leaves his wife out front with Pat, and him and Peter come backstage between sets. Before I know it Bobby is practically getting a blowjob from one of the girls hanging around. I mean with a little more privacy..."

"How can you 'practically' get a blowjob?"

"I mean she's half on his lap, while me and Peter are over here shooting the breeze, she's got his thing out."

"Naw—in the dressing room?"

"I swear to God. I'm thinking, maybe we better go off and leave them in privacy."

"It's a good thing it's his brother who's running for President and not him," I say.

"Listen," Frank points one finger skyward, a cigarette clenched in his fist. It's his signal that he's going to make an important pronouncement, that he wants undivided attention. "Jack Kennedy is going to be the best president since Franklin Delano Roosevelt."

"I'm with ya," Sammy says.

"He'll be good for the Negroes, am I right?"

"Yeah."

"As for the Republicans—who they gonna run?"

"Nixon," I say.

"Nixon—that character. Listen, they talk about *my* mob friends—that Nixon is funded by half of Havana. Miami, Fort Lauderdale, Hialeah. That bunch. And he looks shady."

"Definitely shady."

"Him and McCarthy. Him and McCarthy are the ones who made hay on this Red-hunt business, and they both look like—I don't know, like some kind of thug."

I'm thinking, Bobby Kennedy was sort of in on the McCarthy act, too. But I say nothing.

"Whereas you got a young, glamorous guy with a beautiful wife, a war hero, he's got every Catholic in America voting for him, that means every Italian, every Irishman, every Polack, every—what—Frenchman..."

"All the Negroes," Sammy volunteers.

"All the Negroes—the Jews, he's got the Jewish vote. The guy can't lose. I'll bet ten thousand bucks. Ten thousand bucks. But wait!" he smacks his head. "I forgot the punchline. Here's the whole point of the story. The chick that Bobby is with in the dressing room: blondsville. I mean platinum blond. That's when I get it—this guy would love to make it with Marilyn."

"Frank, who wouldn't? You could say that about any guy in America."

"But don't you see? It's perfect. I get them together, see? I make the introduction, let nature take its course. Now I got Bobby Kennedy eating out of my hand."

"Who cares about Bobby, it's Jack running," I say.

"No, see—what Bobby does, Jack does."

Frank has learned a lot from his buddies in the Mob. Not so much the tactics, because the way the Mob would do it would be to get Bobby Kennedy caught with his pants down in, I don't know, a whorehouse in Moscow, if that's possible. Is there a whorehouse in Moscow? Probably—those fat Soviet fucks have to get laid like everybody else. Say the hookers have a workers collective or something. The People's Prostitute Union Number 5—and it's the same price for everything. I'll have to use that.

He wants loyalty, Frank does. He wants people to be grateful, to return his love with undying loyalty. And he'll do the same for you. That's how he owns people. He gets them to love him. And if he has to pimp for them to earn their love, then he'll go all the way: Marilyn Monroe. Nothing but the best for the next President of the United States.

That night, like a lot of nights, we went to about three more places, closed the last one, stayed til nearly three. I wasn't tired any more. I was beyond tired.

But I finally got away. We had some ladies at the table and the way you get away from Frank is, one of them says she must be going, and you jump up and say, Let me get you a cab. Otherwise you're running out on Frank, you're abandoning him. And that's the worst thing you can do.

I had no intention of getting laid. I dropped the girl off, told the taxi to take me home, and finally got in bed a little before four. And with a day off. I slept til nearly two in the afternoon resolved never to do that again—stay up nearly 48 hours, that is. Frank was right, I needed a driver. And who came to mind was the kid from the day before who made the joke about Adam Clayton Powell.

Chapter 2

1

After being clobbered by the limo's door, Tom can't even walk, much less drive, and gets sent home. Without a third valet, Gene and Kenny have an extra busy and lucrative night parking cars. By the end of the night, Gene has cleared $100 for the first time.

He wakes up at noon in his room in the bad part of Hollywood, a place above a Mexican restaurant and next door to a dry cleaner. The combined smells from both businesses wake him in the midday glare with a headache, as always.

He waits for a phone call, the one that almost always comes a little after 12:20, from his girlfriend, Dana. Brown hair curled in a flip, wearer of sweaters and camel-colored wool skirts, bank teller. She has a half hour for lunch, and often calls him.

But today there is no call. He waits in the sagging, damp bed, dressed in boxer shorts, a sheet tangled around his feet. 12:30 comes and goes. Sometimes Dana goes out to lunch with the other girls, and doesn't call; in that case she usually by the parking lot in the early evening and brings him something to eat.

There's a narrow window beyond his feet. Outside the day has turned into typical Los Angeles winter gloom—broken overcast, and above that a layer of smog. He can't remember the last time he saw a blue sky here. The odor of grease and chemicals exhausted into the alley seems almost visible.

Gene spends his afternoon reading *On the Road*. When he can't stand it in his room anymore, he heads over to the library and reads some more. Paperback in pocket, he makes it down to the parking lot on time at 5:00.

Irv is there talking to some new kid. Gene takes his yellow jacket from the hook in the parking shack.

Kenny is standing there. "A guy was here earlier. I said you come in at five."

"What guy?"

"Don't know. Left you this." Kenny hands him a business card.

"Bobby Blaine," Gene reads. "That's him, that's the other guy who was with Sinatra last night. I never can remember that guy's name."

Irv is waving Gene over; he puts the card in his pants pocket and walks out into the lot. "Kid, lemme see your jacket," Irv says.

Gene suddenly sees what's happening, and freezes in mid-stride.

"C'mon," Irv says, beckoning with his finger. "C'mon, c'mon." He c'mons Gene until he unfreezes and slowly hands over the jacket, which Irv gives to the new kid. The kid slips into it and nods: fits just fine.

Irv takes Gene by the arm and walks him back to the shack. Kenny and the new kid take a few steps in the other direction and turn discretely toward the street. They don't want to watch.

"Irv, if this is about last night, I had nothing to do with that accident. I was in another car completely—I was out here when it happened, following in another car."

"C'mon, kid, it was Sinatra's car, wasn't it? And weren't you watching that car like a hawk all night?"

"I did not crash that car."

"You're through here."

"You're firing me?"

"Don't make a big deal about it. You're a bright kid and sooner or later you'll learn that's it's maybe not such a good idea to have a big mouth."

Gene stands with his mouth open. Finally he stammers, "What about—what about severance pay?"

"I'll show you severance." Irv now shoves him toward the street; Kenny and the new kid have already strolled around the corner toward the restaurant. "Go someplace else and wreck cars." Irv makes a shooing motion. "Go. Don't make me get mad."

Gene stumbles onto the sidewalk, then puts his head down and, by habit, starts up toward Chasen's.

"Not that way!"

He turns and walks back past the parking lot down the side street. Jamming his hands in his pocket, he finds the card from Bobby Blaine. After a few blocks' walk to let himself cool off, he puts a nickel in a pay phone and dials.

"Mister Blaine's answering service."

"Ah..." Gene mumbles. He's never reached an answering service before, he thought it was something in the movies. Well, this is Hollywood. "My... Mr. Blaine asked me to call him." He leaves his name and phone number, picks up some Chinese food, heads home.

His room, which he's almost never in during the evening, is stifling. It heats up after noon from the restaurant's kitchen directly below, and doesn't cool off til midnight no matter how cool the evening is. And it's noisy, with a jukebox in the restaurant so he can hear every Mexican record on it.

After a couple hours, the phone does ring. It's Dana.

"I'm at your parking lot," she says. "They say you were fired?"

"Yeah, I got gypped." He begins to tell her the story, but she interrupts.

"Gene, I'm sorry, but you'll have to tell me the whole thing some other time. I'm here with Greta from the bank. We're on our way to a movie, it starts in a little while—why don't you come with us?"

"Yeah—sure—no wait, I can't. I'm waiting for a call. It might be another job."

"Oh... Are you sure? What other job?"

"I don't know." He wants to ask her to just come over, to step into his arms the way she did the week before, as they waited at a bus stop after a movie—just as the bus was pulling up, she put her arms around him and let him pull her close and kiss her for the first time all evening. He wants her to hold him again and listen to how he was cheated, and then let him fuck her and everything would be all right.

But they hang up and he sinks back onto the bed. Music comes through the window and low clouds mix with smoke from the restaurant's stove. He is awake until the restaurant closes.

2

He takes buses across town, and catches a cab for the last leg of the trip, since he feels it's only proper for somebody coming for an interview in Beverly Hills to arrive in a cab.

Recalling the incident on the street near Chasen's, Gene assumes the main impression he made on Bobby Blaine was that of hilarious jokester. It follows that Blaine wants to hire him as a gag writer—an occupation the existence of which he has only recently learned. Since coming to Hollywood he has become aware of the pyramid of Hollywood scribes: screenwriters at the top, and below them script doctors, dialogue specialists, story artists, gag writers, garden-variety comedians, and, at the bottom, critics and "literary types." Given this hierarchy, Gene feels that breaking in as a gag writer is doing all right, all things considered.

The cab turns onto a cul-de-sac that goes back down the hill a little and stops at the end, in front of a house which looks to Gene comfortingly normal, if big.

After he rings, he hears Blaine's voice startlingly close to the other side of the door: "I'll get it, Mary!" Then the door opens to reveal Bobby Blaine.

He's dressed as he often appears in photographs: a red golf sweater over an open-collar shirt, hair so short it can't be out of place, off-white slacks. "Hello, kid, you're early, aren't you?"

Gene looks anxiously at his watch. "Um, not really."

"That's okay," turning and leaving the door wide open, "Come in, come in. I was out by the pool." Gene shuts the door and follows. The house has not so much a foyer as a lobby; a wide curving staircase and a chandelier create a resemblance to a downtown cinema. Bobby leads him across a marble floor through an open, sunken living room—tan leather couches are built in around a huge burl coffee table, with an enormous stone fireplace at one end, and ashtrays the size of snowshoes rest on oak end tables—to a wall of glass. One of the parts of the wall is a sliding glass door, and on the other side of this is the pool area.

There's a wet bar against a structure on the other side of the pool, and Bobby goes over to it. "Drink?"

"Uh, I'll have what you're having," an attempt at cool bravado.

Bobby looks down at the bar and reaches for a glass and some ice. "First thing, I better know how old ya are."

"Twenty-four," Gene says evenly. He has practiced this response.

"You're twenty-four like I'm Catholic," Bobby retorts. "Come on, tell me the truth, we don't have all day."

"Really, I am," Gene says.

"Let's see your driver's license."

Gene had not anticipated this. He pulls out his wallet, a black leather one he bought at age 16 and which suddenly seems worn and shabby given the surroundings. He fumbles for his license and hands it over. "If it's that big a deal, just give me a Coke," he says.

Bobby looks at him. "It's not about the drink, kid. I just want to make sure you can handle the job."

Gene feels this calls for a quip, but nothing comes to mind. He stands there while Bobby looks at the license, which is fake. It passed muster with Irv, it should do all right with Bobby, supposes Gene. It's not like he checks people's driver's licenses every day. This gives him an idea.

"Once I was stopped by a cop," he begins. "The cop says, 'Do you know how fast you were going?' I said, 'No officer, but if you hum a few bars I can fake it.'"

Bobby makes the smallest possible reaction, still looking at the license. That stank, Gene thinks. He presses on.

"So the cop asks me 'Do you know the speed limit?' and I said, 'I was hoping you'd know. Tell you what, why don't we ask somebody. Hey sir!'" Gene pretends to flag down a passer-by. "'What's the speed limit here?'"

Bobby looks up at Gene skeptically. "Kid," he says.

"The guy says, 'I was only going one mile an hour, honest!' This is a pedestrian, I mean."

"Kid, what are you talking about?"

Gene swallows. "Um. Just kidding around about the license."

Bobby gives him back the license wordlessly.

"How about this one," Gene says, launching into one of his prepared jokes. "A Communist walks into a bar and says, 'I want a beer, but I can't pay.' The bartender says, 'Okay, how about mopping the floor?' Then a beatnik walks in and says, 'I want some wine, but I can't afford it.' The bartender says, 'Fine, just repaint that wall.' Then a priest walks in and says, 'I want a whisky, but I have no money.' The bartender says, 'That's all right, Father, just bless the joint.' Finally a cop walks in, and he sees one guy mopping, the other painting, and the priest performing a blessing. The cop says, 'Man, you sure are cleaning the place up fast after that mob hit here last night.'"

Bobby is standing open-mouthed, staring at Gene blinking in the poolside light. Bobby closes his mouth.

"So—" Gene starts again, but Bobby puts up a quick hand: stop.

Bobby goes over to a chaise longue and sits, leaving Gene at the bar. "Just help yourself, kid." He looks down on Hollywood and the midday glare.

Gene comes over with a glass of something. Bobby points to a nearby lounge chair and Gene sits.

"So what do you think?" Gene asks.

"About what?"

"My material."

"Your material! Well, I'd say, don't give up your day job, but I hear it's a little late for that. In any case, what I have in mind—"

"I know my delivery needs a lot of work, but—"

"Your delivery! Look, kid, leave the gags to me, okay? I mean, the other night, you said one thing, it was funny. Beginner's luck. But don't push it."

"Sure." Gene sips his drink. Bobby looks at him.

"Gimme that." He takes it from Gene, sniffs it, takes a sip. "Whoo-ee! Kid, what'd you put in this? You're no bartender either, that's for sure." He hands it back. "I hope you don't make a habit of this. You ain't a drunk, are you?"

"No, of course not."

"You got any experience besides parking cars?"

"Yeah, I've done some m.c.-ing at clubs in St. Louis and around there," Gene says, as smoothly as he can, "and I was one of the regular opening acts at the Tango Club. That was a strip joint."

Bobby squints at him. "No, not—not in show business. I mean driving. Do you have any other experience driving?"

"Driving?" Gene says dubiously. "Well, yeah, I drove a cab in college, and limos on weekends. And I used to, uh, pick people up at the airport for the club. For my father's country club."

"Country club?" Bobby shrugs. "Fine, so here's the deal. For the next four weekends I have gigs in Vegas, Friday through Sunday night, right? Last show ends about 10:00. But for the next four weeks we're shooting here in L.A. during the week. So I need somebody to drive me between here and Vegas. We go up on Friday morning, come back on Sunday night—and that's all night. And they don't have freeway for most of it, so it's about a ten-hour drive. The main thing is Sunday night—I finish at 10:00, we get in the car, you drive all night to L.A. So, you interested?"

Gene has been listening, frowning, nodding. When Bobby finishes, he sits in the silence for a minute, rearranging his thoughts.

"You want me to drive the car," he says slowly.

"Yeah, drive the car. What did you think?" Bobby sees Gene's mouth grimace and recompose itself. "Hey—I get it—you thought this was like an audition! You come in here with some gags—Ha ha ha!" Bobby is laughing for the first time. "Now that's funny!"

Gene sighs, stands up, carries the glass back to the bar. Bobby turns in his chair and stares at him.

"Kid—what did you think—that I wanted to hire you as a gag writer or something? Oh man! No offense, kid, but I mean, you're a parking lot attendant! In fact, a former parking lot attendant! Geez, everybody wants to break into show business in this town." Bobby stands up and comes over to the bar. "Here—let me fix you a real drink. And you said, 'I know my delivery needs work—!' AH HA HA HA HA. I don't know, kid, maybe you do have a future in it. Ha ha ha, 'delivery needs work.'"

He hands the drink to Gene, who is blushing furiously. "I'm sorry, kid. It's just—Look, I'm sorry I'm laughing. It's just that it's the only real funny thing that's happened to me for a while." He claps Gene on the shoulder. "What's your name again?"

"Gene Kramer. You want to see my license again?"

"Haw haw haw! No, let's not get into the license again. That thing wouldn't fool a blind man! I meant, what's your real given name, is it Genario or Genesius or what?"

"Eugene."

"Of course it is. I was just kidding. Gino! How's that? I'll call you Gino, and then when you make it big, that can be your stage name. So how much do you want? I've never had a driver before so I don't know how much to pay. How much did you make parking cars a week?"

"Three hundred bucks, depending on tips."

"Pfft. If you could make three hundred bucks a week parking cars, the city of Los Angeles would be nothing but parking lots. But of course you want to get all you can. I'll pay you a hundred a weekend. A little more if I need you during the week. Whattaya say?"

"It's a deal, Mr. Blaine."

"Good. Now go get yourself a real driver's license."

3

Dana is not thrilled.

"When am I ever gonna see you?" she asks. They are sitting under greasy fluorescent lights in a hamburger joint on Sunset. She's got a Coke float, and pokes at the floating blob of ice cream with her straw.

Gene, who has just finished his description of the job by taking a large bite out of a hamburger, waves his hands helplessly, chews. In this pause in the conversation, the sounds of other youths in the diner rise to the foreground: "You're not wearing that!" — "He's such a retard!" — "No, come *onnnn*" and in the background, hamburger sizzles and a spatula clangs off a grill.

Gene finally swallows in a tremendous gulp. "It's not any worse than me working six nights a week in the parking lot," he says.

"It's a lot worse," she pouts. "I could go by and see you at the lot if I wanted to. And I always knew where you'd be. If I call in sick we could spend the day together."

"We never spent the day together," he says. "Have I been missing out on something?"

"Well, I haven't called in sick."

"We never spent the day together on Sunday either."

"I go to church with my parents, we've been through that."

He rummages through the french fries, looking for the non-soggy ones. "Dana, first of all, this is a good job. It's easy, I get to meet people, people with a lot of money. Two hundred a week—that's a lotta dough!"

"And what are you going to do with it?" she asks coquettishly.

"Spend it on my cookie," he replies, chucking her under the chin. He loves the way she looks when she's being sweet. Her skin is so pretty, and her chin, which she considers pointy, is in fact simply willful.

"And second of all," he goes on, "this is just like Dean Moriarty in *On the Road*—I go from parking cars to being a real driver, city to city, seeing the country."

"The desert is not the country," Dana says.

"Sure it is—it's all America! It's the real America—out there where everything isn't all straightened out and manicured, where you can see fifty miles, where there's no *fog*, for Chrissakes. I'm sick of this overcast! Vegas is out in the sunshine!"

"Is the car a convertible?"

"No."

"Then what's the difference?" She sips her drink dry, the ice cream clogging the straw at the bottom of the glass. "Well, when *am* I going to see you?"

He sighs. "During the week – in the evenings. There'll be time. And it's not forever, it's only a four-week job. After that, if I'm lucky he'll keep me on, and then I'll be in town most of the time."

They go out into the street. It's early evening and the overcast has darkened into night. Up Sunset they walk to a movie theater and see the new Jerry Lewis movie, *Cinderfella.* Dana detests Jerry Lewis, but Gene loves seeing a grown man making a complete fool of himself and still getting the girl; it reassures him that nothing he could do could possibly be as bad. And Dana is just as pretty as Anna Maria Alberghetti, the co-star. He puts his arm around her as she sits glumly, pursing her lips in distaste. With the arm that's not already draped over Dana's shoulders, he touches her face. Looking at her for a moment, he finds her glaring at Jerry Lewis. Brushing off his hand, she mutters, "Not a chance, not with that monkey up there."

During the intermission before the second feature, Dana asks, "So what's he like, anyway, this Bobby Blaine?"

"Well, he's not a big star—not as big as Frank Sinatra and them, you know—but you should see his house. Marble staircase, marble foyer, big swimming pool."

"Never mind the house, what about him?"

"Ah, well, he's ..." Gene furrows his brow. "I dunno, he just seems like a fairly ordinary guy, kind of talks quick, you know—kind of like you'd expect a comedian to talk. Not refined like an actor."

"You know, I can't remember seeing him in a movie."

"Didn't you see *The Naked and the Dead?* He played both parts! Ha ha!—That's what he said."

"What's that, a blue movie?" she sneers.

"No, it's a war movie—a movie from a famous book by Norman Mailer."

"Pff."

"And he's been on TV. He's like the kind of guy who would be, I don't know, he'd be the friend of the star. Like the sidekick guy. But mainly he's a comedian."

"Hmm. He doesn't sound very famous. I guess I've heard of him but more in connection with Frank Sinatra and that group."

"The Rat Pack. They're going to make a lot of movies together."

"I liked Dean Martin better when he was with Jerry Lewis."

"You hate Jerry Lewis."

"I liked Dean Martin—I hate Jerry Lewis even more now that there's no Dean Martin in it. So what does this guy Bobby Blaine do? Is he a singer?"

"No, he's basically a comedian. A sophisticated one."

"Hmmph. Well, I hope he's funny."

"You know what? He thinks *I'm* funny."

"You? When were you funny?"

"I told him a couple of jokes. I didn't want him to think I was just some dumb driver. Who knows, maybe I could write gags for him."

"Oh brother. Yeah, sure, you'll be in like Flynn."

The monster movie is more conducive to necking. She cuddles into him, as a strange gorilla-cat creature menaces a young couple in a lover's lane. They spend most of the rest of the feature kissing, although this time she doesn't permit him any funny business.

He walks her to her bus stop. His room is closer than her parents' house, only a short bus ride away; he aches to bring her back there, but he can't even bear to think about it. She would only be disgusted with the damp, narrow bed, the cardboard boxes and crates that serve as tables and shelves, the closet without a door. And on top of that, there are the alley's smells and noises. It repels even him.

"You know," he says, "I'll save up the money from this job, and I'll get a decent apartment. Then maybe you could come up sometime."

She stops a few doors from the bus stop, takes him by the hand and pulls him into the shadow of a shop doorway. There she kisses him, not as hard and wantonly as the time before, but sweetly and enthusiastically. "Maybe I could," she says as the bus arrives, and then she gives him a wave goodnight.

Chapter 3

1

On Friday at 7:00 a.m. I pick up Gino in front of his building in lower Hollywood. It isn't too savory looking—some litter on the sidewalk, a fly-trap Mexican restaurant. I figure I'm doing him a favor getting him away from this, even for a weekend.

There he is, yawning on the sidewalk with his hung-over neighbors. "You drive," I say. "Need some coffee first?"

"Don't drink coffee," he yawns.

I shrug. "Okay. Know how to get to 66?"

"Sure," he says.

I get the feeling he actually has no idea. "Through Glendale, right?"

"Sure, sure," he nods.

I guess we'll get there. I get to work on some new material—I do some new stuff every week to keep the act fresh. Just take a few things that happened that week and make a few jokes about them. The Maltz affair has been in the papers—it hasn't broken yet that Frank has fired Maltz, but I figure it will soon. I write two sets of jokes, one based on the general controversy, and another set based on Maltz getting fired. I can use the second set of jokes after Maltz's firing is made public. I like writing topical humor, as long as it's not too political.

We called our three weeks in Las Vegas the Summit, in reference to a big Eisenhower-Kruschev meeting that had taken place in the fall. When Kennedy showed up at our shows in Vegas, we did plenty of jokes about him, but it was all L'il Abner stuff. For example: Frank made this long flowery introduction of Kennedy sitting there in the audience. And while Kennedy's taking a bow, I whisper to Dean, "Say 'It's a real honor, now what was your name again?'" And Dean steps up to the mike and says in his drunken way, "It's such an honor to be in the presence of—" he turns to Frank, "who did you say he was?" and it gets a big laugh.

It wouldn't get a big laugh if I did it, but Dean can do that kind of stuff. We had this bit where we would roll a room service bar cart out on stage. Dean called it the Lunch Cart and he would say "I'm gonna fix myself a sandwich," whereupon he would pour himself a drink. And Frank's line would be, what kinda sandwich you call that? "Ice on rye," Dean would slur.

One night Frank got tired of Dean getting all the laughs. He says to Dean, let's switch lines; you be the straight man for once. "Sure, pallie," Dean says, easy-going as always.

That night they get out there with the Lunch Cart. "I'm gonna make a fruit cordial," Frank says.

"How do you make a fruit cordial?" Dean says.

"Why, be nice to him," Frank says.

Polite laughter. Then Dean just looks at the audience for a *half a second*—and the place goes nuts. See, that is timing.

At the Riviera, I'm on my own. Yes, there's a chance the other guys might drop in, because they're in and out of Vegas too, performing at the Sands. It could happen, and the audience is on edge. So I have to work hard. Even though it's why they're there, I have to make them forget about Frank and Dean and Sammy. I have to grab them and not let their minds wander. Jokes, jokes, jokes, a little singing. But not too much singing, because people will start to say "He ain't exactly Sinatra is he?"

To break the tension one night, off the top of my head I said, "You know we Jews—" and that always gets a laugh, all you have to do is say Jew, wop, dago and they go nuts—"We Jews have a tradition. Every year on Passover we set a place for Elijah just in case he shows up. This is sorta like that—hey, get another microphone out here just in case Elijah shows up!" And the stage manager brought another microphone out and set it next to me.

"Great," I said, "now I've got one for me and one for my friend." And the piano player starts playing a little "Me and My Shadow" which of course is the number Frank and Sammy do together. And I made him stop, I said, "Hold it, there's no friend here yet!" It worked so well I did it every night, and it sort of took the edge off things. You acknowledge what's going on without actually saying it. It gets the audience on your side.

I look out the window and watch the motels and used car lots go by and think, I had a lock on *Slovik*. For about two hours. Now I have to start all over again. This is when I get butterflies, not before I go on stage, but when I have to figure out what my next project is. Because this glow around Frank and the Summit and all—it won't last long.

After a couple of hours, we stop at a diner and get some breakfast. I hand Gene money to pay the bill and I go to the can.

When I come out of the restaurant, he's leaning against the car reading some paperback. He sees me, tosses the book into the shotgun seat and scurries around to open the passenger side for me. Some tourists crossing the parking lot stare at this treatment; their little kid cries, "Look!"

"That's okay, Gino," I say. "You don't have to do that when we're on the road. People probably think I'm putting on airs. Skip the star treatment unless we're in L.A. or Vegas."

"Gotcha." He backs up, points the car toward the highway, guns it left across four lanes of traffic and we're back on the highway.

"What's that you're reading?"

"On the Road."

"What's that, some kind of driving manual? I can see you're really taking this chauffeur thing seriously."

I see him look at me in the rear-view mirror. "No, it's not about— It's not about being a chauffeur."

I lean over and scoop it out of the shotgun seat. "'This is the Bible of the Beat Generation,'" I read from the cover. "'The explosive bestseller that tells all about today's wild youth and their frenetic search for Experience and Sensation'—capitalized yet. Hey, I was just kiddin' you, I heard of this book. It's a beatnik thing, right?"

"Yeah, sorta," he says. He seems a little embarrassed.

I flip over the book and read the back cover. "'Wild drives across America... buying cars, wrecking cars, stealing cars, dumping cars, picking up girls, making love, all-night drinking bouts'—Hey, this is starting to sound familiar—'Jazz joints, wild parties, hot spots. This is the odyssey of the Beat Generation, the frenetic—' There's that word again—'The frenetic young men and their women, restlessly racing from New York to San Francisco,' blah de blah—'in a frantic search for Kicks and Truth.'

"I heard of this, sure. But what's it about?"

"Uh, well, the cover pretty much says it."

"Hey look, I didn't mean to make fun. Really, I'd like to know what it's about."

"Well—It *is* about a couple guys driving back and forth across the country a lot. And they're sort of searching... It's an *existential* search."

"Existential," I repeat, deadpan.

He gives me a quick glance in the mirror. I keep my face serious and just nod.

"It's a search for what's real in the middle of all this stuff they try to hand you. The idea that... you try to free yourself from the dictates of... Well, it's kind of hard to explain."

"No hurry, we still got six hours of driving ahead of us."

"Okay—it's like this. There are various authorities that try to tell you the way the world is. The government, the church, the teacher at school—they all try to instruct you in what's what. And they call it morality. But existentialism is amoral—not in the sense that they're fruits or commies, but in the sense that they decide for themselves what is moral. Not based on what somebody told them, but based on their own experience. And the fact that you have to do this makes for angst."

"Angst? You mean worry? And you feel this because... because why again?"

"Because when you decide for yourself what's right and wrong, you don't have a guide. Without relying on somebody to tell you what's right and wrong, you decide for yourself—and it's this responsibility for deciding that makes for angst."

"Huh." I chew this over. "You got all that from in here?" I hold up *On the Road*.

"No, not in so many words. That's a novel, but it's about people living in an existential universe."

"And they got angst," I say, looking at the cover of the book, which is a sort of collage of kids dancing, driving, making out. "It looks from the cover like they have a pretty good time of it. Maybe it's sort of, Eat, drink and be merry, for tomorrow we die?"

"Yeah, well, see—You're also free."

"Oh yeah?"

"Yeah, if you live your life by your own lights—not by the morality they tell you about in church or whatever—if you make your own decisions, you're free."

"Free to steal cars, get drunk, make out with chicks, that sort of thing?"

"Maybe they emphasized that a little too much on the cover," he says, now a little embarrassed.

We turn north to go through a narrow canyon, settling behind a long line of cars. Gino keeps it in third gear. On the other side of the canyon, a freight train drifts back down toward San Bernardino. Freight trains—this trip was a piece of cake before they cancelled the passenger train.

The road climbs for ten or fifteen miles, then levels off. We drive through a patch of pine trees, and then the landscape opens out to the desert and a stretch of new freeway. It's almost noon and the sun is high. An hour and a half later we eat lunch in Barstow and head out across the desert. The road changes back to ordinary highway, back to freeway, then back again. When we're not on freeway there are bulldozers and trucks working on one side or another. Finally we reach a long stretch of older highway where there's no sign of roadwork and the desert scrub stretches out for miles on either side.

I get drowsy in the warm desert air, nap a little, read. I'm reading a script for a war film about JFK's PT boat and how he managed to get it mowed down by a Jap destroyer. Once it was in pieces he saved all their lives. At least that's the way the script reads.

When the script started going around, Frank was on it like a rug.

"Kennedy's like me!" Sinatra declared one evening at Sardi's.

Silence initially, then the six or seven around the table all sip their drinks. Finally Dean volunteered, "He plays golf."

"He's Catholic," I said.

"What I mean," Sinatra said, "is that we're both coming into this point in our careers where we're set to win the whole megillah—where we're gonna come out on top."

Several solemn nods around the table. Angie Dickenson was there. She said helpfully, "You're both being recognized."

"That's it!" Sinatra said. "Recognition. And everything kind of falling into line."

Yes, they were both coming into their own. But it takes somebody as immodest as Frank to call attention to it. Who else would say something like that—"Kennedy's like me!"

Eventually Sinatra thought better of the idea of starring in *PT-109*. Even he saw that pushing himself into the literal role of JFK would be just too much. But the script is still around, and the better JFK does in the primaries, the more likely it is to get made. I'm looking for a sidekick role. That's my new goal, to get the sidekick role in films, the second lead. I might not ever be a leading man, but I can be his best friend.

"Huh," I say, breaking the silence for the first time in two hours. "Gino, listen to this. You know Kennedy was in the war, right? He was captain of a PT boat."

"Sure—he saved his men when the boat sank."

"Right, so listen. They're on a desert island in Jap territory, okay? And they have to send a message for help without being found by the Japs, see? So you know what they do?"

"What?"

"They write the message on a coconut."

"Huh?"

"Yeah, they carve it on a coconut, and give it to some native character, and tell him to give it to a white man. The native fella takes off in a canoe with it and sooner or later they get rescued. How do you like that."

Gene silently drives on. Then: "Actually, come to think of it, I heard about that from his nephew."

"What? Whose nephew?"

"David Kennedy—JFK's nephew. He told me about it."

"You? Where?"

"Hyannisport, last summer."

"Hyannisport? On Cape Cod? You were never in Hyannisport. What are you telling me?"

"My father has a house back there. Near the Kennedy compound. That's where I met David. I spend summers there. I'm on the swim team with David."

"The swim team?"

Gene nods.

"So your family must be, ah successful."

"Dad's company is one of the major suppliers for McDonnell Aircraft in St. Louis. They supply parts for Air Force jets. Some of the major new test aircraft—they're built by McDonnell, but most of the parts come from his plant—Kramer Aerodynamics."

I purse my lips, look out the window at the sagebrush. Gene goes on, "So our summer house is on Cape Cod—you know how hot it is in St. Louis in the summer—and my father's country club is where I met the Kennedy kids."

"Your father's country club. And this David Kennedy," I say gamely, "what Kennedy is he?"

"His mother is Kennedy's sister."

"Pat—that her name? She's married to Lawford?"

"No—the other one. Jean."

"Well. With connections like that, what were you doing parking cars?"

"My father feels," he says, raising his chin, "that it's important for me to establish myself without his help." He launches into a monologue about how his dad's a self-made man.

I'm thinking, this has to be bullshit. On the swim team with a Kennedy one summer, parking cars in L.A. six months later—come on.

On the other hand, look at him there—driving with his left hand, gesturing with his right, and the more he talks, the more at home he seems—like it's his car, and I'm just a hitchhiker. Regaling me with a war story from my generation, not his own. I chuckle and nod. Let the kid talk. I too was young once.

2

This is the most Gene's ever driven in one day. As the afternoon progresses all he can think of is having a beer and getting in bed.

It gets dark after they cross the state line. There is a small casino on the border, lights flashing bravely in the middle of nowhere. They don't stop, plunging into darkness.

Across another line of hills, they enter a dark valley. But this one is defined by a glow that outlines the hills at the other end. On a horizon where the headlights of cars appear and taillights disappear, light shimmers. Gradually they approach this firmament, and finally, in a sweeping curve to the right, they top the rise and the lights of Las Vegas are before them.

The city is a shining pile of lights in the midst of a vast darkness. On either side of the highway, there's nothing; straight ahead, it seems there's a vast landing strip for cars. Gene forgets his tiredness. He cruises toward the lights like the captain of a DC-3.

The road becomes a four-lane divided highway, and the town starts up out of nowhere. There's an intersection with a state highway, and then everything just starts. Stores and motels and gas stations stand on either side of the street, each one with lights flashing. Ahead, there are even brighter lights.

Bobby has been snoozing. "Mr. Blaine?" Gene speaks up. "We're here."

Bobby's eyes blink open. "Oh. Good." He smacks his lips and reaches for the thermos.

"So which way?"

"Just stay on this road, it goes right past everything. Watch out for the Riviera, it's past the Sands and the Dunes. It's on the right." He pours coffee into the cap of the thermos and gulps it down. "Hoo boy. Hey, how you doing? Want some coffee?"

Gene blinks, shakes his head. A second later he clears his throat and manages to say, "No thanks."

"Tired? I'll bet you are. You ever been in Vegas? Did I ask you that?"

Gene shakes his head again. "No, I haven't."

"Well, it's just a town, except it has a lot of fancy joints. Get yourself a cheap motel room a block or two off the main drag here. Here, I'll give you forty bucks for the weekend for your motel and your meals. If you want my advice, walk around, take in movies all day, but don't get started in the casinos."

"Okay."

"Here I'm talking to you like your mother. Well, do what you want. But you'll probably enjoy yourself more if you just go to the movies. I won't need you during the weekend at all; I just stay at the hotel. I do shows on Friday night and Saturday night and a final show at nine on Sunday night. That's over at ten, so you have to meet me at the Riviera about ten thirty. Okay?"

When they reach the Riviera, Bobby directs him to the main entrance. Bobby gets out with his briefcase and a garment bag, and introduces Gene to the head bellman. "This kid will pick up my car at about ten on Sunday night. Gino, pick up the car then and gas it up and come back here. Wait right here and I'll come out, ten thirty, like I said. Don't do anything I wouldn't do." With that, he disappears into the hotel.

Gene gets a knapsack out of the trunk and an attendant roars away with the car. He's left standing on the driveway. He asks the bellman for directions to a cheap motel, walks a few blocks, registers for a five-dollar-a-night room, and collapses fully clothed on the bed.

He sleeps until the maid wakes him up, barging into the room at 9:00 a.m. Seeing him sprawled out on the bed in his clothes, she shrieks, thinking it's a dead body. The sound catapults Gene into the air like a startled cat; he lands on his feet next to the bed. This transformation from stiff to upright man frightens the maid further, and she screams again.

Gene sits down heavily on the bed. "Stop that screaming!" he begs, clamping his hands over his ears. "Christ, I thought it was the Bomb."

The maid, a young Mexican woman, is leaning against the doorframe, having dropped her cleaning supplies in a heap. She's hanging on to her chest as if to keep her heart from leaping out. "Dios mio!" she exclaims. "Man, why'd you scare me like that?"

"Please," Gene begs. "It's all right. Just calm down."

"Man, what you doing in here?!" the maid demands.

Gene looks around, getting his bearings. "This is my room. I paid for this room."

"Oh man," the girl says. "You surprised me. People hardly ever spend the night in this motel. I didn't see a car, and they didn't tell me there was somebody here." She starts to back out and close the door. "I'll come back later." Her cleaning supplies have fallen in the doorway, and she has to open the door again to clear them out. "Sorry!" she says, finally succeeding in closing the door.

Gene rubs his face and goes to the bathroom. He takes a shower and puts on some clean clothes. When he opens the door to go outside, the desert sunlight filling the parking lot practically stuns him. But he ventures forth; it's still late February, the air isn't very hot at all.

He finds the maid vacuuming the room next door. "Hey there!" he shouts over the noise. She looks up at him outlined against the brightness of the parking lot, and startled, drops the vacuum wand. Frustrated, he shouts, "Can you just shut that thing off for a second?"

She turns off the vacuum. "What?"

"I just wanted to tell you, you can clean my room now."

"Oh, you're the guy from 11."

"Yeah, remember me?"

"Yeah, sorry I woke you up," she says suspiciously. "I said that."

"Is there a place to eat around here?"

"There's a coffee shop on the corner, just walk toward the Strip."

"Thanks."

"You know how to find the Strip, don't you?" she asks, arms folded.

"That's the only thing I know how to find," he says. "By the way—I'll be staying another night, so don't wake me up tomorrow."

"I don't work Sundays," she says, and leans down to turn on the vacuum again, dismissing him.

3

Saturday night there's always a big crowd, liquored up, ready to blow money and eager for a good time. They want to laugh; if they're laughing, it proves to them and everybody around them, look, I'm having a good time. So they're easy.

Friday night crowds are tougher; depending on the venue, they're either tired from work, or they've traveled some distance to get where you are, the resort or whatever. They're grouchy and tense, and you have to work to relax them. It's almost like they're daring you to entertain them, and if you don't, they can be murder.

Compared to Friday night crowds, Saturday audiences are like a nice drunk compared to a mean drunk. But because of that, sometimes you don't work as hard as you should. They laugh at everything, so you get lazy. You feel like if you took a leak on stage they'd give you an ovation.

But I'm a professional, and a professional works hard and stays sharp. I always give the best show I can. That's why I don't drink before I go on. After—that's a different story. The "Lunch Cart" indeed! See, the Lunch Cart was basically a Saturday night crowd idea. The idea that you're on stage with your friends, boozing and cutting up, and the audience has the privilege of sitting in. That you're acting in your everyday party mode, sort of giving the audience a ringside seat to your glamorous life. Where Frank is one of the boys and we can kid him if we don't take it too far.

It's important to Frank that he maintain his persona as one of the guys, somebody who might call you up on Sunday morning and ask if you can round out a foursome. Somebody who you could rag on for hitting three balls in a row into the sand trap; who might, for the duration of the afternoon, accept a mocking nickname like "Sandy." That's why he hates the news stories that depict him as a bully, as a petty tyrant. He roughs up some waldo and it's in the gossip columns a day or two later, SINATRA ON THE RAMPAGE AGAIN, STOMPS PARKING ATTENDANT. It doesn't matter that it's true; to him this is persecution. Because unbeknownst to the gossip columnist, he's already had a change of heart and sent the guy flowers in the hospital and paid his bill. And that never gets published.

So on Saturday night at the Riviera, I'm on stage. I decide not to use the jokes I prepared about Maltz—the fact that he's gotten canned hasn't been in the papers so I leave it alone. I've got the shtick going with the microphone "for my friend in case he shows up" even though I well know that Frank is in Chicago at a JFK fundraiser and Dean is sitting at home in Beverly Hills watching movies on TV. I'm building to the point in the act where I "realize" nobody is going to show up and I start singing "Some day he'll come aloooooooong, the man I love" and burlesque it to death. That's the end of the bit.

But I'm not there yet. I'm building to it. I'm three-quarters of the way through the show, telling a series of jokes about an Eskimo, a broad, and a polar bear. Which has nothing to do with anything but it lets me tell spade jokes without calling a spade a spade, if you know what I mean. All the Eskimo jokes are spade jokes from years ago. Enlightened entertainers like me never tell spade jokes anymore, after all, this is 1960. You can say anything about Eskimos, though.

"So they're in the igloo," I'm saying, to easy Saturday laughter. "And Nanook is thinking, 'Finally.' He says, 'I've killed a polar bear for you. I've skinned the bear and I've cooked you bear for supper. But to get the full experience you have to lie down on this polar bear hide.' And the girl says, 'Oh, it's very comfortable.' And he says, 'You have to feel how soft it is. You have to feel it with your whole body.'" Beat, frustrated yet eager expression, another beat. "'If you know what I mean.'

"But Nanook—he has never seen a woman naked before. It's cold up there, you know?"

I pause for the laugh, and suddenly I see something that nearly throws me off completely. Not fifteen feet from the stage, there's Donny Timson, sitting with Jerry Wald, a big producer from Warners.

Who is Donny Timson? A Brit—of course, with a name like that—who's trying to break in over here. He sings, he dances—they still have that whole Music Hall tradition—but he has this strange persona. I mean, I'm not one to judge, but his persona is like this vicious little fruit who goes to a lot of trouble to prove he's not a fruit by constantly bragging about all the girls he's balled. It's really strange. You see guys making fruit jokes, and you see guys doing fruit acts—like this kid Paul Lynde—but I've never seen somebody combine them.

Now, for the last month or two, I've been hearing this guy Timson's name mentioned whenever I find a part I want to try for. Though to me we're completely different, we seem to be trying for the same parts. So to see him out in the audience, sitting with a producer I'd love to have fifteen minutes with, is a little shock.

I continue on automatic pilot. "I mean, how often do they take all their clothes off? Sure, they're tough, but come on!"

I force myself to look away from Timson. How long has he been here? How could I not have noticed him before? "And the blonde says, 'You mean take my clothes off? No friggin' way!'"

Big laugh. You can't say certain words on stage, but you can say something that stands in for them, and whenever you do, it gets a big laugh. My eyes stray over to Timson's table. He's leaning over and saying something to Wald. Fuck him—he's *commenting*. He's analyzing my act.

I get the Eskimo shtick out of the way as soon as possible and immediately say, "Of course, you talk about cold—You ever been to England? Oh man! They don't call them blue bloods for nothing!"

The audience laughs mildly, slightly thrown by this sudden transition.

"You know how they heat the room? They got a little box on the heater, and you put in a *shilling...*" I stress the word *shilling* in a way that makes the audience laugh, like a shilling is some kind of coin only a homo would use. "You put in a *shilling* and the heat comes on for an hour. What if you run out of change? Can you see going down to the candy store on the corner, 'I say old boy, could you change a *quid?* I've got to heat my room and I've run out of *shillings.'*

"What really happens, of course, is that the shilling goes down a tube into the basement, where they've got this old guy in a miner's helmet standing on a pile of coal, and whenever a coin comes down the chute, he picks it up and puts it in his pocket and dumps another shovelful of coal on the fire."

I'm improvising wildly. Most of the audience is following me, or at least pretending to. I can see some of them are thinking, Jeez, is that true or not? Maybe that is the way it really happens over there. A guy in the cellar.

"An English guy came to Vegas, and instead of staying at a classy joint like this he rents a motel room out on the highway—the kind where they've got those vibrating beds—and he puts a shilling into the little box by the bed and the whole thing starts going *bzzzrrrrrrrrrrrrrrrrrrr!*

"'I say—bloody strange way to heat a room.'" This slays them. I risk a glance over at Timson. He's laughing too. I've got to get meaner on this.

"So he starts getting undressed for bed, but the room's not getting any warmer. The bed has quit vibrating and it's freezing in there. Now, you'd think this would make him feel at home but this is Vegas. You know how they say 'It's a dry heat?' Well, here it's a dry cold!"

That stank. I better go with the "how to make an Englishman feel at home" idea.

"So you've got a Brit in Vegas," I go on quickly. "How do you make him feel at home? Well, first, serve him really bad food. Everybody knows the food over there stinks. So get him something really awful. To a Brit, liver and onions is a feast, you've got to get much worse than that. You have to give him jellied mincemeat truffle or something.... I think they serve that over at the Tropicana." Rimshot.

"Next you've got to line up everybody you know with bad skin and bad teeth and dandruff. You know, the British are famous for being fastidious, but the fact is, well, the sun never shines there, you know? So no matter how neat they are, they're..." I quickly try to think up some British-y word for it. "They're *wan.* You know what wan means, don't you? It just means pale. Because they never see the damn sun!

"'I say old boy, what's that glowing object in the sky?' 'I don't know, I've *never seen it.'* 'But just feel the heat—jolly good! If only it would stay like this—do you have any *shillings?'"*

Out on the town on Saturday night, Gene has a few handicaps. First, he's a scrawny kid in appearance, and in fact is only 20. Vegas is surprisingly tight-assed about checking his I.D., which isn't fooling anybody. Finally when he does get a beer, it's because the bartender feels sorry for him. "Not even a good fake," the guy says, tossing Gene's driver's license back at him. "But I'll give you a beer if you stand over there and keep your nose clean."

Gene takes his fake I.D. and his beer and stands where directed, behind a pillar on which there is a little ledge for him to rest his drink. The bar is part of an older Fremont St. hotel. There are a few slot machines, but they're older models, and the décor hasn't been upgraded since the war. The paint isn't quite peeling, but high on a wall, Gene spots a scrap of faded crepe paper, on which he can just make out the letters V-I-C-T-O-R— Apparently the remains of a long-ago V-J celebration.

A few middle-aged couples and a uniformed soldier and his girl are patrons, and one booth contains four women who look to be in their 30s. Their hair set in perms, each wears bright red lipstick, smokes a cigarette, and sips a drink. They're talking as loudly and freely as any male foursome on the town—Gene thinks they're maybe wives from Santa Barbara or Costa Mesa, on a vacation from marriage; or perhaps divorcées-in-the-making, taking advantage of Nevada's famous divorce laws.

Consuming his beer slowly, Gene decides to stay put instead of searching for another place that will serve him. Over the course of an hour, during which the barkeep serves him another beer without comment, he watches the population of the bar ebb and flow. The soldier and his girlfriend are joined by a like couple; they share a drink, then leave. Two skinny women with short hair wearing cowgirl outfits stand at the bar drinking whiskeys. A group of three men and two women, dressed up a little but talking loudly enough to indicate they've already had a few rounds, settle into another booth. They enter into mock disagreements with each other and try to enlist other patrons in the disputes. "Is this or is this not a genuine diamond?!" demands one woman, shoving her hand in the face of a quiet guy sitting at a nearby table. He smiles and shrugs as if to say, "I don't know, I don't care, and don't bother me—but no offense." Gene admires the eloquence of this gesture, sees it as part of the acquired grace of the grown-up: To sit alone in a bar and keep your dignity and amiability when surrounded by fools.

Gene catches one of the putative divorcées looking at him, not just once, but twice. Mindful of the bartender's request and not knowing what else to do anyway, he stands his ground, nursing the second beer. A while later the foursome prepares to leave, and the woman who caught Gene's eye approaches him. She's a brunette, thirty at most, he thinks, and pretty. He composes his face into a friendly grin that James Dean might display.

The woman arrives in front of Gene, accompanied by a faint atmosphere of tobacco, scotch and perfume, holding a virginal cigarette between her fingers. "Got a light?" she says.

Gene does not have a light, but fortunately the hotel has placed bowls of matchbooks every three feet around the premises. He nervously manages to strike a match and hold it to the tip of the cigarette. This is the most grown-up thing that has ever happened to him.

The woman removes the cigarette, now imprinted with her bright red lipstick, and blows smoke off to the side. "Thanks." Gene is still holding the lit match. She looks at him wryly. "Better put that out," she says. "You might burn your fingers."

He shakes out the match, the movement seeming to wake him from his stupor. "Staying at the hotel?" he asks.

"This dump?" She takes another puff, throws her head back and expels smoke straight up. "Not a chance. You?"

"I'm at the Riviera," he says. "My firm has a suite there."

"Your firm?! What firm is that, the Little League?" She turns her head to spot one of her friends, and her body swivels after. She rejoins her group, and two seconds after they've gone out the door, he hears them explode in laughter.

On Sunday morning, Gene wakes up on his own. No housekeeper barges in, no families load noisily into station wagons; the place is quiet. As the girl had said, nobody actually spends the night there.

The coffee shop down the block is still busy, with mostly single men, card players alongside night workers, smoking cigarettes at the counter and staring blankly ahead as their coffee cups are filled over and over again. Gene orders the same thing as the day before: bacon, eggs, potatoes, no coffee, thanks. Coffee is another one of the talismans of adulthood which he hasn't adopted yet.

The mid-morning sky is laced with thin white clouds, high up against the deep blue backdrop. No rain has fallen, but the air is actually cool.

Feeling already bored with the walk up the strip to downtown, he heads off at an angle. Off to the west, or is it the north, there are mountains, dry and brown, like the ones they passed on the drive up. They're much too far away to approach, but he heads in that direction anyway, figuring they'll make it easy to find his way back. Of course, the buildings on the strip are the tallest in town, visible from anywhere, so he can't get lost.

He walks through a few blocks of small businesses and into a deserted industrial area. Large blank buildings alternate with auto wrecking yards and vast parking lots full of buses and trucks. There's nothing in particular to see, but Gene tries to relish the grittiness of this side of town, since it's the Real America too. He wants to learn to be comfortable in any environment, the grittier the better. Kerouac's characters never seem to reject anything they pass through in *On the Road*, even the ugliest landscapes, as if grit was redeemed by its genuineness. On the other hand, he feels Kerouac would have enjoyed the garishness of the casinos just as much, even if he would also have made some Buddhist comment about the misery underlying all the glitter.

The auto lots give way to small, dusty houses. Here, too, is misery. It's a poor area, and there seem to be a lot of Mexicans around. But Gene adopts an amiable, non-threatening expression, thinking if there's any time he's safe, it's on Sunday morning. It helps that a number of people from the neighborhood are walking in the same direction. Some look at him curiously but don't speak. They cross a thoroughfare together and come to a large Catholic church. Feeling more anonymous than he really is, Gene goes in with the crowd.

He stands in back, together with the young mothers walking slowly back and forth with babies. The congregation stands as the service begins and the priest, his back mostly to the crowd, speaks in Latin. Seen from the back of the church, the priest is so far away and so small against the ornate altar that it's like looking through binoculars the wrong way. This distance, combined with the rising mid-day warmth and the Latin—

mumbled in unison from time to time by the crowd—quickly blunts Gene's attentiveness.

He is calculating how he can wander out without being noticed, when he sees, not thirty feet away in a back corner of the church, the motel maid who crashed into his room the day before. She is facing the altar, wearing a head scarf and an expression only partly attentive, and chewing gum. Her straight black hair pours down her back from the scarf. She's wearing a light blue flower print dress, modestly calf-length, and a dark blue sweater. Standing with her arms folded, the way she had when he interrupted her cleaning, her gaze wanders around the church, taking in the stained-glass windows, the ranks of heads and shoulders, the small children standing in pews looking back at her. Gene maintains his distance, standing several

feet away and slightly behind her, outside what he gauges to be her peripheral vision, and peers at her as much as he dares.

5

"Look at that," Bobby says, gesturing ahead at the black emptiness. "Not a light except for cars. It's like we're going through outer space."

Sunday night, on the way back to L.A. Gene can smell the whiskey, faintly, in the back seat. He thinks about a cop stopping them and smelling the booze, but a cop ought to be able to tell the difference between a drunk driver and a passenger who's drinking. As if there were a cop, or anything, out in the middle of nowhere. There really is not a single light, not even a glow outlining the horizon.

Bobby sighs. "Well, I'll tell ya, Gino. I struck out last night. I had a very nice young lady at my table for a few minutes and I blew it."

"What happened?"

"It was after the last show—about 1:30. I do two shows a night, one at nine, the other at midnight. I usually see somebody I know in the audience and go sit with them after the last show, say hello, find out what they're up to."

"Show business people?"

"Precisely. And here's Rock Hudson and his manager, and a couple other fellas, and a few women. And things being the way they are, it's a little hard to tell who's with who. If you know what I mean... No, why would you... Well, skip it. Anyway I go and sit with them, and I wind up sitting next to this beautiful girl, who turns out to be a starlet at

Columbia. She looks just like that girl, what's her name, Kim Novak. Only it's not her."

There's a short pause, which gives Gene a chance to ask, "I've always wondered, just what is a starlet anyway?"

Bobby laughs. "A starlet, my boy, is a bite-sized star, and they come twelve to a box. No, I'm kidding. A starlet is a young actress under her first contract. It's usually for a year with an option for another year, and the purpose basically is to get them into the business and expose them to various people in high places... Oh boy, listen to me. You could read a lot between the lines here."

"So she's with Rock Hudson, getting exposure," Gene prompts him.

"Precisely. The point is that she and Rock Hudson are seen together. But they're not exactly together, because... well, some show business people are... Ah, never mind. But suffice to say I figure I got a chance with her. I'm not the best-looking guy at the table, but the others are, I don't know what they are, dancers or something, if you know what I mean. And I had just done my act and gone over big, and people are coming up to the table for an autograph. I'm playing the star, turning on the charm. She's laughing at my jokes. Finally I have a chance to say, 'Whatta you figure we can go to the Sands, get a drink there, just the two of us?' I tell you, she gives me one big smile and says, 'That would be lovely, but I'm married.'

"So she's married, but that hasn't stopped half the dames in Las Vegas from kicking up their heels while their husbands are losing their shirts at craps, you know? So I say, 'Oh, and where is your husband?' And she says, 'He's in San Quentin ever since he murdered the last man who tried to ask me out.'"

Gene laughs.

"Yeah, it's funny now," Bobby says.

There's a short silence. "You're not married," Gene says.

"Hmm? No." There's a short silence, and Gene grows embarrassed that he asked, but then Bobby remarks casually, "Kind of hard when you're in show business. So... how'd you make out?"

"Oh... fine," Gene replies coolly. "I got laid."

"You did?! Oh man! Listen to this, I'm giving you a sob story and the whole time you're holding out on me. Let's hear it."

"I was having a drink in a place on Fremont St.—kind of an old place."

"The El Rancho?"

"That's it. And there was a table of four women. One of them was giving me looks, and when the rest got up to go, she comes up to me and says, 'Got a light?' And we talked a while, and then we went upstairs."

"Oh man!" Bobby exclaims again. "I don't believe it. Don't tell me—she's a divorcee."

"Well, her divorce is coming through, you know."

"Right, right. And she's probably about 27."

"I'm not sure. She looked younger than that."

"Oh Jesus. You're killing me. You know, kid, I never know whether to believe a damn thing you say. I'm bombing with Kim Novak's twin sister and meanwhile some sexy divorcee comes up to *you*. It's a brutal world," shaking his head. "Tell me the truth, you're bullshitting me, right? Did that really happen?"

"Absolutely," Gene says in his most sincere voice.

They zoom into the night. Bobby drops off to sleep around the state line, and they ease down past Baker and Barstow, small constellations of lights in unbroken blackness. At this late hour, there are almost no other cars on the road; the Imperial sweeps past trucks in the right lane. Gene is alone with the feel of the wheel in his hands, the sound of the engine, the edge of the soft light cast by the headlights, and the barely perceptible outlines of mountains. He fiddles with the vents until the cold desert air defeats the smell of Bobby's whiskey, but he doesn't let the car get too cold.

Piloting the car through the darkness, his passenger safe in the backseat, Gene feels an intoxicating mixture of power and maturity. He has advanced in the world beyond mere parking lot attendant; he's the driver for a Hollywood star. Soon he'll chauffeur other stars, perhaps drive them with Bobby from movie studio to restaurant to agent's offices. He'll listen to them, to their business talk and their joshing around. Perhaps—who knows?—he'll soak up enough of the atmosphere to really become a gag writer.

At the same time, he feels he's eased into some essential Beat existence. He is literally On The Road. He's getting a chance to see what Kerouac is talking about—going from one place to another, living life in constant motion, meeting girls, driving, driving, driving. Seeing America on ground level, the good and the bad. A Kerouackian line comes to him—*alone in the darkness like a Chinese poet.* Is that in the book, or has Kerouac's voice simply sunk in deeply enough that Gene's thinking like him? The thought makes him happy, and he repeats the line to himself over and over.

Chapter 4

1

As soon as Frank told me about the *Make Nice for Daddy* project, I called my agent and asked him to get me a copy of the script. He asked me to be patient. "These things take a few days, you know."

"Philly, this is the jet age. Things happen fast."

"I can't just send them a typist, Bobby. I wish I could but I can't."

I know he can't. Philly isn't connected to one of the large talent agencies. He's someone I've been with since I came out to Hollywood five years ago, before I could attract the attention of the large talent outfits, and now that I'm more successful, I've been loyal to him. "Okay Philly, just do your best."

That was last Tuesday. Now on Monday morning, I'm in the dressing room trying to get some sleep while they're shooting a close-up of Akim. I'm having a dream about a girl, only we're not in a bedroom, we're on a stage in a big auditorium. We're going to bed together and maybe we're in a play but there's no audience. She's sitting down on the bed taking off her stockings...

A studio messenger knocks loudly on the door and barges in. "Mr. Blaine? Package for you." It's the script for *Make Nice for Daddy.*

I tear it open. It's like Frank said, a sex comedy set in an office. Daddy is a gruff industrialist with a heart of gold; his pride n' joy is an uptight manager with glasses and her hair in a bun. That's brilliant— Marilyn playing against type. The ramrod office manager who lets her hair down, but only in the second act. Then there's the equally prissy junior executive type who thinks he's going to get her, and the more down-to-earth guy who everybody knows really will get her. That's Frank's role, clearly; he seems a little old for it, it's more for somebody like Tony Curtis or Paul Newman, but then again, Marilyn ain't no spring chicken either.

But as I race through the script, I don't really see a sidekick part. Eventually I get to the scene where the two rivals get drunk together and become pals. So that's it—no sidekick role; instead, the second lead. The junior executive who loses the girl but who gets plenty of screen time with all three other characters. This is wonderful. If I'm not getting *Slovik,* this would be the biggest part I've ever done.

I don't have a line this morning. It's just a reaction shot while Akim is talking on the phone. I stand patiently while the cameraman checks a few things. It's not this role I'm thinking about; I'm thinking about the second lead in *Make Nice for Daddy.*

At lunch I find a phone and call my agent. "Philly, I got the script. The script you sent me. Yeah, did you read it? It's the second lead! I'm perfect for the second lead!"

That evening I go to Villa Capri for a drink, hoping to run into somebody who has some juice for this part. I take a seat at the bar and I haven't been there five minutes before Tony Curtis stops in with some young chicky. They stop to say hello.

"Hey Bobby! I hear you're the star of the act." He means our Las Vegas "Summit."

"Yeah, you know, without me those guys would never get on and off the stage. Especially off! How do *you* do," I say, turning to the girl, a bleached blonde with a suntan darker than Tarzan, and stacked. Despite the presentation, she's kind of unwholesome-looking. A second glance points up the need for some dental work.

"Oh, so sorry, this is Nadia. Don't tell anybody," he stage-whispers, "but she's Rumanian. Like from behind the Iron Curtain."

"Is that so. Well, welcome to the Free World, Nadia."

"Senk you."

"I'm giving her all the secrets I know. Just don't breathe a word," Tony says, turning away.

"I won't," loud stage whisper.

"You can't be too careful!" Even louder whisper, over his shoulder as they go to a booth.

I finish my drink, talk to a few more people, order another. A good guy, Tony, if a little fascinated by his own success. Chasing the starlets while he can. That whole sex jackpot aspect of Hollywood has never happened for me. Not that I'm above it—on the contrary, I'm just not a big enough star. What I told Gino the other night about how I struck out at Rock Hudson's table is pretty typical. Then he has to go and ask am I married.

Of course, when I was younger, before I went to Hollywood, things were different. When I was in radio in New York, during the war, I cut a good figure, I attracted the dames. And one in particular… But that just leads to a bad memory, which has to do with why I'm not married. I don't like to think about it.

I finish my drink and I'm preparing to go when in comes Don Tragge, the *Daily News* columnist.

"Hey Bobby. What's cookin'?"

"Mister Tragge. What are you doing slumming with the actors?"

"Somebody's gotta dish your dirt. Otherwise how would people like Sinatra ever communicate with the people who they're not speaking to?"

"Frank's speaking to everybody as far as I know." Except for Maltz, I say to myself.

"So Bobby, whattaya hear about this new project? I heard you're up for a part."

"Which project is that?"

"Come on, Bobby. Frank and Marilyn—*Make Nice for Daddy.*"

"I took a look at the script," I say evenly, though I want to shake him and say "You heard I'm up for a part? From who? Who said that?" But I can't act like a kid who's just been told he might get to start for the varsity. I have to play it cool. In fact, we're both digging for information in our own ways.

"Frank and Marilyn together," he muses vaguely, fishing.

"That would be something, wouldn't it? Of course, nothing's a sure thing. You're talking to the person who probably knows the least."

"I heard it has a certain international flavor."

"No kidding. Well, Tony Curtis is over there with some Rumanian bird. Maybe she's up for it."

"No, a certain British personage."

Christ, not Timson. I see Timson and Jerry Wald sitting together in Vegas on Saturday and two days later the guy is practically in the cast. Now I have to act like it's no big thing.

"British, Rumanian, Chinese—what's the difference. It ain't a national secret." I toss back the last of my drink. "But listen—I'm serious about that Rumanian chick. Have you heard her sing?"

"Sing? Aw, you're bullshitting me!" He claps me on the back and moves on. "Be good, Bobby."

I depart the place in a bad mood. Word has gotten out about this picture, but somehow Timson's name has gotten attached. I saw him last weekend with the producer; now Tragge knows something. Clearly I need to turn up the fire on this as soon as possible.

2

I get my chance a few days later. Frank and Dean return to the set to shoot scenes with me and Akim. Dean is in a funk, worried about some TV deal. He stays in his dressing room except when he's actually on camera. Frank and I spend most of our time playing cards with the crew. I'm not much for cards but I get on this incredibly lucky streak. By the end of the day I'm up about a hundred bucks. Most of it's Frank's but I make a mental note to send a bottle of Scotch to the crew so they won't feel like some successful movie actor took their money. You don't want to get those lighting guys mad at you. They can make you look like the Wolfman if they feel like it.

As I've been hoping, Frank grabs me at the end of the day. We ride in his car to Puccini, the restaurant he owns with Dean.

"Hey!" Frank says, settling back in the upholstery. "You know who I got a call from the other day? The Secret Service."

"Oh yeah? They're in the same department as the IRS, you know. Didn't you pay your taxes?"

"They don't care about that. This was the presidential security detail. They wanted to arrange security at my house for when Jack visits."

"Since when do they follow him around? Aren't they getting a little ahead of events?"

"Apparently it's a well-kept secret that they shadow all the major candidates. Nothing major like they do with the President, you understand. They just sort of go through the house and do a check. Kind a dry run for the real thing."

"So you're having Kennedy at your house."

"Right before the convention, probably—you know they're having the convention in Los Angeles—he'll come out for a day or two, a little R and R as they say."

"Or a little J & B," I venture. I don't want Frank to think I'm making fun of Kennedy, but it's an old joke anyway. Frank chuckles a little, but he's already thinking of something else, like the ambassadorship to Italy.

We get to the restaurant, Frank performing his ritual of tipping everybody right and left, even though they're his employees. He has a strange, imperial way of spreading cash around. He never does it himself, he has Hank or somebody else carry a roll of cash, and when he wants to tip somebody, he turns to Hank and says "Duke him a hundred" or "Duke him a fifty." So we have all these people salaaming before Frank, with Hank distributing C notes in his wake. Furthermore, there are always a few tourists who come to the place on the off chance that Frank might walk in. They squeal and he comes over to their table, signs an autograph, has the waiter bring over a round of drinks. I stand off to the side watching this, shooting the breeze with the bartender. Finally we sit down, Frank with his back to the room, in the very last booth.

He has Kennedy on the brain. No matter what we talk about, the film we're shooting, his record label, his kids, the talk keeps veering back to JFK and the convention this summer and how Frank is going to do his best, his very best, to see that Jack gets elected.

At long last I get a chance to bring up the new picture. "So Frank—I got a chance to look at that *Make Nice for Daddy* script."

He lights a cigarette. I wait for him to settle back again. "Yeah?"

This isn't the enthusiasm I expected, but I press on. "I thought it was a terrific part for you. And, well I don't have to tell you this, the scenes between your character and Marilyn, they're great. They're funny and yet they're classy. It could be a great project."

Frank is nodding patiently. "So you liked it?"

"Yeah—but you know what I was thinking? This is the kind of classy comedy that Cary Grant does. Like that picture—what was it— 'Mr. Blanding's Dream House' or something. And yet there's no way he could be in this film. You know why? Because Marilyn has this completely *American* image. And the whole situation, her father the tycoon, the aggressive young executive, the dame in the office—it's a completely *American* situation." My point being that some English twit would be as out of place in the movie as an Arab in a synagogue.

"I guess that cuts out Peter for the part," he quips.

"Peter! I thought you were doing it."

"Oh sure," he says. "But you know he's becoming an American citizen, right? The President's brother-in-law has to be a citizen, otherwise, after the inauguration, they won't let him sleep with Pat."

I just laugh at this.

"But I'll bet you weren't reading the script just so you could sing 'God Bless America,'" Frank adds.

"Of course, of course. I was looking at that second lead role, Frank. I'd give anything to get that part."

"Another good part for an American," he says, taking a big sip of his martini. Intimating that he knows the Timson rumors too. He sits back in his chair. "Bobby, I understand completely. The *Slovik* deal didn't pan out, and you're looking for your next gig. Hell, we both are! I was counting on *Slovik*, too. If it weren't for that louse Maltz... Lemme tell you, McCarthy may be history, but J. Edgar is still taking this stuff seriously. You don't want to fuck up when J. Edgar Hoover is involved."

I nod vaguely. It seems as if poor Albert Maltz is now to blame for the whole thing, in Frank's mind, at least.

Frank changes the subject. "You're still doing those gigs at the Riviera every weekend, right? How's that going?"

"Terrific, and Frank, I have to thank you. You remember you said last week for me to get a kid to drive me to and from? Well, I did, and it's working out great. You should have seen me on Monday morning, well rested, fit as a fiddle. All thanks to you."

"Why, that's fine, Bobby. Glad I could help." There's nothing Frank likes better than to hear that some advice he gave has worked out.

"Nice kid, good driver. Kind of a bullshitter. But a nice kid."

"Well, good, Say, I wonder if I can ask you a little favor. Since you're going to be up in Vegas, I was wondering if you wouldn't mind picking something up for me."

"Picking up something? Sure, why not."

"Just a package. The kind of thing you wouldn't want to send through the mail, you know. But since you're driving, I thought it would be perfect."

"No problem whatsoever."

"The thing is, you want to keep an eye on it. You go to take a leak, the kid watches the car, right? And he doesn't mess around with things?"

"No, if I tell him to do something, he does it. A good kid, like I said."

"Fine. That's fine. Someone will contact you. You take the package home, and I'll have somebody get it."

"Say no more, Frank. It's done."

"That's good. I knew I could count on you, Bobby." He gathers up his cigarettes and lighter and we get up. "I have a recording industry thing to go to—can I drop you anywhere?"

"My car's back at the studio. I'll just take a cab there."

"No, I'll have the service car take you. Carlo! Have someone take Mr. Blaine back to Warner Brothers." He gathers up a few matchbooks from the coat check to pass out like souvenirs; it's like a joke that he constantly promotes his restaurant. Turning to me at the door, he says, "Thanks again, Bobby. It's good to have a friend like you."

3

"For somebody who just works weekends, you sure are busy these days," Dana complains.

The day after Gene's return to L.A., after the first trip to Las Vegas, he slept all day following the all-night drive. He went Tuesday to buy the suit that Bobby had given him money for, and sat in his room for the rest of the time in case Bobby wanted him.

"I have to stick around in case he calls," Gene says.

"You're just going to sit in there all week long?" Dana's voice squeaks indignantly.

"Look, I'm picking up my suit on Thursday. Why don't we go out Thursday night, you can see how it looks."

"No, I'm supposed to go skating with Greta. Why can't we go out tomorrow?"

"We can, we can—but I want you to see the suit. It won't be ready till Thursday."

"I don't care, I just want to see you."

So they go out on Wednesday, to a theater in downtown L.A., with Gene ducking out of the movie every half hour to check for phone calls. By the time the movie ends, she's had it.

"Go on home and wait for a call from your boyfriend, why don't you?" she says loudly in the theater lobby. She heads for the door.

Following her to the bus stop, he pleads with her to change her mind. He'll pay for them to get into the movie all over again. But she's too angry.

"It's like we're on a date and you're spending the whole time making eyes at some other girl. When you're out with me, you're out with me. You pay attention to me. Now it's nice that you got a job and all, but he's not paying you enough to be on pins and needles like this. And if I were your landlord I'd be sick of it too. He's gonna throw you out, bugging him like this for messages."

"So what, it's a fleabag anyway. I said I'd get a new apartment."

"Yeah, you get a new place at the end of a four-week job, and then what are you going to do?"

"Maybe it'll go on longer than that."

"I don't need this new apartment, new suit, new job, Hollywood junk. I just want you, okay?" But when Gene takes this as the end of the argument and tries to take her in his arms, she pushes him away. "No, enough, I'm mad." And she stays mad, no matter what he says, until the bus comes.

Gene is only mildly surprised. The girls in *On the Road,* except for the narrator's angelic Mexican girl Terry in the first part of the book, are all bitches. They all yell and scream and throw things and the men just laugh and take them in their arms anyway, seemingly in possession of something the women want even more than they want to stay mad.

Kerouac—or his narrator—seems to experience both hilarity and sadness simultaneously. In the middle of a party, the guy suddenly feels lonely. In the middle of nowhere, he perceives the presence of friendly spirits and universal wisdom holding the world together. So many people, to Kerouac, are "sad"—even if they're not drunk. Sometimes this feels like another word for loneliness, or a sort of shyness the Kerouac narrator seems unable to shake. Other times he seems to link it to the condition of the whole world and everyone in it, so that despite all the frantic traveling and drinking and music and even sex, everyone is ultimately alone and sad.

This makes Gene uneasy. As far as existentialism is concerned, he likes the part about freedom; the angst he would rather do without. He feels he's had enough already; he wants to get to the rule-breaking, hell-raising, joy-riding part of being an adult. Now as Dana boards the bus he just gives her a big smile and bow, which she ignores.

She's mad because she can't see me more often, he tells himself. What could be better?

4

Gino and I drive to Las Vegas again.

We stop in Victorville for coffee—I've started making him drink any coffee that was drinkable so as to get him used to it—when I tell him about the special errand. "The thing is, on our way back, one of us is going to have to stick with the car all the time. So we'll get a thermos and some sandwiches and some potato chips and that way we can get back all in one piece."

"What is it that we're going to carry?" he asks.

"It's probably something like a gold record which Frank got and Jack Entratter had hanging in his office, and Frank wants it back. I don't know. It's better for us both not to know, so don't ask. Don't even think about it."

The truth is, though I don't know myself what it is, I have a pretty good idea. What else gets imported or exported from Las Vegas except dough? It comes in with the tourists like fleas on rats, and goes out in as wire transfers to bank accounts in Detroit, Chicago, Cleveland, New Jersey. Or it goes out in suitcases to certain individuals or organizations. What Frank Sinatra has exactly to do with all this is anybody's guess, but I'm content to let Frank worry about that.

That night at the Riviera, between shows, there's a knock on my dressing room door. "What, already?" I call out. I look at my wrist, I'm not due on for half an hour.

I go to the door and open it. There are two guys in suits. They aren't mobsters, I'm thinking—more like cops.

"Mr. Blaine?" asks the little one. He's only a little taller than me, middle-aged, with wide shoulders that make him look like a retired Irish bantamweight. He holds up a badge. "FBI."

"Come in," I say. The first guy walks in, the other one has to duck his head in the doorway. Jeez, he's tall.

There's a couch over to one side. My suitcases are sitting next to it. Naturally my first thought is about this secret errand Frank has asked me to do. That was quick, I think. At least I haven't been given the package yet.

"May we sit down? I'm Agent Wilson. This is Agent Corley."

"Hello," I finally manage, standing next to my makeup chair, the lighted mirrors at my back.

"No need to be nervous, sir. I'll get straight to the point. We're asking some questions about Communist influence in the entertainment industry."

I blink. "Still?"

"There is no end to vigilance against subversion," the tall guy, Corley, says in a bored voice.

"What is this about? I've got a show in a few minutes, so please tell me what's on your minds."

"There's a John Ronald Timson, a British citizen, known as 'Donny,' currently in this country," says Wilson.

"Donny Timson? Yeah?"

"We're investigating his connections to Communist front organizations... An organization known as Writers for a Democratic World."

"That means nothing to me. You're saying Timson's a writer? It's news to me."

"He's a writer in the sense that he creates his routines," Corley sneers. He says "routines" like you'd say "masturbation," like it's something dirty. I can see this guy as a member of the Penn State basketball team, trying to eke out a C in his Senior English class. He has to write a paper on *The Scarlet Letter* and can hardly bring himself to say the word "adultery."

"He writes his own material. Okay, I guess that makes me a writer too. What can I do for you gentlemen? Like I say, I have a show to do."

Aside from looking at each other, they don't move. "We just want your cooperation, Mr. Blaine."

"What I mean is, since I don't know Timson, I've never heard of this Writer's Democratic Union or —"

"'Writers for a Democratic World.'"

"Whatever it is, how can I possibly be of help to you?"

"We have information that Mr. Timson is recruiting for this organization. If he approaches you, we'd appreciate knowing."

"If he approaches me! I don't even know him. I mean, I may have met him at a party once…"

"You met him on May 4, 1959, at the '21' Club in New York City," Corley interjects, his finger on a page in his little notebook

"Is that a fact. Boy, you guys would come in handy when I get audited. 'What's this receipt for?' 'I don't remember, but just ask Agent Curley here-'"

"It's Agent Corley."

"Are you guys done? I would really appreciate it if you got out of here."

Wilson, the short one, is sitting on the couch with his legs crossed, like he's watching TV in his den. "Mr. Blaine," he says, "We appreciate your cooperation." He uncrosses his legs and stands up. "Here's my card. Like I say, just a phone call from you would be very helpful."

He holds out the card as the other fellow unbends his body from the couch and stands. I look at them for a moment, and then, more because I'm standing between them and the door, take the card and stand aside.

"Thank you, Mr. Blaine," they both say, and let themselves out soundlessly.

Chapter 5

1

When he checks into the motel on Friday night, Gene buys a postcard in the tiny office and writes Dana a romantic yet humorous message—the written equivalent, he hopes, of kidding her and making her smile and feel like being nice again. But the little stamp machine in the office is broken, so Gene takes the postcard to his room.

It's lying on the desk when the door explodes open at 9:00 on the dot. Fortunately Gene's not still in bed, but in the bathroom.

"Maid!" yells out the Mexican girl, the same one as before.

"Hello! I'm here! I'm in here!" Gene calls.

"Oh—sorry," her voice retreats and the door shuts.

He finishes washing while listening to the sound of the vacuum cleaner next door. While he's shaving, he can hear her clanking in the bathroom, separated only by the thin wall. He runs water, she runs water. She flushes, he flushes unnecessarily. He gets dressed in silence—maybe she's making the bed.

He leaves his room. Next door is propped open with a bucket holding cleanser, sponges, aerosol sprays. Gene knocks loudly and pushes open the door, heavy on its pneumatic arm. She's finishing the bed and looks up, startled.

"You can clean my room now," Gene says, leaning in the doorway. "Next door."

She frowns, then turns away without stopping what she's doing. "You again. Why are you sleeping here, man?"

He laughs. "It's a motel. You're supposed to sleep here."

"Nobody else does." She tucks the bedspread around the pillows with four short, measured chops with the side of her hand.

"What's your name?" he asks.

She picks up the vacuum cleaner and thrusts its hoses and attachments under her arm, all in one motion. She advances toward him, forcing him to back out of the door as she reaches it. She picks up her cleaning implements, brushing past him as the door closes. "Dolores," she says over her shoulder, going down to his room.

"I'm Gino."

"Gino, what are you, Italian?" She puts the bucket down and unlocks the door of his room.

"Yeah."

They go into his room; she props the door open with the bucket full of supplies. Putting the vacuum cleaner down, she faces him, thrusting her chin out. "If you don't mind, I'd like to work without you watching me."

"Sorry. I'll go get breakfast."

"Bye." She lifts her bucket and the door swings closed, shutting him out.

Gene goes for breakfast at the same place, then walks the morning away among the casinos, restaurants and gas stations. It's another sunny morning, not yet hot; and he wanders up busy streets and down deserted back alleys, finding nothing but addled tourists and heaps of garbage. Once he passes a busy hamburger stand located on a corner behind two big hotels. Even though it's barely 10:00 a.m. the place is packed with hotel and casino workers on some kind of early lunch break. He wonders what the tips are like at the big hotels. He's already encountered their parking valets, who spirit away Bobby's car when they arrive at the Riviera; he makes a mental note to ask them.

Parking cars is as low as he wants to go, though. Manning the front desk would be more like it. He can see himself in a suit, standing behind the heavy mahogany counter, saying "Yes sir—room nine forty-two.

We'll have your bags brought up, sir. Enjoy your stay at the Sands." Then, in a few years, a manager.

His destiny had been elsewhere. Gene's father owned a busy small-town hardware store that everyone assumed he would inherit. When Gene was nine his father went off the road after a few late-night beers following a church-league basketball game. An uncle took over the store until Gene was old enough to assume command.

But Gene had acquired little interest in tools and even less in their use. To the boy, a drill was a funny object with a turning handle, equivalent to his mother's eggbeater; it could be admired only for its moving parts, the clattery noise it made, and other abstract qualities. But when his uncle took him in hand to teach its real use, Gene became dubious. He couldn't understand how a man chose, among the infinite points on a board, the exact spot to apply the drill. When his uncle explained the potential relationship between a carpenter's measurements and his arithmetic homework, Gene's sense of vertigo became even worse. Numbers belonged in school, not arrayed on concrete objects to suggest where those things might irreversibly be sawed in two. When Gene miscalculated and lopped off a two-by-four in the wrong place, his uncle pronounced it "ruined," and Gene's heart sank. He dropped the saw on the workbench and moaned in a panicky voice, "I can't!" Taken aback, his uncle pointed to the pile of lumber and said it didn't really matter. But Gene was upset not so much for being criticized as out of sympathy for the wood.

His disinclination toward hardware, lack of talent in sports, and preference for reading science fiction comics flummoxed his family. Gene suffered for several years under a general air of disappointment. By contrast, when he turned fifteen and began to show an enthusiastic interest in girls, his uncle was so relieved that Gene was off the hook, as far as hardware was concerned. Now he didn't intend to get anywhere near it if he could help it.

He finds his way back to the motel a little before noon. The maid is hauling her tools across the parking lot toward a closet at the end of the row of rooms. He rushes up, grabs the vacuum cleaner.

At first she is startled, but then, with a raised eyebrow, she lets him carry it. "You still here?"

"I'm spending the weekend."

"I hope you see more of Las Vegas than this."

"I'm not trying to get anywhere, just killing time."

"That must be nice." She takes the vacuum cleaner from him and puts it away, along with the other things. Taking off her smock, she reaches into the pocket and pulls out a postcard. "I found this in your room—I thought you left so I was going to give it to the old man. This to your girlfriend?"

"No, my cousin."

"Some cousin. 'Baby, you're the'—what is this - 'gonest little chicky.' What does that mean?"

"It's just a joke between us," pocketing the postcard. "How about some lunch?"

She shuts the door of the closet and heads back across the parking lot. "I bring mine," she says. "And I have to get on to my next job."

He has to stride fast to keep up with her. "You have another job after this one?"

"I do the books at my cousin's shop. My real cousin," she says. "Excuse me."

She goes into the motel's office, comes out after a few minutes. "He wants to know if you're bothering me," she says to Gene. They walk down the driveway and toward the Strip.

"Am I bothering you?" He looks back to see the motel's proprietor, an elderly Swede, watching them from the office doorway. Gene smiles reassuringly at the guy.

"So far all you've done is carry my vacuum cleaner and offered me lunch. I guess you're harmless."

"Let's have lunch, then I'll pay for you to take a taxi to your next job."

"Ijole. What are you talking about, man?" she asks crossly. "If you can afford that, why are you staying in that motel? What do you want from me? Let me alone, okay?" They reach the coffee shop on the corner. "Go eat your hamburger. I'm catching my bus. I don't like hamburgers anyway."

She has the light and hurries across the wide boulevard, leaving Gene on the corner. He goes inside and sits in a booth by the window. As he sits waiting for his hamburger, he watches her sitting on the bench, eating her lunch and reading a paperback. Finally the bus arrives and takes her away.

Now this is sad, Gene reflects, as the hamburger is put before him, bristling with lettuce and pickles. It's like in On the Road when Sal and Terry are just getting together, so suspicious of each other. He eats his lunch feeling romantic and sad and excited that there's a Mexican girl in his life, too.

2

It's Saturday afternoon and I'm by the pool at the Sands with Sammy. Not exactly by the pool—sitting at the bar that looks out over the pool. They don't actually let Negroes swim in the pool here, whether they're headlining the joint or not. While Sammy probably has no intention of swimming, he would like to get some sun. But the closest they let him get to the pool is sitting at a patio table under an umbrella at the bar adjacent to the pool. Fully clothed, so that nobody gets the wrong idea.

Sammy is wearing enormous sunglasses and a yellow Hawaiian shirt with orange and red flowers. Even though he's sitting behind the railing that designates the area belonging to the bar, not the pool, he has a towel draped around his neck—his way of indicating that, as far as he's concerned, he's poolside. He might just go swimming if he decides he wants to.

For myself I'm wearing a golf shirt and slacks and a cap from Pebble Beach. Not that they let Jews join Pebble Beach either, but I did play there at some celebrity benefit.

From behind the shades, Sammy is checking out the talent. "Dig her," he grins, a cigarette hopping up and down on his lips. I turn around and see a redhead in a green bikini. She walks down the diving board and daintily dives off.

I turn back around, sip my drink and set it back down on the metal table.

"You need another one?" he asks. "Your ice has melted. Here—Mr. Perkins, bring another for my guest, please."

"Yes, sir." Aside from Sammy, the only Negroes here are the help. Sammy always calls them Mister as an example to the rest of us.

"So whattaya hear about this *Make Nice* picture?" I ask, but before I can even finish talking, Sammy interrupts.

"Dig, there she is again," Sammy nods toward the pool again.

I don't turn around. "I thought you were engaged," I smile.

"I am, but May's in Sweden making a movie."

"One of those rip-roaring Swedish comedies, I guess?"

"Haw haw! Yes, man, a comedy. They need the laughs."

"So how's that going?" I ask. Sammy's fiancé, May Britt, is not just white, she's a gorgeous Swedish actress, which is about as white as you can get.

"Lovely, it's going lovely. She's now a civil rights hero in her country."

"For getting engaged to you?"

"Naw, man, I'm kidding you. The Swedes are cool, man. They have maybe six Negroes in the entire country, and they're all African ambassadors. I'd be the first non-ambassadorial Negro."

"What, don't tell me you're thinking of moving there."

"And give up all this? Next year they may let me sit *by* the damn pool," he says, but quietly.

"Ha ha."

"No, I'm a patriotic American. I'd never leave here. Not like those guys who go to Paris, James Baldwin and such. Can you see me speaking French? No, man."

"Who's James Baldwin?"

"A writer cat." Sammy puts out his cigarette and lights another. "A genius. A fantastic writer. But he doesn't dig the way Negroes are treated here," Sammy explains, speaking quietly again. "You know. And I can dig that. The man wants to live in a place where he doesn't get bothered, where the fact that he's a Negro doesn't make a difference.

"But you know, look at this." He waves his arm. "Sunshine, broads, a full bar, you should see my suite here. Baldwin probably has to live in, what do you call it, a garret. And you think they have swimming pools in Sweden?"

"I guess they do."

"Yeah, to skate on! They play ice hockey on the swimming pools, you dig?"

"Aw, come on, what about all those pictures you see in magazines of gorgeous Swedish dames in swimsuits?"

"My opinion is, they shoot those photos in Italy or someplace."

"Well, you sound like a patriotic American to me," I say.

"Absolutely."

"But hey, let me ask you something. Have you heard about any kind of investigation going on? Like a few years ago—the Hollywood blacklist thing. You think it's over with, but what I hear, it's still going on, just more quietly."

"Hmmm," he drawls. His sunglasses reflect the scene in the pool, the drinks on the table, and me.

I venture, "A guy I know—you know Dick Shawn? Don't say this to anybody else, but he got a visit from some FBI guys."

Sammy purses his lips.

"They wanted to know if he had any dirt on other entertainers. They came to his dressing room at the Sands, can you believe that?"

Sammy takes an elaborate drag from the cigarette and holds it in front of his face. He could be posing for a Lucky Strike ad. Finally he says, "Yeah, they came to me too."

"To you!"

He puffs. "The asked me about May," he says in a pained voice. "They asked me things like, did she and I talk about politics. Does she support civil rights for Negroes. Do I know what her politics are—her politics in Sweden! I said, 'Man, I would not know a Swedish politic if it bit me on the ass.'"

I sit there absorbing this. This has nothing to do with this Timson thing, or with any investigation of writers or comedians. What the hell.

Sammy shakes his head. "I'll tell you one thing. May and I are getting married this September. I don't care if it's America or Sweden or Timbuktu."

"You love each other."

"That's right, man. We love each other."

3

On Sunday evening Gene's in the Imperial outside the Riviera, thermos and gas tank full, a bag of sandwiches and candy bars beside him on the seat as ordered. He notices a security man in a blazer has been standing near the car since he got back from the gas station. The guy stands silently by, not acknowledging Gene, just waiting.

When Bobby comes out, carrying his garment bag as usual, he's followed by two more men in blazers, one of them with a gray Samsonite suitcase.

"Gino, let these men have the keys for a second," Bobby says.

Gene starts to get out to walk around and open the trunk, but one of the men is suddenly standing in his way. The thug holds out his hand for the keys. "I'll get it," the guy says. Gene hands over the keys and sinks back into his seat.

The trunk is opened, the Samsonite is put inside, the trunk is slammed shut. "Thanks, fellas," Bobby says. He hands Gene the keys, gives the leader a twenty and climbs in. "Let's go."

They head up the Strip, make the U-turn, cruise past the hotel on the other side.

"Nice and easy," Bobby says. "No big hurry. You got the sandwiches? Good. Only thing we'll stop for is gas."

Gene is both taken aback and excited by the smooth actions of the security men. They drive in silence as the lights of the city recede behind them.

Finally Gene offers in a Bogart drawl, "I don't know nothin'."

Bobby has to chuckle. "That's right, you don't," he says.

Judging from last week, Gene expects that Bobby feels like talking after his Sunday night appearance, so he says, "I saw in the paper last week about that guy—what was his name—Albert Mertz?—who wrote a script for a movie for Frank Sinatra."

"Maltz. Mertz is the guy on *I Love Lucy*. So what about him?"

"Well, it said that he wrote this script, and it was his first script since being banned for being a Communist."

"*Was* a Communist. In the 30s and 40s. When Russia was our ally."

"It said that Frank Sinatra was going to give the guy a chance, but then the guy decided not to."

Bobby nods. It had come out in the papers the right way—Maltz released a statement last week saying, more or less, that he had realized he was too hot a property and was going to move to Acapulco and write a historical novel set in Mexico, or some b.s. like that. Of course, the reporters had speculated plenty about Sinatra dumping Maltz because of the Kennedy association, but Maltz had promptly shut up and disappeared, and the story quickly died.

All Bobby says is, "Something like that."

"So why doesn't he just make an announcement that he's not a Communist anymore—that it was all a big mistake and he's going to be a good American from now on. Even if it's not true—he could lie and say, 'I was wrong. I'm not a red anymore, I love America.' But he's lying, down deep he still believes in Communism."

"Well, precisely. That's why some people don't want him to work."

"But if the script is okay—that's his whole contribution, right? Once it's done, where's the danger?"

"You're right. The script is the script, and what does it matter where it comes from. That's why people use a front. It's not fooling anybody in the industry. You have a script supposedly by Joe Blow. Everybody knows it was really written by a blacklisted guy, but as long as it's not official and nobody really talks about it, it's okay."

"So Maltz could have used a front."

"Maybe, but he doesn't want to. He wants to use his real name, and why not? He's not ashamed of his work. He wants to be able to take his little boy to the movies and say 'Look, your daddy wrote this. That's not Joe Blow's name up there. Look, it's daddy's name.' And that's maybe why he doesn't make a big announcement about his patriotism either. Maybe it *would* be a lie—I don't know, I don't know the man—but maybe he just doesn't want to lie. Maybe, for him, being a liar is worse than being on the blacklist."

Gene drives through the night, the mostly downhill grade keeping them from running low on gas before Victorville. While the attendant is filling the tank, Bobby goes to the bathroom and leaves Gene with the car; then Gene goes while Bobby settles himself in the backseat again.

It's three tanks of gas to get up to Vegas, only two to come back to sea level. They get to Bobby's house about four o'clock in the morning. Bobby, rocked awake by the Imperial starting and stopping in the Hollywood streets, directs Gene up the driveway. He unlocks the garage door himself and has Gene drive right in, then closes the door behind them.

They carry the luggage in, Gene with Bobby's garment bag and his own duffel bag, Bobby with the Samsonite, which he carries straight upstairs. "Put my garment bag down anyplace," he says over his shoulder.

When Bobby comes downstairs, Gene is standing indecisively in the living room. "How about a drink?" Bobby says. "I'll give you some brandy, and you can sack out on the couch. I have to leave for the studio at 7:00, but Mary comes in at 8:00 and she can fix you some breakfast. Is that okay? Would you mind staying here till she gets here? She fixes some terrific pancakes."

"Uh, okay. You mean to keep an eye on … yeah."

Bobby holds a finger to his lips and goes over to the bar. "Keep an eye on nothing. I just would feel better if there's someone here."

He pours a double for each of them, finds a blanket and hands it to Gene. "Take your shoes off before you lie down on the couch. There's a bathroom off the kitchen. If I think of anything else in the morning I'll leave you a note if you're not up. Nighty-night, Gino." Carrying his drink, he heads for the stairs.

Anchored by the brandy, Gene sleeps soundly on the couch until kitchen noises wake him up. He blearily pulls on his shoes and makes his way across the shag carpeting toward the kitchen. The maid gives him some pancakes and bacon and an envelope. There's his pay for the weekend and a note. It asks him to come back to the house around four when Mary leaves, until Bobby can return an hour or so later. "Invite your girlfriend for a swim if you want. (But no wild parties! Ha ha!) I'll see you around 6 or 7 and drive you home."

4

"Are you sure you can afford this?" Dana wonders. She holds Gene's hand in the backseat of a taxi.

"Sure I can. My room's only $60 a month; I'm getting a hundred a weekend on this job. What else am I gonna spend it on?"

It's four o'clock and the taxi is rising into the hills. Sun has finally burned off the overcast, and Dana is looking forward to this proffered pool date with a mixture of pleasure and anxiety. She's just a girl from Pasadena; she's never met a Hollywood star before, much less been in one's house. The closest she's come is one New Year's Day afternoon, following the Rose Parade, when Soupy Sales was at the next table in a Pasadena diner.

"You're sure we're not invited to dinner?"

"The note didn't say anything about that."

"And he'll be back when?"

"He said between six and seven."

"It'll be dark then."

"And he'll drive us home. Don't worry—I was a little nervous about coming here the first time, too, but he's just a regular guy. I think he just wants to be nice. The pool's there and it's a nice day so why not use it."

Gene hasn't said anything at all about the suitcase, of course, and he feels pleasure in the secret. In his note, Bobby hadn't reminded him not to mention it; he hadn't needed to. Gene understood.

They arrive at the house a few minutes after four; the maid lets them in and directs them to the poolside cabana. They change and dip into the pool; they take turns performing on the diving board; there's enough sun for them to lie in twin chaise lounge chairs, drinking cokes. When the sun goes down, Gene goes to change his clothes, but Dana plunges into the pool again. She begins swimming back and forth, executing a neat kick turn at the end of each lap. When Gene comes out of the cabana, dressed in sports clothes and drying his hair with a towel, he stands beside the pool watching her go back and forth. She finally stops, grinning and breathing heavily, at the side next to him. "It's really heated!" she exclaims. "Almost too warm for somebody swimming laps."

"I never knew you were a swimmer like that."

"There were teams at all the city pools in Pasadena. I did it all the way through junior high and high school. For a while I thought I was going to get a swimming scholarship to a college." She smiles ruefully. "But I didn't."

Gene hears the doorbell ringing. "That must be him," Gene says.

"Oh jeez," Dana exclaims. "I'm not ready. Gimme that towel."

He tosses the towel on the side of the pool and trots into the house and across the living room. Glancing at the clock, he sees it's not even 6:00. That's all right, he thinks. Bobby can have a look at how pretty my girl is in her swimsuit.

He pulls open the door only to be confronted with a tall, handsome man dressed in a gold sweater and slacks. He's smoking a cigarette and doesn't seem surprised to see Gene. "Oh, hello," the man says with a British accent. "I don't know if you're expecting me. I'm Peter Lawford."

Gene shakes himself out of his frozen pose. "Uh, hello. I'm Gene Kramer." They shake hands.

Lawford puffs on his cigarette. "Bobby told me you might be here guarding the place," he says. "I'm to meet him here. Do you mind if I come in?"

"Oh, sorry." Gene steps aside. "I think Mr. Blaine will be here soon."

"Thank you."

Gene says, "Er... Would you like to wait in the living room?"

Lawford is looking across the room and out toward the pool. "Hello," he says, more to himself than to Gene. Then, turning to Gene, "I see you've been enjoying the swimming. Marvelous, isn't it?"

Gene follows Lawford's gaze and sees Dana, dripping in her maroon one-piece swimsuit, bending over in profile, wrapping her hair in a towel. Her figure is silhouetted against the evening sky.

"Oh yes—that's my... my fiancé. Let me introduce you."

They go across the room and out the glass door just as Dana straightens up and sees them. She sees Lawford and, like Gene had, freezes.

Lawford goes up to her and extends his hand warmly. "How do you do? Your young man was kind enough to let me in."

"Oh... hello..."

"Um, Dana, this is Peter Lawford. Mr. Lawford, this is Dana Grezilanik—my fiancé."

Lawford steps on Gene's last word. "So pleased to meet you."

"How... do... you... do," Dana stutters.

"I see Bobby's pool is finally getting some use."

"Oh, yes. We were... just swimming."

"Of course. I hope I'm not intruding."

"Oh, not at all. We were just getting out. Um..."

"Shall we sit down?" Lawford motions her to the twin chaise lounges. He takes her hand and smoothly helps her into it, then sits down on the other, facing her. She can't take her eyes off him. Gene wanders over, but the closest chair is thirty feet away. Finally he takes up a standing position behind Dana. Lawford's looks are striking, he has to admit.

"So are you in the industry, my dear?"

"Um, beg pardon?"

"In films. The film industry. That's what we call it, just 'the industry.'"

"Oh, no. I work at a bank."

"Really! And you've never considered getting into pictures? Perhaps you should."

She seems to be recovering some of her self-possession. "Oh really, flattery will get you nowhere," she says, smiling.

"Oh blast. I was hoping it would."

Gene clears his throat.

"Oh, would you like something to drink?" Dana asks. "Gene, didn't you say there was a poolside bar?"

"It's not open, though," Gene says quickly. "But I can offer you a Coke from the fridge."

"Oh, I'm sure Mr. Lawford doesn't drink Coke!"

"Nonsense, I heartily endorse it. But I don't want to trouble you."

"It's no trouble," Dana says. "Would you mind... honey?"

"No trouble at all," Gene says crossly, heading across the concrete. Behind him, he hears Lawford say, "I really *do* endorse it," followed by Dana's laugh.

By the time he gets back, carrying three Cokes—even though he doesn't want one, it looks more like he's getting a drink for them all, rather than serving Mr. Big Shot—Lawford is twelve inches closer to Dana and is holding her hand. She's looking into his eyes, mesmerized.

"And she said, 'But I'm nervous with all these people around,'" Lawford is saying in an intimate tone. "But I just took her hand like this and said, 'Don't worry darling, just pretend we're on the beach at Waikiki and we're the only ones here. That's not a klieg light, it's the moon. Those aren't people out there, they're palm trees. If you listen closely, you can hear the ocean lapping on the shore nearby. Just imagine we're the only ones here.' And I nodded at the director, and he said 'Action' very quietly, and we said our lines and kissed and it was just like I said. She was marvelous."

Dana lets out her breath in a little gasp.

"And that was Elizabeth Taylor's first screen kiss," Lawford concludes.

"Here's the Coke," Gene says loudly. He hands one to Dana, and it goes right through her hands, the bottle shattering on the concrete.

"Oh God!" Dana says. "Gene, why don't you watch what you're doing!" The soda fizzes out around the legs of the chaise lounge.

"Don't stand up, dear, you'll cut yourself," says Lawford. He bends over and quickly scoops her into his arms.

"Oh my," she says.

"I haven't swept a girl off her feet like this in quite a while," Lawford grins. "Now where is it you get dressed?"

"Over there," Dana says, latching her hands behind Lawford's neck. Gene stands dumbly, holding a Coke in each hand, as the star carries his girlfriend over to the cabana.

They're almost at the door before he hears Bobby's voice behind them, "Peter, where are you going with that girl!?"

"Oh hello, Bobby," Peter says, swinging back toward them with a big grin. "We broke a bottle and I didn't want missy to cut her pretty feet."

"Fine, Peter, just put her down so she can get dressed."

The mood is broken. Dana alights and scampers into the cabana. Peter wanders genially back to Bobby, pulling a cigarette from a case and lighting it. "Just being chivalrous," he says.

"I'll sweep up the glass," Gene says.

"Don't bother. Mary will get it tomorrow. Just as long as I know it's here—it's the bottles I don't know about that are the trouble. I presume you've introduced yourselves?"

"Yes indeed, I was just telling old war stories to Jim and his girl here."

"His name's Gene, Peter. Come on, I've got to drive these kids back, so let's get our business over with. Excuse us for a few minutes, Gino." Bobby leads Peter into the house. Just before going through the patio door, Peter turns around and gestures vaguely with his cigarette, a sort of pointing gesture. Gene doesn't know if it means "Sorry" or "Cheerio" or "Take that."

Gene sets the bottles down and sits on the chaise lounge. Dana comes out of the cabana in a flash, smiling at Gene. "Where'd they go?" she asks.

"Upstairs."

She shakes her hair so it falls the right way on her shoulders. "My god! That must be what they mean when they say Kennedy has charisma."

"Let me see," Gene says, looking into her face. He regards her closely. "Yes, it's all right."

"What?"

"Oh, you had something on your face a minute ago."

"On my face! What?"

"I don't know. A leaf, maybe. From the pool."

"I did not."

"Or maybe it was a bug."

"You're nuts! I didn't have anything on my face," she says, rising. "You're just jealous."

"Jealous? Of a big Hollywood star? Of course not."

"You have to spoil it."

"You know, I'm sure he'll give you a ride back himself, in case you don't want to come with me."

She sighs and takes his hand, sitting down again. Gene waits for her to say something. Finally she says, "I'm sorry. I'll come with you. Just don't be mean to me, all right?"

They sit by the pool, looking sadly at the shadowy water. The sun has been down for some time and the sky is almost dark, and lights are standing out against the hills around and below them and in the city in the distance. Gene sees how deflated Dana is, and reaches out and strokes her hair, but she doesn't respond.

Through the glass wall over her shoulder, he sees Peter Lawford come downstairs with the suitcase, followed by Bobby. They say a few words as Bobby lets him out, and then Gene hears a sports car start up and drive away.

Bobby comes out on the patio. "You kids should have turned the lights on," he says. He flips a switch near the door and the dismal water is suddenly illuminated. Gene introduces Dana to Bobby, who says, "Glad to see you survived Peter's wolf act. I was sure I'd get here before him, but he was on time for once in his life. Let me give you a lift. You kids just sit in the back. I'll be your chauffeur."

"Oh no—I'll sit up front with you," Gene protests.

"Just get in the back! Pretend you're on your way to the Academy Awards."

They walk through the house and out the front door. "It's a beautiful car, Mr. Blaine," Dana says politely.

"Ah, well, Gino hasn't scratched it up yet."

They drive down the hill, Gene sulking. Dana glances over at him in annoyance. "He's never actually driven me," she offers. "We ride buses."

Bobby looks in the rear view mirror at Gene, who stares glumly ahead. He makes small talk with Dana until they pull up in front of her house.

Gene, sitting on the curb side, rouses himself to open the door and climb out. Then he bends down. "Want to get out on this side? No, I'll open your door." He goes around and lets Dana out on the street side.

She shakes Bobby's hand through the driver's window and thanks him. "You come back to my pool, okay?" he says. "I'll make sure there aren't any sharks next time."

Gene gets into the shotgun seat and they drive off.

"Hey, cheer up, okay?" Bobby says. "You're not the first guy whose girl's head was turned by Peter Lawford. He even beats out Sinatra, you know that? In an even contest, the girls choose Peter every time."

Gene sighs. "Sorry," he says.

"Not that she's not a nice girl. She's a very nice girl... Oh, listen. Are you free tomorrow?"

"Uh, sure."

"Can you drive me around? I don't have to be on the set the rest of the week and I need to see some people. If I don't have to park and all, it'll be one less thing for me to worry about."

"Sure."

"I'm already working on my next role. Working on getting it, that is. They wrap this picture by the end of the month and Frank's next project starts immediately. That's the picture I'm trying to get into next. So tomorrow I meet with some people who can help me get the part."

Bobby pulls up in front of Gene's building. Music from the jukebox in the Mexican restaurant blares when Gene opens his door. "I'll pick you up at 9:00. And wear that suit."

Chapter 6

1

My agent, Philly Snider, has a chair that creaks. Not the desk chair he sits in, but his client chair. It's a godawful Scandinavian job, upholstered in dark green burlap of some kind, and it was originally designed to go up, down, tilt back and forth, and do everything short of churn butter. Now mostly what it does is creak.

I sit on this piece of junk, right ankle over left knee, my left foot planted in a thick blue carpet, a sort of very dark turquoise. The chair and the carpet, and everything else in the office except the pictures on the walls and Philly's desk, date from his move into this office five years ago. He was having a good couple of years and took the opportunity to move out of Hollywood and over to Fairfax to the second floor of a small office building where a few other agents had their offices. The only thing is that those other agents moved, for various reasons, since then and now Philly shares the building with dentists, doctors, a lawyer and two chiropractors. You come down the hall and there's a faint smell of that stuff they use to fill teeth.

Philly is on the phone with somebody from Warners. I don't like what I'm hearing on his end of the conversation.

"I've got the script on my desk right here... right in front of me... I see. 'Norman Krasna Project.' Since when do they name things after the writer? What does that mean?... Uh huh. Uh huh. Well, I don't care what you call it as long as... 'Make Nice'... Yeah, sure, it sounds great. Look, I don't care! What are you telling me? ... But I thought it was supposed to shoot next month... Oh, I see. Yes, sure.

"Is Overbeck still producing? Can you tell me that, or is it a state secret? Fine." Philly nods to me. Dick Overbeck handles a lot of Warners' borderline stuff. He does B pictures with an aging star, or with young players the studio hopes will go someplace. It would be a little surprising for him to put Sinatra and Monroe together, but Frank probably wants somebody he can control.

"What about my boy here? You know *Esquire's* doing a feature on him? I just talked to the writer... Gay Talese, who else?"

A patent lie, but that's what agents are for.

"Because he's an up and comer, that's why... What does that mean? Sheldon. Sheldon... Listen to me here. Bobby is getting hot. That's all I want you to remember. He's getting hot. By November he'll be hot... Yeah, him and Kennedy! Sure, ha *haaa!* ... Ah ha ha ha ha! That's terrible... Now Sheldon, make nice! Ha *haaa*, 'Make Nice.' Sure. Sure. Sure. Love to Judy. You too. Thanks, Shel. *Good*-bye!"

Philly always says "*Good*-bye" at the end of phone conversations, a mannerism left over from his days as a small town radio host during the war. Philly Snider, the only Jew in Beloit, Wisconsin, presenting the Sunday morning classical music concert from a sweatbox of a studio behind the screen of the town's movie theater.

I've been looking out the window at the hazy sunshine, the tops of a few trees, the side of a commercial building down the street, a faded ad on the bricks for "Tip Top Tooth Powder, 5¢." Now I turn back to Philly. The chair shrieks like an El train going around a curve.

Philly leans back. "It's the damnedest thing, Bobby. First he pretends he doesn't know what I'm talking about. I say 'A Norman Krasna script I got right here, *Make Nice for Daddy property Warner Brothers Studios Inc. copyright nineteen hundred and sixty.* You're the executive in charge of production and you're telling me you haven't heard of it?'"

"Philly, I was here, I heard your end of it. Tell me what *he* said."

"Then he says 'Yeah sure, that Norman Krasna thing.' Then he tells me they're not sure about the title, that's why he wasn't sure what I meant. He says they're probably changing the title to *Make Nice* because they don't want people to get confused with the Danny Thomas show. *Make* Room *for Daddy… Make* Nice *for Daddy…* What confusion is that? I thought that was the point!

"Anyway, he says they're just referring to it right now as the 'Norman Krasna Project' until they decide. I tell him I don't care what they call it as long as they at least test you. But they don't even have a director yet!"

"What the hell, I thought they were shooting next month."

"That's what I said. He's saying they might use a blacklisted guy. Suddenly they're out of directors… I dunno. It's the damnedest thing."

"A blacklisted guy! But that's why Frank's not doing *Private Slovik* in the first place!"

"Apparently there's a big difference between using a blacklisted writer and a blacklisted director, as long as the director doesn't use his real name."

"There is?" I haven't told Philly about the visit to my dressing room by the FBI yet, but maybe it's time to. I quickly fill him in.

"Democratic Writers for a… what? Better World?" Philly echoes when I'm done. "What the fuck is that?"

"Never heard of it. But it seems like I can take the bait, screw Timson, get the part…"

"Where's the catch?" Philly completes my thought.

I grimace. "It just seems so cutthroat. It's one thing to manipulate someone into doing you a favor, it's another to stab somebody in the back."

Philly purses his lips, looks down at a pile of unopened mail sitting in front of him. He touches the stack of envelopes—just fiddles with the corner of one envelope. His finger brushes the corner up and down, like the paw of a curious kitten.

"I screw somebody to get ahead, what does that make me? A prick. I've never done that. And especially this blacklist thing. It stinks."

Philly is nodding patiently.

"I played all those mob clubs for years, but do they own me? No. When the time came, when Sam Giancana offered to lend me money for a house, I turned him down, in the nicest way possible. That's why they don't own me. And I've never stabbed somebody in the back. Somebody likes my act, they hire me, great. They like some other guy, fine. Next time I'll be funnier than him and maybe they'll hire me."

He's still fiddling with his mail. He brushes his finger up the stack of envelopes and back down. I realize it's a stack of bills. He sighs. "You're absolutely right, Bobby. They should hire you because you're funnier than the next guy. But people get hired for lots of reasons. Sometimes because, frankly, the guy they wanted is not quite available and you're the second choice."

"Why should I be the second choice? Am I the second choice?"

"I'm just hypothesizing. There are many factors that you and I will never know about. But we do know about one factor. The acceptability, or palatability shall we say, of this Timson character. What do you know about him?"

"Nothing—nothing that everybody doesn't know. He's been in a couple of British movies nobody saw, he did that USO tour to Berlin, *Life* published that photo that everybody got such a kick out of, Warners' signed him last year and has been looking for something to put him in. Plus this Communist thing, which could be complete bullshit as far as we know."

Philly picks up the stack of bills and lines up the edges with a *thwack* on his desk. Then he sets the pile down gently. "All I'm saying—the palatability—just one factor."

We fall silent.

Finally he says, "You talked to Frank."

"He's mum," I say. "You know what his response was? He asked me to do *him* a favor."

"What favor?"

"This is strictly *entre nous,* okay? He asked me to carry a suitcase full of cash from Vegas back to my house. To be picked up by Peter Lawford."

"Jesus Christ. What did you say?

"Say? I did it. I brought it back in my car Sunday; Peter picked it up last night. Probably some cash for Kennedy. I don't even know if it was cash, I didn't ask—don't mention this to *anybody.*"

"Bobby, you think I'm a fool? But what about the picture? Did he say anything about the picture?"

I shake my head. "Precisely. What about the picture."

"Look," Philly says. "I'm having lunch today with Jerry Wald. Maybe he knows something. They're so up in the air about this, maybe Jerry will end up producing."

"Why didn't you say so? Jerry will know something. I'm an old pal of Jerry's. Take me along."

"I'd love to, Bobby, but this is all business. He's signing one of my starlets—Sherlyn Reese. She's gonna be the next Kim Novak. We'll be negotiating. But I'll come downstairs with you."

Gino is in the car at the curb, reading his book. Next to him in the traffic lane there's a taxi letting out some old lady on her way to one of the doctor's offices in the building.

"This here's a passenger zone," the taxi driver is saying to Gino.

"So I'm picking somebody up. Look, here he is."

Gino comes around to the passenger side to open my door, but I go to the front of the car and give a hand to the old dame. "Sorry, ma'am."

She nods, then keeps nodding. She's nodding and shaking all over, in fact—some condition she has. The taxi driver looks like he's ready to hand her off to me, but I quickly hand him a sawbuck and say, "Do me a favor, move the cab backward a few feet so we can get out, then come back and make sure this lady gets all the way in the right office." I hang on to the old lady while the cabbie backs up.

Philly shakes my free hand. "There's your good deed for the day."

"Yeah, now do one for me. Call Gay Talese. Maybe he really does want to do a feature for me for *Esquire!*"

"Ha haaa!"

I hand the old gal off to the taxi driver and we take off down Sunset. Jerry Wald is the archetypal Hollywood producer on the make, and though his career has faltered along with the traditional studio system in the last few years, he's still got plenty of juice. Jerry can talk to Overbeck, put in a good word for me. Meanwhile Frank is in town and likes taking lunch at his own restaurant if he's got nothing better to do. If I run into him I'll just say, I saw Peter last night. Just to let him know the mission has been accomplished, though Peter calls Frank practically every day.

Puccini is dead, populated only by a couple of tourists and some chick who wants to meet Frank and asks me if he'll be here today. How should I know, I answer. I eat in the bar, trying to put as much distance as possible between me and these other seekers.

There's a game show on the TV. Boy, there's something I wouldn't do if you held a gun to my head. Doing TV is one thing—comedies, specials, talk shows; I've subbed for Jack Paar on the Tonight Show a few times, it's not a bad gig. I suppose in my darkest days I might be reduced to doing a soap opera. But please, God, never let me have to do a game show.

By 12:30 Frank has not appeared. I pay and leave, standing a moment while the doorman trots around the side to tell Gino to bring the car around.

Gino pulls up, and right behind him Frank pulls up in his big Lincoln. He has none other than Dick Overbeck with him.

"Bobby, you know Dick Overbeck, don't you?"

"I haven't had the pleasure yet. How do you do."

Overbeck doesn't look like a Hollywood type at all. He wears heavy black glasses and wing-tips; he looks like one of those extras sitting in the background of a scene in a bar near Grand Central Station. "Happy to meet you, Bobby. I hear you and Frank are getting to be a regular act together."

"Dick, when we did Vegas last month, Bobby was the funniest guy in the act. The *only* funny guy."

"Yeah, except for the lines I wrote for you, then you were the funniest."

"You didn't get a chance to see one of the shows, did you?" Frank asks Overbeck.

"I couldn't get in! You guys had 'em all sold out."

Frank turns in the direction of the door; he wants to eat. "See you down on the set, Bobby."

I seize Overbeck's hand and don't let go. "Dick, I'm playing the Riviera in Las Vegas for the next two weekends. Come on up and see me, I'll make sure you get the best seat in the house."

"Thanks, Bobby, maybe I'll do that. Say, have you had lunch?"

"Well, I—"

Frank, who considers me already dismissed, is waiting next to the restaurant door as it's held open by one of his minions. He clears his throat loudly.

Dick looks back and forth from Frank to me. Now he's the one who hasn't dropped the handshake. He realizes he's erred in inviting me for lunch but he doesn't know how to get out of it.

Suddenly Gino pipes up, "You have your interview with Gay Talese in thirty minutes, Mr. Blaine."

Overbeck's eyebrows shoot up. "Gay Talese? Really?"

"Oh yeah," I mumble, "for, uh…"

"*Esquire* magazine!" Gino puts in. "A feature interview."

"Is that so? Well, Bobby, sounds like you've hit the big time. Sinatra film, *Esquire* interview…"

"Dick, you got a hungry man here!" Frank calls.

"I'll be seeing you." Overbeck reshakes my hand and follows Frank into the restaurant. I watch them go and then climb into the car. Gino slams the door and gets into the driver's seat.

We pull away and I say, "Thank you, Gino. That was very timely." I'm shaking my head. One moment I'm explaining to him what an agent is, the next he's bailing me out. This kid is amazing.

2

"What's the matter?"

Dana wanted to look especially nice because they're not just going to a movie like always, they're going to a café for a poetry reading. She doesn't know how one dresses for a poetry reading but she figures it's like a recital of some sort, so she dresses up a little. Also because Gene had told her he was going to wear his suit. Dana is wearing a crisp light blue dress. She's carrying an off-white patent leather purse that glows like a little moon. And her shoes are robin's egg blue. When she sees him approaching in the coffee shop where they met, he looks so nice, and she feels encouraged. She slips off the stool to give him a kiss, and that's when he freezes. He's looking her up and down.

"What is it? What's wrong with you?" she hisses. She turns away and plops herself back on the stool.

He sits down next to her. "I'm sorry," he said. "I guess I thought you would wear something—darker."

"Darker? I don't understand."

"We're going to a poetry reading, not—not a church picnic."

"What do you want me to do, dress like some beatnik? You kill me. What are you dressed for? The opera?"

"This is a very stylish suit."

"Sure it is. I'm sure all the bongo players wear them."

They ride the bus out to Venice and find the café, situated in the middle of a block full of closed shops. The place is so unassuming it's hard to tell if it's even open.

"It's a café?" Dana asks. "It looks like a bar. Are you sure we can get in?"

"We'll get in." Gene holds the door open for her and guides her in. Inside the place looks like a bar, too, though it is called the Tres Amis Café. But there is an empty wine bottle on each table, a candle stuck in its neck, and the place is half full of people mostly wearing black. A tiny stage huddles against one wall. To Gene's relief, no one challenges them, and he chooses a table where he feels Dana's fashion *faux pas* will be the least conspicuous.

A pony-tailed waitress approaches them, dressed in a horizontally-striped shirt and Capri pants like a ragtag refuge from the café dance scene in *An American in Paris*. "*Bon soir.* What would you kids like to drink?"

"*Un thé,*" Dana pronounces in her best high-school French.

"Whatzat?"

"We'll have some red wine," Gene says hurriedly. "A carafe."

"Oh. You kids legal? Sure you are," she says, turning on her heel.

"I don't think they're really French," Gene whispers to Dana.

"How was I to know," she pouts. She smoothes her skirt out and takes in the other patrons, a collection of slouching, chino-clad men with beards outlining their chins and women in black sweaters and dark red lipstick. All are smoking cigarettes. Some are talking, others are staring resolutely at nothing. They project an air of boredom if not sophistication, but Gene is sitting bright-eyed, expectant, like he expects Dean Moriarty to come crashing in any moment.

The waitress brings the carafe of wine and a list. "Here's the sign-up list for reading."

Gene and Dana look at her for a minute and then Gene says, "Oh, we're not here to read. We're just here as audience."

"Oh, well, good for you. That'll be two bucks."

"You mean there's a discount for poets?"

"No, then it's three bucks."

Gene pours the wine into heavy-bottomed tumblers. He's happy, even though nothing's happening. "Fun, huh?"

"It's different," she says sullenly.

"You'd rather go see *North by Northwest*? That's for squares. This is going to be cool."

"You're funny. Sometimes you talk about how great Hollywood is, how far above everybody else all those movie stars are. Now you say it's for squares."

"It's not all square; Cary Grant is square."

"Is that so. I guess all the *suavité* I see here outclasses Cary Grant." She picks up her glass and peers into it. "I think there's a bug in this."

Gene sits attentively, trying to attune himself to what's going on, which is precisely nothing. Aside from a quiet jazz record playing through speakers and the few conversations, there is almost no stimulation. Gene wishes he could go over to the other patrons—real beatniks!—and absorb their coolness. Bringing Dana might have been a mistake. She doesn't understand the possibilities, the beauty that is hidden within these sad characters, the potential that the person who eventually stands at the microphone will speak the truth so perfectly they'll all become enlightened.

Voices are raised at a table near the stage, where a man and a woman have been talking. "You think I'm just a bum, is that what you think? 'Get a job, Jack. Clean the kitchen, Jack.' While I'm trying to do my work!"

The woman speaks to him urgently yet quietly, trying to calm him, but he isn't having any of it.

"I should have known you'd be a bitch like all the rest," he says loudly, leaning back, throwing his arms wide.

His companion stands suddenly and reaches over the tiny table. She's tall and she looms over him, reaching out to push him over.

"Hey, wait a minute," he says more quietly. "Wait." They struggle together, the man balanced on the two rear legs of his chair. Finally both of them crash to a heap in front of the stage. The man is still holding a bottle of beer. "You bitch, get off me."

She leaps up and delivers a swift kick between her boyfriend's legs. A strangled groan indicates she's hit the target. As she seizes her purse and stomps out of the café, two women sitting at another table clap sarcastically.

No one comes to help the man on the floor, curled in a fetal position. The jazz continues to play on the speakers. After a few minutes, the man uncurls and sits upright on the floor. He locates his beer, which he has managed to keep upright all this time, and takes a long, morose swig. Then he pulls a small notebook from the pocket of his jacket, opens it and begins to read:

> You never make my eggs the way I like them
> You interrupt my creative process all the time

You go around emptying my ashtrays even while I'm in
the middle of a smoke
You ask me where I've been like it's a test—
I should have known you'd be a bitch like all the rest.

At first you said you loved my tattered haircut
You said you'd give me head whenever I wanted
You said you liked it, you said I was your favorite lover,
You took me into your house, made me your guest—
I should have known you'd be a bitch like all the rest.

Gene listens open-mouthed. It's not what he expected, but it feels uncensored, frenetic, truthful. He steals a look over at Dana; she is scowling.

After ten or twelve stanzas, all delivered from the floor, the man finishes his poem. He stands up and takes a bow; the applause lasts about eight seconds, or not counting Gene's enthusiastic response, about four.

"That's Jack Santini," says a man who has taken the stage. "Nice going, Jack. You gave me an idea: I think we're going to make everybody sit on the floor to read tonight. Extra credit if you do it in the lotus position... Next up is Laura Ferrebouef."

One of the two women sitting together rises. She steps onto the stage, then sits down cross-legged. "I'll compromise," she chirps.

"Try it on your knees," calls a male voice. She smiles weakly.

"Gene, let's go," Dana hisses.

"No—are you kidding? I bet you'll like this."

The woman on stage opens a large, heavy black volume. She sits in silence for several seconds. Then with a toss of her head she flings her straight, black hair over her shoulder and intones, "Blossom Highway."

"You mean *bosom* highway," the same man sneers. She reads:

Yellow and white stripes like flowers
Grow all the way from your house to mine
And every time I travel that road I pick them
A huge bouquet of road daisies for your room
You accept them like you accept my body
Like they belong to you
And I want you to travel up and down my highway
And wherever you stop flowers grow...

Dana stands up, picking up her purse. Gene doesn't even notice until she's brushing past him on her way to the door. He turns but self-consciousness keeps him from calling out to her. He stumbles to his feet, the chair scraping. Everyone looks up in annoyance and the woman stops reading. "Do you mind?" her companion says.

Gene stands next to his table digging out a dollar for a tip. "Sorry," he says, throwing it on the table and rushing out.

He sees Dana heading toward the bus stop and hurries after her. "Hey wait," he says, catching up. She's walking pretty fast and he practically has to trot to keep up with her. "What's the matter?"

"Why did you leave?" she asks. "Wasn't it smutty enough for you? Isn't that what you came for?"

"Of course not..."

"I'm not going to sit there and listen to that. When you said it was a poetry reading, I thought it was going to be something high class. I should have known it would be some stupid beatnik thing."

"Why do you say stupid? It wasn't stupid. Jerry Lewis is stupid."

"Jerry Lewis is Shakespeare compared to those people."

"It's more underground..."

"That's what it felt like, all right. Well, I don't want to be underground." They've reached the corner and Dana waves at a taxi. "Go on back, maybe you can make some time with one of those beatnik girls."

"Dana!" The taxi has arrived, and he finds himself opening the door for her.

"Good night!" she says, closing the door behind her. The taxi takes off, leaving Gene standing in the intersection. A car honks at him and he retreats to the sidewalk. After a few minutes he starts walking, away from the café, back toward Hollywood.

3

"You know, everybody says the beatniks are reds. But it's not true. They believe in free love, after all. Right? Don't they? But in Russia, there's no free love. And that's because you have to get approval from a committee. Here's a Russian asking a girl for a date. 'Comrade Natasha, please to accompany me to the worker's collective dance this Saturday night.' 'Not so fast, comrade Ivan. Where is your permit?' 'My permit! Of course. Wait just a minute.' And he goes off to the Worker's Committee for Romance and Labor.

"Of course there's a line and it takes him two hours. Finally he gets to the front of the line and says, 'Quick, I need permit for date with Natasha Boobinsky.' And they stamp his papers, and he hurries back to Natasha and then they go to the dance. And when they get there, there's a band, but they're not playing. They're just sitting on the bandstand drinking vodka. And Ivan goes up to the bandleader and says, 'Comrade, why aren't you playing?' And the band leader looks down at him and says, 'Sorry, comrade, this week music is rationed.'

"And that's why I say the beatniks are not reds. You ever see anybody standing in line to date a beatnik girl? No, I think I'll take Natasha Boobinsky... Sure, I'd even wait in line... None of that free love for me..."

"No, the beatniks are okay. They're 'cool,' right? Everything's 'cool.' And everything's poetry. I was at the butcher's, I'm reading off my little list. And I was telling him 'Three pounds of hamburger, some calf's liver, and six chicken breasts. Wrap it all up for me.' And behind the counter he's got a beatnik assistant. That's right, a beatnik butcher's assistant. Instead of the little paper hat he's wearing a beret... And he's getting my chicken breasts and he says, 'Man, can I have your list?' 'Whattaya mean—my shopping list?' 'Yeah, man—I collect them. It's *found poetry.*'

So I say, okay, and I hand it over. And he stands there behind the counter and says, 'Hamburger three *pounds.* Calf's liver one *pound.* And I got some *ground round...*'

"I take my order and I say, 'Now I'm going down*town...*'"

This is just the beginning. Gino told me about his expedition to the poetry reading this morning while we were driving up to Vegas, and I got this idea—a beatnik butcher. A butcher in a beret. And I started developing it. This is my first tryout of the material. And sure enough, there in the audience is Dick Overbeck.

"My butcher is a good guy to know. Once I asked him, 'How should I dress a duck for a party of twelve" and he says, 'Is it a formal party?' and I say sure..."

There is anticipatory laughter in the audience. You cannot beat a joke with a duck in it to break people up. "What's the matter? ... You'd think there was something wrong with my rug. No, actually, this is not a rug. I couldn't afford one, so they made me keep my hair. Where was I?

"'How do I dress a duck for a party of twelve?' and he says, 'Is it a formal party? Then the duck should wear a tuxedo too.'

"Did I say the butcher's name is Leopold?—they used to call him the Butcher of the Congo!" That was improvised.

"So I asked around a little and I find out, the beatnik assistant is his nephew. It's his brother's kid, and his brother was a college professor, so maybe that's where he gets some of his crazy ideas. One day, he tells me, his nephew comes in and says, 'Uncle Leopold, I'm going to be bringing my lunch from now on.' 'What's wrong with your lunch here? What's wrong with a sausage on a roll? That's what I have every day for thirty years. What, it's not good enough for you?' And the kid says, 'It's not that, it's very good. But I have become a vegetarian.'

"That's right, a vegetarian butcher! I tell Leo, 'I know you want him to follow in your footsteps, but look at it this way. He's still learning the trade, right? He's still a good butcher?' 'I guess so. But he's also apologizing to the meat.' 'He's what??' 'He's apologizing to the meat.' 'Well, why does he do that?' 'He says that's what the Indians did. When they killed a buffalo, they'd apologize to the buffalo.' So he's at the meat grinder putting in a thigh saying, 'I'm sorry, I'm sorry.'"

There's no big punch line to this bit—it's just a succession of ideas that are funny. A butcher who's a beatnik, who's a vegetarian. The crowd is laughing, anyway. Overbeck is laughing.

"So one day I'm in the shop, and Leo is helping me, and from the back of the shop I hear, *whack!* 'I'm sorry.' *Whack!* 'I'm sorry.'

"The beatniks are intellectuals. Did you know that? That's why they go in for some of this stuff like vegetarianism and existentialism. You know what an existentialist is, don't you? An existentialist is an egghead with a bad hangover. He's sitting at the breakfast table holding his head, going 'Why am I alive?'

"Some of you didn't get that, I see. Haven't you heard the word angst? Angst is that stuff they put in sauces to make them rich. That's why French chefs are so grouchy all the time. 'Thees sauce—it ees not really sauce… it has not the angst.'

"Are you following me? You have to have angst to have real French cooking, but once you do, you worry over whether it's French enough. It's not enough that the Germans lost the war, they left their angst behind. This is what is known as an existential paradox... That's what Noah had on the ark: a pair o' ducks, a pair o' sheep, a pair o' lions… After they got the lions on there, they had to go out and get more sheep.

"No, really, the French take all this philosophy stuff very seriously. And they're all in analysis—every Parisian has a shrink. But they take a different approach than the Freudians. If you're Austrian, you go to resolve your conflicts. 'Doctor, I had a dream about sleeping with my mother.' 'Oh, Mister Blaine, you are fery sick. Ve must get to the bottom of this.' But the French see everything differently. 'Doctor, I had a dream about sleeping with my mother.' 'But what ees wrong with zat? I too had a dream about sleeping with your mozzeh... She ees a very attractive woman, your mozzeh...'

After the show I send word out to Overbeck to wait a minute for me and I'll join him. I wipe my face and step into the hallway outside my dressing room, hurrying to close the door behind me. Plunging blindly down the hall, I practically run over the FBI agent Wilson. "Oh, Mr. Blaine!" he says. Big grin. "A word."

Corley hovers behind his boss like Ichabod Crane. Together they look like a good cop-bad cop team of morticians about to hand you the bill for your mother's funeral.

"I'm in a rush, you guys."

"No, listen to this one," Wilson insists. "Why did the truck driver win the golf tournament?"

"Oy. Okay, I'll bite."

"Because he had longer drives. Ha! How about this: Two Boy Scouts are lost in the woods, and they come across a bear. One of them climbs a tree and the other runs away; the bear catches the kid in the tree and eats him. When the kid who ran finally reaches civilization and tells what happened-"

"This is already making me late."

"Just listen. They ask him what happened and he says—no, that's not it. They ask, 'How did you decide to run instead of climbing a tree?' and he says, 'I'm afraid of heights.'"

"Is that it? Look, you guys, I have to go." I brush past them and head for the ballroom.

"Have you thought about that other issue, Mr. Blaine?"

"Yeah, look—why don't you guys wait for me in my dressing room? I have to come back there anyway to change clothes, right? So I really will come back." I'm backing away down the hall. "Maybe in a half hour. Hey, Curley—the microfilm's in the cold cream, okay? Look really carefully."

I turn and trot down the backstage hallway, hearing over my shoulder, "It's *Corley.*"

Overbeck is waiting patiently at his table, smoking cigarettes and smiling vacantly at the guy playing piano to the after-show crowd. He stands up when I come over.

"Sit down, sit down—Dick, thanks for meeting me."

"Great act, Bobby. Funny."

"Thanks—what are you drinking?"

"Scotch."

"Fine, same for me—put it all on my tab, miss—So who else have you seen in town?"

"Oh, let's see. I just saw Debbie Reynolds… And last night I saw Jonathan Winters. Oh man, that guy! He has this aircraft pilot thing he does—and he does all the voices—oh God. I thought I'd piss my pants."

"Absolutely, a great comic," I say. This guy Winters has come from out of nowhere and suddenly he's a big thing. People can't stop telling me about him.

"Oh man. I never laughed so hard."

"He is funny. So hey, you a golfer?"

"There's this thing," Overbeck says, "he's the pilot and all the engines have gone out… heh… And he's saying, 'Uh, ladies and gentlemen, here at Skinner Airways we're always at the forefront of innovation, so we'd like to call your attention to our new quiet engine technology…' Oh man."

"Yeah, heh heh." The waitress brings the drinks, putting an end to this debacle. "So, Dick—you're working with Frank now."

"Well, we'll see. We'll see." He takes a big sip.

This is not the response I expected, but I maintain my casual smile. "I know the project isn't exactly written in stone, but you are producing, right? I mean, it's public knowledge."

"Yeah, well… it's hard to say."

"Dick, come on—I've seen the script. Philly Snider, my agent, talked to Sheldon Eisenberg. It's not top secret."

Dick slouches, looking for his cigarettes. He's still smiling, but half of it is a grimace. He pulls out his pack, extracts a cigarette and lights it. Finally he says, "Well, Bobby, you're right. There's no reason to be coy. But I just want to make sure we're on the same page. Tell me what you know about the project and I'll see what else I can fill in." He blows smoke toward the ceiling.

"Fair enough." I take a drink, thinking, I may as well have gotten interrogated by the FBI. "Frank and Marilyn. There's a Norman Krasna script called *Make Nice for Daddy*, or maybe it's just *Make Nice* at this point. You're the producer of record. They're supposed to start shooting next month because Marilyn has to shoot that cowboy movie out here this summer. And since I'm asking you to be frank, let me be: No surprise, I'm angling for the second lead. I'm sure it's obvious to everybody in the universe but there you go, all my cards are on the table. Now what am I missing?"

Dick is staring at his glass with a sad, bemused smile, nodding as I talk. "Oh, and one more thing," I add. "There's this guy Donny Timson angling for the same part. Which everybody in the universe also knows. There. That's it." I take a gulp of my drink.

Dick eases himself out of his slouch, tapping his cigarette in the ashtray. "Well, Bobby, you are exactly right... as of three weeks ago. But things have changed."

"What things?" I say, keeping my voice as light as possible. The piano player picks this moment to start singing "It Was Just One of Those Things."

Putting his cigarette in his mouth, Dick pushes his glasses up the bridge of his nose and then holds out a finger. "First thing. Frank is no longer in the picture."

"You mean no longer *in* the picture, or no longer associated with the project?"

"No longer in the cast."

"Is that so. When did that happen?"

"I don't know, two or three weeks ago. Two weeks ago."

I think back. It was only ten days ago that I went to Frank to lobby for the part and in response he asked me to do him a favor. So I did it. And now it turns out that the whole time he knew he wasn't even going to be in it. "Son of a gun. Okay, what else?"

"Number two is—and I wouldn't have mentioned this but you brought it up—the studio wants Timson in something. They've had him on contract since last year and they want to recover something on their investment. Word is they're going to renew his option but if he flops, then that's it for him.

"Timson's not a bad guy," Overbeck shrugs, but despite his smile I can tell he's uncomfortable. "Likes to drink, but…"

I'm holding my whiskey glass tightly, I realize. I relax my grip and draw aimlessly on the tablecloth with my finger. But my hand wanders back to the glass. "Who's making the decision? I'm sure you're casting it, but who's deciding about this Timson?"

"Shel Eisenberg, more'n likely."

"So what were—" I start, then stop myself. I was going to ask him what he and Frank were meeting about at Puccini three days ago, but it's none of my business and he won't tell me. "So you still might end up working with Frank," I say, as if what we're really talking about is his chances, not mine.

"Yeah, hope so," he says with false cheer.

"New project?"

"I'm sworn to secrecy. That's why I was being cute at first. But this Krasna picture, that's another matter. And in fact he's still associated with that. He might co-produce, and he wants to sing the title song." His cigarette is bobbing up and down in his mouth, the smoke drifting between us.

"So," I nod. I want to take a deep breath to relax, but the smoke is bothering me. Frank *might* produce. He'll sing the title song, whoop-de-do. Is it his project or not?

I go on, "If Frank's not going to be the lead, who is? Not this Timson guy, please."

Dick shrugs. He taps the cigarette into the ashtray again and glances at me. "Easy on that glass, Bobby," he says, his voice kinder. "I think they put it on your bill if you break one."

I relax my clench on the glass and discover it's empty. I don't remember drinking it all. My hand is wet, I don't know if it's from the glass sweating or me sweating. I wipe my hand on a napkin and sit back in my chair and try to relax.

"Bobby, I wouldn't worry. Frank thinks a lot of you."

"Yeah?" I don't trust my voice.

"He told me he depends on you. You're the hub of the wheel, he says. The whole act revolves around you. Take you out, and you take out the heart. You know—I saw you on Jack Paar a few months ago—you were subbing for Jack. And essentially what you do as the host is what you did for the Summit act. You make everything work. That's what he said."

"Is that so. Nice to hear that." I lick my lips. Something's not right here. Suddenly I'm seized by a coughing fit. I pull my handkerchief out of my pocket and hack into it, red-faced.

Overbeck puts out his cigarette and touches my sleeve. "You okay, Bobby?"

I take a deep breath. "Sorry about that. Got a little stuffy in here. Smoke got to me, maybe."

The waitress comes back. "Another round for you gentlemen?"

"No—no thanks," I say. I give her a sawbuck.

"You've had a long evening," he says. "I'll let you go. I just want to say one thing, Bobby. People like Frank, Jerry Wald, Shel—they're *machers*. They make things move, they pull all the levers. You and me, we're the little people."

"Yeah." I suddenly remember the FBI guys cooling their heels in the dressing room.

"And don't worry about this Timson. What I hear is, he's not on firm ground."

"You can say that again."

"How's that?"

"Nothing—I'll say good night. Thanks for coming to see my act."

"All right, Bobby. Take care of yourself. And Bobby—great show."

Still sweating, the whiskey making my head feel like a hot balloon, I head back to the dressing room. I just hope Agent Wilson doesn't try any more of his material on me.

Wilson is sitting on the couch, his hands sunk in his pockets, and Corley is standing to examine the framed photos high on the walls. Fred Astaire, Bob Hope, Judy Garland, Elvis Presley. He whirls when I come in.

"Don't worry, Fred!" Agent Wilson calls out gaily. "It's only our host."

"Hope you boys made yourselves at home." I go over to the chair in front of the mirror and start taking off my makeup.

"Just like the three bears," Wilson says. He stands and comes over to the mirror and watches me delightedly.

I look at him reflected next to me. "You mean like Goldilocks. It was Goldilocks who was breaking and entering. It was the bears' house."

"Sure, sure—So, Mr. Blaine, have you given any thought to that matter?"

I bury my face in the towel, scrubbing my face with it and breathing hard. I scrub so hard it makes my eyes water, or maybe it's just the whiskey. Tossing the towel down on the table, I study my face in the mirror. My mouth is turned downwards in a grimace; I look like my stomach feels. "As a matter of fact, I have."

Wilson's grin drops and becomes a half smile. Corley sits down on the couch and pulls out a notebook. "And what have you been thinking?" Wilson asks softly.

"This guy Timson," I say, turning from the mirror. "I'm remembering more about our meeting." I take off my jacket and tie and start unhooking my cufflinks.

"Uh, huh." Wilson's eyes sparkle like a beauty contestant's before they announce the winner.

"It was when you said—at '21.' We were sitting at a table with some other people—I don't really remember who. You probably know better than me."

"Go ahead."

I put the cufflinks in my pocket and start unbuttoning my shirt. I barely remember meeting Timson, I sure as hell can't remember what we talked about. What would be plausible?

"I was telling him about subbing for Jack Paar—I think I'd just done it for the first time. And we started talking about TV work and the strike that happened a year or two ago. And he started talking about how it was important to keep things in perspective and how the TV union, what is it, AFTRA, how AFTRA was really in the pockets of the network and the whole strike was just a charade. But still he wouldn't work during the strike because of his beliefs. 'And what are those?' I asked—more to be polite than anything else. I mean, I didn't give a flipped pancake about his beliefs, but it seemed important to him, so I just let him talk."

"Sure, sure," Wilson says. "So what did he say?"

"Oh, the usual—I mean, what you'd expect someone to say. Sort of clichéd actually. About how there had to be some resistance to the blacklist and people had to pull together on everything."

"I see. Anything else?"

"You're getting powder on your butt," I say.

"Damn," he says amiably, looking in the mirror over his shoulder. He picks up a clean towel and whacks himself in the fanny with it. Then he folds it carefully and puts it right back where it came from.

"And he mentioned this organization—what was it you called it?"

"Writers for a Democratic World," pipes up Corley. He's as alert as a retriever, scribbling into his notebook. I strip off my shirt and undershirt and toss them on the couch next to him. He looks down at them suspiciously.

There's still some tension in Wilson, I see. He's like an audience waiting for the big punch line, patient and gleeful at the same time. I haven't quite hit the target yet.

"What else can I tell you?" I shrug, standing there in my shorts.

"How did he seem to you?" Wilson asks intently. He is leaning against the counter by my makeup kit.

"He's a drunk, that's what I hear," I answer. "He sure seemed drunk that night."

"Yes, but did he seem..." Wilson's hands float vaguely in the air, trying to express the shape of someone who's a pinko.

"Suspicious?" croaks Corley.

"Damned suspicious. Talking about the union and fighting the blacklist and the importance of pulling together. I would definitely say Donny Timson is a suspicious character. Suspicious as hell."

"Did he mention any names?" Wilson asks casually.

"Oh, no," I say. I throw the trousers on the couch and snatch another pair from the back of a chair where they've been hanging. "That's where I draw the line. You guys are getting Timson, that's it. I wouldn't give you Dwight Eisenhower if I saw him sitting on Khrushchev's lap."

Wilson nods, smiling all the time. "That's all right, Mr. Blaine. You've been very helpful."

They let themselves out. I hop into my pants and my shoes and go out to get drunk.

Chapter 7

1

After Dana fled the poetry reading on Thursday night, Gene walked all the way home, muttering to himself the brilliant things he should have said or done that might have salvaged the situation. He tromped across the city for two hours and fell into his bed, disgusted, confused and horny. It was too late to call her at her house, and she wasn't allowed to take personal calls at work.

So he tried her at home late on a windy Friday afternoon, when he and Bobby stopped in Baker. Plopping quarters into a pay phone mounted on the cinderblock wall of a diner, he waited nervously as trucks ground their way up the strip of diners and gas stations.

He doesn't know what he would say to her. He doesn't even know why she'd gotten angry at the poetry reading. But when he is finally able to get through to her house, her mother says Dana's not home. At 6:30 on a Friday evening.

Now as he strides the Las Vegas sidewalks, a little more slowly than he had walked that Thursday night, he wonders what's gone wrong. Only a few weeks before, when he was still parking cars, things were going beautifully. He had come to think of their dates, over the last two and a half months or so, as a sort of military campaign that had been making slow but steady progress. Their first kiss was the landing at Normandy. He captured Paris the first time she let him feel her tits. The tortuous but ultimately successful effort to finger her snatch was the Battle of the Bulge. And now, when he had Berlin practically within sight, Peter Lawford has come marching in like the Russians and loused everything up.

Things hadn't been the same between them since that evening. Though he laughed it off with Bobby—who had seemed terribly relieved Peter hadn't actually captured Berlin—the feeling of getting aced out stuck with him. And if he couldn't get Lawford's presence out of his mind, then what about Dana? She must be thinking about his debonair b.s. every minute. Being with Gene probably only reminds her of the discrepancy.

And she'd been right about how the job driving Bobby had kept them from seeing each other. They have time for one date a week, and even a phone call is long distance on the weekend. An argument on Thursday takes a long time to iron out.

Then there's the uncertainty of what he'll do once this job is over with. Next weekend is the last of Bobby's contract at the Riviera; he hasn't said anything about extending the arrangement. It looks like he'll have to find something else. He's thinking maybe Irv will take him back at the parking lot. Then he and Dana can fall back into a routine, her calling him during her lunch hour, setting up a movie date for a Wednesday or Thursday.

Or maybe her reaction to the poetry reading is a sign. In his mind, if you don't get something, you don't stomp out the door and down the street. You shrug and say, let's skip it next time. Maybe she's just a square, he thinks, and feels cheerful since it means he's less of one. Maybe she's just not cut out for the demands of the beatnik life.

The more he thinks about it, the more impossible it is for Gene to imagine Dana as a beatnik's girlfriend. She's too critical, too insistent on propriety. His fake I.D. actually bothers her, not because it doesn't work, but because it constitutes a lie. More important, she doesn't put out; she wants to wait to make love until they are at least engaged. Gene feels this runs counter to the beat spirit. The girls in *On the Road* were always putting out, and for more than one guy. Gene admires this liberality, and would gladly join in if only he could convince Dana or anyone else to play along. He thinks that if Dana could read the book she might get it too, but he doesn't want to risk the opposite reaction, her cutting sarcasm.

He times his walk to arrive downtown a little before noon, and goes into a bookstore he's passed before. There he buys *The Dharma Bums* for fresh inspiration, and starts reading it as he walks back to his motel.

Letting himself into his room, he knows he'll see it has been made up by Dolores, the maid, whom he avoided this morning by leaving extra early. The room is made up, but he's surprised to find her inside, kneeling next to the bed, trying to see behind it.

"Hello," Gene says.

"Oh!" She quickly gets up. "Sorry to come in like this. I'm looking for something I lost."

"Oh? What?" He puts his book down on the desk.

The door on its pneumatic arm shuts behind him, suddenly drenching the room in shadow. Dolores moves swiftly to the window, only a step away in this tiny room, and yanks the curtains open. "My necklace."

"Necklace? What does it look like?"

"A gold chain with a little *milagro* on it—a little, what do you say, charm."

Gene gets down on his hands and knees and peers under the bed. "Why don't you open the door, it'll give more light." She does so, but he still can't see. He stands up. "Here, I'll lift it and you look." Before she can say anything, he puts his hands under the edge of the bed frame—it's just a steel double bed, it doesn't weigh much—and lifts the end right off the ground.

She gives a surprised look and then searches the space underneath. "*Ijole,* I should have you do that for every bed while I vacuum. Look! There it is." She snatches the necklace from the floor. "Thank you. I'm so happy."

Gene sets the bed down. "Let me see it." He goes up to her and takes the necklace from her excited hands. Holding it up to the light, he sees a chain with a St. Christopher medal hanging alongside a little metal leg. "A leg?" he says. He's never seen a leg charm before.

He looks back at her and smiles. "Turn around. Hold your hair up." He opens the catch and then fastens the necklace around her neck.

"It's for my mother, her leg is bad," she says.

"There." Standing close to her, he can smell her hair. It smells of dust, beauty parlor chemicals, Lemon Pledge. He wants to put his hands on her shoulders, but she goes to stand in front of the mirror. She rearranges her heavy brown hair and then slips the medal under the neckline of her dress.

"Thanks," she says, smoothing her hands against her dress.

Gene stands there for just a moment looking at her, then goes to the door and opens it for her. She takes a step toward it, looking up at him. Then he says, "How about going to lunch with me?"

She arches her eyebrows, purses her lips, and to his surprise says "Okay. If you can eat tacos. You know what a taco is, don't you?"

"Oh, I know what a taco is." He's eaten dozens of them from the Mexican joint in his building.

They go to a taco stand hidden behind a car wash, a couple of blocks off the strip. It's lunchtime and the place is crowded with hotel and casino workers, mostly dressed in the uniforms of janitors, maids and mechanics. They carry greasy paper bags over to a picnic table and sit down.

"Don't you have to go to your other job?" Gene asks.

"Yeah, but it's not a busy time, so it's okay if I get there late. It's my cousin."

"Oh yeah, your *real* cousin," Gene jokes, echoing her words from the week before.

"Yeah, my real cousin, what do you think?" she asks, instantly irritated.

"I was just kidding. So you said you do the books there? And you work at the motel. Do you have any other jobs?"

She picks a bit of lettuce from her lips, and swallows before answering. "No, I go to community college. I'm taking accounting classes. Some day I'll be a CPA. Then I won't have to clean rooms no more. Any more," she corrects herself.

Gene nods. "I was going to Harvard for a while." Juice is dribbling down his chin.

"Harvard, what's that?"

"Harvard University," he says, a little taken aback. He wipes his mouth with the back of his hand.

"Oh. Where's that?"

"New York, where d'ya think?"

She hands him a paper napkin and proceeds to wipe her own hands, folding and refolding a napkin to uncover unused spots, and using those to wipe between her fingers. Then she picks up another taco.

"So how come you come to Vegas every weekend? You a gambler?"

"No," Gene says, not explaining that he's underage for the casinos. "I'm a writer for one of the big comedians. Bobby Blaine. You ever hear of him?" he adds uncertainly.

"No. You're a writer for a comedian? What does that mean?"

"They don't make up everything they say, you know. One guy isn't funny enough. They have to have two or three guys writing material for them, that's why they're so funny."

"Okay, tell me a joke." She wipes her lips, then takes another big bite.

"Er, okay. Let's see, here's a good one. The government is getting ready to shoot the first man into space," Gene begins, trying to remember one of the jokes he had prepared for his non-audition with Bobby a few weeks before. "But before they send up the man, they send up a dog. Off he goes…"

"*Pobrecito!* The poor little thing," she adds, translating.

"He… he orbits the earth a few times, then splashes down in the ocean, and when they open the capsule, lo and behold, the dog can talk! The effect of outer space has made the dog a genius. So they send up a monkey—"

"Wait," she says, waving both hands. "The outer space has made the dog talk? What is that?"

"I don't know, it's—space radiation or something. Just pretend. So they shoot up a monkey. And when the monkey gets back, he can do nuclear physics and speak ten languages. So everybody is thinking, wow, if the dog comes back like a man, and the monkey comes back a genius, what'll happen to the man when he goes up? He's going to evolve so far, he'll be like a god! Who knows what powers he'll have?

"So they take their best test pilot. He's a real straight arrow, he's never smoked, never drunk, never been married. All he's done his whole life is train for this flight. The day arrives and they shoot him into space. Everyone waits expectantly. He splashes down and they rush to retrieve the capsule. The frogmen open it up, and inside are two blondes, one's pouring a martini and the other is lighting his cigarette, and the astronaut has turned into Frank Sinatra."

"That's it?" Dolores asks, her mouth full.

"Get it, the guy has evolved into the highest form of life on earth."

"Tsk," she says, "I can see why you have to stay at the Cactus with jokes like that." She balls up the paper wrappers and starts wiping off her fingers again, using a clean paper napkin. "Besides, who likes Frank Sinatra?"

"You don't like Frank Sinatra?" Gene's finishing his last taco, but she snatches the wrapper right out from under him, leaving him only an already stained napkin.

"I like Richie Valens. Did. He got killed."

"But jazz is where it's at," Gene says, lowering his voice to what he thinks has some kind of beatnik cool.

She stops cleaning up the table and gives him an are-you-crazy? look, then gets up and carries the paper over to a trash can. "I gotta go," she says shortly.

Gene stands up, smiling, and walks with her to the bus stop. He doesn't care whether she likes Sinatra or not. He's thinking of the way her bare neck looked when he fastened her necklace, of the way everything got quiet when that happened, back in his little motel room.

Gene spends another Sunday walking around town, and stopping once in a while to read Kerouac. His characters never seem to worry much about work or settling down. While Gene is only barely more employed than they are, he's stumped by their approach to their endless free time. They seem to regard their unemployed activities—wandering the countryside, reading mystical poetry, getting drunk with each other—as some kind of occupation. Never at a loss for something to do, even doing nothing is a kind of activity for them, as they seem constantly to think deep thoughts about philosophy and life.

It's because they've been to college, he reasons. They've been to college and studied poetry and Buddhism and all that stuff.

Then again, he's pretty sure they don't teach that stuff in college. The hero of *The Dharma Bums*, Japhy Rider, is some kind of mountain-climbing, poetry-writing, Buddha-preaching genius. The character's whole explanation for these skills is that he grew up on a farm. Gene is hard pressed to reconcile this notion with his memory of the farm boys he went to high school with. Mostly they sulked at the bottom of the stairwell leading to the woodshop, smoking cigarettes and tormenting the weak. Others went in for musical productions and the school newspaper, and enjoyed dances. But none of them were interested in poetry or knew what Buddhism was. Neither did Gene, until he started reading Kerouac.

That's what gets him. Now everybody reads Kerouac and wants to be a beatnik. But Kerouac had no Kerouac to read; Japhy Rider somehow made the leap from farm boy to Buddhist mountaineer. Gene wants to make the leap, too—maybe not that leap, but some leap.

Dolores knows how to get from maid to accountant. Gene wants to go from small-town boy to California hepcat—if only he knew how.

He finds himself on the edges of downtown, in what appears to be a sort of Chinatown, though it's hard to discern. There are no pagoda roofs or big signs for tourists written in a fake-Chinese alphabet, just a few stores with signs in real Chinese characters. Gene stops in the shade of an awning outside a restaurant, and looks around him. Even here, half the faces are white. He notices a grocery store across the street selling duck and something called bok choy. On a low brick building next door, he notices a distinctive tiled roof. A brass plaque on the wall says, below some Chinese characters, BUDDHIST CHURCH.

Gene is electrified. While the characters in Kerouac's books never go to anything called a Buddhist Church, they must have learned about Buddhism someplace.

He crosses the street to examine the sign more closely, but it lists no service times. There's a door but it's closed, and he's too timid even to try the doorknob. Two Chinese men come walking down the sidewalk, and one gives Gene a suspicious glance as they pass. That's enough to get Gene moving again, off the block and closer to downtown. He goes into the library, takes out his copy of *The Dharma Bums,* and sits down to read.

2

By Sunday night, when I climb into the back seat of my Imperial for the drive back to L.A., I've been drinking for 48 hours, more or less. It's been a long time since I went on a binge like this and I've found out that I'm not sure I know how to do it anymore. Knowing I had four shows to do, two on Saturday and Sunday each, I tried to moderate my intake. In fact, I tried to stop. But like in that interview, I mean that conversation, with Overbeck on Friday night, my hand kept wandering back to the glass.

Still, I made it through the weekend. Aside from a little nausea on Saturday night during the early show, I was fine. The show *must* go on.

Maybe that early show was a little on the short side. It just gave the piano player a chance to show his stuff.

Now, in the car, when I can drink all I want to, I suddenly don't feel like it. I open the flask, which I had filled right after the show, and the smell of whiskey turns my stomach. I roll down the window and fling the damn thing out onto Las Vegas Boulevard, almost nailing a trio of drunken soldiers.

Gino glances back at me in the rearview mirror. "Lose something?" he asks. "Want to go back?"

"No thanks. I've had it."

"Okayyy," he drawls.

"Wish I weren't *coming* back."

He purses his lips and says nothing. We head out into the dark desert.

I haven't bothered to roll up the window yet and the air feels good. It was a hot day today, middle of March. The air coming in through the window is warm. Gino doesn't have his window open, though. I roll mine up and slump in a corner of the back seat.

I've been thinking of what to do when I get back to L.A. Should I go see Frank? What for? Hey Frank, you know that part you sort of hinted at in a movie that you decided to have nothing to do with? Can I have that part, huh, Frank? Can I appear as the schlemiel in a Cary Grant - Marilyn Monroe movie, *con su permisso?* Oh, you want me to do you a favor first. What is it, Frank? You want me to stab somebody in the back? Oh, literally, I see.

Have I been muttering? I'm usually not a mutterer when I'm drunk, but I haven't been this drunk in a while. I better strike up a real conversation, just to keep myself in the real world.

"Hey, Gino."

"Yeah?"

I pause for a few seconds, trying to think of what to say, and he takes my silence to mean he's offended me, so he says, "I mean, yes Mr. Blaine."

I cough. "That's all right, Gino. We don't insist on propriety on Sunday night. Sunday night is the end of a long weekend." I draw it out, lo - oo - ong, making it sound like I'm speaking of four or five days at least.

He nods. We're deep in the desert now. There's a moon, and I can see the mountains against the sky. The tail lights of the car ahead disappear and all I can see is a lot of sagebrush and whatnot; I don't make any reflection in the window at all. I stretch and cough and wonder if I'll be able to sleep. I don't feel like it.

I sigh. "I'm glad that's over. The weekend, I mean."

"One more weekend on your engagement, though," he replies.

"My engagement, that's right. You ever wonder why they call it an engagement?"

"No, why?"

Silence. I can't think of a punch line, but I can't stand the silence, either. I should have held on to the flask—then I'd be able to sleep, maybe. "It just means, a short period of togetherness," I say, lamely. "Like 'We have engaged the enemy.'"

"Oh, uh huh." I can hear the expectation in his voice of a punch line but too many seconds tick by and I leave the joke just dying there. Sometimes you have to. "Listen. What do you do by yourself all weekend?"

"I'm seeing this, uh, this woman," he says. "The one I told you about a couple weeks ago?"

My lips seem stuck together, and when I part them, it makes an unpleasant smacking sound. I cough. "The divorcee?"

"That's right. Her name's Elaine."

"Tsk," I respond. "Yeah. Sure." I pause. Whenever someone stops talking, the hum of the car fills up the silence. I straighten up so I can see the greenish light of the dashboard, just to keep from getting disoriented and woozy.

"She's getting one of those Nevada divorces," he says. "We see each other every Saturday."

"Sure, I remember," I say. I let another couple of seconds go by. "But give it to me straight, that's just bullshit, right? You're just pulling my leg."

"Swear to God," he says happily.

I can't say how, but somehow I know he's lying. Even though my brain is working like a cheap watch dipped in mud, I come to the realization that Gino's one of these guys who just bullshits everybody all the time. There's something too perfect about his stories, like the one about—what was it—being on the swim team with a Kennedy cousin? Hearing first-hand about PT-109 after playing touch football with Jack? Now this extended fib about balling some divorcee every Saturday.

I rub my hand over my face and let out a long breath. "Do me a favor," I finally say. "It doesn't make any difference to me whether or not you're making time with some chick or who she is. Just don't bullshit me about anything that has to do with me, okay?"

His face, reflecting the light from the dashboard, takes on a pained expression. "Well... Yeah, sure. I wouldn't do that."

"Divorcee, no divorcee, I don't care. Just don't pull my leg when it counts."

He swallows. "I don't," he finally says.

"Good."

A bus passes by, followed by a stream of five cars trailing along behind it. We pass them in a series of whooshes, shoom, shoom, shoom, shoom, shoom. Then silence. The Imperial is so quiet back here.

A while later I'm jarred by the slowing of the car. I lift my head, blinking at motel signs and coffee shops.

"Whuuugh," I say, smacking my lips. "Guess I fell asleep."

"This is Baker," Gino says helpfully.

"Unnnnnngh. Shit. Let's stop, okay? That coffee shop we stopped in on the way up. Christ, I'm thirsty. Do you have anything?—a bottle of soda, something?"

"Thermos of coffee." He hands it over the seat, not looking.

My eyes are like bits of concrete. I manage to pour some coffee into the thermos cap, but it's too hot to drink so I blow on it, then slurp some. "God, this isn't helping... where's that coffee shop? It doesn't matter, stop here, stop anyplace."

"You feel okay?"

"Yeah, I— No, I don't. Here, the gas station, fine. Christ."

We pull up to some gas pumps and I throw open the car door and stagger out. The gasoline fumes put the capper on my attack of nausea, and I throw up into a thirty-gallon drum they use as a garbage can.

After a minute Gino comes up with a paper cup of water. "Want some water?"

"Yeah." I swish my mouth with it and spit it out. I'm still thirsty but I'm afraid to swallow anything. I throw the half-full paper cup into the garbage can; water splashes back at us. Suddenly I'm seized with loathing, of the garbage, the gas station, the FBI, and most of all myself. "Christ! What a fucking shithead I am!"

Gino is standing there, probably thinking I've just said the first smart thing all night. But what he says is, "Oh, everybody gets drunk and throws up once in a while."

I slump against the fender of the car. "It's not that. Jesus, I have to get away from these fucking gasoline fumes. Fill the car up, okay? I have to... I'm going to get a soda."

I go into the tiny gas station office and get a 7-Up out of the cooler and gulp some of it down. Then I grab the bathroom key from a hook on the wall and shuffle around to the side of the building. The bathroom has seen better days, but at least it doesn't stink. I splash water on my face, over and over again. I get it all down the front of my shirt and pants and down the back of my neck. If there were room to stick my head under the faucet, I would, but they've got one of those tiny little gas station sinks and I wouldn't want to stick my face in it anyway, it's cruddy.

When I've had enough of a bath I try to straighten myself out. I can hardly see myself in the cracked mirror, but that's probably all to the good. When I see how wet I am, I go out to the car. Gino is already done with the gas and is waiting patiently in the driver's seat. "Give me the keys," I say; he complies with a surprised look. I get a change of clothes out of the suitcase in the trunk and retreat to the bathroom again. I change clothes, tossing the wet ones in the trunk. I even change my shoes.

Then I come around and get in the car, not in the back, but in the shotgun seat. After what Gino's seen me go through just now, for the moment I can't play the Hollywood star. I hand him the keys and he gets behind the wheel.

"Sorry about that," I say. "Guess I had a little too much... I feel a little better now."

We head back out across the desert. The moon is straight overhead and you can see everything—the mountains, the underbrush. Out of the corner of my eye I see a coyote, fifty yards off the highway, just sitting watching the traffic plain as day. Sometimes there's a little light way off in the middle of nowhere, some miner's cabin or something; otherwise we may as well be driving across the bottom of the sea.

I think of something Overbeck said—about me guest hosting for Paar and how similar it is to my role in the act. He thinks it's a compliment. I was sitting at Sardi's one night about a year ago at a table that included Noel Coward and Sheila Graham. And at that time Coward was hosting a talk show on CBS, a show that wasn't really working. Coward didn't understand that, once you delivered straight lines for the guests—whom he mostly considered inferior to him—and they said their joke, that as the host it was not your job to come back and top them with something that was also mildly insulting. It wasn't going well.

Steve Allen came up to the table—he had only recently been replaced as the Tonight Show host by Paar. He complimented Noel on his show, just being a good sport to someone in the same line of work. But Noel was drunk, and he tore into Steve and the whole talk show business, said that in order to be a good talk show host all you have to do is be a wanker, a kiss-ass, feeding lines to the guests, that the right person to do an "omnibus programme"—which I guess was British for talk show—was an omnibus conductor. And a lot of other witty and mean things, supposedly about himself, but really about people like Steve who were happy being talk show hosts rather than miserable like Noel. Steve, as mild-mannered as they come, just swallowed and turned on his heel. Sheila and I glanced at each other; I knew she was a friend of Steve's. A couple of days later, an equivocal item appeared in her column about Noel's show, and a few weeks later he was off the air and had gone back to New York.

But a lot of people in the film industry agree with Noel. Doing a talk show is a job for a bus conductor. Just call out the stops—This is Como, Perry Como. What's your new record, Perry? Where are you playing in Vegas? And what do you think about JFK's chances? That was Perry Como; next is Sherman, Allen Sherman. Watch your step.

And as we creep across the desert floor, all I can think of is, Jack Paar, Steve Allen—they never made it in movies.

3

"Like I said, next weekend is the last trip," Gene says irritably.

"And that's not what I'm talking about," counters Dana. "I'm talking about how you're gone already."

They're crossing L.A. on another bus, going to see a movie in Hollywood. The theater isn't that far from Gene's room, but Dana won't ride a bus into Hollywood by herself, so he has to meet her at a bus stop downtown. They've already missed one connection and at this rate it looks like they'll be late for the movie.

"I go away for the weekend, I'm here all week. It's not my fault we only get together once a week."

"You know it's been nice weather the last two weekends. We could have gone to the beach. But you're off in Las Vegas. What do you do there, anyway?"

They've been arguing since she got off the bus from Pasadena.

"Well, I tried to call you on Friday, you know that?" Gene says. "While we were on the road, we stopped and I called your house from a pay phone. At 6:30 your mom says you're out."

"I was, I was with Sharon and our friends. What are you, suspicious? What do you expect me to do, stay home all weekend? You never called before."

"It's long distance."

"What do you do with all your money, anyway? You're making a hundred a week and more on this job. Are you gambling or something?"

"I'm saving it. I opened a savings account."

"Well okay," she says, unable to disapprove of that. "Saving it for what?"

"A trip, maybe. Across the country."

"Oh, now you're Jack Kerouac again."

"Or maybe just up to San Francisco. I want to see it."

"I went there with my cousins. It's okay, but it's not that big. It's not as big as Los Angeles."

Their bus heaves its way down Sunset Blvd.

"I don't know why we had to come all the way out here anyway. All the movies are playing downtown."

"No they're not, not this movie."

"What's so great about this movie?"

"It's a Swedish movie, it's cool."

"They better speak in English. I can't stand those little lines, what do you call them, subtitles."

"What? You can read."

"If I want to read, I'll read a book."

"Well, you know what, we're late anyway," Gene frets.

Then he neglects to ring for a stop and they wind up going two blocks past the theater. When they disembark, Gene just stands on the sidewalk, cars roaring past. Gene wants to feel free and uncomplicated like Kerouac in *The Dharma Bums*, always knowing what to do, gladly hitching up the coast in trains and trucks. Tonight he wanted a cool

European film and then an existential post-movie conversation, maybe over a glass of red wine at a beatnik cafe which might magically appear. Instead finds himself stranded on Sunset Blvd. in Hollywood on a cold March evening, arguing with a bank teller in a beige winter coat, the sunlight fading in the western sky over the red tail lights of cars.

They trudge back down the street in the direction of the theater and go into a diner. The diner is full; as far as the eye can see, every booth is filled with teenagers, tourists, and the single men who populate Hollywood, their newspapers spread out on a table. Gene and Dana hesitate in the entryway, watching waitresses rush back and forth carrying dirty plates, pots of coffee, milkshakes in both hands.

"We may as well wait a little," Gene says uncertainly. None of the staff has given them the slightest nod of recognition, as if they're invisible. A table clears as a family gets up to go, but that just makes the area near the door more crowded. Gene and Dana are separated by the roiling children as she squeezes herself into a corner next to a cigarette machine and Gene presses himself against a coat rack. This strategy makes them so invisible that the hostess again fails to address them when she's finished ringing up the departing family.

He won't look at Dana, and he can't think of what to do to get someone's attention. He tries a faint "Excuse me" when the waitress comes barreling past again, but she ignores him; when she comes back again with more plates of food for the same table, he tries louder. Finally she snaps, "The hostess will seat you," but there's no hostess in sight.

It's one thing to be essentially invisible as a parking valet or, slightly less so, as Bobby's driver, but here he should be treated like just another customer. What's wrong with them? And it's not just the diner staff, it's Dana standing there silently waiting for him to do the grown-up thing, though he has no idea what that is.

Finally the hostess, a girl hardly older than them, with straight brown hair and freckles, appears and seats them at the table the family vacated. It's still dirty and they sit there waiting.

"At least we're not standing anymore," Gene says.

Dana glances at him and then back to the point in space where she has decided to fix her gaze.

It's a good thing they have a long time to wait until the next showing of the movie, since they are served in excruciating steps. First the table is cleared by the same hostess. Then a few minutes later they are given menus. Later, water arrives. After they've been sitting for twenty minutes, one of the harried waitresses presents herself. "What can I get you kids?"

All they want is coffee and pie. She glumly writes this down and walks off without a word.

The diner clears out rather suddenly. Within five minutes, they are almost the only ones in the place. If for no other reason, their order finally arrives: the coffee cold, the pie congealed. They each take one bite and put their forks down.

"Why are we here?" Dana mutters furiously. "What kind of joke is this? Are we on Candid Camera or something? Why don't you take me someplace nice to dinner?"

"I took you someplace nice on your birthday."

"And I paid for my bus fare. That was very memorable."

"Oh, sorry—I'm sure Peter Lawford will take you much nicer places."

"Oh, shut up about that, will you? Are you ever going to let me live that down?"

Finally they get to the theater just as the first show is letting out. They make way for the stream of people leaving and then Dana goes up to the candy counter. She orders a bag of popcorn and when Gene tries to pay for it, she doesn't let him.

They take their seats in the dim light of the theater. *The Seventh Seal* starts, and right away, Dana snorts in annoyance. "Oh, it's in black and white!"

"It's more artistic," he hisses.

"Probably they just can't afford color." She watches a few more minutes and then blurts out, "What in the world is this? Why aren't they talking?"

"It's artistic."

"Would you stop saying that?"

"Well, shut up yourself."

They sit in silence. A man rides past a horrible dead body, and begins to play chess with a ghostly figure. A procession of flagellants makes its way through a village. Gene watches, open-mouthed. This movie is like something from another world.

He's completely wrapped up in it when suddenly Dana heaves herself to her feet and down the row and disappears up the aisle. He gapes at her empty seat. Is she just going to the restroom? No, she's taken her coat. She's walking out.

He catches up to her halfway to the corner. "Where are you going?"

"I'm sorry, Gene. I'm sorry I'm not sophisticated enough to enjoy your wonderful European cinema."

"It's not that hard to understand."

"I can't believe we waited two hours to look at a bunch of people dressed in rags, and in black and white no less."

"You'd rather see Cary Grant, I guess."

"I sure would."

"European movies are cooler."

"And that's another thing," she says, still walking. "You've changed. You used to be satisfied with an Elvis movie and a soda. Now everything has to be cool. All your beatnik stuff. You know what, I don't think it's cool. I just think it's dirty. The language is dirty and the people are dirty. You were much nicer when you were a new kid in town from Kansas."

"Missouri."

They reach a major cross street. She charges across the intersection. Trailing after her, Gene sees there's a bus approaching from the south, one that will take her to a transfer point in Glendale and back to Pasadena. Dana stumbles on the curb and catches herself on the lightpost; she scrambles over to the bus stop and tries to wave at the bus while simultaneously digging in her purse. "What are you doing?!" Gene shouts over the noise of the traffic.

"What's it look like?"

"Well, fine!" Gene says, throwing up his hands. "Go home! I can't do anything right."

"Just shut up, Gene," Dana says. "This was a waste of time. Seeing you at all is a waste of time."

The bus pulls up with a deafening whoosh. Dana hoists herself up the stairs and looks down at Gene for a moment. All Gene can do is glare back at her. Then the doors close and the bus pulls away with a roar.

Gene turns away from the disappearing bus and walks tensely back to the corner. When the light changes, he doesn't do anything, just stands there. He doesn't know what to do next, where to go; he's afraid for a few minutes to cross the street. Finally he walks home alone through the cold night.

Chapter 8

1

"Look at this, the sun's barely set. We hit the Nevada state line and look how light it is," I say.

Right hand casually yet steadily at the twelve o'clock position on the steering wheel, Gino dutifully looks around at the mountains and the sky.

"I mean I guess we've only been doing this a month, but hey," I say. "We're gettin' the hang of it. Too bad this is the last trip... Thought about what you're going to do next?"

"Yeah," he says. "I was gonna try to get on back at the parking lot, but now I'm actually thinking about finding something in Las Vegas."

"Is that so. What about your girlfriend?"

He shakes his head. "That's all over."

"What happened?"

"We had a fight the other night, and then when I talked to her on the phone yesterday, she said she didn't want to see me anymore." He shrugs. "That's okay. Things weren't going so good lately."

I'm silent, watching the light change over the sand and scrub.

He goes on: "I mean, I read a lot, and I want to find out about Buddhism and all, and poetry, and she just doesn't. I think she wants somebody who works in a bank like her."

"It didn't have anything to do with what happened with Peter, did it? Because then I'd feel responsible."

"No, nothing like that... We're just on different paths."

Listen to this kid—different paths. Poetry. Buddhism, for crying out loud. "Well," I say, "you know, if you're not ready to settle down, that's okay. You're not even 21. When are you going to be 21?"

"End of July."

"Hey, you gotta lot of wild oats to sow. Don't feel bad. You're gonna have a great time on your own. Listen—how'd you like to see my show tonight?"

He smiles. "Hey... no kidding? Sure I would."

"Then that's great. I'll comp you. That means you get in free," I say quickly in response to a quizzical look.

We sail into town as the sky gets dark and all the lights come on. When we pull up to the Riv and get out together, he takes my garment bag from the trunk along with his little bag, barely bigger than a briefcase. We go inside and check in.

In my dressing room there are a couple of messages. The important one is from Philly—says he's going to be in the audience tonight, wishes me luck on the last weekend here. That's good, it means he's here trying to get me another gig.

I send word out to the house manager to comp Gino and get him a halfway decent table—not like he's a VIP, just what we call a "friend of the family" table—for when your mother's rabbi or some such person comes to town. He'll be over on the side a little but with a good view.

While I dress, I should be thinking about my act, running over the set list. But these FBI visits make me nervous. Those two feds won't be satisfied with what I gave them last time.

I review my conversation with Sammy. It makes sense that they're snooping around him because of the marriage angle, but Sammy is also friendly with the civil rights movement, which is something the government can't decide what to do with.

Christ, maybe they're going to ask me about Sammy. I'll tell them to go to hell. No way will I ever stoop that low. It's one thing to stab in the back somebody you're competing with. It's another to screw a guy you've worked with—somebody who, if he's not exactly a pal, is a colleague, a damn good performer, and a guy with guts. More guts than I have. Just wait until it gets in the press about his engagement to May Britt; the gefilte fish will really hit the fan then.

But can I really tell them to go to hell? The blacklist is still alive and well, as Albert Maltz demonstrated a couple months ago. At this point in my career, can I really afford to piss off anybody?

Fortunately no federal agents invade my dressing room before the show. The call comes and I go on stage. I've retained a lot of the beatnik material. As for Gino, I don't remember he's in the audience until I'm in the middle of the butcher bit, and when I'm doing the vegetarian beatnik butcher apologizing to the meat, I can hear a familiar laugh over to the left, and I remember he's out there.

After the show I go out in the house and sit down with Philly. The piano player segues from the that's-all-folks music to some standard as I see Gino and wave him over to Philly's table. If Frank has some ape sitting around while he gabs, why can't I have my driver? He's better company than Frank's goombah.

"Philly, this is Gino. He's my entourage. No, seriously—he's just doing some driving for me. He gets me back and forth between L.A. and here in one piece."

"Pleased to meet you, Mr. Snider," says Gino politely.

"Hello, Gino, I remember you picking up Bobby at my office. You Italian?"

"Who isn't?" he says smoothly. I chuckle to myself. If this kid actually had any talent, he'd be dangerous.

He sits down a little away from us, just where one of Frank's bodyguards would sit—far enough away to be almost at the next table, close enough to make it look like a party. A waiter comes by; we order a round, and I tell the guy to add Gino's tab to mine.

"Ya done good, Bobby," says my agent. "They want you back for three days in May."

I look at him. "Three days in May? And which days would those be?"

"Ah... The seventh through the ninth."

"What are you telling me? That's Monday through Wednesday. That's it?"

He grins and shrugs. "I didn't tell you the good part yet. They want you for two weekends at their place in Reno, too. Bobby, it ain't chicken feed," he says when he sees my reaction. "You're gonna headline in Reno."

"In August, I suppose?"

"No, in May as well. You can thank me later. Now about that movie we've been talking about. You know, it's the damnedest thing—"

"Philly, please don't get started on the fact that it's damned. I know that already. Just tell me what's so damned about it."

"Well, you know how it started out—a terrific project. Then what happens—they're not sure about the title. Then they're not sure about the script. Then Frank drops out. So now what do you think happened?"

"I hope you're gonna tell me."

"Okay, it's this. There ain't no *Make Nice,* for Daddy or for anybody else. Now it's called *Let's Make Love.* Still Marilyn. Still a Norman Krasna script. Still no Frank. But in fact it's a completely different movie. There's no daddy, there's no big-business setting. Or rather the business setting is way off to the side. It's completely different."

"And no more second lead for me."

"Oh, there's a second lead, all right, but you ain't getting it. Timson is doing it. That's it. Sorry to be so direct, Bobby, but that's the way it goes."

"Christ, Philly, what happened?"

"Nothin' happened. It's a singing and dancing role. It's completely different, like I said."

"You mean it's a musical. With Marilyn?"

"She can sing—so they say."

"And Frank?"

"Frank has zilch to do with it, as far as I can tell. Jerry Wald is producing."

"But this script—the *Make Nice for Daddy* script—Frank owned that script, he was going to produce…"

"He didn't own it, he had an option, and when he decided not to do it, he dropped the option too. Jerry still had Marilyn on the line, though, and the writer. So Norman dug something else out of a drawer, and whatshisname, Arthur Miller is going to doctor it and play up Marilyn's part, so she doesn't come off like some dance hall girl in a western. They're going to shoot it quick, in seven weeks, and then do that cowboy movie out here in the desert. Hey, you know who they got for that? They got Gable."

"Never mind about that. So I got nothing."

He shrugs. "Way I hear it, it's better that you didn't get it. Arthur Miller is practically going to rewrite Timson's part out."

"I'm sitting right here with Dick Overbeck last week and he's telling me Frank is still producing. He says Frank might sing the title song."

"Smoke screen. I think Jerry wanted people to think it would be Frank's project, in order to keep Marilyn in the game long enough to get her signed for it. And Overbeck went along with the charade under orders. You weren't the only one they were kidding."

"For Chrissake—all the hours I spent working this thing. And for what? I could get indicted for—" I shut up and glance over at Gino. He plays dumb, good for him. "Well, for the rest of the day's laughs, come see the late show."

"Very funny show, Bobby!" Philly says, happy to have a subject he can say something good about.

Doesn't he understand what a disaster this is? First I lost *Slovik*. Now I lost *Make Nice*—not that I ever had it—in fact, judging from the evidence, I'm not even sure at this point that it existed. I've been spending my time chasing a ghost.

There's a commotion at the entrance. I hear a burst of laughter, male and female, and then the unmistakable sound of Dean Martin's voice yelling "Fore!" The heads of everyone in the room swivel in that direction. In comes a bunch of people—Dean, Frank, Ed Torres the boss of the Riviera, Jack Entratter who runs the Sands, the producer Jerry Wald, some more folks, a couple of goombahs, three or four dames.

It's so much like a staged entrance, the quarter-full room applauds as the entourage comes in our direction. Frank holds up his hands. "Quiet! Quiet!"

Everyone shuts up, even the piano player. Glowering at the tourists, Frank points to him. "There's a man working here. He's a professional. He's the show here, not me, so let's have a little respect."

He turns to the thunderstruck piano player and says, "Go ahead, buddy. Sorry to interrupt your show." The guy nods—almost bows from his seat, really—and starts up with a soft version of "I've Got the World on a String."

Smiling like the Pope, Frank leads his retinue to our table. "Bobby!" he says. "Sorry I missed your show. Philly! How's your clyde?"

"Swingin', Frank. You missed a great show."

They all sit down around us. Frank points to me. "I was just telling Leo here—" Leo Durocher, former manager of the Giants and now a broadcaster, is among the group—"that you are the funniest guy in Vegas tonight."

"And that was without seeing your show," Dean puts in. "Imagine if he'd seen it."

"We'd all be dead by now!" Durocher says.

"Dead! What are you saying?" Frank yelps. I realize he's drunk.

"Because he was slaying 'em," Durocher explains, a little loudly.

"That's right!" Philly says, ever the cheerleader.

"Well, when's he coming back, Ed?" Frank demands of Torres, who books the place.

"In, uh, what did we just agree to, Philly?"

"In May."

"Well, hell, get him back here sooner. What's wrong with April?"

"Well, nothing…"

"Get him back in April."

"Sure, Frank." I know nothing will come of this—it's just Frank showing off and the guys letting him. They let him deal blackjack at the Sands, too.

Dean asks Entratter, "Hey, how's my boy Dick doing?" This is in reference to a running joke that Dick Shawn is one of Dean's protégés or something, when actually has nothing to do with him. The reason it's a joke is that it's well known that Dean never gives anybody a leg up; if an ambitious young comic or a singer even so much as tells him "Nice show," you can bet that kid will never appear on the same bill as Dean. Typical of Dean to make a joke on himself that's really a joke on the rest of the world.

While they go over a bit that Dick Shawn had done while headlining the Sands during the week, Frank is regaling Jerry Wald and Philly with tales of last month's marathon, even though you'd have to be living in Pago Pago not to know the story already. "We'd shoot during the day, do two shows, and then play cards all night. And did we walk through those shows? Not once! We gave those people their money's worth." He interrupts the other conversation. "Jack! Jack, you tell 'em. Did we phone in our show even once?"

"Absolutely not, Frank. You guys were troupers every night."

"Frank, I was there," Jerry says. "You were brilliant. You all were."

"Hey, thank this guy right here," Frank claps me on the shoulder. "Bobby was the hub of the wheel. It all revolved around Bobby."

Jack smiles tolerantly. He must have heard this from Frank over and over. Probably all he's thinking is, you bet, it made us five million bucks.

"We're wrapping up the picture next week," Frank says. "Right, Bobby?"

"I shot my last scenes on Wednesday."

"What you got lined up next, Bobby?" asks Wald.

I try not to let my face fall. Is he kidding? He must have known I was angling for a part in his Marilyn picture. What's he trying to do, rub it in?

I laugh weakly and look at Philly, hoping he can bail me out.

"I heard *Esquire's* doing a feature interview with Bobby," says Frank, to my horror. I can't believe this completely bullshit story, which started as a joke between me and Philly, is still alive.

"Hey, I heard about that," Jerry nods. "Who's that doing the interview, Norman Mailer?"

"Gay Talese," says a voice. Everyone glances in that direction—it's Gino. I had forgotten about him. He's sitting right between me and Dean, in the huddle that formed around our table. I can see Dean looking at him thinking: another poseur. It's not possible for Gino to even get out without causing a disturbance, so I just shoot him a look that says shaddup.

Frank has glanced at Gino, not recognized him, and turned back to me. "How about that!" Frank exclaims. *"Esquire* asked me and I had to say I was too busy. Who do they go to? Bobby. See what I'm telling you, Ed. Bobby's on the rise, you need to get him here as much as possible. Forget that guy … what's his name."

Everyone stares open-mouthed at Frank while he searches for the name, except Dean, who blows smoke toward the ceiling, and Ed Torres, who smiles vacantly.

"Jerry Lewis?" asks one of the girls. Dean coughs.

"Buddy Hackett?" from another.

"Jonathan Winters?" from Durocher.

"No!" exclaims Frank. "I know. Bob Newhart."

"Oh, *him,*" drawls Dean, and everybody laughs. Even I crack a smile. Nobody knows what Dean meant by saying Oh *him.* It probably doesn't mean anything. It's just his timing and the way he says it. Amazing comic.

"He does this phone thing," Durocher says helpfully.

"Yeah, I know," Frank says. He seems suddenly anxious, even disoriented for a moment, though he can't have had that much to drink. I know what he's thinking: The damn dago is funnier than I am.

"What's your next picture, Frank?" asks Torres, playing the host, trying to keep the conversation going.

"I may not be making a picture for a few months," he says. "Once we wrap *Ocean's*, I'm going to be working for JFK."

"Doing what?"

"Cultural attaché," Dean says with heavy irony.

"I want to organize Hollywood and the entertainment industry behind Kennedy," Frank says. "The convention's in L.A. in July and I want a big industry presence. We need to show the world the town is behind Jack."

"What about this picture I hear Marilyn is doing?" Entratter asks. "I heard you were involved in that."

"The Misfits? No, no, they got Clark Gable for that."

"No, the other picture they're shooting first. The comedy."

"That's Jerry's picture," Frank says quickly, nodding to Wald, avoiding my eyes.

"I heard Cary Grant," Torres says.

"We're looking at a lot of people," says Wald. "Because of the songs, we need somebody who can sing and dance and cut up a little. But a leading man type," he adds unnecessarily, looking at me. I could kill him.

"Well, there goes *my* big chance," I deadpan.

Frank guffaws, a little too loudly. "Yeah, Jerry," he laughs, "you had Bobby going there for a minute."

"Bobby can lead," Philly says, with a big grin to show everybody he's really joking.

"Into a commercial," Dean says.

"I been working a *lot* on my dancing," I protest, going along with the joke.

"He can lead there, too," Dean says.

"It's better than following," Frank says in a mincing voice, throwing a limp wrist.

"Nah, we got to get you and Marilyn together in a picture," says Jerry Wald to Frank. It's one time I'm grateful the spotlight's been shifted off me.

"Wouldn't that be dynamite?" says Philly.

"Hey Frank," asks Durocher, "is Marilyn behind Kennedy too?"

This really breaks them all up.

"No, really," Frank says. He really is plastered, God knows why. He turns to me and gets that sincere-drunk-fatherly look. "Bobby, the perfect thing is gonna come along for you some day."

Christ, not this again. "I know, Frank."

"Just make sure you have exact change, because it might be a bus," Durocher says. They all break up laughing again.

"Bobby's career is in great shape," Frank is protesting now. "Isn't it, Bobby? Look at you—headlining at the Riviera. How's he drawing, Ed?"

"Great, Frank," says Torres—too tactful to add: but only because everybody thinks you might come by and visit.

"And you're gonna have him back, right?"

"Absolutely."

I think: maybe if Frank is drunk, and everybody else is, nobody will remember this. In any case I wish I were.

"No," Frank goes on in his merciless way, "a big chance is like if I take this kid here," and he points at Gino—everyone looks at the kid as if he were some specimen brought back from space—"I take this kid here and put *him* in a movie. That'd be his big chance.

"*This* is your big chance, Bobby!" he says, sweeping his arm out to include the whole room, and narrowly missing the bouffant hairdo of one of the dames. "Oh, I'm sorry, sweetheart, did I mess up your hair?"

"Will you really put me in a movie?" Gino pipes up.

Frank turns and looks at him. "No, kid, that was just an example. Who are you, anyway?"

Gino swallows. For a second I think he's going to come up with another line of bullshit. But he finally croaks, "I'm Mr. Blaine's driver."

"His driver! Get outta here!" Frank says, suddenly reacting as if he's being spied on.

"Mr. Blaine invited me to his show," he says in a strangled voice.

"Oh yeah?" Frank flares. "Who else do you paper your audience with? Your milkman?"

"Looks like you blew your big chance, kid," deadpans Dean.

"Scram, Gino," I say. "I'll see you for the ride home."

There's an awkward moment while he looks for an escape, but everyone's packed so tightly that there's hardly even room for him to stand up, much less leave. Dean has him boxed in on one side, and one of Frank's goombahs is on the other. Dean isn't going to move a muscle, so finally the thug bestirs himself.

"G'wan, beat it," Frank snaps. I'm afraid this will cause the thug to give Gino more of an impetus than he needs, but the bodyguard confines himself to a threatening look as Gino scuttles away.

So much for my effort to be the big shot. A chill descends on the party. The dames are looking away from me, as if my shame were contagious.

"I had Kennedy at my show," Frank says, oblivious.

"Yeah, but he was comped," Dean says. Everybody attempts to laugh, but there's a tangible air of embarrassment. Even Dean seems a little guarded. Nothing causes him concern, but if things are going to get nasty, he'd just as soon go upstairs and watch TV.

"Hey," Wald says. "You see that new comic Don Rickles? He insults people. Just stay out of his line of fire," Wald says. "Lucky for me he didn't know who I was."

"Who are you anyway?" Dean asks. "Aren't you Bobby's milkman?"

"Come on," Frank says suddenly. "Let's blow."

"Come back and see Bobby's show," Torres smiles.

"A great show," says Philly.

"Are *you* the milkman?" Dean asks him.

"Come on," Frank says, rising. Like the Red Sea, his bodyguards and all the dames and hangers-on stand up and part for him to come through, then close up in his wake as he proceeds out of the room.

Dean stands up last. With the others across the room, he winks at me. "Don't worry about it, Bobby," he says, lighting a cigarette. "The war isn't over." He picks up his drink and trails after the group, calling, "Hey Frank, you forgot your elephant gun."

Philly and I are left standing next to my table. Slowly we sit down amidst the litter of drinks, dirty ashtrays and scrambled chairs and tables. It's like Fifth Avenue after a parade has gone past. "I don't even know which drink's mine," I finally say.

"Waitress," Philly calls.

"No, never mind, Philly. I'm going back to my dressing room. Thanks for coming to the show."

It's a long walk back to the dressing room. In the hallway I look at my watch. An hour and a half until the next show. And two more days of shows after that. And after that, what? Just wait around until Jack Paar needs a sub again? Become the maitre d' at Puccini? Maybe I can go back to Atlantic City and work in the mob joints again. Or I could continue my career as a bagman. There's lots of security there.

I open the door to the dressing room and there are the two FBI agents. "Oh, Christ!" I exclaim. "Larry and Curly."

"It's Corley," the tall one says. "And Agent Wilson."

"Hello, Mr. Blaine," says Wilson, cheerful as ever. "We just came for a chat."

"Well, you're in luck—talking what I do for a living. Two shows a night, live on stage. But you'll have to buy a ticket, and they don't sell 'em in the dressing rooms, so why don't you buzz off."

"Come on," Wilson says. "We can help each other."

"Yeah. I've seen the way you guys help me. I get any more help from you and Donny Timson will be up for an Academy Award."

"You can have a say in that, Mr. Blaine."

"I've had my say with you guys. I want you out of here."

Wilson looks offended, as if I've just insulted Mamie Eisenhower. "Now, really—"

"Yes, really—unless you've got a search warrant. Otherwise the hotel security is gonna throw you guys out just like you were a couple of off-duty deputies from Mississippi."

"Don't get tough with us," says Corley in a tough-guy voice.

"Don't worry, Curley. They won't leave any marks." I pick up the phone. "Get me casino security, please. Hello, this is Bobby Blaine's dressing room. Yeah, backstage of the Sunset Room. I have a couple of unwanted guests here whom I'd like to have leave, but they don't seem to know where the door is. Yeah. Thanks."

I put down the phone. "There's going to be four football linemen with Italian last names here in about thirty seconds, you guys. You better scoot."

Wilson stands up from the couch, dusting off his hands. "Mr. Blaine, think for a minute. You need us. You want to be opening for Soupy Sales in Elko this time next year?"

"I need you? What a fucking laugh! Let me tell you something, you transparent shmuck. I'm perfectly capable of fucking up my own career without your help. In the last month I've lost two film roles and I've been demoted from Vegas to Reno. So what more can you do? Get the hell out!"

"All right, Mr. Blaine. But don't expect any more help from us."

"My God! It doesn't understand!— Enough, leave! Go peddle your fish elsewhere!"

I go over to the door and open it. There are four palookas in black suits, one of them with his hand raised to knock on the door. He lowers his hand and says, "Something the matter, Mr. Blaine?"

"These men were just leaving. They say they're cops, so you might want to be gentle with them. Otherwise I never want to see them again."

"Yes, sir. Gentlemen?"

The two agents exit, looking extremely pissed. As he passes me, Corley mutters, *"Gei tren zich!"*

"Same to you, you fake!" I scream, slamming the door. The nerve of that guy, to tell me in Yiddish to go fuck myself. There's a magazine on top of a pile on the coffee table with a picture of Frank on the cover; I pick it up and throw it across the room.

2

After Gene leaves the Sunset Room, his first impulse is to go back upstairs to his room. It's a much larger room than the one at the Cactus Motel, with a huge bed, a nice television, and a series of chests and desks that run the length of the opposite wall. But there's nothing to do up there except sleep, and with the lights out, the lights of the Strip filter through the thick curtains, flashing weirdly on the walls and ceiling. So he goes downstairs again, wandering around the casino and then out into the illuminated night.

After several weekends of doing little but walking around Las Vegas, he's now familiar with the town. He heads downtown on his usual route, walking past the other Strip resorts and then the smaller, peeling buildings until he reaches the brightness of Fremont St. He looks around inside a huge souvenir shop and goes into some of the casinos.

All he wants is distraction from the embarrassment of being sent away, like a little kid, from the group of adults sitting around Bobby and Frank Sinatra. All he did was sit silently and then try to say something funny. He had known Sinatra wasn't really talking about putting him in a movie; he was just trying to lighten the mood. Sinatra was the one who had pointed to him in the first place; why did he then object to Gene opening his mouth?

That voice snarling "Get outta here … g'wan, beat it" echoes in his head along with the rest of the conversation. Frank Sinatra, the big star—

who grandly asked for respect for the piano player as a fellow "professional"—had put him in his place.

Probably he shouldn't have told the truth when asked to identify himself. If it were anyone else, such as Dolores, he would have stretched the truth, said something about being one of Bobby's writers. In fact, hadn't Bobby used in his routine all kinds of Beatnik stuff he'd got from Gene?

But at the last moment he had reacted with caution and told the truth. What does he really know about being a gag writer? He was sitting among a bunch of men whose business depended in part on gag writers and others; they could have discovered his ruse in a second, and that could have been much more embarrassing. For Bobby as well as himself.

Gene feels ready to go to a drive-away car agency and get a car going across the country. Like the hero of *On the Road* he'd make a mad dash for the opposite ocean, finding kicks and truth. The problem is that he still won't be 21 for a few months, and he has the feeling the car agency, not to mention the bartenders along the way, would insist on that qualification.

For the first time, he feels bored enough, or irritated enough, to want to gamble. Figuring his suit lends him a few years among the crowd of casually dressed tourists, he strides up to a teller's cage in one of the casinos, hands the man a twenty, and asks for quarters. The man glances at him, but raises no objection. Gene takes the orange rolls to a bank of slots and spends the next half hour steadily plunking them into the machines. Every five or ten tries, a few quarters come back; once he wins more than ten dollars' worth and is slightly ahead. His midwestern conscience tells him to stop playing at that point so that he can truthfully say he beat the house. But he keeps on. Once the motions of inserting a quarter and pulling the lever have become automatic, he's able to step outside himself and admire the figure he makes at the machine, suited and playing steadily, his eyes on the rolling cherries, sevens, grapes and whatall.

Finally the quarters are exhausted. He has brought another twenty dollar bill; excited by the prospect of daring to lose so much money, he gets two more rolls of quarters and steadily loses those, too, at an even faster rate.

He steps away from the machine feeling edgy and exhilarated. There's a tingling in his fingers, his eyes are shining and his shoulder is a little sore from pulling the lever dozens of times. He's almost shaking.

The crowd in the casino has grown larger, and people brush him as they walk past. He's jumpy, as if his reflexes have been somehow sharpened by the machine. He feels like picking a fight with someone just to show how fast he can move.

He walks around the casino in this jittery mood. He doesn't have any more money with him, though, so he can't play any more. He goes out onto Fremont St. and walks up and down, then back down the Strip.

By the time he reaches the Riviera again, he feels tired, but his experience of losing money has restored his self-image as a hard-boiled man. He considers the options a suave adult would have upon returning to his deluxe hotel room after a turn in the casinos. Call room service for a bottle of scotch, perhaps, or bribe some staff member to send up a call girl. But he doesn't drink scotch, has no idea whom to approach for a call girl, and can't afford either one anyway. So he takes the only remaining option: he turns on the TV, an amenity the Cactus lacks. The Tonight Show is on, but Gene has trouble focusing on the conversation with some New York swell he's never heard of. He keeps going back to the windows to gaze down on the Strip.

On Saturday morning, Gene returns to the Cactus Motel, carrying his small suitcase. Over his shoulder he carries his suit in a plastic garment bag supplied by the Riviera. He steps into the empty office, where the only sounds, from a fan and a television, are coming from the doorway leading to the owner's apartment.

Gene rings the desk bell, but nothing happens. He rings again and thinks he hears the noise of someone stirring. The old man who runs the place, whom Gene has seen on his previous visits, begins coughing and hacking, still hidden in his lair. When he quiets down but doesn't appear, Gene rings one more time.

"No vacancy!" shouts the owner.

"Whattaya mean, the place is empty."

"We don't open until five."

Gene carries his bags outside the office where a roof over the driveway offers shade from the spring sunshine. He stands for a minute in the scrap of cooler morning air, sweating from his walk from the Strip.

He notices Dolores come out of one motel room and lug her cleaning supplies down to another. Carrying his bags across the parking lot, he walks down to her and says hello.

"Don't talk to me, I'm busy," she says, trying to shut the door on him.

He jams his suitcase in the door. "I just want to put my bags in a room. Say, number 11."

"So go ahead."

"He won't give me a key, he says the office is closed."

"Then go get lost," she says, trying to kick his bag out.

"Aw, come on," he says, pushing back on the suitcase with his foot. "Just let me in number 11, that's all I ask," he says.

"All right, if you promise to leave me alone." She opens the door and pushes past him, walks down to 11, unlocks the door and throws it open. Gene has to lunge to catch it before it closes. "I didn't clean it yet, so just put your bags in the corner and beat it."

"What's eating you?"

She makes a frustrated sound, more a *pfft* than a sigh, and answers, "Just mad." But instead of going back to work, she leans against the outside wall of the unit and crosses her arms. Gene puts down his suitcase, lets the door of the room close, and stands outside with her.

"It's my father," she says. "I'm really serious about my studies. I'm going to be an accountant. He says sure, sure, but actually he just wants me to get married and get out of the house."

"Are you engaged or something?"

"No, I don't even have a boyfriend," she shrugs. "I mean, he doesn't say that, but that's what he's thinking. He doesn't understand, he thinks all I have to do is get married and have babies and everything's all right. Like my brothers' wives." She shakes her head. "Maybe it's fine for them but I want more than that. I don't want to be just another *mamacita*. I'm going to make something out of my life. At this rate it'll take me a couple more years just to get the credits to transfer to the university. I can do it if I live at home, but not if I have to move out."

She glances toward the office, and Gene follows her gaze. There's no sign of the owner, but she says, "I should get back to work."

"So your father doesn't want you to be an accountant?" Gene persists. He shifts his position so he's facing her, blocking her view of the office.

"He just doesn't think it's important. That's not even what we were arguing about—we were arguing over me giving up my room so my brother and his wife can move in because she's pregnant. I have to move in with the *niños*. Then I won't have any peace. Oh, it's a long story, why should you care." She shakes her head again and says, "Don't you think it's a good idea to want to climb up in the world?"

"Sure," he says. "I was parking cars last month. Now I'm a gag writer."

She rolls her eyes and begins walking back to her work. "Sure, sure," she says. "I tried to tell that stupid astronaut joke to people and they don't get it at all."

"It's in the delivery."

"Yeah, well, maybe you better get to work, too."

"So you don't have a boyfriend?"

Ignoring his question, she unlocks the door to number 6 and goes inside.

"Maybe I could help," he says, following her into the room. "Make the bed or something, I mean." He picks up a corner of the mussed bed linen, tugs on it tentatively.

Watching him, she says, "No, just pull it off. No, don't ball up the bedspread too, that doesn't get washed. Or the blanket either." She's been standing in the door holding it open; now she steps away from the door and it shuts. "Here, the bottom sheet and the top sheet and the pillowcase, that's all."

"Yeah." Her thick hair is tied back in a ponytail but still bunches up around her face as she bends down and yanks off the linens. Bending down, he says, "What's this, then?"

"That's the mattress pad. Keep that on there. Oh, you're not helping."

She reaches past him to tuck in the corner of the mattress pad again. When she straightens up, he puts his hands on her shoulders. She looks very surprised, even before he draws her to him and kisses her.

She lets him kiss her and then backs away a little, though not far enough that he has to drop his hands. Her back is to the window and shadows fall across her face. He kisses her again briefly.

She laughs a little. "I thought you were going to do that." She steps away, precluding yet another kiss. "What about you? Where's your girlfriend? Or your cousin or whoever it is."

"I don't have a girlfriend," he says. "Not now."

"Well," she says, "I have work to do."

He stolls toward the door. "Want to have lunch?"

She balls up the linens and tosses them at his feet. "Okay."

On Sunday night, as usual, Gene asks the bellman to have the car brought around, takes it to get gassed, fills the thermos with coffee, and meets Bobby as usual.

"What the heck happened to you?" Bobby asks as soon as he sees Gene waiting in the front seat. "I call you on Saturday and you've checked out."

"I spent Friday night here, but I decided to save money and go back to the cheap place for last night," Gene says.

"What for? I thought you had some money saved up."

"It's just more my style," Gene said evenly. "I guess I was used to it. This place is great, but I felt a little out of place."

Bobby pays the bell staff, tipping them more than usual because it was his last night, and climbed into the front seat with Gene. They take off. "Look," Bobby says. "If it was about Friday night—I really owe you an apology. Frank was absolutely out of line. In fact, I called your room the next day to tell you I'd talked to him and he was sorry. I had no idea something like that would happen."

"I should have kept my mouth shut."

Bobby sighs. "Well—you were out of your league. But I don't blame you. It's tough to just sit there like a bump on a log. Believe me, I know."

They drive out of town in silence. The lights of Las Vegas recede behind them.

"It sounded like the part in the movie didn't work out for you," Gene says.

"No," Bobby says quietly.

"Well..." Gene says. "I hope they change their minds."

Bobby smiles and reaches forward to pat Gene on the shoulder. "Thanks, Gino. I appreciate that."

"I wanted to tell you," Gene says, "I've decided to move to Vegas."

"Oh yeah?"

"I mean, unless you want me to keep driving for you. And the next time you have a... an engagement up here, of course, I'll be glad to do this again. But I think I want to move up here."

Bobby is nodding. "Okay, why not. Lots of work up here."

They drive some more in silence. Then Gene says, "To tell you the truth—I met a girl up here."

"Ah," Bobby smiles. "That explains it."

"Since Dana and I broke up, you know..."

"You didn't waste any time," Bobby says. "More power to ya. May I get another job as fast as you got another girlfriend."

"She's not even my girlfriend yet."

"No? So you're a gambler. Well, that's what Las Vegas is for."

Gene likes this, smiles behind the wheel.

Chapter 9

1

A clear blue desert sky, filled with the light of a sun in the southeast still climbing toward its mid-spring zenith. What clouds there are dot the sky sparsely, taking up little space, shading nobody in the warm Las Vegas morning.

Gene shades his eyes and looks up into this sky—really to the roof of the office of the Cactus Motel. It's early April, and he arrived in the city on the bus the day before.

"Mr. Gustafson? Hello?" Gene calls out. The owner of the motel is up there pounding away with a hammer. The pounding continues for a moment, then is interrupted by a hacking cough. Then silence.

Gene backs away into the parking lot to try to see the man, and walks in an arc to get the sun out of his eyes.

"Mr. Gustafson?"

The owner, whom Gene has encountered several times in the office, is maybe seventy; he is dressed, as always, in khaki-colored work clothes. He wipes his mouth with his sleeve and puts the hammer down, half in annoyance, half in exhaustion. "Whattaya want?"

"I'm Gene Kramer. I talked to you yesterday when I checked in. About the monthly rate."

No answer from Gustafson, who seems to be trying to catch his breath.

"You said to see you tomorrow about it. I mean, that's today."

Gustafson manages, "Can't you see I'm busy up here? Wind last week knocked off some shingles," before embarking on another coughing jag.

Gene stands in the parking lot, looking down at the black asphalt, then up at the roof, waiting for the coughing to stop. "You okay?"

"I—" More coughing.

Gene walks up to the long wooden stepladder, steps onto it, and climbs. The roof is peaked and covered with wooden shingles. Gustafson stops coughing in time to see Gene mount the roof and ease himself across the shingles in his direction. "Hey, you can't come up here!" He hocks and spits over the side of the roof onto the street.

Gene settles himself next to the man. Gustafson isn't smoking up there, but his clothes still exude a bitter tobacco smell. "You don't sound so good. You sure you should be up here?"

"I'm fine, I—" He coughs briefly. "Get outta here. You don't belong up here."

"Just wanted to see if you were okay."

"Bullshit!" the old man shouts. Gene flinches. "All I need is for you to fall off and sue me. The insurance doesn't allow you up here. Get down!"

"I have to talk to you about the monthly rate."

"The— " Gustafson is seized with a coughing fit. He doubles over, waves the hammer blindly as if in self-defense. Then he puts the hammer down and pounds his fist on the roof.

Gene looks down at the parking lot. The lot was half-full when he walked to the soda machine at 11:00 the night before. It's empty now. Nobody spends the night there.

Finally Gustafson regains his breath and sits panting. He wipes his mouth again.

"They sent me out here from Chicago for my health. Got TB back there. They said it would clear up out here."

"Oh, uh huh," Gene says politely, gauging the distance between himself and Gustafson's breath.

"Don't worry, I don't have TB anymore," Gustafson sneers. "Just... just my lungs are kind of weak." He picks up the hammer and a nail, pounds the nail home with two little taps and four sharp whacks. "Uughh," he groans, putting the hammer down again. "Got no breath. It's like trying to hammer nails on Mt. Everest." He rests, wheezing.

The hammer suddenly begins to slide down the roof, and Gene grabs it before it can get away. He touches one of the shingles that has come loose; it has worked its way out at an angle. Picking up a couple of nails, Gene works the shingle back under the row of shingles above it, and awkwardly nails it down. He smiles at Gustafson, who watches him silently. Nearby there is a gap where a shingle has fallen. Gene reaches for a new shingle from a nearby pile, works it into place, and hammers it down. Gustafson purses his lips, then looks off into the distance and sighs, his first truly controlled breath.

"I can finish this," Gene offers.

Gustafson says "Mmm," a low rumble, then says "Hell." Begins to ease himself down toward the ladder. After he steps onto it and descends a step, he looks up at Gene and says, "Gonna need to paint those, too."

"Sure."

The owner descends, coughing gently at first, then harder.

By one o'clock, Gene has completed the roofing job. He hangs the ladder on two big brackets along a side wall behind the motel. Nearby is a tool room and janitor's closet. Shelves full of peeling cans and bottles line the wall, and there is a filthy metal sink with a bucket-and-wringer beneath it.

He washes his hands and face in the sink, locks the room with the keys Gustafson had handed him, and goes back to the office and faces the front counter like any other guest. "All finished," Gene calls out. After a few moments, he hears a chair creak, and Gustafson comes out through an open doorway. Gene can see a couch and a bookcase through there; apparently this is where Gustafson lives.

"Ya do the painting?"

"I did a coat."

They walk out into the parking lot until Gustafson can see the sloping roof. "Aungh. Can't see shit from here, but I guess it looks like you painted it."

"Want me to go get the ladder so you can climb up again?"

"Aw hell. I wouldn't survive another trip up there. Forget it." He heads back toward the office.

"So about that monthly rate," Gene says, tagging along.

Gustafson coughs, hocks, clears his throat. "Yah. Well. You're pretty handy, seems like."

"Used to do this stuff at the country club," Gene says. "Did all sorts of stuff—lifeguard, golf caddy, grounds keeping, handyman stuff."

"Country club?"

"Sure. My dad was the head groundskeeper."

"Groundskeeper. Do any plumbing?"

"Well, there was a lot of hoses and valves and such associated with watering the grounds, of course, and also the filter, um, pump, on the swimming pool. And then, yeah, the showers in the locker rooms—we had to completely replace those. So yeah." He hopes that made some sense.

Gustafson sniffs, clears his throat, coughs, sniffs again. "Yah. Well. This ain't no country club. But seems like there's always something that needs to be done. I figure, weekly rate is forty a week, you do all the work, it's a wash. You do all the work in return for lodging. Take room number 12. Stay in it and fix it."

"Fix it? What's wrong with it?"

"Plumbing's been screwed up for a year. Haven't been able to use it. Open the door and you'll find out real quick."

"I can't stay in a room where the toilet doesn't work. That's no good."

"Well, take it or leave it." They go inside the office, and Gustafson heads back into his den without looking back at Gene.

"Look," Gene says. "I'll stay in another room and do the work—it's not like the place is full—I know. Got any other rooms that aren't rentable?"

"Well... the bed frame is cracked in 8. I don't rent that one out too much."

"There. And I want a dollar an hour on top of it."

Gustafson turns and makes a shooing motion. "Absolutely not. Forget the whole thing. You owe me forty bucks for the week."

Gene swallows. He only has fifty dollars in his pocket; he has planned to earn money parking cars at the Riviera, where Bobby Blaine has promised to give him a reference, but that won't be until the end of the week. He can't make it all week on ten dollars.

"Mr. Gustafson," he says. "Be fair. You're getting skilled labor here. Plumbing, carpentry, general handyman work."

"Skilled my eye! You swing a hammer like a girl."

"I can't live on nothing. You won't be sorry, Mr. Gustafson."

"Fifty cents plus the room."

"Seventy-five."

"How long you gonna be here?"

"All summer," Gene replies without thinking.

The old man wipes his mouth. The stubble on his face is uneven. "Yah. Okay. Keep the key to the storage room, I got another one. Here's the key to 12. And 8—move your stuff in there. You need parts or materials, you let me know. There's a hardware store I go to over on Tropicana. I got an account there. What'd you say your name was again?"

Outside in the parking lot, Gene sees Dolores carrying her implements down to the housekeeping closet. He trots over to her, grabs the vacuum.

"Oh, it's you. I thought I saw you on the roof but I thought, 'Why the heck would he be on the roof?'"

"I got a job here. I'm the new handyman."

"You? Here?" she says with surprise.

"I was coming every weekend. But I've moved to Las Vegas now. I got here on the bus yesterday."

She frowns as she puts away her cleaning supplies, takes the vacuum from him without a word.

"How about having lunch?" he asks.

Locking the closet, she purses her lips. Then she turns and looks at him for a moment, before marching past him across the parking lot. He trails after her, ducking in the midday sun as if it were rain beating down.

In the office, she steps into the niche where the time clock is. From there she can see into Gustafson's apartment, where he sits in an armchair watching a golf tournament on TV. "Mr. Gustafson?" she calls over the announcers' voices. "You gave Gene a job working here?"

"Yah." The old man doesn't look up. He lifts a yellowish glass of iced tea from a metal TV tray. "You done? Punch out."

"How much is he gonna work here?"

"Long enough to screw something up, then he's out. I'm watching this. Punch out, you hear? I'm not paying you to stand there watching television."

She stands there, hands on hips. Gene is nearby, leaning on the counter. She goes "Tsk" and seems to decide something. Turning to Gene, she whispers, "Here, I'll show you something." She takes two time cards from the rack. Putting a piece of carbon paper between them, she winks at Gene and punches the cards. "See? Every week I get two cards, I put the carbon, and bing, I punch the card. Now I got my own copy. Bye, Mr. Gustafson," she adds loudly.

The two emerge from the office and walk up the street. "He is such a pain in the you-know-what," she says.

"Why do you do that with the two cards?"

"So he don't cheat me."

"You want to have lunch?"

"No, I'm going home, I have to watch the babies."

"Let's go out sometime, then."

"What makes you think I want to do anything with you?"

He frowns. "You did kiss me a few weeks ago."

"You did that. I didn't do anything."

That's not how he remembers it. "Then how about going to the movies sometime?"

"The movies? Who has time for that?" She swings her purse on its leather handles, making it turn a full circle in the air. "I hope you didn't move to Las Vegas just because you kissed me once. That would be pretty stupid. What makes you think I want to spend time with you at all?" They have reached the corner, with her bus stop across the street. The light changes and she strides into the intersection.

He steps off the curb with her and she holds up a hand. "Stay here. Don't follow me!" she shouts, startling him so that he rocks back on his heels. By the time he's recovered, she's across the street and the light is changing. He watches her walk toward the bus stop, eyeing her muscular calves beneath the blue maid's uniform. Then he turns and walks east toward the Strip.

He finds the employment office at the Riv and drops the name given to him by Bobby. The personnel man makes a call, says a few words, hangs up, and says, "Sure, no problem. Come a half hour early to get a uniform and a locker. Then report to Billy Harrison at the valet desk at six. Start Friday."

In the lobby, he finds the telephones and looks in the directory for the public library. They must have some books on plumbing.

2

"Bobby, things are great. You wouldn't believe how great."

It's eleven in the morning, and I'm sitting by my pool dressed in a golf sweater and slacks, barefoot, a drink in my hand and a towel over my head. A wet towel, for my head is pounding. The sound of the vacuum cleaner in the house is like a dentist's drill.

"Philly," I say into the phone. "Don't start."

"Bobby! You have no idea. May I be struck down if I don't have six great things to tell you."

"I'm waiting. What else do I have to do? I've been sitting here by my pool for, what? I haven't worked since I did that weekend at the place on Sunset two weeks ago."

"They loved you. You had 'em falling off their chairs. You're going back there."

"When?"

"They're not sure, but it'll happen, it'll happen."

"Well, you really had me going there, Philly. I thought for a minute you were telling me about some work and I got all excited. But you'll warn me first, right?"

"Yeah, sure, Bobby, listen to this. You know you're back at the Riviera next month: a weekend in Reno, mid-week in Vegas, then back to Reno."

"I hope those aren't three of the six things. We knew about that weeks ago."

"I'm not even counting that. Listen to this. I got you at the Cal-Neva up in Tahoe at the end of May."

"Yeah, and? Am I headlining?"

"No, opening... *for Judy Garland!*" He shouts the last part. "Judy Garland, Bobby! You know what kind of crowd that will bring? She's not doing Reno, she's not doing Vegas. She's doing Tahoe as a personal favor to Frank."

"Opening."

"It's her only appearance in the western United States for months."

"Okay, but look, you have to jump on it then, you have to say, look, the place was packed when Bobby was out there, he slayed 'em, they sold drinks up the wazoo, get Bobby back as a headliner. I need to headline, Philly!"

Suddenly I see myself—a Hollywood hack, sitting by his pool with a towel on his head, but half rising out of his chair, and yelling at the phone *I need to headline!* I lower the phone, say out loud, "What the fuck am I doing?" and put my drink down.

Philly is saying, "What was that, Bobby?"

"Hold on a minute, Philly. Just hang on."

I put the phone down next to my drink, take off my sweater, and fully clothed, dive into the pool. The heater isn't on, and the water is freezing. Every one of my blood vessels contracts; I feel like my head's going to pop off. My hands numb on the metal ladder, I climb out and yell toward the phone, "Hang on another second, Philly!" and walk dripping into the cabana, where I strip off my clothes, towel off, and put on a robe. Then I walk back out into the sun, feeling almost human again.

"Sorry, Philly, a delivery man came. Now where were we?"

"Opening for Judy Garland at the Cal-Neva, May 20th and 21st."

"Okay, good job, Philly. What else?"

"You're hosting the Tonight Show, Friday next week. Jack Paar is taking the day off and you're subbing."

"Friday? Why that Friday?"

"It's Good Friday. A Christian thing, you know. The day the Jews killed Christ."

"Oh, wonderful."

"I'm going to try to get them to consider you the designated backup man there. And you know Paar. He's already walked out this year once, maybe he'll throw another tantrum. You see what I'm getting at?"

"So you're sending a Jew out there on Good Friday? What do you think, maybe I should wear side curls and a shawl? Or should I just wear a yellow star?"

"Come on, Bobby, nobody's going to think twice about it."

"I'll go out there with a hammer and nails and say, 'We got him once, but he rose from the dead, the scamp! This time I'll get him for sure!'"

"Bobby, please."

"'Just call the Jews—we kill Christ dead!'"

"Bobby, stop. Even I'm offended."

"Got any Muslim holidays you can book me into? Or do you just want to wait until Christmas Eve?"

"Bobby, please. The Tonight Show is the Tonight Show. Just do your monologue and stay away from religion. You don't want to exacerbate the issue."

"I know I've said this, but I'll say it again. I do not want to become a talk show jockey. For one thing, it's not that much money. For another—"

"Not that much? You kidding? Paar gets six thousand a week!"

"And as a sub I get five hundred a night. What is that? Peanuts."

"It's exposure, that's what it is! Three hundred people might see you at the Riviera. Three *million* people see you on the Tonight Show!"

"Yeah, I'm sure a lot of good Catholics are going to be watching."

"Come on. You love New York. You told me you love going back there. Good memories, right?"

"Good and bad."

"You can't still be carrying a torch, not after all this time."

"Never mind."

He sighs. "Do the vegetarian beatnik butcher. No, on second thought, better stay away from any jokes about the butcher. I don't know, you'll think of something. *Mein gott!* That reminds me. The best thing! They want to make a record of you, a comedy record. Everybody's doing these."

"Who wants me to?"

"What is it... Capitol Records. They want to sign you to a record contract."

This is the first decent thing he's had all day. "Philly, that is good."

"Of course it is."

"Is that a done deal?"

"Practically!"

"My own record, that's swell."

"More like a series of records."

"They want to sign me to a multi-record contract? or whatever you call it? That's unbelievable!"

"Right. Well, it's not just you. It's you and Frank, you and Dean, you and Sammy—you get the idea."

"Wait a minute, what?"

"It's the Rat Pack series—and you'll be introducing. You'll be on every record. Like this: on Frank's record, you act like the m.c., you welcome the audience, tell a couple of jokes, then introduce Frank. After a few songs, you come on again, tell a couple jokes, introduce the next song. Same thing with Dino, only he tells some jokes too. You get the idea. It's basically recreating the Las Vegas Summit shows in the privacy of your own living room. Gives mom and pop back in Kansas the idea that they were there."

"So I'm m.c.-ing record albums. That's something I've never heard of."

"This is in its infancy, Bobby. It's a whole new model."

I chew over that phrase. "That sounds like what they say at the nude drawing class at the art college."

"Ha *haaa!* That's a good one, Bobby. No, it's something I got from *Variety.* TV, movies, records, live appearances, they're all different exposure models."

"Now it's 'exposure models.'" My headache seems to be getting worse, but I don't want to jump into the pool again. For one thing, this is the only robe I have, and I've got nothing on underneath. If I take the robe off to jump into the pool, I'd be skinny dipping. Then we'd really have a new exposure model.

"Okay, what is that, three things. Three more things like this and I'm through."

"I lied, there is only one more thing."

"Thank God."

"You know that rumor last month, the one about Gay Talese doing a profile on you for *Esquire?* Well, he's not doing it."

"I know that, Philly, I was there when you made up the rumor."

"Yeah, and it didn't hurt. Because right now Gay Talese instead is doing a lead-in for the Rome Olympics, he's covering the young boxers. Cassius Clay, is that a name for the screen or what? He could be the next Tarzan."

"I think Cassius Clay is a Negro, Philly. But what's it got to do with me?"

"Oh. Well, in any case, having Talese off in Rome makes it look like he was going to do you, but he took this Olympics story instead. For all anyone knows, he can do you when he gets back."

"Yeah, I'm sure that's on a lot of people's minds. Is that it?"

"No, wait for it. So as I was saying, it all started me thinking, well, there are other writers and other magazines, so I called a few editors to try to interest them in the story. But no dice."

"You're going to tell me one of these days, I can feel it."

"You know how *Make Nice for Daddy* became just *Make Nice* and then turned into *Let's Make Love*. Which they're shooting now—"

"Boy, we're just revisiting all my failures here, aren't we?"

"— with Marilyn Monroe and Yves Montand, if you please, and the other man whose name you told me never to mention."

He means Timson. "Very kind of you to remember that."

"So finally here it is. *Look* magazine is doing a series of articles 'on Hollywood *by* Hollywood.' Which means they're going to get famous stars to write about each other. Which means you."

"So someone is writing about me."

"No. You are writing about someone. You are going to the set of *Let's Make Love* and you are going to write about the Movie Queen and her Playwright Husband, Arthur Miller, who is doctoring the script for Miss Monroe, and you are going to write between the lines of the romance between Miss Monroe and Monsieur Montand that is happening right under the nose of Mister Miller and Monsieur's equally famous actress wife, Simone Signoret."

"Holy Moses... Philly... You want me to go to the set and write about ... Look, first of all, where did you get the idea that I'm a journalist? I can write a joke, but... my spelling alone..."

"A ghost writer will take care of it all. All you have to do is go on the set and get Marilyn to start talking."

"And then I'm supposed to write about ... No, Philly. Really. And with Timson there the whole time?"

"Forget him. You think Marilyn is tough to work with? That guy showed up drunk the first day and Arthur Miller has been merrily cutting out his part ever since. He'll be lucky if he winds up in the finished product at all. Be glad it wasn't you."

"Except I'm not a drunk and I wouldn't have fucked it up."

"You're not a singer and dancer either, which is why you didn't get it. But that's water under the bridge. Don't you see, Bobby? You're making like I'm rubbing your nose in your biggest failure. Quite the contrary, this is a chance to make some hay. You're not in the film, but for the reader of *Look* magazine, you are... You're there on the set, writing in the first person, and because you're a Hollywood star like the rest of them... well, almost... they open up to you. You can relate to them, you're not asking them crap like 'What's it like to wait around on the set all day?' because you *know*, you've been there. Instead you're asking them confidentially to share details that only insiders talk about, like—"

"Like Marilyn getting boffed by her co-star."

"No, haven't you been listening? That's between the lines. The ghost writer will handle that stuff. Don Tragge from the *Daily News*, that's who it is—you know him. What you do is industry gossip, the insider stuff. Their next projects... Will she ever really work with Frank Sinatra... The challenge the famous playwright faces as he becomes a screenwriter... That's the stuff."

"What am I, Louella Parsons?"

"Can't you see sitting down with Arthur Miller and comparing writing for the stage versus writing for the screen? Sitting down with Yves Montand and comparing what it's like working in Hollywood versus France?"

"Sitting down with Marilyn Monroe and comparing her husband with her lover?"

Silence from Philly. A crow suddenly launches himself from the top of one of my trees, squawking his way toward Sunset Blvd. "I shouldn't have mentioned that at all," Philly says finally.

"And this is paying me what?"

"Don't ask that, Bobby. You know what? You don't want to know. You figure it out by the hour, you may as well be waiting tables. But they publish your picture along with your byline in *Look* magazine, that's the important part."

"Is it a whole new exposure model, Philly? I'm going to say it so you won't get a chance to."

"Yes, precisely. It is. Exposure! That's the important thing. All you have to do is say the word. Then the wheels start turning and next week you're on the set. Tragge's on call."

"Just to make sure you're not taking this exposure thing too literally, Philly—What is the one thing I will never do, no matter how much 'exposure' it is? Even if I have to do a telethon, if I have to do a supermarket opening, if I have to put on a clown suit and do an afternoon live kid's show, what will I never, ever, ever do?"

"Bobby..."

"Never, Philly?"

He sighs. "A game show."

"Thank you. All right, call *Look,* tell them okay. I'll go down and get a notebook and a pencil and a little tag to stick in my hat that says CUB REPORTER."

"Good man, Bobby. *Good* bye."

3

Gene throws himself into the purgatory that is number 12, where almost everything needs repair or replacement. He puts the mattress out for the garbage man, removes the metal bed frame, dumps the ruined carpet and pad. Beneath the pad is a damaged wood floor, warped and partially rotted. As for the bathroom, the toilet is entirely missing, along with some tiles from all around where the toilet is supposed to be. He finds the toilet in several pieces in a bin behind the motel.

Standing with Gustafson in the doorway of number 12, Gene begins, "Floor's messed up."

Gustafson sighs. "What'd ya expect?"

"I think the right thing to do is replace the lousy parts of the floor and the baseboards. You probably want it done to code, and—"

Gustafson barks out a laugh. "Code! You think there's a city code for a two-bit place like this? City inspectors only shake down the big places. They don't bother with small fry like me. Nothing in it for them."

"You can't just lay down new carpet on top of this."

"The hell I can't. I can slap a rug down there, and the trash that will use this room for one hour won't notice or care there's anything wrong with the floor."

This is the first time Gene has heard the owner acknowledge that the motel is patronized mostly by hookers and their clients. It's one thing for Dolores to refer to the fact that "nobody spends the whole night here," another for the old Swede to own up to it.

"So you don't want me to move into this unit when it's cleaned up?"

"As long as I'm getting my money's worth out of you, you can stay on the roof as far as I'm concerned. As for the floor, I'll rot sooner than that floor will. And when I'm dead I won't care what happens to it." The old man turns to go out and stops at the window. He turns to go, and then stops to peer at the window frame. "What the hell is this?"

"I sort of bent the frame trying to open the window. It stank so bad in there."

The old man peers at him with disdain. "You do know what the hell you're doing, right?"

"All I did was try to open the window," Gene says.

"In other words, you don't know what the hell you're doing." He shakes his head. "So far all you've done is tear things up. You tore up the window and the bed and the carpet. A retard could have done as much." With that, the owner is seized with a coughing fit that drives him out of the unit. He makes his way across the parking lot, weaving across the asphalt like a little boat tacking against a fierce wind.

Gene stands in the doorway of the unit for a few moments, sighing. He has a strong urge to pack his stuff and move on. There are plenty of crappy little motels to stay in, and he can probably survive on what he'll make parking cars on the weekend.

Dolores comes down the walkway. "Hey, Smelly," she says cheerfully, then laughs at his reaction. "Oh, don't look so downtrodden. Me, I've put up with him for two years. I need the money. You can walk out anytime you want," she adds, as if reading his thoughts. "You look like you'd make a good bus boy."

That does it. He's staying.

4

Tragge—rhymes with Maggie—is waiting in the bar when I get there.

"I've already got the title," he grins. Setting his drink down so he can use both hands, and spreading his fingers in a gesture that looks like he's placing letters on a theater marquee, he says, "'*Mon*roe... *Mont*and... *Mon dieu!*'" His cigarette waggles up and down in his mouth as he speaks. "Whattya think?"

I wave the bartender over and order. This is getting off on the wrong foot. "Don, listen. I'm not above having a little fun with this, but this is *Look* magazine. It's not some cheapo scandal sheet."

"Yeah, it's an expensive scandal sheet. If you call seventy-five cents expensive."

"Second of all, and let's put all our cards on the table here, I've heard the rumors about Marilyn getting it on with Yves Montand, and so has everybody, and we just don't have to get into it. I mean, it's not necessary, and thirdly, people have their private lives. Even reporters."

"You're wrong there, Bobby," he says, raising his glass to me. "Reporters have no lives." He tosses the last of the drink down.

The lunch traffic is really emptying out now. Behind us in the dining room are empty tables with dirty dishes and full ashtrays. But in one of the banquet rooms in the back, I can still hear a large party going on. "Hey Bill," I say to the bartender, while Tragge lights another one, "what's going on back there?"

"Bunch of local politicians—the county committee or some such. They come in here all the time now that the convention's coming to town."

Holding his glass and his cigarette in the same hand, Tragge says, "I think we have to talk to Marilyn first thing. Or maybe not first—after all, she usually doesn't get to the set real early—but she has to be our highest priority. *Look* magazine isn't sending us over there because of Yves Montand."

"I heard the angle was The Movie Queen And The Playwright. And Arthur Miller has got to be interesting to talk to."

He shrugs, nods. "That raises the level, bringing this intellectual in. Also the Frenchies. But you gotta have Marilyn in there. And it's not going to be easy. Word is, last week she locked herself in her dressing room. So they improvised a scene with Bing Crosby who happened to be on the lot."

"I can't believe the studio wants to have a reporter down there on the set."

"They don't—that's why they got you. You're going to write a puff piece. What else are you gonna do, write an exposé? And never work at MGM again?"

"I never worked there once."

"But still, you're not burning any bridges. I'll see to it. I don't want to be *persona non grata* there either. Hey, speaking of which," he says, lighting another cigarette, "what happened to that *Make Nice* picture anyway?"

I can see Tragge is going to be a pain in the ass. "Don, come on."

"What's the matter, Bobby?"

"I have to spell it out for you? Give me a break."

"But what happened?"

I heave a sigh. "It was a con, that's what happened. A big con job Jerry Wald set up. He got Marilyn to sign up for a picture, and then at the last moment, he switches stars and scripts on her. And they pulled the same con job on the studio, once they got the green light, bingo, suddenly it's a musical. Or a sex comedy, one or the other."

"They conned Marilyn, they conned the studio..." He trails off, watching me through the smoke.

Finally I say, "Why don't we leave me out of it."

He arches an eyebrow, sips his drink. "Here's how we'll do it," he says. "Way I see it, you don't want to be burdened taking notes. You just have the conversation, I'll sit behind you in the dark taking notes. I won't say a word."

There's a ruckus in the back of the restaurant as the politicians' lunch breaks up. Tragge turns on his stool to look. "Here it comes, the Democratic party," he says. "Hey, get it? The Democratic party."

I ignore him, for coming through the restaurant, his head bobbing above a school of red-faced local pols, is Peter Lawford. Smiling and nodding and making his way toward the door as quickly as possible, but they're practically hanging on him, eager to soak up his celebrity. Peter spots me and claps me on the shoulder, relieved.

"Bobby," he says brightly. "You're a welcome sight, old boy. For a minute I thought I was in some Midwestern hofbrau. Now it comes back to me, I'm still in Los Angeles, thank God."

I introduce Tragge to Peter.

"Pe - ter Lawford," Tragge sings out. "I hear you've become a citizen of these United States."

"Perhaps not of all of them," Peter says. "I was rather hoping they'd just let me become a citizen of California and New York and we could agree to let the rest go."

"Ha! That's a good one. You're a Democrat, I take it?"

"It seems to be a family tradition."

"Don, we'll be in touch," I say. "Let's plan to meet at the studio first thing Monday." I throw a twenty on the bar and stand up. "Need a ride, Peter?" I say.

"Anywhere but here," he says. "A little peace and quiet would be nice."

They bring the car around and, remembering Gino and his sad tales of parking cars, I tip the guy ten bucks before climbing in. We head out Sunset Blvd. "You still living in Santa Monica? I know a little place out that way," I tell Peter. "Nobody ever goes there."

"Sounds marvelous."

"Who was that little man you were with at Capri?" Peter wants to know.

"Don Tragge, *Daily News* columnist. We're going to work on an article together."

"Really? I didn't know you were a journalist."

I explain the idea behind the celebrities-interviewing-other-celebrities piece.

"Why, that's great, Bobby," Peter says. "But I'm surprised they didn't send you to interview Frank."

"But he doesn't have a project now, right? He's just working on JFK's campaign."

"Quite right, along with yours truly. Sometimes I don't know who's the real brother-in-law. Jack certainly spends more time with Frank than with me."

"What are they cooking up?"

"Well, of course the Democratic convention will be held here in July. And Frank and I are positively pounding the pavement trying to drum up Hollywood support. All the actors and directors and writers we can get—anyone with a name at all—we want them somewhere in front of a camera endorsing Jack Kennedy."

"They have to be famous? So that's why you haven't asked me yet."

"Oh, don't be silly, Bobby, of course you're wanted. In fact, Frank's putting together some events related to the convention, I'm sure he'll want you to m.c. or do something."

"Well, you let him know I'll be glad to help in any way."

"Thank you, Bobby, I appreciate that. Listen, I have a tux to pick up at Devore's. Can you just drop me up here on Vine?"

"Sure." I'm thinking, this guy is in the same boat as me. He's scraping by, clinging to Frank's coattails. Being married to JFK's sister isn't helping him one bit, except with Frank—if not for that, he'd just be an aging matinee idol.

"Well, here we are. Thanks for rescuing me from those Democrats."

"Sounds like something else you'll have to get used to."

"I'm afraid you're right. Right, then, ciao, Bobby." He slams the door and strides into the tailor shop.

5

The low point of Gene's week is Thursday, when he finally works himself up to tackling the plumbing problem. Despite having carefully turned off all the water to the hotel, he is sprayed with filth when he uncaps the pipes.

After he cleans himself off, it takes all his determination to go back and clean up the mess. The incident reminds him of just why he hates handiwork—the whole hidden world of the messy systems behind walls and under floors, the necessity of getting his hands dirty. It's just what he tried to avoid by not hanging around his dad's hardware store. Forcing himself into the work, he cleans up the filthy bathroom several times over using heavy amounts of Dolores' supplies.

The next morning, Gene is sitting outside number 12 in the sun, trying to put the toilet back together with the help of a library book, when Dolores arrives to clean the room next door.

"Most people have the toilet *in* the bathroom," she observes.

"This is what you call a dry run."

"Let me see what it looks like in here—oh, man, look at that floor. That's bad."

"He won't fix it, either."

"See, he's cheap."

"At least all the stuff in there that stank so bad is gone. I think the floor will look a little better once it finally dries out."

"Hmm," she says. "Maybe that means number 11 won't stink now."

"Maybe so," he says, turning a wrench.

"You want to come check?" she offers.

Gene wipes his brow on the back of his wrist and squints up at her. Wiping his hands on his pants, he goes smiling after her into number 11. He lets the door shut; she doesn't object. They stand in the dimness quietly.

"Seems a little better," she offers. She's facing into the center of the room, but when he puts his hand on her shoulder, she turns to face him.

This time she definitely kisses back.

On Friday evening, with seventy-eight cents remaining in his pocket, Gene reports for work at the Riviera, and his life seems to improve immediately. He had been a little worried about being the outsider in a group of hardened, experienced valets who would compete with him for tips. But most of the other valet parkers have been on the job only a few weeks. They're set on becoming waiters or dealers inside; none of them have as much experience as Gene. Despite working all week long at the

148

motel, he feels light on his feet. For every car he fetches, he gathers in five- and ten-dollar bills. After tipping back to the parking manager at 4:00 a.m., Gene has made $85. The next night, Saturday, is even better.

He sleeps late on Sunday morning. Lying contentedly in the slanting bed with its broken frame, he reflects on his good fortune. He made almost $200 for the weekend at the Riv; considering he isn't paying anything for lodging, this is a stupendous amount. He's got one job with a guaranteed room, another that's good money. It doesn't matter that they're both temporary; it's just how he wants it. The beatnik's itinerant life, as depicted in *On the Road* and *The Dharma Bums,* is not just a dream to him anymore. He tasted it when driving Bobby Blaine back and forth from Hollywood to Vegas; it seemed to infect the rest of his life, coming between him and Dana and leading him completely out of California. Even as he settles into his new Las Vegas life, he can foresee at the end of the summer another leave-taking, another journey to an unfamiliar town, another temporary job, temporary housing, temporary girlfriend.

And yet, having established himself with the right amount of security and insecurity, Gene knows he doesn't have a complete handle on the beatnik lifestyle. He still feels like a kid, whereas Kerouac's characters all seem like men. Not only are they grown up, with access to women, booze, cars and everything else Gene yearns for, they seem possessed of other-worldly knowledge not taught in schools. The strange Buddhism depicted in *The Dharma Bums,* for example—where in the world do you learn that? The soul-deep, nearly religious relation to jazz music, which evidently has the power to sweep men into profound trances—what does it take to appreciate music on that level? And most of all, the courage to leap into the unknown, to go from coast to coast without enough money for gas; to be so confident of your attractiveness that you are unable to be tied down to a single woman; to hop freights or to climb the Sierras with little more than a thin bedroll (he wonders: what is a "bedroll"?); to drive through a foreign country, subjecting yourself to all kinds of fetid experiences, and even smoking marijuana— where do adults get such self-assurance? Where do they even learn to drink like that? Who's going to teach Gene these things?

He already suspects that Las Vegas, or anywhere besides San Francisco and New York, is an unlikely place to find either Buddhists or beatniks to tutor him in their ways. Kerouac makes Denver, for example, seem like the coolest place in the universe. Gene came through Denver on the way to California, and is unable to picture the continuous party depicted by Kerouac. This discrepancy suggests to him that Kerouackian bliss depends less on a particular location—his characters, after all, move on from place to place and have fun just about everywhere—than on raw self-confidence and a sort of native ability to appreciate the possibilities of things. Perhaps if he really had the Kerouac spirit, Las Vegas would be as good a place as any to be.

Chapter 10

It's a funny thing pulling up to the gate at MGM and giving my name. They look at a list, wave me and Tragge in, and we find our way to Stage 14. So simple. Like I told Philly, I've never worked at MGM. Now I am—in a manner of speaking.

We climb out of the car. It's a pleasant April morning, with the sun already poking through the overcast. Ever since the day I rescued Peter from the Democrats and he said he wanted to go to Santa Monica, then changed his mind, I've been wanting to go out there. This would be a good time. The fog burning off, the cool sea air. A nice little walk along the palisades—if that's what they call them.

Long after there's any reason to, I stand gripping the car door handle. The last, tenuous link to my nice, safe house. "So how *do* you interview somebody for an article, Don?" I say.

He's already shambling over to the sound stage. "Come on, Bobby, coffee's gettin' cold."

We go through an opening in the huge doors, leaving the morning behind. Inside we ask around and find an assistant director. The A.D. goes to find the publicist. The publicist is a gray little froglike guy, part department store floorwalker, part Peter Lorre. "Don," says the man, exuding annoyance. "Didn't you get my message?"

Tragge completely ignores his question. "Bobby, this is Pierce Hawkins, unit publicist. You know what a unit publicist is, don't you?"

"I'm terribly sorry but we must reschedule," Hawkins says. "Today will not do."

"A unit publicist," Tragge continues, "is just like one of those guys you meet if you go to Russia. They say they're assigning you a personal tour guide, but he's really in the secret police. Ostensibly the idea is that the tour guide's going to help you see things. In fact, it's the opposite—his job is to make sure you *don't* see things. Hawkins is supposed to be a publicist, but he's really here to prevent us from seeing anything or talking to anybody he doesn't approve."

"Today," Hawkins says, more loudly, "will be impossible."

"What's the matter, Hawkins, didn't they give you the good kibble today? We just want to talk to the director, the actors, and the writer. That won't be too much trouble, will it?"

This argument is ended only by the approach of George Cukor, the director. Tragge's seen him coming and quickly shakes Cukor's hand and pulls me over.

"Mr. Cukor! Don Tragge of *Look* magazine! And Bobby Blaine—you know Bobby."

Cukor, dressed in a short-sleeved white shirt and khaki trousers, is in his 60s, and is small but trim, like a retired tennis star. His balding head is cut just right, suggesting he is professional but not too square. "I know you fellows are here for an interview," he says, taking off at a fast clip. We follow in his wake like tin cans tied behind a car, leaving Hawkins in the dust. "And ordinarily I'd give you five minutes and kick you out. But it seems we're due to fall behind schedule today—again—so I have the feeling we've got plenty of time."

Tragge jerks his head at me as if to say *Take him up on it, and fast.*

"Well," I croak, "if you've got a few minutes to tell us about the picture you're making, we'd really appreciate it."

"I think the readers of *Look* are in for a real treat—just like the moviegoers of America are with this movie." A glint in his eye betrays this seeming bullshit as pointed sarcasm. Tragge is already furiously taking notes.

Cukor starts in by telling us about the story. The plot of *Let's Make Love* concerns a famous playboy billionaire, played by Montand. About to become the subject of a satirical Off-Broadway play, he goes down to the theater himself to protest. But before he can get a word in edgewise, he meets a cast member, Monroe, and is smitten. A moment later he is mistaken for an auditioning actor who is there to try out for the part of the billionaire—in other words, to play himself, even though they don't recognize him. He gets the part and proceeds to woo Monroe. Once she starts returning his affections, he gets scared and thinks she's really after his money—and then it runs out of gas. I wonder how they're going to pump some life into the story to keep it from dying before the third act. That's a question for Arthur Miller, though—he's the one doctoring the script. I decide to get to the point.

"You've worked with the greatest actresses," I say. "Judy Garland. Bette Davis. Ava Gardner. Katherine Hepburn. Now Marilyn Monroe is the greatest star of our age. How does she stack up—er, let me rephrase that—how does she compare to them?"

Cukor purses his lips. "I think she is best compared to Judy Holliday," he says in a diplomatic tone. "Judy has a wonderful comic sense, and is such a joy to work with. Marilyn… is also an excellent comic actress and she is… also blonde."

I say, "What struck me, when I heard about the movie, is that the unique angle is the combination of this very continental type, Montand, with a very American type, Monroe. How are they on camera together? Do the sparks fly?"

"Sparks positively fly," he says in the same droll tone. "Just the word for it. Their romantic interest in each other—that is to say, the characters—is very believable."

"And how's the shooting going, generally? I've heard there is a little script rewriting going on."

"Any picture changes in the execution," he says blandly. "We have a fine script, though." He pauses, purses his lips again, blinking. "Norman Krasna," he remembers finally. "His work is well known."

"Even more for the scripts that didn't make it to the screen," mutters Tragge.

"But to get back to Miss Monroe," I say loudly. "Sometimes great actresses are difficult to work with. In your opinion, is it true that, the greater the actress, the more temperamental she is?"

"I don't know what you mean. Everyone I've worked with has been marvelous. Including the cast of this picture," he adds.

He is clearly determined not to rock the boat. But two can play at this game. "You're speaking, of course, of Miss Monroe's widely known professionalism and dependability."

"Yes," he says, now sounding remote. Have I pressed too hard? "Miss Monroe works very hard. I don't think most people realize that. She's worked very hard on her craft, and her success is a testament to it. She prepares very carefully."

"I see." I look around the sound stage theatrically. "Is that where she is now—preparing?"

"Of course. And speaking of which, I have some work of my own to do. So if you will excuse me?"

He walks a few steps toward a couple of crew members who are doing something to the lights. They confer. "Give me 2A!" one of the crew shouts, and a light comes on. "Thank you. Give me 3A."

I turn to Tragge, who is studiously scribbling. He holds up a hand, stilling me while he writes down Cukor's words.

Hawkins has been hovering. "Listen, Mr. Blaine, I was told to cooperate with you, and I expect the same in return."

"What'd I do?" I shrug.

"We don't need any rotten press about this picture," he says. "In fact, with this cast, we don't need any press at all about this picture. It sells itself."

"Speak for yourself, Mac," Tragge says, finishing his notes. "Now where's Montand? Hey, Hawkins—listen to this line: 'Monroe... Montand... mon dieu!'"

Hawkins virtually curls his lip. "I expected such," he hisses.

"Make way!" someone shouts. "Watch out! Coming through!"

A man in a yellow suit—yes, a banana-yellow jacket and trousers—topped by a yellow ten-gallon hat—and wearing white tennis shoes—barges through the set. He is carrying something out in front of him, arms extended stiffly as if it were a bomb. As the guy blows past, I see that he is carrying merely a big paper cup with a lid. It's just coffee.

"Monsieur Montand's personal assistant," the publicist drawls. "A clown."

"Speak for yourself," Tragge says again. By the end of the day I'm sure it's one of his favorite lines.

We follow the man—his glowing suit leading us through the recesses of the sound stage—into the makeup room. A tall man is reclining in the chair, festooned with towels, a makeup artist hovering over his face like a hummingbird and manicurists working him over on both sides. The yellow-suited man buzzes around them crying "Coffee! Coffee!"

The man in the chair emits a groan. "Clarice," he says. "Wait a minute." Or actually he says min-*eet,* in a French accent. The makeup artist pauses, and the man struggles to sit up. "Somebody help me with thees fucking chair," he cries. The makeup artist presses a pedal, and the chair gives a *ker-chunk!* and propels the man into a standing position in an instant. Towels drift off him as he stands there blinking. It is, of course, Yves Montand.

The yellow-suited man springs to a position in front of Montand and proffers the paper cup. "Coffee!" he proclaims.

Montand takes the cup absently, peering at Tragge and me. "Are you from the police?" he demands. The women break into laughter.

"Relax, we're your friends," I say. "We're from the press."

He clutches his temples. "It's still an interrogation... I'm innocent, I swear! I disown the weapon, I disavow the knowledge, I disem..." he falters. "I dis... You're sure you're not the police?" The women are howling.

"We just came to talk to you about *Let's Make Love,* your role, and what it's like working with Marilyn Monroe." I think I'm sounding a little too much like a radio announcer.

He lifts the lid of the coffee container gingerly, as if he expects a tarantula to jump out. Closing the lid without drinking any, he sits down on the edge of the chair with a sigh. "I play zee billionaire. Who becomes an actor to be close to the woman he is in love with. When she finds out his real *identité,* he becomes suspicious, afraid she wants only his money. After that I forget. Anyway, in the play-within-ze-play, I get to sing and dance, which I enjoy very much. And there are also the comic scenes where Bing Crosby teaches the billionaire how to sing, Gene Kelly teaches him how to dance, and another man teaches him to be funny. Who is that... Meelton Barrel."

He means Milton Berle. "What's it like acting with Miss Monroe?"

"She is very sincere with the other actors," he says thoughtfully. "Maybe that is not the right word. Now let me think. You know, before I started this picture, before I came to Hollywood in fact, I think like everybody else, that Marilyn Monroe is just a sexy broad. She is like Jayne Mansfield, very sexy, but her acting must not be good. Then to prepare for this picture, I see *Some Like It Hot.* And I realize, she is not just the sexy broad. She is a great comic actress. So I anticipate to see what she is like to work with."

"Yes, and...?"

"I mean like this. Some actors, you see them on the screen, or on the stage, from the audience. And you think to yourself, 'I am seeing the mask.' You understand? What's the English word?"

"The façade. But mask is fine. Go on."

"Voilá, you see only the façade. And it's fine, it's enough, but as a professional I can see the difference. I see they are only presenting the façade. They are not giving their spirit. That's what I mean when I say I already know, *Some Like It Hot*, she is a great actress, because she is giving her spirit. Now working with her I see it, she is giving the spirit. You know, she takes her acting very seriously."

"Yes, Mr. Cukor said the same."

"See, he can see it, ze great director. A great honor to work with him."

"What is Marilyn Monroe really like as a person?"

Montand pauses, perhaps growing a little impatient with the incessant talk about Monroe and wanting a little more publicity for himself. "Sincere," he finally says, almost in a tone of regret. "Vulnerable. Serious. Even in the comedy. She wants so badly to be taken seriously. That's what people don't realize. They think she is satisfied with the façade, with the figure of the dress going *psshhh* up around her ears. She is not. And so she studies very hard. She wants to be a great actress."

We discuss acting in Hollywood versus Europe; what projects his wife, Simone Signoret, is involved in; and how he likes the weather. Behind me I hear the sound of Tragge scribbling like a demon. There must be smoke rising from his pencil tip.

Somehow we get on the nature of comedy.

"And that second, that in-*stant* of recognition, where the audience suddenly realizes that the subject of your comedy—it doesn't matter if you're doing a pratfall or singing a funny line in a song, or if you've just made a point that is at once strange and iron-*ic*—zey realize that the subject of your comedy is really yourself, and themselves, all together—in fact, ze human heart—dzat is what I call ze Comic Moment."

Pretentious. "Do you have some favorite comic moments?" I ask, trying to puncture his balloon.

As I hoped, he gives me a pained look. "It is not like a souvenir to put in your bag," he says. "It is an effect psychological."

Suddenly the little guy in the yellow suit, who has been sitting there on a couch the whole time, pipes up. "Freud called it the Moment of

Horror! To see a man who slips on the ice is to see yourself—not just slipping on the ice, but dying. You're confronting your own death!"

Everyone turns to look at him. His legs don't even reach the floor, and he's smiling weirdly.

"Then why laugh?" Montand asks seriously.

"What choice have you got?" the man cries, as if that's the punch line of a terrific joke. He actually bounces on the couch with glee.

Montand rubs his eyes. "The studio gave me this man as my valet," he says. "He's named Freddie. Every day he has something like this to say. I ask, 'Are you sure you aren't lost? Are you positive they're not making a... a cowboy clown movie or something on another stage?' In fact he tells me he's the head of valets here. He says he's the best they've got."

"Personal Assistant," Freddie corrects him. "It's been Personal Assistant since 1958."

Considering Montand is best known for his cabaret-type performances, I ask if he's planning on playing Vegas.

"Oh la la," he actually says. "I was taken there once. You fly over hundreds of miles of desert, zen suddenly, in the middle of no-*where* is this place. And the whole is like Montmarte, or rather, like a certain area of Marseille where you do not go. And they brought me to ze casino and—Well, what can I say, it is not to my taste. I prefer Monte Carlo or at least Biarritz. I hope the American people will allow me this preference.

"You see, Mr. Blaine," he says, patronizing me now, "once a performer has reached a cer-*tain* level, he does not wish to play in what you call the sticks. But look, it's the same for you. Now you work for a large American magazine, whereas perhaps you started on a newspaper in a small vill-*age*. You would not wish to go back to that small newspaper. I'm sure Mr. Tragge understands," Montand adds, nodding over my shoulder. In addition to the continuous scrawling, it sounds like Tragge is trying to keep from bursting into laughter.

"Oh yeah," he allows himself.

"Don interviewed me one year ago when I first came to this country." Montand says. "So you are breaking in a new reporter, Don? He's a little serious."

"Yes, he's brand new. He's doing fine for his first day, wouldn't you say?" He finishes writing and closes his notebook with a merry expression.

We go out of the dressing room into the shadows of the sound stage. "You louse," I say. "I'll get you for this."

"Relax, Bobby," he says. "So you're not known on the continent. But it'll read great in the piece. We'll put in a zinger from you, okay? It doesn't matter that you didn't come up with it on the spot—just phone it in sometime this week. We'll make it seem funny that the guy from France didn't recognize the Hollywood star."

Hawkins, the publicist, looms up out of the shadows. "Hello, Hawkins," Tragge calls. "We're doing great, thanks to you."

"I want you out of here."

"So where you keeping Marilyn?"

Hawkins seems to expand with this request, like one of those big lizards that flare out their side vents to seem more menacing. "She's in conference."

"I'll bet she is. 'Mirror, mirror, on the wall. Which head shrinker should I call?' That kind of conference, Hawkins?"

"I'm calling the studio guards right now."

"We'd settle for hubby. Arthur Miller around?"

Hawkins deflates a little. "He might be available."

Looking ostentatiously at his watch, Tragge drawls, "It might be all we have time for."

Hawkins leads us out of the sound stage, across an alley full of ladders and lumber and discarded stage flats, and into another stage. The overhead lights are on in here, and the Klieg lights and scaffolding and cranes stand quiet. "Better get what we can," Tragge whispers to me. "I have a feeling Madame is nowhere around."

Arthur Miller—of all the people on this picture, he's the only one who actually intimidates me a little. We're alike in some ways—about the same age and we're both Jews. But while I was busting my ass telling jokes to old farts in the Catskills, he was writing brilliant drama and becoming the toast of Broadway. Then to top it all off—to show that nothing's out of reach in this country for a smart Jew with glasses—he married Marilyn Monroe. As if the Pulitzer Prize and all the other awards and honors were not enough, he gets the greatest prize of all, the Queen of the Shiksas.

After crossing the sound stage, we enter a corridor and stop before an unmarked gray metal door. I can hear someone typing inside. Hawkins knocks quietly, and the typing stops. Hawkins opens the door.

"Mr. Miller," he says unctuously, "these are the gentlemen I mentioned."

There stands Arthur Miller, wearing a modest brown suit with a white shirt and tie, the familiar black eyeglasses resting on a nose of some prominence. Curly brown hair, now receding. He smiles politely — for all its ordinariness, the face that won Marilyn.. He shakes hands with us and motions toward a couch. Beyond the desk where Miller is working, the wall is lined with makeup mirrors. The studio has hidden him away in an empty dressing room. "I see they've given you the first class accommodations," I joke.

He doesn't even smile. "What can I do for you fellows?" he asks pleasantly enough, but he seems reserved. I explain our mission and he tells us the story of the film, the same as the others. I ask him about his wife's singing and dancing and he says it's fine. I ask him what kind of work he's doing on the script, and he just says, "Officially, none. Off the record?" he raises an eyebrow at Tragge, who gives a slightly pained nod in return. "Off the record, I've just fiddled a little with it, to tell you the truth. It wasn't much to start with. It's like a poorly designed house — you're not going to make it a brilliant piece of architecture just by knocking out a wall or painting it blue. Mainly I'm concerned with some of the dialogue. Making it..." He almost rolls his eyes. "A little more dignified," he finishes.

"Okay, enough of that. Now I'll go back on the record. *Let's Make Love* is a delightful comic fantasy which the American public is going to enjoy very much."

"So no big changes?" I ask, so I can hear all about how he's practically eliminating Timson's part.

"None at all. It's a wonderful script," he says. "Anything else I can tell you?"

He's hardly told us anything. "We don't want to keep you from your work," I say. "But to tell you the truth, it's starting to look unlikely we'll talk to Miss Monroe today. I'd like to ask you a little about her — the public is of course very curious, and as her husband you know her best of all."

He looks at me. His face is no longer pleasant. The silence grows uncomfortable. "Of course, we don't want to intrude," I say lamely.

"Bobby Blaine," he says, pronouncing my name with some distaste. "You're a talkative fellow, I hear."

What the hell does he mean? "It's my job," I say.

"We all do some talking as part of our job," he says. "Look at me, being interviewed. I'm not even on this picture, but somehow it's part of the job description. Very well. I'm speaking of the kind of talking that is strictly extracurricular. Very much off the job, though some people think we all have a duty to talk to little men in blue suits and black shoes."

Word must have gotten back to him that I blabbed about Timson. I sit there thunderstruck.

Tragge has stopped scribbling. He looks at me curiously.

"I don't have much use," Miller goes on, "for backstabbers, though I'm told it's pretty standard for Hollywood. I wouldn't know—I'm used to Broadway and New York. We have it there too, of course, but not like this. But then again, we're small potatoes—or so they keep reminding me out here. Now I see what people mean by that."

"I ..." is all I can say.

"I see," he goes on, "why some people get a foothold in Hollywood when they never did on Broadway. Backstabbing's a way of life here. And if some feds come along and give you a bigger knife to wield, so much the better. Yes, we're definitely in the minor leagues compared to the major-league finking that goes on out here. Well, what do you say, Bobby? No longer so talkative?"

I blush crimson. Talk about the hot seat—the FBI has nothing on this guy. "I think you may have missed your calling," I manage. "You'd make a terrific district attorney."

"Oh no, no," he says, standing up. "I neither prosecute nor demand a sentence. You're on your own there."

Tragge and I have to stand up. Miller shakes Tragge's hand and says, "Drop a line if you need any more, Mr. Tragge. Some other day." Then he turns back to his desk, as if I'm not even in the room.

Tragge and I slink out of there, find my car and go to a bar, all without speaking. He's going to get an explanation but is willing to wait until I've had a chance to pull myself together. After a couple of drinks, I make up some kind of story not having to do with the FBI and definitely not mentioning Timson—though Tragge, with his contacts, has probably already heard something. He doesn't press me, just lets me talk, doesn't make any notes. When I'm done, he shrugs and orders another round. And when the article finally comes out several months later when the film is released, the parts that quote Miller make it seem like we had a great interview. Tragge turns out to be a more decent guy, all around, than I expected.

Chapter 11

1

Gene works on number 12 for ten straight days, with the assistance of a couple of Dolores' cousins. One of them knows how to plaster walls; the other knows how to lay carpet. Gene pays them five bucks each plus a few beers, does the plumbing and the painting himself, and by Friday of the second week, the room is almost ready.

Gustafson visits from time to time, hacking his way across the parking lot to stand in the doorway and block the light. He likes to point out that if he wanted to hire wetbacks he would, but if he can get a white boy to pay for the wetback and do the work at the same time, he's coming out ahead.

But Gene is making plenty on Friday and Saturday parking cars at the Riviera. Taking the free room into account, he's doing quite well. Gustafson doesn't know, or doesn't care, about the other job. He doesn't care about anything, which is the other thing he likes reminding Gene of.

"It's a good thing you fixed the toilet in here," Gustafson says. "That way they have a place to crap." He means Dolores' cousins. "They ain't coming into the office to take a crap, hear me?"

"Yeah, sure," Gene mumbles. He has realized the old man's visits tend to terminate with a coughing fit that drives him back to his lair. The more he talks, the sooner the geezer will start hacking.

Gustafson pauses to light a cigarette. "I'm inspecting this unit when you're done. If it ain't done right, I'm kicking you right out on your keister."

"'Done right?'" Gene echoes. "Inspect all you want. I've seen the other rooms. It's going to look better than them."

"Well, of course it looks better if it's just been painted. I—" Then the coughing begins and Gustafson departs.

At five o'clock Gene knocks off, punches his time card, and goes to his room to take a shower and change clothes. Then he walks the six blocks to the Riviera. Night is coming later as spring progresses, but he still walks in darkness until he reaches the Strip and its blazing lights.

The night is a slow one, for some reason. Even after ten o'clock, when trade picks up, he still spends at least half the time just sitting on the bench and playing five card stud for pennies with Barney, the future professional poker player. There's a small TV in the parking shack. It shows mostly snow and isn't worth watching, but they keep it on for the sound. Slumping on the bench, Gene isn't really listening as the "Tonight Show" music starts and the announcer goes into his patter. "Frooooooommm New York! The Tonight Show starring Jack Paar. Our guest host tonight is comedian Bobby Blaine. Bobby's guests tonight—"

Gene perks up. "Hey, I know that guy."

"Call," Barney says, tossing a few pennies into the pot.

Gene stands up and peers at the TV. "Bobby Blaine, I know him."

"Yeah, sure, he tipped you a sawbuck once. Me too. Come on, play."

Gene tosses down his cards, still looking at the snow. "I got nothing."

"Ha!" Barney spits out. "Three of a kind."

The announcer is introducing Bobby, who emerges dimly into the snowy image like a polar explorer. After the applause stops, Bobby says it's great to be back in New York, that the warmth of Southern California is nice, but frankly he'd prefer to be able to see where he was going. No, really, it's true what they say about sunny California. It's just that the smog is so bad you can't find your way. That's why they have those maps to the stars' houses—they aren't for tourists, they're for the people who live there.

This line of humor seems to be doing fairly well, but Bobby switches into the routine about his butcher's vegetarian assistant. "Hey, I know this part!" Gene says. "I was with him when he dreamed this up, I swear to God."

"Sure, sure, come on and play."

"Didn't I tell you we were going back and forth to L.A., working on material? I developed this stuff about the vegetarian butcher with him."

The phone in the shack rings and Gene picks it up and listens. "Yeah," he says. He turns to Barney. "The red Cadillac—you get it."

"Me? Whatever you say, cowboy." Barney trots off, perfectly happy to fetch a car if Gene is giving up his turn to watch TV.

The next morning, Gene finds Dolores at work. "Hey, Bobby Blaine was on the Tonight Show last night—did you see it?"

She looks at him, unamused. "You want to talk to me, help me make the bed."

He steps inside, remembering to prop the door open with the vacuum cleaner. She is still careful not to be with him with the door closed. "Did you see it?"

"I wasn't watching TV last night," she says. "I was at church. Don't you know it was Good Friday?"

He goes to help her with the bedmaking. "Oh… no, I didn't. Geez, maybe that's why it was so slow."

"Geez, maybe so," she says wryly.

Together they finish with the bed, and then she pushes him toward the door. "Beat it, I don't have time to waste with you today." She picks up her bucket and vacuum and herds him before her to the next room. She goes inside, not propping the door open, so that the pneumatic gizmo almost slams it in Gene's face.

He catches the door right before it shuts. Poking his head in, he sees her disappear into the bathroom. "Hey!"

"I said beat it."

"I said hey."

"Why don't you let me work?"

"Because I like you."

"Good for you."

"Let's go to a movie tonight."

"No, it was Good Friday last night—Jesus is in the tomb! I can't go to a movie."

"So let's go in a few days. Or next weekend."

"Why don't you go paint something?" she yells.

He frowns. "What's wrong with you?"

She appears in the bathroom doorway, pulling on bright green rubber gloves. "Listen, Gene, you're nice. It's nothing personal. But my mama didn't raise me to go out with a handyman, I'm sorry. Or a parking lot attendant. Or a beatnik, for that matter."

"You're the one who's about to clean the toilet," Gene replies.

"Yeah, well, I'm not just some maid. I'm going to be an accountant."

"This isn't exactly going to be my career, either."

"Then don't you go out and get a real job? You work at that big casino, you got that show business buddy—so you say. Why don't they hire you as a desk clerk at the hotel or something? That don't take a college degree. Now, for the last time, go away, before I throw something."

2

On Monday Gene is putting up the towel racks and cleaning room 12 a final time when a truck comes with the new mattress. He helps the driver get it out of the truck and into the room, stripping off its plastic wrapping.

"Good for another few thousand tricks," the driver remarks, turning back to his truck.

"What makes you say that?" Gene asks. He knows the motel's reputation, but he wants to hear it from a local.

"Oh, no offense. But most of these little motels around here are used for just one thing. That ain't no secret."

"I guess, but—I just haven't been around town long. Just a few weeks."

"Oh yeah?"

"Yeah, I—I'm the owner's grandson," he blurts. They come out into the driveway.

"Oh, the old man has a family. Well, I guess there's nothing he can do about it—the clientele, I mean."

"Yeah, um… Granddad… hasn't been too well. We thought the desert air would be better for his health, and it is, but …." He lets his sentence trail off as the driver slams down the door of the truck and latches it.

"Yeah, I know," the driver says, taking off his gloves and walking around to the cab. "That cough. Well, whattya gonna do. See you," the man says, climbing into the truck.

Gene steps back as the truck starts up and bumps out of the parking lot.

He stands on the hot asphalt for a minute. Gustafson's grandson! That's the first whopper he's told in a while. Gene laughs to himself as he walks across the lot. Dolores has gotten as far as room 7.

"Hey," he calls out, opening the door with his pass key. "I got more work for you."

"Thanks a lot," she says sarcastically.

"The bed's here, in number 12. Needs linens."

"Yes, Mister Stinky."

"Hey, the room doesn't stink anymore."

"Yeah, you probably just got used to it."

"See for yourself." He goes over to the office. He wants Gustafson to see the finished room. The old man has already reneged on his promise to let Gene move into number 12 after he had made it habitable; now he wants it earning money, of course.

The owner is watching TV in his living room as usual, regarding the screen through a cigarette haze.

"Hey, Mr. Gustafson, they brought the mattress for number 12. Dolores is going to make the bed, and you can rent it out starting tonight. I thought you might want to take a look at it."

The old man takes his cigarette out of his mouth long enough to say, "Wait a minute."

Gene looks around the apartment with distaste. It's full of useless heavy furniture—like a huge china cabinet—hauled down from some northern city. A game show is on, and the host is asking for synonyms for "livid."

"Blushing," Gustafson says.

"Flushed," Gene suggests.

"You should know, toilet boy," Gustafson cackles. A commercial comes on and he hauls his frame out of the chair. His brown trousers are flecked with ash. "Well, how long's it been? Three weeks? Took you long enough."

"It hasn't even been two weeks," Gene protests.

"Guess time flies when you're having fun."

Gene leads the way into the sunlight, finding the hot asphalt of the parking lot smells fresh in comparison to Gustafson's apartment. They walk across to the open door of number 12. Gustafson goes inside, carrying his cigarette. "Stinks like paint," he grumbles, exhaling smoke into the just-painted room. "Guess they won't care." He makes his way around the room, stamping on the carpet, exercising the plumbing in the bathroom, whanging his fist on the towel rack. "That towel rack's on too high."

"It's just where it was before."

"You take it off and put it lower. About six inches lower. Man hits himself on it like this." He splays his hand on the wall, feeling the paint. "Feels dry. Okay, I guess it's good enough for my distinguished clientele."

Gene thinks, I guess that's about as close as he gets to a compliment. They walk back across the parking lot, Gustafson now wheezing.

"I'm going to paint some of the exterior now," Gene says. "The eaves and the trim that you said never got done."

"Okay. Don't use expensive paint, now. Get the cheapest they got." They reach the office door and Gustafson turns to Gene. "Well, whatta you want? A medal?"

Gene sighs. "Just my week's pay." He suddenly sees smoke coming from the office. "Hey, what's that?"

"Oh Jesus!" Gustafson cries. "Get the—the fire, the fire extinguisher, quick!"

"Where is it?"

"Behind the counter! Move, goddammit!"

Gene runs behind the counter, finds a red fire extinguisher lying on its side under some phone books, and rushes into the apartment. It's just the wastecan—a metal one, luckily. The fire's out in ten seconds, leaving a lot of smoke.

"Damn you!" the old man shouts from the office door. "Open a goddamn window in there! Christ almighty, you almost burned the place down!"

"Me! What did I do?"

"You must have knocked the ashtray into the wastebasket. Goddammit to hell!"

Gene puts the fire extinguisher down and goes back for the blackened wastecan. He carries it out to the street and comes back to open windows.

"There's no other damage," he says, looking around.

"Just to you, you no-good bum. I oughta have you arrested."

"Mr. Gustafson, I didn't knock over your ashtray. You must have done it when you got up out of the chair."

"The hell I—!" The owner is seized by a coughing fit. Gene turns away angrily, walks halfway across the parking lot, comes back and waits for the coughing to stop. Gustafson manages to heave himself back into his armchair.

Gene stands in the office, his arms on the counter. When Gustafson is finally quiet, he says, "Mr. Gustafson, I want my pay."

"You go to hell!"

"You owe me forty-five fifty. And seven bucks for supplies."

"Get the hell out. You're lucky I don't call the police."

Gene slaps the counter in disgust. "The police! Fine— I'll, I'll, accuse you. I'll have you charged with theft!"

"You grimy bum! Piece of shit!" The old man is racked with coughs again.

Dolores pokes her head in. "What's going on? Was there a fire?"

"He knocked his ashtray into the wastecan, and he's blaming me."

She comes into the office and peers over the counter into Gustafson's apartment. The owner is doubled over in the armchair, alternately coughing and struggling for breath. "Man, why don't he stop?"

"He's always doing that."

"Not like this." She steps around the counter and goes up to the old man. "Mr. Gustafson? You all right?"

The old man raises a hand, waves her away, then waves the hand furiously in the air in that motion Gene's seen before, the one that reminds him of a drowning man waving for help. He comes closer just as the old man slides out of the chair onto the floor, gasping.

"Ai!" Dolores cries. "Gene, call an ambulance. Mr. Gustafson! Mr. Gustafson! Gene, move!"

Chapter 12

1

I thought the Tonight Show went well, all things considered. Of course I didn't use the jokes about the Christ-killing Jews. I just talked about beatniks and vegetarians, and threw in some new stuff about cops. Actually the cop bit is about Curley and Larry, those FBI agents— whatever their names were. I can't directly make fun of the FBI or the red scare, or the blacklist without ending up on it, so the routine's about getting a speeding ticket. It doesn't matter—a cop is a cop. They act the same way whether they've stopped you for speeding or for subverting the country.

The next morning I'm at Bloomingdale's, making my way among the perfume counters, looking for Chanel. Philly asked me to pick some up for his wife.

The place is busy with a Saturday morning crowd, casually dressed, plus a few ladies of a certain age in their white gloves. A lot of women with children, maybe come to pick up some nice clothes for the Easter service; not many men. I wouldn't say I'm inconspicuous in my charcoal suit, but nobody's asking for my autograph either. People don't recognize me, even the morning after I do the Tonight Show.

Then, just as I spot the right counter, all my attention suddenly shifts. Time stops for a second; the Chanel counter and all the others fade. The only thing in sharp focus is the girl in the yellow dress, forty feet away, coming down the aisle toward me.

A bell rings in my mind: Lucy.

And for the moment that time stops, it is her. She's twenty-three again and it's 1945 and she's coming toward me in her yellow dress, smiling a smile meant just for me.

Then a cash register rings loudly in my ear, the spell is broken, time starts up again, and it's not Lucy, of course. It's just a pretty girl in a dress that is similar to the yellow Lucy wore, and her hair is the same length but a little lighter. And it's not 1945 either.

As I step toward the perfume counter a baby stroller comes out of nowhere and I practically break my neck to keep from smashing into it. "Sorry, sorry," I gasp to the startled parents.

The girl is gone when I look back, but what's the difference? It wasn't her, it could never be her. I pull up to the counter like a boat with a broken mast.

"Can I help you, sir?" asks a salesgirl.

I raise my head and try to focus. "Eh…"

"Parlais-vous Francais?" she asks brightly.

"Er—no, no, I speak English just fine, thanks. I was just… woolgathering for a minute. I need to get some Chanel no. 5, that's all."

"Certainly. A gift for a lady? This atomizer is very popular now."

"Fine, fine." I crane my neck now, but of course the girl in the yellow dress is completely out of sight; by now, she could be out on Lexington Avenue. It's not her, not her, I tell myself over and over.

Lucy, the real Lucy, is indeed out of sight, someplace on Long Island, or maybe Cape Cod or somewhere equally picturesque. Or she could be busting broncos in Wyoming, for all I know. I only know she was on Long Island ten or twelve years ago. After the wedding to the orthodontist.

And before that she was in Riverside Heights, finishing her degree at Columbia, and before that she did a hitch in the service, like lots of good girls, wearing a smart brown uniform. That was how I met her, in her Army-doll outfit, accompanied by three others in identical dress, at the Rainbow Room.

It was a Friday night early in 1945, and the place was packed with servicemen, their girls, and the older swells, with a few women in uniform thrown in. I was m.c.-ing that night for a national radio broadcast of the goings-on in New York. From about 1937 to '47 you could tune in a radio anyplace across the country at night and pick up a dance band being broadcast live from some nightspot, and I had a great gig announcing these things. It was my first national exposure, not that anybody pays attention to the announcer—especially since it was my job to be smooth and anonymous, and I didn't get to tell a single joke. What made it a great gig was sitting up on the bandstand near the conductor, eyeing the crowd, tapping my toes along with the music and picking out the dames. All I had to do was break in from time to time with a few sentences of description of the tremendous room and the wonderful view and the beautiful patrons, so that some factory worker in Michigan or some farm wife in Tennessee could visualize what it was like to be young and dancing to Tommy Dorsey at the Rainbow Room, your arms around someone beautiful and sophisticated, a martini in your system and the lights of New York spread at your feet.

It was during one of these flights of fancy that I noticed them—the four cards, I called 'em. Like any good Army squad, as represented in all movies, they were a matched set of Americans—a blonde off the farm, a girl with jet-black hair from Chicago, a redhead from out west, and a Jewish American Princess from Brooklyn—equalized by the uniform. The maitre 'd put them at a table on the edge of the dance floor so the guys in the band could see their legs, poking out from under those brown woolen skirts like so many French fries. But I had the best view.

When the broadcast ended, I quickly got to know 'em. "Norma," I said to the girl from Missouri, "I see you as the queen o' clubs."

"Ooo," she said. "What kind of clubs? Country clubs?"

"Uh…. yeah, yeah, that's right—you got a lotta golf in Missouri, huh? Sure, you're the queen of the country clubs. And you, Chicago—"

"Linda," her redhead pal put in.

"Lieutenant Linda, ta you," she said, snapping her gum, *with* a cigarette in her mouth.

"You're the ace o' spades."

That broke up her pals. "She's black Irish all right!" screamed Norma.

"Red, where you from?"

"It's Jacqueline. Golden, Colorado."

"Ah, well, if they mined diamonds out there instead of gold, you'd be the jack of diamonds." This on account of her looking, what's the nice way of putting it? Mannish. But in the uniform, who could object?

"Dat's haa," Lt. Linda confirmed.

"Haw!" Jacqueline laughed. "Maybe I'll get a tattoo." That just sent them all into further paroxysms—all except the dark-haired beauty on the end. She knew what was coming.

"And what do we call you?" I turned to her.

"Just Lucy," she said, extending her hand.

I kissed it. "No, you're the queen of hearts." The others applauded, like it was the punch line.

Just at that moment I got a stroke of luck. A slow song started and some guy in a pencil-thin mustache came up and asked Lt. Linda for a dance. The other two got up to dance together—nobody thinks anything of it because they're WACs, right, they're sacrificing for the country. That left me and the princess. I asked her to do me the honor, and she could hardly say no.

"Hey, we're the same height," I said, sweeping her onto the dance floor.

"Well, lucky me," she replied.

"Whattya do with the Women's Army Corps?"

"Supplies clerk. The whole gang of us are. I sent sixty carloads of corn today from Winnetka Kansas to Oakland, and the entire tomato output of Kern County, California to points east."

"I'll call you next time I feel like a salad."

"And what'd you do to defend our flag today?" she asked.

"Did magic tricks at the Army hospital on Governors Island."

"Magic? No kiddin'?"

"Yeah, I am kiddin.' I couldn't do a magic trick if I had a magic lamp. No, I'm strictly a comic. I did go out there once and told some jokes, but they said it hurt when they laughed, so I got fired."

"You should come over to our unit sometime. We could use a laugh."

"No—You look like you're always smiling."

"Oh, boy. Now isn't that a nice thing to say. You're a smooth one all right."

"Brooklyn?"

"Right the first time. You?"

"South Philly."

"Oh. Well, I guess there is a war on."

"Yeah, all kinds get thrown together."

You see how it went. The Battle of the Bulge was barely a month old, and the only guys coming back were in pieces, so the ratio was something like twenty-three love-starved gals for every decent-looking guy in a tux—which is what all the musicians, singers and comics wore. That was our war uniform, but aside from a few stray bullets fired by loan sharks, we were unlikely to get shot, blown up, or bombed. The women appreciated those odds.

It wasn't all that, of course. We hit it off that night—by which I mean, we went to bed together. People in January of 1945 didn't waste time. Do you want me to tell you how our lovemaking was? I won't, but right then and there I stopped trying to seduce other women. Odds or no odds, she hooked me.

Hell yes, I was in love. *We* were in love. To this I still swear—we fell in love *with each other*. She may have had some swain fighting his way up Italy, a guy she had dumped, that is. In fact, he never figured in the picture, then or after, though he may have come back in one piece. And there was nobody else for me, either.

Taking the bag from the salesgirl, I leave the perfume counter and head for the door. Outside, sun is streaming across Lexington Avenue.

It's been four years since I've been to New York. Now that TV production has started moving out to Hollywood, and the nightclubs are closing or cutting back on live entertainment, there's not much work here anymore. Anybody ambitious heads out to California when they get a chance. But being back here on a nice spring day—man, there's nothing like it.

I'm in no hurry, since I have only 15 blocks to cover and my lunch appointment is still an hour away. I stroll downtown, cutting over to Park Avenue. There are new office buildings going up all over, and already completed ones I've never seen. Shops are open, with people from the East Side popping in and out of them. I pass the Waldorf and the line of cabs in front, the drivers reading the *Post* while they wait for fares.

In the middle of the day, Grand Central is quiet, with a few servicemen and tourists. Now they have a false ceiling in place, but in 1945 in the Grand Concourse all you had to do is look straight up and lo, they had constellations painted on the ceiling, the stars themselves little lightbulbs.

So romantic, she laughed. But on Valentine's Day, everything is. We ron-day-voo'd here in the great hall, and shared a compartment on the Empire State Limited up to Niagara Falls. Not only did I not have a gig up there—an "engagement," Lucy liked to call it—I had actually given up two bookings to take the trip.

But what an idyll it was. Rocked to sleep all the way up the Hudson, we did not actually make love on the train. There was plenty of time for that in the suite I'd booked. Though the plan was for us to check in and then see the falls, we never even made it out of the room the day we arrived, nor the next day until well after noon. Taking into account the few hours we slept, I count a whole day of whoopee. Only when the sun started approaching the horizon on the second day did we stagger out in time for a cocktail. And we weren't the only ones, of course: the place was full of honeymooners, as well as couples masquerading as such, like us. The only difference was the rings on the fingers of the new brides.

I asked Lucy if she felt strange not having one—a ring, that is. "Not on your life," she said. "Haven't you seen the expression on their faces? That's not smugness—it's regret. They're looking over at us and thinking, 'Geez, did I really need to get married to get some lovin'? Look at them, they're having the time of their lives. Meanwhile who is this guy I got myself tied down to?' No, there's plenty more second thoughts over on that side, believe me."

"Still…" I said, feeling a little uneasy, "Don't think I wouldn't if you wanted to."

She turned to me, took my hand, and looked deep into my eyes. That pretty much made everything else go away. When she looked at me like that, whatever she said to me would bypass my brain and go straight to lesser organs, from the throat to the heart on downward. And she knew it, too. "Bobby," she said, "I've got what I want."

"So do I," I said.

"Except right now I could use some more of it," she added. "Shall we?" And it was back upstairs for another round.

Would it surprise you if I said that at that moment, looking into her eyes like that, I almost choked up? I'd had dames before, good-looking ones, too—there was a war on, like I said. But no one ever took my hand and looked at me like that. So how could I not think she loved me?

I walk down the ramp from the Grand Concourse to the lower level and the Oyster Bar. Talk about something from old New York—here's this place that's underground so the fish would stay fresh in the days before air conditioning. It's getting a little tattered, and I wouldn't be surprised if they replaced it with a hamburger grill one of these days, but for the time being, it's here. I get a table and order some strong coffee to clear my head. This reminiscing is just what I try to avoid.

David Schlain comes in. Schlain—née Schlansky—is a producer. He'd like me to say Broadway producer, and in fact we had a show on Broadway once. But mostly it's off-Broadway, out-of-town stuff, the Catskills circuit, and what's left of burlesque.

"We're ordering lunch, waiter—And how are you getting along, David?"

"Not so bad, not so bad. Wait til you hear about this new show. But after, after lunch. I saw you on the Tonight Show—man, that Phyllis Diller, what a card. What else are you doing in town? When are you going back?"

"Going back on Sunday."

"Why, whattaya got? Something in Vegas?"

"Well, no, but—"

"Stay around. See how it feels. If I can get you in this show, you'll have to buy an apartment, it'll run so long. But after lunch for business!"

"It does feel good to be in New York. Very... nostalgic."

"Yeah, well... Plenty of changes in town. Did you know, they finally shut down the Empire—or rather, it's going to be a straight movie house now. That was the last real burlesque. Nothing left now but strip shows."

"Where you also have your hand in, don't tell me."

"Where don't I have my hand. What did Lancaster say in that movie? 'My right hand hasn't seen my left hand for thirty years.'"

"Great line."

"*Sweet Smell of Success.* Hell of a movie. It flopped, nobody went to see it. Odets wrote the screenplay, you know that?"

"Don't remind me, I tried to get on it."

"You woulda been great in the Tony Curtis part."

"I keep hearing things like that."

David isn't trying to needle me; no reason to. Hollywood and Broadway are different worlds—as Arthur Miller was kind enough to point out—and except for the Catskills, whatever live performing I do tends to be in the state of Nevada. We worked together once, in a show he produced in 1954, an Army comedy called "The Liberators." It was about Italian and Irish gangsters who get into the service for the theft and smuggling opportunities and wind up working together to liberate Italy. It was a surprise hit that got me a year and a half of good work in a featured role (I played Italian). But between the Anti-Defamation League complaining about Italian "gangster stereotypes" and that fact that by 1955 people were tired of war pictures, it never made it to the screen. Almost my big break! I had to wait another five years.

We have lunch, talking about actors, producers, writers, hits and flops. Not until the coffee comes do I bring it up.

"Okay, David, so what's your next big thing?"

"Your next big thing, Bobby—*your* next big thing. It's a musical. About two guys: a Jew and a spade. The Jew's a comic, the spade's a dancer, and they both sing. They start out in vaudeville, see, and all through the first act they're competing to see who can get better billing. At the end of the first act they're thrown together, they're forced to team up, and they become bigger than they ever would have alone. But there's jealousy, see? Another vaudeville performer, a rival, *he* wants to be the biggest. So he gets some cracker sheriff to bring them up on charges. But their girlfriends team up too, see, and help them—"

"Hold on, now," I say.

"You haven't heard the half of it. Who do you think I want for the spade?"

"Don't tell me. Sammy Davis Jr."

"Gee, how'd you guess? Of course Sammy Davis Jr.! Whom you've worked with now already. Okay. So I mentioned their girlfriends. Well, the girls, the Jewish one and the colored one, are both tap dancers, and halfway through the first act they have this dynamite tap dancing war, *while singing about how they've had it with men.* It's like 'Gonna wash that man right out of my hair' crossed with the scene where the Jets and the Sharks have that dance-battle in the gymnasium. Each girl has a chorus of a dozen others right behind her."

David is waving his arms in excitement, half rising out of his seat. "Think of it—thirteen tap-dancing Jewish girls versus thirteen tap-dancing *shwartzes.* It's a guaranteed show-stopper. *You want to know,*" he plows ahead, waving down my attempts to interrupt, "*where* I'm gonna find a stage that big. And I'll tell you: 'Flower Drum Song' just closed."

"Well—"

"And in answer to your next question, yes, there are plenty of Jewish girls who can sing and dance. How do I know? Because I happen to live in an apartment right underneath at least ten of them."

"David, listen—"

"Now when the girls actually do get together with the guys at the end of the first act, that's your love conflict resolved right there." While speaking, he takes the white handkerchief from his breast pocket and mops his forehead. It's not hot down here; David has broken into a sweat through sheer excitement. "Then in the second act, they've got the wedding all planned, see, and we're gonna see both weddings happen at once, the Jewish wedding on the East Side, and the Negro wedding in Harlem, and you've got a fantastic double-chorus scene where you hear the Negro bridesmaids singing about how great the wedding is gonna be, and then the chorus of Jewish bridesmaids sing their verse only we change the harmony from gospel to klezmer, and at opposite edges of the stage we have the nervous bridegrooms…" He puts the salt shaker on one corner of the table and the pepper shaker on the other.

"David," I groan. He loves these counterpoint scenes.

"Big climax of the number," he shouts. "The brides enter"—the mustard and catsup—"Everyone's singing their asses off, and at the last minute, right before the ceremony starts, a private detective, actually hired by the villain, comes running onto the stage, right up to the rabbi and yells, 'This woman cannot marry this man!'" David shakes his handkerchief in his fist like it's an urgent message on a battlefield. "And you say 'Whattsamatter?' And he says, 'I have proof positive this woman is of the Negro race!'"

"You mean I've got the other fellow's girl?"

"No, Bobby, don't you see? Your girl has been passing. She's, what do they say, high yellow or whatever. She's been passing as white."

"Wow. Let me guess what happens next—we leave the show boat, strike off on our own, and twenty years later, she's the star of Broadway, while Sammy and his bride are … well, assuming *his* girl wasn't really passing as colored …"

"Bobby, listen, listen!" he says. "Comedy, dames, singing and dancing, and best of all, it's patriotic. Not patriotic like these anti-Communist cocksuckers today," he says, just as intently but lowering his voice, "but patriotic like an old Frank Capra movie—it's about the little guy who triumphs because of free speech and a fair trial and all the other stuff he's got coming to him. And most of all, it's about two underdogs who work together for both their good. Like our hit, you know? The micks and the wops worked together. Here the Jews and the spades work together."

"Are you sure you don't have a Siamese king, a cockney flower girl, or con artist selling band uniforms in there someplace?"

"Bobby, you haven't even asked me the title." His voice has taken on a pleading tone.

"Oy. Okay, hit me."

"'Fry and Fish'!"

"What?"

"Fry and Fish! That's the characters' names! And that's the name of their act! 'Fry and Fish'! Like *Fryin' fish*," he explains unnecessarily, even gesturing with his hand as if he's holding a skillet.

I'm speechless for a moment. Finally I stammer: "I'm Fish?"

"Yeah. Whattaya think?" He sits back in his chair and mops his forehead.

I take a deep breath. "First of all, I won't deny it's a... an intriguing idea. A Jew and a Negro singing and dancing together. It works when Sammy does it with Judy Garland, it even works with Peter Lawford, so why not with a Jew. I almost follow you. And the whole—ah—theme, is nice. Jews and Negroes teaming up together. Just fine."

"It's better than fine."

"Let me talk, okay? First of all, I have worked with Sammy, and I want you to know one thing. There is not a man on God's green earth who can keep up with him when it comes to dancing. Or if there is, it's another colored tap dancer. You put me in there with Sammy Davis and it would be like handing me a bat and telling me to go up against Sandy Koufax. There's no chance."

"So Gene Kelly you're not. I told you, you're the comic, you don't have to do that much dancing together."

"We would the way you described it. Second of all, and more important, I don't know if the country is ready for a show about the Jews and the Negroes teaming up together. They weren't even ready for the Italians and the Irish to team up together."

"Broadway was ready," David says gravely. "Hollywood may not have been ready, but Broadway was ready eight years ago, and it's ready now. After all, what have half the shows been about for the last fifteen years? 'South Pacific'—racial tolerance and intermarriage. 'Show Boat'— same thing. 'The King and I' ...'West Side Story'—same thing."

"That's four shows in fifteen years. None of them had tap-dancing. Even if you find some high-minded people crazy enough to invest—"

"I already have! The show is twenty percent subscribed right now."

"Even if you find the investors, can you honestly tell me people are going to shell out ten bucks to see two dozen tap dancers in this day and age?"

"Bobby, it's a risk. Of course it is. There hasn't been a sure thing yet on Broadway. If I came to you—what, a year and a half ago—and tried to sell you on the idea of a show about a crazy nun who becomes a nanny to a bunch of singing brats and falls in love with their father—and oh, by the way, there's Nazis in it—you would have told me to hit the road. But 'Sound of Music' is the hit of the year."

"You're wrong there. Singing nuns are always a sure thing." I sigh and lean back in my chair, pursing my lips. "All right, look, David. I hate to be the pessimist. But look at it my way: I could spend six months rehearsing and trying out the show, only to have it close in one week when it gets to Broadway."

"And who's hurt? Not you—you're getting two thousand a week."

"Let me finish. My career's at a delicate point right now. The right vehicle could make me a real star; the wrong one, at best, is a waste of six months of my time, and in six months I can miss a lot."

David frowns. "You think it's that bad."

"I didn't say that."

"You think the idea stinks. I offer you the lead in a Broadway musical that can—"

"David, David, I said the idea was all right."

He shakes his head. "'A waste of time,' you said. Well, let me tell you something, Bobby. It's Sammy who's gonna carry the show. On the face of it, the show has two leads, but in fact, it's a vehicle for Sammy Davis. So now what do you think? You said you're not in his league. You're right about that, Bobby."

"David, don't get sore."

"You think any show that depends on Sammy Davis Jr. is going to flop? It's not possible! And I offer you the lead opposite him, and you tell me it's a waste of your precious time. Well, tell me, Mister Big Shot— just what are you so busy with?"

"I've got engagements."

"You've got engagements! You think I don't talk to Philly Snider? I know what engagements you've got. Two weekends in Reno, that's what you've got."

Now I'm mad too. But I try to stay calm. "Have you approached Sammy, David?"

There's a long pause while he looks at me across the table. At first I think he's going to explode, but instead, after a moment, he deflates visibly.

"That's what I wanted you to do," he says.

"I see," I say evenly. Do I ever. This show isn't about Fish and Fry. It's about Fry, just like, no matter what Dean did, Martin and Lewis was really all about Jerry Lewis.

"You've worked with him, you're pals, part of that Rat Pack or whatever. I thought you could take him the idea."

"Sure." I take a sip of water. "Of course I'd have to give the secret Rat Pack member handshake before I handed him the script. Otherwise it's no good."

"All right, Bobby. Maybe I got a little sore. I need you. I thought maybe we could help each other."

There's no more water in my glass, so I put the glass on the table. Finally I say, "Why don't we do this. Send Philly a tape of the songs. If they're good, I'll talk to Sammy."

"Fine, Bobby, fine. That's all I ask." David extends his hand. "Shake my hand. Are we friends? Good man."

That's where we leave it. David picks up the check and we shake hands at the door of the Oyster Bar. He heads for the subway and I go up through the Grand Concourse again, out to 42nd St.

2

Gene sits in the corridor of the Las Vegas emergency hospital. He's been sitting there for three hours, since they brought Gustafson in the ambulance.

Gene got there by taxi. He took the money from the motel's petty cash, figuring it was a motel-related expense. After all, somebody has to represent the old man.

The hospital is old and everything seems dusty and undersized. There isn't even a proper waiting room for emergency, so he's sitting in the corridor next to a little table holding a few old magazines, all of which he paged through in the first hour. At the end of the hallway, through an open window, he can hear construction equipment. Like everything else old in Las Vegas, the hospital is about to be replaced by a newer, larger version.

Gene slumps in the creaky wooden chair and contemplates the pale green wall across from him. Despite having nothing to do as he waits to be informed of Gustafson's condition, he isn't bored. He feels in an odd state of suspension. Something's happening.

When the ambulance arrived at the motel, Gene led the attendants to Gustafson's gasping carcass. They ministered to him while Gene stood nearby, wringing his hands.

"Has he had a heart attack?" Gene finally asked.

"Maybe so," one medic said. "Who are you? Relation?"

Gene had blinked. "He's my grandfather," he said anxiously, echoing his words to the truck driver earlier that morning.

"Well, we're going to have to bring him to the hospital. He have insurance?"

"I guess so. It should be in his wallet. I'm just visiting from Missouri."

At that moment a cop had driven up to assess the situation. Gene seized the moment. "Help," he said. "Granddad had a heart attack!"

Since then, at every juncture, Gene has taken the opportunity to inform everyone of his supposed relationship to Gustafson. The most crucial moment came when the admitting clerk had called him over. Gene solemnly repeated his claim and the clerk typed it all up without question. Name of patient: Karl August Gustafson. Nearest relative: Gene Kramer. Relation: Grandson. Address: Cactus Motel.

Now he sits waiting, his mind calmly going over the details. Gustafson is his mother's father, thus the different last name. They're from Chicago—Gustafson had said as much. Granddad moved out here several years ago and bought the motel, Gene wasn't sure when because he was just a kid then. There is little more to fill in. There might be letters in Gustafson's room that will supply the name of his "mother." As for actual contacts with family members, Gene wonders how frequently, if ever, the old man wrote or called. He's never seen any letters lying around when he was in the office nosing around or gazing into Gustafson's apartment.

A nurse comes out of a doorway. "You're with Mr. Gustafson?"

"I'm his grandson," Gene says loudly, standing up.

"The doctor would like to see you."

Gene follows her through the door into a large room where two empty gurneys are parked near a nurse's desk. "Please wait here a moment." The nurse walks to one of several curtained-off places, sticks her head in and says something, then pulls the curtain aside for a white-coated doctor, a swarthy, middle-aged man in short sleeves. As he shakes Gene's hand, his grip is strong. "I'm Dr. Schwartz," he said, his breath smelling of cigarettes.

"Gene Kramer. I'm Mr. Gustafson's grandson. How is he? Did he have a heart attack?" Gene asks with concern in his voice.

"Seems so. Has he had these attacks before?"

"Well, I think so. He's always coughing, and he's out of breath a lot. Any little bit of exercise and he's out of breath."

The doctor was nodding. "Well, he pulled through, but he needs to stay here for a while."

"I see. Well, I'm calling the insurance company as soon as I get home."

"Have you called his family?"

"I wasn't able to reach Mom yet," Gene says earnestly. "But I'll call her after I get back to the motel. Granddad owns a motel. I need to get back there soon, you know, to keep it open—unless you think I should stay here."

"No, you can get back there now. But your grandfather's awake, if you want to see him for a second."

He has no choice but to follow the doctor. The doctor parts the curtain and motions Gene inside. Gustafson is propped up slightly, breathing through an oxygen mask. "He has to keep that on for several days," the doctor says.

Gene goes a little closer to the bed. "Hi, Granddad," he smiles.

The old man looks sharply in Gene's direction.

"The doctor says you're going to be fine. Don't worry," Gene says. "How long will you have to keep him?" he asks, turning to the doctor.

"At least two weeks. Maybe even three or four."

"Good thing we have good insurance. They're going to take care of you, Granddad. Don't you worry."

Gustafson's eyes widen and he starts to say something, but it's muffled by the oxygen mask. When he reaches up to pull it aside, the nurses restrain him.

"I better go," Gene says. "One thing, doctor," he adds, motioning for the doctor to follow him back to the nurses station. "Granddad's been a little bit confused lately," he says in a soft voice. "Sometimes, you know, he forgets things."

"I see. Has he been examined for senility?"

"I'm not sure, but he certainly seems a lot—well, mentally weaker than he used to be. Sometimes he doesn't even recognize me. I'll say 'Granddad, it's me, Gene—don't you even recognize your own grandson?'"

"I know how it is," the doctor says. "My grandfather went through the same thing. I'm sorry to say there's not much we can do about it. Maybe give them something if they become agitated."

"I understand," Gene says. "Whatever you have to do."

"We'll take good care of him," the doctor assures Gene. He shakes his hand and claps him on his back, incidentally propelling him toward the door.

"I'll stop by tomorrow," Gene says, walking backward, then turns and goes.

3

It's about 1:30 and the Saturday crowd is at its thickest. The fine blue sky of morning has become a glare, and I walk down toward the Public Library and the park next to it, to see if I can get some shade.

Just walking two blocks is difficult. I get stuck behind a family of four kids eating ice cream cones, their mother busily trying to keep the kids in line and the ice cream off their shirts, and their father struggling with a tourist map. They're like a living Norman Rockwell painting called Small-Towners in the Big City. With a constant stream of pedestrians coming the other way on the same sidewalk, I know I'll never get past, unless I walk right over them. So I force myself to slow down, stroll a little.

In fact, all I need to do is walk off lunch. So why am I hurrying? Because even before we started arguing, David's spiel made me nervous. It was pretty much the same idea that David's been coming up with for years—people from different backgrounds or cultures band together and triumph over adversity. He kept trying it out even before "The Liberators," got one hit with that show, and ever since then he's been recycling it. Not that people never recycle ideas in show business, but David has a real one-track mind.

But his desperation is showing. Sure, he'd like to get Sammy Davis Jr. for his show—he'd like to get him for any show—so would every other Broadway producer. And as bait he comes up with this ridiculous idea that is some kind of cross between "Show Boat" and "West Side Story" and "The Liberators" and God knows what else. And he puts on a big act and expects me to be excited by the idea. Not just excited—grateful.

And what bugs me is that, underneath all the skepticism I showed, part of me wants to go for it. A co-starring role with Sammy on Broadway? It may not be a major motion picture, but it's sure to be a hit, and then this time the picture would follow. Against my better judgment, I want to believe David's spiel. I want it all to be true. I want to be a Broadway star, strutting across the stage, taking a curtain call. So what if seventy-five percent of the applause is really for Sammy?

As I stand at a light, still hemmed in by the freckled family, I see a friend standing across the street buying peanuts at a hot dog cart. "Hey, Feldman! Simon Feldman!"

He looks around, up, down, left, right, everywhere but right across the street.

"Over here, dumkopf! Over here!" The light finally changes and I scurry across, doing an end-run around the Hoosiers. "What, you, buying peanuts on a Saturday? And from a hot dog vendor? Feldman, if your mother were here she'd bat those peanuts right out of your hand."

"Bobby Blavitsky! What are you doing in New York?"

"I did the Tonight Show last night."

"Oh yeah? How'd it go? Here, come into the park."

"It went fine, what could go wrong. What are you doing these days?"

"I'm still at the New Century."

"Times Square, huh? Burlesque?"

"Is it ever. 'It's burlesque, only it's less and less.' That's the kind of joke I do, thank you for the straight line. And the crowd! They could care less. Half winos, the other half Shriners from Iowa who heard this is what you do in the big city but they can't figure out why. Have a peanut."

"Girls?"

"All you could want. I think I'm a little old for them, though. You're more their type. Better bring some one dollar bills though. Maybe a five for the one you really like."

"I get it."

"No, come by. It would be an honor. Do five minutes, I can take a break, it'll be a bigger honor. There's honor among thieves, so if you steal the show you'll be doing me the biggest honor of all. Hey, that's enough peanuts for you."

"Feldman, you're killing me."

"Killing is my business." He shakes my hand. "New Century, anytime after nine." He turns and walks off. I look down in my hand and it's full of empty peanut shells.

I think I'll pass on going up the Empire State Building. Lucy and I went up there together. We did all the corny things you could do back then. The Palisades. Boating in Central Park. Take the Staten Island Ferry back and forth for a nickel. At night she would bring her WAC pals to whatever show I was MC-ing. New York was a wonderful place for young lovers back in 1945, especially young lovers who were not worried about being separated by the war. I was 4-F, on account of having TB as a kid, so nobody was going to draft me. We had all the time in the world. So we thought.

I was starting to make some dough in radio and I could afford nice things for her. Like the yellow dress that was hanging one day in the window of this very shop on Fifth Avenue.

We were like kids for the rest of the war, and I was in town almost the whole time; if I had to go and do a USO show somewhere, we picked up right where we left off. On V-J day we walked down Broadway with a million others, her in her uniform, all of us feeling like we had won the war personally. When the crowd in Times Square started to get a little rough, we went to the Waldorf Astoria, sat in the bar until we were pissed, then went up to a room and celebrated in our own way. My God—it's good there was a riot outside on the streets, otherwise they certainly would have called the police to our room.

She was shortly discharged, and went back to Columbia University to finish her degree. We generally saw each other at my place, a one bedroom apartment on Murray Hill, but it was a little small. So when we wanted to really spend a day in bed together, I'd get us a room at the Waldorf or the Plaza, and it would be almost like V-J day again.

I started doing radio full time with NBC, MC-ing benefit dinners for this and that charity, and also started to do a comedy act in nightclubs. Nobody remembers it, but I was on the bill at the 500 Club in Atlantic City the night Martin and Lewis brought the house down for the first time. They packed the place for weeks. I was a fly on the wall, which was good in its way. I certainly got to know Dean and the guys around him, Jerry less so. When they finally left, for bigger and better things, it was like a big ocean liner had passed by, and by comparison it made my own little boat seem small.

I got ambitious after that, appearing all over, glad-handing agents and theater managers. I met Philly, who was representing some top radio stars, and who had an idea this television thing might turn out to be something. He got me my first TV gig—as a weatherman. And I did a couple of small roles on Sid Caesar and so forth.

Lucy and I continued seeing each other. But the atmosphere began to change. During the war, there was a sort of suspension of peacetime reality. You could have an affair, or ten affairs, and nobody thought of the future. But once the war was over, you could no longer pretend there was no tomorrow. Everybody who came back alive had a tomorrow, and started settling down.

Nothing wrong with that. I asked her to marry me before the year was out. We were in the Waldorf again. It was in November—I'll never forget the day, it was the 14th, a week before her birthday. I couldn't wait til her birthday to pop the question because she was going out of town to her grandmother's for Thanksgiving. So before we made love, I had champagne brought up, and without too much ado brought out the ring and asked her to marry me.

She must have known the moment would come. She kissed me and very reasonably explained that she loved me very much but that her education was very important to her father and to her, and that she absolutely wanted to marry me, but had promised her father that she would not do such a thing until she graduated in three years.

I said, "All right, let's get married in three years, but let's get engaged now."

She said, "Bobby, I love you, but God knows what three years will bring."

186

"Three years?" I said. "I know what three years will bring—I'll love you three times as much as I do now. I'll love you three million times more. I don't care. Promise me now."

She put her arms around me. "I hate promises. I love you. Which would you rather have, me or a promise?"

"What the hell, Lucy? All I've told you is that I'm crazy about you and I want you to stay with me forever. Don't you want to?"

She put her lips close to my ear. She knew it drove me nuts for her to whisper to me. Why, then, was she saying things like, "I want you. I want this."

I never thought I would take her hand away from between my legs, but I did then. "Lucy, I have to understand. You don't want to get married to me?"

She released me, walked over to the table where the champagne was sitting, and finished the rest of her glass in one gulp. "Bobby, you'll just have to ask me in three years."

Three years, of course, brought other things.

I started touring more, doing nightclubs from New York to Kansas City. Every time I came back, she would see me, of course—but it was different. We were growing up; no longer wartime lovers thrown together, we both had wider horizons. Though she was a couple of years older than the standard college student, so were most of the returning G.I.s, and Columbia was full of them. So she was meeting lots of men who, though still in their 20s, had seen the world, fought a war, and had more gravity than a smart-aleck comedian. At first I was positive she wasn't seeing anybody else. Then I left for two months on a barnstorming tour of the Midwest, and when I came back, I wasn't sure anymore.

And I didn't ask her. I was ashamed to, since I had had my dalliances on the road, most particularly with a dancer named Virginia. That girl was about as far from Lucy as you could get—blonde, Midwestern and about as sophisticated as a hot dog at the county fair. She had legs for days, though, and though she seemed to tower over me, we hit it off. We spent most of the tour together. Sure, we broke up right on schedule two days before the train back to New York. She ended up going back to Decatur and I spent two days on the train drunk, swimming back to my Lucy and my New York.

When we met again it was obvious that things weren't the same, but at least we were together in some way. I became pretty certain she was seeing someone else—not regularly, and not in town. But once in a while I wouldn't be able to get in touch with her for a weekend or, once, for a whole week. When we saw each other after one of these breaks, she would pay me extra attention—so accustomed to gauging an audience's moods and reactions, how could I not notice it when she varied her attention to me? After a while, I learned to exploit those times. Like a movie star who knows a producer will put up with her prima donna ways, I became more demanding after Lucy's absences. A weekend without her was worth an extra blow job; two whole weeks and I put it to her ass. Her tacit acceptance of this arrangement, her willingness to accede to my admittedly hostile wishes, failed to bring us closer. Instead it reduced our time in the sack to a form of exchange, where each of us paid the other what was owed.

So we started to see each other less, and the times we saw each other began to be reduced to sexual hijinks. Both of us were drinking more— not that everybody wasn't, in the late 40s—and so we would get a little sloshed and then get down and dirty. Afterward, we'd hardly say a word. I'd ask her what was going on in school, and she'd ask me news from the Stork Club. I'd say let's go down there now and find out, and she'd say she had an early class. And we'd part before eleven p.m. I'd go down to the Stork Club on my own, or do a few minutes at a nightclub where a friend was M.C.-ing, just to get her out of my system. At those times, the few minutes on stage, with a half-drunken audience guffawing at my tawdry attempts to entertain them, were not unlike what had just passed between me and Lucy in some midtown hotel.

I find myself far down 5th Ave. as evening comes—almost to Greenwich Village. I have dinner at a little Italian joint, just sitting and resting. I've been on my feet all day. I still have time to kill before going to see Feldman and his strippers, so I see a movie. Afterward I take a cab to Times Square.

The warm day has turned into a warm evening, and the crowds are out. Tourists, conventioneers, soldiers and sailors, hustlers, pool sharks, bums, the broad spectrum of the underside of America wandering beneath the bright lights and crazy signs like tourists on a day trip to hell. Avid, leering, hungry, drunken, excited, and the younger they are, the worse they take it. Worst are the young sailors, so young they couldn't grow a mustache for a million dollars, determined to become jaded grownups all in one night.

No, I take it back—worst are the five-year-old boys, pattering around Times Square with their parents way past their Midwestern bedtimes, goggle-eyed from all the lights and noise. One family pauses at the window of a souvenir shop; Mother and Sis go inside while Dad busies himself lighting a cigarette. He leaves Junior momentarily unattended, and I watch the kid innocently walk next door to a strip joint—in fact, the New Century, where I'm headed. A barker is yelling, "Come on in! It's air-conditioned! Come on in and see the show!" and the little boy happily tries to accept the invitation before his father sees what's happening and yanks him away from the doors.

"Don't you ever wander away like that!" the father yells.

"But he said 'Come on in,'" the lad protests.

But I'm of age, and there's no one to divert me, so I go in where Junior couldn't. Admission is five bucks—seems kind of high, but I haven't been to a joint like this in years, and perhaps this is the Saturday-night-sucker price. There's a faded lobby, strangely overlit, with the ghost of a popcorn stand. Like most of the strip joints, it was a movie theater, and before that, maybe, vaudeville. Now it's vaudeville again, in a way.

A blonde girl is on stage doing her best imitation of a strip-tease dancer. Maybe they have the less experienced talent early in the evening, I think, for she bears about the same resemblance to a professional stripper as a semipro ballplayer does to Mickey Mantle. She's got the equipment, but it's not at all clear she knows how to use it.

I look around. Theater seats fill up the back half of the house; closer to the stage, there are tables and chairs. About twenty guys sit around, most of them in the seats; three Shriners slump at one of the tables, drinking watered-down booze. Paint's peeling off the walls, but you can't see it much because there's almost no lighting in the house. A sleepy kid about Gene's age sits on a stool and runs a big pink spotlight with one hand, glancing down from time to time to a paperback he's holding in the other. To top it all off, there's no band, just a record that sounds like they recorded the Nelson Riddle Orchestra while dragging them behind a high-speed train.

A cocktail waitress comes up to me and asks me, in a thick Brooklyn accent, if I'd like to be seated and have a drink. "I'm here to meet a friend," I say, looking her over. She's a redhead, wearing a black leotard. I don't know what that's supposed to suggest—ballet dancer? Beatnik? She wouldn't look half bad in a nice outfit.

The first girl finishes her dance and we give her a hand—a few of us do. Immediately, another record starts and another girl emerges, no better than the first. During her act, a troop of young men come in, evidently a bachelor party, crowding around a table near me. This livens things up considerably. The blonde girl who was dancing when I came in appears in a waitress outfit and comes to take their orders, and they spend several minutes, while strippers come and go on the stage, in a bawdy palaver. It quickly becomes clear that the girl's real strength is as a waitress, because she gets them to order a collection of complicated, expensive drinks it would take an advanced degree from bartending school to prepare.

As they complete this negotiation, the dancer on stage finishes up to a burst of mad recorded trumpets. Enter Feldman. He's wearing a tuxedo so worn it appears fragile and soft, like Abraham Lincoln's coat in a historical exhibit. The spotlight operator appears in front of the stage and hoists a microphone stand onto it just as Feldman hits his mark, already carrying the microphone itself in his hand, its black cord trailing off into the wings.

"Ladies and Gentlemen, that was Kitty LaFarce. I think I got that right. Right, Kitty? Oh, it's Latrice. A thousand apologies. Let's give her a big hand, ladies and gentleman.

"You'll notice I say ladies and gentlemen even though there are no ladies out there. Wait a minute, I better check. The last time I said that the pitcher from a ladies baseball team clocked me with an ice cube." He shields his eyes from the spotlight, which has graciously turned from pink to white. "Just as I thought, no ladies. Except you, miss," he says to the waitress taking care of the Shriners. "Please excuse me if I don't include you as part of the audience. She's heard my jokes so many times, she fills in for me when I'm sick. Puts on the tuxedo, the whole bit. When I come back, I have to serve drinks for a night to make it even. Yeah, I put on her outfit. It's only fair. No one minds.

"Hey, we got a group here tonight. Welcome to the club, gentlemen. Where you boys from?"

"Jersey," a couple of them blurt.

"Mississippi?" he says, cupping his ear.

"Jersey!" they all shout.

"Mississippi, a wonderful state. It's wonderful of you to come all the way up here. We freed the slaves here a few years back, boys, so it may be a little strange for you. If you see a Negro driving a car, don't chase him. He's not an escaped slave. He's a free man."

By now Feldman has me dying. "See, this guy gets it," he says, motioning to me.

"You're killing me," I laugh.

"Isn't this a terrific audience?" he says. "You can all learn from this man. Actually he's a friend of mine. Ladies and gentlemen, just back from the coast, where he shot a new movie with Frank Sinatra and Dean Martin: Bobby Blaine. Stand up and take a bow, Bobby. Now sit down, this is my show. Where was I?

"Dean Martin, you know, he's a lovely fella. He used to live in the neighborhood. As a young man he'd come in to help around the house. Hey, you don't believe me, I can't help it. We'd have him clean the tropical fish tank—we had a fish tank the size of a car. In fact, it was a car. When the old Mercury stopped running, we tore out the seats, locked the doors, pumped her full o' water, and there you are. Dean would put on a snorkel and get in there and clean the butts out of the ashtrays. And while he'd clean it, he'd say, 'That's an angel fish, that's a catfish, that's a goldfish... *that's a moray.*' And the rest is history. Well, where do you *think* he got the idea?

"Frank Sinatra. A lovely man. He travels with a whole entourage, you know. He's got a bodyguard and a guy drives his car. He's got a couple of other guys just to keep him company, laugh at his jokes. It's good to have a little backup, you know? Because Mr. Sinatra, he's his own man, and sometimes people take things the wrong way, and an argument starts. And like I said, those other guys, they're there strictly for backup. They let him take a few shots before they fight back. Oh, you thought they were there to protect him? No, they're there for him to fight *with*. I don't want to say he's argumentative, but for a while he was getting in so many fights that the legal bills were killing him. So now he brings along his own combatants. It makes everybody much more comfortable. And finally there's a guy with a checkbook in case they do any damage. You can't be too careful.

"Where was I? We've got the most beautiful girls in the world here, fellas. Here in New York, I mean. They just don't necessarily work here. But they do stop in for drinks once in a while. A few weeks ago a couple dames came in during one of the dance numbers. They sat back a while and watched and one said to the other, 'It's a shame they way they expose their bodies.' And the other said, 'Yes, and the songs are so short!'

"So...ahhhhhhh," he lets out a breath in a ragged sigh as the joke dies. "Back on stage after her recent retirement during the Pleistocene Era, it's the one, the only, let's have a big hand for... What? Whattaya mean she's not ready yet? I'm dying out here. Oh crimeny. Where was I?"

Feldman strokes his chin for a moment. The bags under his eyes are big enough to take on a week-long trip. He sighs. "You know, the Russians don't have it so bad. They got Khrushchev. He's not such a bad guy. One Russian's talking to another and says, 'Comrade, I know you've been a police informant for the last twenty years. You've reported on your boss, your co-workers, and your family. And you've been paid by the government. But now I hear you're informing on me. Aren't we best friends? How could you do such a thing?' And his friend says, 'But your wife pays better.'

"I mentioned Khrushchev. He's a lot better than Stalin. With Stalin the only people who could get real coffee were the highest party members. Now anybody who's a party member can get coffee. You just have to sign up to go pick it in Cuba. Sure, they grow it there. There and in Columbia. That's Columbia in South America, not the District of Columbia. Not Columbia University. Not Columbia, South Carolina. Is she ready yet?

"All right, without further ado, the one, the only, Miss Pussy Willow!"

Feldman gingerly steps down off the stage and sits down at my table. Directly, the waitress brings him a highball as another noisy record starts.

"That was good, Feldman," I tell him, as Miss Pussy Willow enters behind him.

"Bobby," he says negatively, waving me off. He picks up the drink and slugs back half of it, then lights a cigarette.

"You killed me with that Mississippi joke."

"Yeah, but after that I stank. The Dean Martin one wasn't bad. But the Sinatra bit stank. And then I was off my rhythm."

"Can't go wrong with a commie joke," I say encouragingly.

"Thank God for the commies," he says, raising his glass again. "Here's to 'em—and their enemies. If Russia ever gets blown up, half the comics in this country would commit suicide."

"You know who I saw today? David Schlain."

"He got another brand-new, can't-miss idea for the exact same Broadway show?" Feldman shakes his head. "A nicer guy you couldn't meet. And he doesn't realize he shoulda quit while he was ahead."

"I don't think he ever got ahead, actually," I say. "He was so in debt by the time 'The Liberators' was a hit that he spent everything paying back people from five years, and then the rest of it he sank into the next show."

"Presto, he's a schmuck." Feldman finishes his drink. "What are you having?"

"This is enough for me," I said, rattling the melting ice in my drink.

"What? Since when?"

"I'm cutting back a little. But don't let me stop you."

"You're making me feel old," he says, signaling the waitress again. "So who else you seen here?"

"Nobody. I'm lucky I ran into you. You know what I spent my whole day doing? Just wandering around and thinking about old times. This city does it to me."

"Yeah, you had a good run here. But it's good you got out. There's not so much work anymore. Look at me. I'm lucky to have this and a few bar mitzvahs a month."

"Hey, this is going to sound crazy," I say. "But you remember my old flame, Lucy. Seems like everywhere I went, I couldn't get her out of my mind."

"Lucy, sure. You know, I was wondering if you heard. I wasn't going to bring it up, but since you have..."

"What? Tell me what?"

"I heard a couple months ago—she got divorced from that doctor on Long Island. Not a couple months ago—a while back. I just heard a couple months ago, from Feinstein, you remember him. I ran into him at the Plaza. I was doing a bar mitzvah, he was working a wedding reception. Still doing that business with the doves."

Feinstein had been a magician, and apparently still was. "What about Lucy?"

"Feinstein was her husband's relative, you know. And he told me they split up a few years ago. He didn't remember exactly when."

"Is that so. Any idea what happened to her?"

"Nah. So you're still carrying a flame, Bobby? You can't fool me. Old Bobby, never changes. Well, I wish I could tell you more."

Up on stage, the girl is down to a g-string. She has a bit of life in her and the table of guys from New Jersey is cheering her on like they're at a football game. Feldman, with his back to her, picks up his new drink, toasts me and my loneliness, and taking a gulp, swallows elaborately.

Chapter 13

1

With the old man still in the hospital, Gene and Dolores have been cleaning his place. Having discovered, on encountering his bed, that Gustafson had a little incontinence problem, Gene has been dealing with Gustafson's bedroom like any of the other rooms he's worked on, replacing the carpet and the whole bed—which was a piece of junk—and repainting.

Gustafson has been in the hospital for three weeks when a truck delivers a new bed for the owner's apartment, along with a couple of mattresses for other rooms. From the walkway in front of the guest rooms, Dolores pauses as she passes from one room to the next carrying her cleaning things, and shields her eyes as she watches Gene and the driver lift the new bedframe from the truck.

"Sure is good of you to do this for your grandfather," the driver says. "Lot of kids wouldn't lift a finger."

"Well, I came out to help, you know."

They put the frame down outside the office and go back to the truck to get the mattresses. "You figure to inherit the joint?" the driver asks.

"Jeez, I don't know. I'm not sure I'd want to stay in the business. I'm going back to Harvard in September."

"Harvard, really. Yeah, you don't wanna stick around here, then. But you could sell the joint."

After the truck leaves, Gene tugs and shoves one of the mattresses into Gustafson's bedroom and flops it onto the bed. Then he locks up the office and takes off walking.

On the day of Gustafson's collapse, he'd left the hospital and returned to the motel around 4:00 in the afternoon. Dolores had cleaned up the mess in the apartment from the fire and the invasion of the ambulance attendants, and locked everything up before leaving. Gene self-consciously let himself into the office and stood for several minutes amid the silence and the lingering odor of smoke. He phoned the parking office of the Riviera, said he'd been called out of town on a family emergency, in fact was at the airport right that minute. He asked them if he could have his job back when he came back in the few weeks, but they hung up without answering.

Then he unlocked the cash register, turned on the neon signs that said VACANCY, and planted himself on the stool behind the counter.

His first customers, checking in just before 5:00, had been two women who were clearly prostitutes. One had a bouffant hairdo, the other a ponytail, but they both had tough, humorless expressions, like soldiers going into battle. "We always get 5 and 6," one of them informed him, meaning two rooms in the middle of the main row. They paid without an extra word and repaired to their rooms. Twenty minutes later, as the sun was beginning to set, a taxi pulled up in front and the women came out of their respective doorways like figures on a cuckoo clock, now wearing short skirts and lots of makeup. The taxi took them away.

After that, a succession of single men arrived. A truck driver told him of a hard trip from Texas carrying chickens. A beaten-down man in a wrinkled suit and a ten-year-old car seemed to be a salesman; like the prostitutes, he had nothing to say, looking as if the effort to make conversation would mean the difference between breaking down in the office or reaching the sanctuary of room number 3. A jumpy young man arrived next, carrying nothing but a rucksack, like someone out of a Kerouac book. Gene wanted to talk to him, but when he asked the man where he was coming in from, he merely got a suspicious look and a grunt.

Then a couple checked in, and another. He was in the act of giving the second man change for a ten when the man suddenly turned and slapped his companion hard across the face, when all she'd asked was whether they were going to get anything to eat. As the woman shrank back, her hand to her face, the man turned and viciously said, "Gimme my money, man, or do you want some trouble?" Gene watched as the man shoved the woman out of the office and across the parking lot to their room. A little later, the men from these couples left separately, on foot, heading in the direction of the Strip, while the women remained in their rooms.

That evening Gene was host to a full complement of the underside of Las Vegas—hookers, vagabonds, ex-cons, small-time hoods. Six or seven men went into one of the rooms, and the next morning the Sunday maid told Gene they had a regular poker game in there; she cleaned up fifteen empty bottles of liquor and almost three cases of beer bottles. Taxis continually pulled into the driveway, letting off prostitutes and their clients, then picking them back up again twenty or thirty minutes later.

The other visitors on Saturday night were the police. They were "checking to see if everything was quiet." They questioned him about what had become of Gustafson, and satisfied by Gene's explanation, one of the cops went back to the car. The other put his thick hands on the counter, splaying his fingers as if testing the counter's strength. He was middle aged, and his uniform had a sergeant's stripes. Every part of him—his neck, his arms, his eyes—bulged out, as if he stored brutality in his flesh.

"Old man Gustafson's been running this place for six years," the cop said. "We know him pretty well. Come to see him every week. Just to keep the peace, you know?"

"Sure," Gene said. He had an idea what was coming.

"He usually has an envelope for us. Did he mention anything like that before his heart attack?"

"He didn't, exactly, but maybe he keeps it in a certain place for you. Would you have any idea where that is?" Gene said politely.

The cop smiled, after a fashion. "Under the drawer in the cash register."

Gene opened the register and lifted the steel money tray with its slots for bills and coins. There was a lot of stuff under there, pieces of paper with phone numbers, receipts from workmen, and business cards from cab companies. Gene found a small white envelope and held it up. "This look like it?"

The cop snatched it away from him. "What the fuck are you trying to do, send a semaphore? Next time, just slide it across the counter if you know what's good for you," the cop said, his voice infused with professional menace.

"Sorry."

"My number's here," the cop said, stuffing the envelope in his uniform pocket and tossing a card across the counter to Gene. "Any trouble, you call that number."

"That the police station, the, uh, precinct?" Gene asked, picking up the card and looking at it.

The cop had already turned to the door, and he stopped and turned back slowly. "Just call the number, ya fuckin' meatball."

The police cruiser did swing by once during the night, but didn't stop, and since the first night, the police had come in only at the same time on Saturday nights. Gene asked Gustafson, on one of his visits to the hospital, how much to put in the envelope. Still weak, the old man had wheezed, "A hundred."

As he tends the motel by himself, Gene sometimes tries to tell himself that Gustafson will appreciate what he's done, keeping the place going. By looking at records from the past year, he can see that business is up slightly, if only because the formerly unusable number 12 is now being rented several times a week. One of Gene's managerial decisions is to charge two dollars more a night for that room because it is "remodeled."

Other nights, he feels a creeping dread of Gustafson's return, his reaction to Gene's renovation of his rooms. Gene had heard that people sometimes come back from heart attacks and other dire episodes somehow changed, but Gene has seen no evidence of this in his visits to the hospital. Instead, the old man uses his scant energy to beg Gene to bring him cigarettes. Since he's remodeling the old man's apartment mainly because it stinks so badly of cigarette smoke, Gene never complies.

He also looks askance at the motel's patrons. His Midwestern upbringing was both sheltered from life's seamy side and condemning of it. A favorite phrase of both his father and his uncle had been "I don't approve of that kind of behavior," whether they meant spitting on the sidewalk or adultery. So Gene feels an inherited disdain for the motel's customers who are engaged in tawdry and often illegal dealings. But at the same time, he feels complicit. If keeping a house of prostitution weren't enough, surely bribing the police is itself a crime.

So, as much as possible, he tries to ignore what's really going on. He may be handing out motel rooms to hookers, but he tells himself that his involvement ends there.

But the patrons constantly try to involve him further in their dealings. The sullen silence of the first night's guests dissolved once they realized he wasn't a cop. Now they make constant requests that Gene considers outside any reasonable expectation. They ask him to make change for hundred dollar bills, hold mysterious envelopes until someone calls for them, let them store personal belongings in a non-existent storage room, give them medical advice. Most often they ask him to give them money, although they always refer to this as some sort of loan. Gene has resisted all these pleas. He even managed to say no to a young woman with three kids who drove up to ask only for five bucks for gas to get her "the rest of the way to L.A." He felt bad about saying no, although he felt less bad the fifth time he heard the same story.

Sometimes he feels like an extremely minor but highly annoyed deity, unable to grant the prayers of his supplicants and all the more grouchy because of it. In more sympathetic moods, he feels like some sort of dejected social worker, and wonders why anybody would get a college degree in this kind of thing.

The worst incident began when a woman—one of his semi-regulars—returned to the office about four hours after checking in, to ask Gene for some clean sheets. This is the one thing he has decided to do: offer one change of clean linen per shift to each room. But the woman was back for the second time, and wouldn't take no for an answer.

She was a little younger than the average Cactus hooker, but ugly. She wore a shabby pink sweater, and both the sweater and the woman retained just enough youth that Gene could imagine that, at some point, they'd both seen better days. Gene wondered if there was some kind of point-of-no-return for prostitutes, past which being young, or even being good-looking, would no longer avail.

"You don' unnerstan', when I checked into the room the sheets were dirty," said the woman, who was also drunk.

"No they weren't," sighed Gene. "And besides, I already gave you a new set of sheets tonight."

"No, see, here it is," she persisted. "There's two beds, see, and you gave me the sheets for the one. And then the other one, it was dirty when I took off the cover."

"You're in number nine, aren't you? There's only one bed in number nine."

"No, I'm in nummer... nummer ten," she said at random.

"No you're not," Gene said. "And there's only one bed in number ten as well."

"Well shit—pardon my French, mister, I'm sorry, mister..." she whined, swerving from a sly approach to a pathetic one. Gene sighed. It had been a long night already.

"I can't give you any more sheets," he said. "Now get out of the office. Go back to your room, or go stand in the middle of the street for all I care, but get out of here!"

"Mister, mister, why you yellin' at me? All I'm asking for is a bed... I mean some sheets... I'm sorry. You're not mad at me, are you?"

Gene clenched his fists and, out of sheer frustration, shook them at nothing in particular. The woman's face took on a horrible expression of fear and pain, and Gene felt like apologizing until he realized her expression had nothing to do with him. She staggered.

"God, mother Mary, help me," she bleated.

"What's the matter?" Gene said.

"Shit... God help me..." She tried to hold onto the counter, then fell.

Gene rushed around the counter. "What's wrong? What's wrong?"

"Don't call the police," she rasped, curling up into a fetal position. She turned away from him enough that he could see, seeping through her pants, a slowly spreading stain of blood.

Gene went back around the counter and seized the phone, then hesitated. Should he call the number given to him by the menacing sergeant, or an ambulance? Another look at the bleeding woman was enough for him to decide. He dialed 0 and begged them to send an ambulance.

As Gene hung up, the woman's pimp came into the office and began screaming and kicking at the woman. "What the fuck are you doing?" the man shouted. "Get up, bitch!"

"Stop that!" Gene yelled.

"Mind your own business, boy!" the man spat, still kicking at the woman as if trying to propel her out the door with his feet.

"She's on the floor of my office!" Gene shouted back. "How is it not my business?"

"Shut up or I'll shut you up!"

Gene realized that if ever there was a time to call the sergeant's number, this was it. He swiftly dialed, yelling, "I'm calling the cops!" Strangely, this elicited no reaction from the pimp, who continued to kick and berate the woman.

A mumbling voice answered the phone. "Yeah?"

"This is the Cactus Motel!" Gene said. "Is this Sergeant Carlisle?"

"No," said the voice. "Who's this?"

"I was given this number by Sergeant Carlisle. I need help."

"What's goin' on?" asked the voice, unperturbed. Gene explained breathlessly. "Yeah, okay. Cactus Motel? Uhhh.... let me see here." There was a long moment of silence; then the voice returned. "Help is on the way," the man on the phone said, and hung up.

As the beating continued, a beat-up green station wagon turned into the driveway and stopped in front of the office. A tired-looking man climbed out and opened the office door. The man froze when he saw the mêlée. Over his shoulder, Gene glimpsed a woman and a baby in the car.

Swell, he thought. The first family that's ever stopped here, and this is what they see.

Two taxicabs arrived next, bearing prostitutes and their clients. The taxi drivers honked at the station wagon because they couldn't get into the driveway. The tourist turned from the beating going on in front of his eyes and looked at the cabs, then back to the fight. Shocked, he remained frozen, still holding open the door.

Then two unmarked cars screamed to a stop. Four men in suits burst out, crowded into the office like a football team, and physically picked up the pimp and carried him out still kicking and screaming. They threw him into one of the cars and both cars roared away.

A moment later, the ambulance arrived, and the attendants rushed past the tourist into the office. The hookers, having given up being driven into the parking lot, paid off the taxi drivers and marched indignantly past the station wagon, followed by degenerate-looking johns.

The shocked tourist watched them parade past, then turned to his wife still sitting in the car.

"Honey," he said, "I think we better try to find another place."

Oblivious of the chaos, she called back, "Do they have a *vacancy?* Did you *ask?*"

Still holding open the door, the man turned back to Gene. Between them, the ambulance attendants worked over the crumpled prostitute. The tourist looked down at her, up at Gene, and back at his wife. Finally, he looked speechlessly back to Gene.

Gene stared back at him for a moment, the man's beseeching expression just as helpless as any of his guests'—and just as clear. Without moving from his place, Gene reached over and flipped the switch that turned on the word NO on the motel's sign. "Sorry," he said. "No vacancy."

Dolores herself was unimpressed when Gene related the incident the next day. The only thing that surprised her was that he had called Sergeant Carlisle's emergency number. "I don't think Gustafson ever had to do that. I bet he'll be mad," was her verdict.

"Is that all you can say?"

"She left her stuff, you know. Just a purse and a couple things. In case she comes back for it. Here." She handed over a battered pink vinyl purse.

It now sits behind the counter in the office. Gene doesn't want to look inside.

2

It's three weeks after Gustafson's collapse. Gene and Dolores are eating lunch together at the dinette table in Gustafson's kitchen. They meet here every day now after finishing their morning's work.

"I'm going to work on number 7 next week," Gene says. "Probably just repainting."

"There's damaged tile in the bathroom," Dolores says.

"Unless it's an actual hole, I think I'll leave it."

She shrugs, picking up a piece of lettuce that fell from her sandwich. She looks around the room—the maple china cabinet full of knicknacks instead of tableware, the brown armchair with the cigarette burns and exhausted upholstery.

"That armchair stinks," she says. "You should just throw it out."

"A new one's too expensive."

"Let him sit on a kitchen chair. At least he couldn't set it on fire." She takes a bite of sandwich, then licks mustard from her little finger onto her lips. "He's lucky you even go see him at all."

"He's mad because I won't bring him cigarettes."

She shakes her head. "It's funny you deal with him when you don't have to. I'm so tired of living with my family."

She takes a napkin from a metal holder and wipes her fingers. Leaning back in her chair, she crosses her arms. "I had to move into the little room with the niños. That's bad enough. But now they're always making jokes about it—all about me having my own kids someday and when's it gonna happen? I said, the sooner the better because when I'm married I won't have to live in this house any more. Then my father starts calling me a little princess and says in Mexico people live ten to a room and love it. Lately he's threatening to send me back there to live with his brother—my uncle. In some kind of, what you say—tenement."

"Have you ever been there?"

"Just when I was a little kid, I don't hardly remember it, but it doesn't matter. I'm not going there. I'll just have to stay in the little room until I can afford to move out." She stands up, taking their plates to the sink.

"So how about going to a movie this afternoon?"

Washing the plates, she doesn't answer. He's been trying to get her to go to a movie for weeks, hoping to establish their relationship beyond the workplace.

"We could go to a late afternoon show. You could get a bus, meet me downtown." Silence. "There's some good things on. There's a John Wayne movie… I think, a Jerry Lewis movie… All kinds of stuff."

She leans against the sink, crossing her arms again. "All right, just to get you to stop bothering me. Let's go to a movie."

"You're really going to do it?"

"Yes, sure. Find out the time." She smiles.

"I'm no longer just the handyman, is that it?"

She rolls her eyes. "You've shown something in the last few weeks," she says. "Some responsibility. And yes, at least I can tell my parents I'm going out with the desk clerk instead of the handyman."

Gene walks steadily toward downtown through the midafternoon heat. It's been more than a week since he's finished reading *The Dharma Bums,* and he doesn't feel any closer to being a beatnik than when he was parking cars in Hollywood. Farther away, if anything—he finds himself stuck at a job and acting responsible, instead of taking off on the road or, as in the book, climbing mountains. He's unclear about what mountain climbing has to do with being a beatnik, and since being a Buddhist seems to have to do with getting drunk and playing footsie with Chinese girls, he doesn't get that either.

In the Yellow Pages under Churches, however, he finds a listing for a Buddhist temple—the same one he'd passed on a walk some days before. It took him a couple of days to work up the courage to call the number, which was answered by a man with a strong but understandable accent. "You want to learn Buddha? Okay, you come Saturday? I tell you about Buddha. Ask for Lee, that's me."

He arrives at the brick building in the tiny Las Vegas Chinatown and rings a doorbell. After a couple of minutes the door opens, and a middle-aged Chinese man stands there, unexpectedly dressed in the uniform of a hotel valet. "I'm Lee," the man says. "Come in."

Gene finds himself in a small courtyard—the high brick wall is only that, not the wall of a building. A few steps across a concrete space, worn wooden steps lead into a building with little curved roofs above the doorway.

Mr. Lee leads him into a different building and then into an office. He sits behind a wooden desk with small stacks of papers arranged into neat piles, and motions Gene to sit in one of the worn chairs. "So you want to know about Buddha."

Gene swallows. "I read in Jack Kerouac's book about the Dharma Bums," he says.

Mr. Lee looks at him with an uncomprehending smile. "'Dharma Bums?'" he echoes.

Gene pulls the paperback from the back pocket of his pants. "It's in here," he says. "About Buddhism and yabyum." He hands the book over.

"Hmmm?" Mr. Lee examines the book gingerly. The copy on the back of the book is not much different from the stuff on the cover of *On the Road* about wild parties and racing cars, and Gene waits in embarrassed silence.

"Mm," Mr. Lee says, handing the book back. "But this book is a novel. It's not about Buddha."

Gene opens the book and flips a few pages. "Listen," he says. "There's something in here about the Diamond Sutra."

"Oh?"

Gene reads: "'I reminded myself of the line in the Diamond Sutra that says, "Practice charity without holding in mind any conceptions about charity, for charity after all is just a word." I was very devout in those days and was practicing my religious devotions almost to perfection...' Um.... 'I really believed in the reality of charity and kindness and humility and zeal and neutral tranquility and wisdom and ecstasy, and I believed that I was an oldtime bhikku in modern clothes wandering the world... in order to turn the wheel of the True Meaning, or Dharma, and gain merit for myself as a future Buddha (Awakener) and as a future Hero in Paradise.'

"Let's see... " He turns a page. "I want to find the part about yabyum."

Mr. Lee waits patiently.

"Here it is.

"'Here's what yabyum is, Smith,' said Japhy, and he sat crosslegged on the pillow on the floor and motioned to Princess, who came over and sat down on him facing him with her arms about his neck and they sat like that saying nothing for a while. Japhy wasn't at all nervous and embarrassed and just sat there in perfect form just as he was supposed to do. 'This is what they do in the temples of Tibet. It's a holy ceremony, it's done just like this in front of chanting priests. People pray and recite Om Mani Pahdme Hum, which means Amen the Thunderbolt in the Dark Void. I'm the thunderbolt and Princess is the dark void, you see.'"

Mr. Lee has listened with arched eyebrows and pursed lips. He sighs. "This is not real Buddhism," he says.

"It's not?"

"No. I can see you're disappointed. You like this book, okay. But I ask you: Do you understand Buddha from this book? No. This book doesn't help you understand. But even if this is not real Buddhism, for some reason you read it and you want to understand. You are curious. So you come here. Good."

"So can you tell me what... what it involves?"

Mr. Lee sighs and nods. "I tell you in four words."

"Okay."

"Be good to people."

"That's it?"

"In a nut. Of course there are many thousands of books of dharma—you know that word at least," he said, nodding at the copy of *The Dharma Bums*. "You know what it means? Dharma means the law, or maybe better, the teaching. The wisdom of Buddha. So, many thousands of books—but maybe today you only have time to learn one thing, so I tell you one thing: Be good to people." He watches as Gene digests this. "Put another way," Mr. Lee says. "Compassion."

"Compassion," Gene echoes uncertainly.

"Okay, I tell you another thing. Buddha says there are four facts which describe the world. We call them the four noble truths. Ready? First thing, everywhere there is suffering. Second thing, people suffer because of desires. Third thing, therefore remove suffering by removing desires. Fourth thing, the way to remove desires is by eightfold path."

"Eightfold path?" Gene echoes, dismayed.

"See, eight is too many for you today. You just remember 'be good to people.' You just remember compassion."

Gene's brows are furrowed. "Say again about the suffering."

Mr. Lee shrugs. "Suffering is everywhere. Look around, you can't go five minutes without seeing it."

"Yeah," Gene says, thinking of the motel's nightly spectacle of grief. "That's definitely true."

"I work at Desert Inn. I see gamblers, men losing all their money, then they want to kill themselves. I see people drunk, fighting. Suffering all the time.

"Buddhist way is the way to end suffering. Therefore compassion. Never mind the other three noble truths. You just remember compassion." Mr. Lee sits back in his chair with a smile. The light from the window glints off his nametag.

Gene asks, "You work at the Desert Inn?"

Mr. Lee nods. "Bellboy. I start at five." He stands up. "Here, you want a book? This one is pretty good." He hands over a thin booklet simply titled "Life," by K. L. Lee. "I wrote it. But it was translated by American professor, so no excuses for the English. Four noble truths are in there. But you just remember 'be good to people.'"

He guides Gene out the door and through the courtyard.

Still not quite believing that Kerouac got it so wrong, Gene asks, "Can I come back again and maybe talk to the minister?"

"I'm the minister," Mr. Lee says. "I'm Buddhist priest."

Holding the door, Gene looks back at him.

"Priest and bellboy." Mr. Lee presses his palms together and bows.

* * *

In midafternoon on the following Tuesday, Gene meets Dolores on a downtown corner. To his pleasure, she's put on something nice, a simple light blue dress.

"Good, you're here," she says by way of greeting.

"You look nice," Gene says. He doesn't say he's been standing there, closely eyeing the faces on each bus, for more than half an hour. When she got off the bus, he feels so happy that he almost hugs her.

They see a western with John Wayne as a sheriff and Dean Martin as his alcoholic deputy. Their hands link, and they try a few kisses. It doesn't feel quite right, though, not the way it felt with Dana. It seems strange to be with Dolores in a theater.

But when the movie ends, he walks her to her bus stop. There they kiss again, lightly, and all the strangeness disappears. She says she'll go to a movie with him again sometime.

3

It's a hell of a long trip from L.A. to Reno when you're driving alone. But I had time, so I drove up 99 and stayed at some motel between Fresno and Sacramento. Then the trip over the mountains has nice scenery for a while. But then where are you—Reno.

The gigs there went great, at least. They don't get nearly as many top-flight performers, and somebody from Sinatra's circle is treated like royalty, so the place was packed. I used some new material about race relations, inspired by Feldman's "don't chase the Negroes" bit. Of course it's not as blatant as Feldman's act. What I do is suggest that, since America is considering electing its first Catholic president, why not go all the way and have a Jewish president? And as the first Jewish presidential candidate, my platform is basically to apologize up one side and down the other for being Jewish—it's "elect me because I'm actually just like you." Subtle—too subtle for Times Square, it's perfect for the casino audiences who consider themselves a little sophisticated.

A little.

I even got a nice review in the Reno Donkey-Gazette or whatever it's called. I'm back there next weekend as well, with this gig in Vegas in between.

Compared to the drive *to* Reno, the drive from Reno to Vegas is shorter but much more boring. First, it's the most blasted landscape known to man—literally. Part of the route goes by the nuclear bomb test site. Second, I'm driving south, right into the glare, all day long, wearing the darkest sunglasses I can find.

Just when I think it can't get any worse, I come upon a military convoy. I can't pass it, no matter how fast I go, because it stretches for more than a mile. For thirty miles I have to plod along, before they all pull over and take a collective leak. The resulting flash flood takes out the town of Pahrump.

All the driving reminds me of Gene. I haven't seen him since dropping him off in L.A. for the last time. But I heard he moved to Vegas as promised, I don't know why. Considering where he was living in Hollywood, he probably was willing to take any excuse to get away. I guess he's parking cars at the Riv now. Funny if I drive up and there he was to take the keys from me.

But when I finally reach the Riv at five in the afternoon, there's no sign of him. Subsequent inquiries reveal he quit a few weeks before. They give me an address, and when I go looking for it the next day in a row of body shops, strip clubs and tourist courts, there I find a shabby motel, and Gene in the office, painting the wall. "Hey, Gino!"

Does he look surprised. "Mr. Blaine!" he exclaims. "I'll be darned."

"I checked in at the Riv last night," I say. "I'm working there this week. They told me I might find you here."

"Chief handyman, desk clerk, and temporary manager," he says, trying to salute with the paintbrush. "Priest and bellboy," he adds, for some reason.

"How'd you land this gig?"

"I got a job as the handyman here, and I parked cars at the Riviera on the weekends. Then the old guy who owns this place keeled over, and I just kind of stepped in. Actually he's my grandfather," he adds.

"You mean, that's what you *tell* everybody, that he's your grandfather," I say, looking around at the place. Talk about a dump. "That's the way you've squared it with everybody, that you're stepping in for your old grampa? What's the deal?"

He laughs. "No deal. Really, I'm just filling in until he gets back from the hospital."

A woman in a pink uniform comes into the office—I guess she's the maid. But Gene brightens up and steps aside to give her room; he does everything but wag his tail.

"Oh!" he says. "Mr. Blaine, this is Dolores. She works here too. Dolores, this is Mr. Bobby Blaine. He's the comedian I was telling you about—the guy I drove back and forth from here to L.A."

Now I see why he's sticking around here—he's trying to make time with this girl.

She doesn't seem so sure, about him or me. I extend my hand and say pleased to meet you. She nods and says "How do you do?" with a self-possession that gives me a hint of what Gino sees in her.

"We're sort of running this place together," Gene says.

"I'm just doing my regular job," she says flatly, as if she wants to make plain her neutrality.

"Hey, why don't you take a break one night and come see my show? Both of you—it's all on me. I'd get you a great table and comp everything."

That seems to stump both of them. After blinking for a few seconds, they speak simultaneously. "I don't think I could..." she says, while he blurts out, "But there's no one else to man the office."

I look at her—she seems more tempted than he is. "Gino saw my show a couple months ago. You liked it, didn't you, Gino?"

"Sure, but..." He looks at her. "It would be a lot of fun. Mr. Blaine's very funny."

She shakes her head. "I really shouldn't. But thank you. It's very nice of you."

"Then—what about coming in the afternoon and going swimming? You kids would like that." I look over at Gino and wink. "Peter Lawford will be nowhere in the vicinity, I promise."

"Hey, that would be great," he says. "We're both off in the afternoon."

"Well..." she says, before finally agreeing.

4

Dressed a little nicely for a swimming date, Gene and Dolores leave the Cactus Motel a few days later and walk toward the Strip. It's midafternoon as they walk along the baking sidewalks, the heat coming at them from above and below. Gene has purchased a new pair of Keds for the occasion, and they make squeaking noises clearly audible above the traffic. He carries his swimsuit in a rolled-up towel; Dolores carries a plastic beach bag.

They turn onto the Strip and blend into the tourist crowds.

"Do you ever come down here?" Gene asks.

"Lots of times," she says.

"Okay," he nods. They walk a few more yards and he asks, "What for?"

"Man, what do you think? Not to play blackjack. To get a job."

The big hotels are two to a block, and the blocks are half a mile long. Or sometimes there's only one to a block, and then a quarter mile of sand, with just a bare sidewalk leading through it like an oil pipeline. And it is a pipeline, of sorts—everyone on it is a tourist bringing money to the casinos. Parents herd their kids along, adults and children alike wearing souvenirs of attractions en route: Carlsbad Caverns, Grand Canyon, Hoover Dam. Gene sees none of the deeply tanned and weathered Las Vegas types that haunt downtown. Only tourists walk the Strip, and all the faces are sunburned and white.

"So what happened?" Gene persists. "Did you get a job?"

She shrugs. "Mmm. I decided to stay at the Cactus. I don't have some inspector lady walking around after me giving me a hard time. And it's just less work."

When they reach the Riv, Gene calls up to Bobby's room. Based on his experience of staying here for exactly one night, Gene points out details of the lobby and the entrance to the casino. Dolores barely responds; she's looking around, but with a nervous alertness.

After a few minutes, Bobby steps out of an elevator. "There you are! All ready?" He leads them down a hallway with guest rooms on either side. "The pool's down this way. I think. Never been there myself."

Dolores says, "Thank you again for the invitation, Mr. Blaine."

"Don't mention it! Oh, Charlie," Bobby says, stopping a young man in a blazer. "These are my guests. I invited them to swim in the pool, and I reserved a cabana for them."

"Yes sir," the man says. "You should see Ted. He's the director out there."

"Fine, fine, thanks." They walk to the end of the hallway, where a door leads outside. "This is it. Come on, I think there's a desk or something out here."

They go over to a booth where a kid is handing out towels. Bobby asks for Ted and the kid says he'll be back in a minute. Bobby looks at his watch and says, "Well, kids, I wish I could stay and get a suntan, but I have a meeting with someone, and I wouldn't want to get sunstroke before my show. So have fun." With a smile, he disappears back into the hotel.

Dolores looks at Gene; a little taken aback by Bobby's quick exit, he shrugs and looks out over the pool area. The pool is big, oddly shaped, and includes a remote area shaded with what look like palm fronds. People crowd the vast apron and patio areas, the sun beating down on them.

Turning to the towel boy, Gene says, "Mr. Blaine said he reserved a cabana for us. Can you tell us where that is?"

Glancing at them skeptically, the kid consults a clipboard. "Mr. Blaine? Number 2," he says. "Over there." He goes back to folding towels.

Dodging small children, they walk across the concrete, past rows of chaise lounges, toward a series of gaudily painted doorways. The "cabana" turns out to be only a small dressing room with a couple of lounge chairs on a square of carpet in front of it. Dolores goes in and changes first while Gene waits in a scrap of shade cast by the structure. He thinks the towel boy gave them a funny look, but tells himself the kid was probably just busy.

Dolores emerges, dressed in a light green one-piece swimsuit. Gene tells her she looks nice, and she smiles briefly, but resumes her alert posture, looking around the pool area as if trying to spot someone. "What are you looking for?" Gene asks. She just shakes her head.

Gene's in the dressing room only a minute; while he's in there he thinks he hears Dolores speak. "You say something?" he calls, but gets no answer. When he comes out, Dolores is standing with folded arms next to a different man in a blazer.

"You're with this person?" the man asks him. His name tag says Ron.

"I'm... with this young lady, yes," Gene answers uncertainly.

"May I see your room key?" the man asks.

"We're... guests of a guest. Bobby Blaine. He's, uh, entertaining here. He invited us. What's the matter?"

"Our facilities are only for our guests," the man says, glancing at Dolores. She is not looking at either of them.

"But we were invited. I'm sure Mr. Blaine wouldn't have invited us to use your pool if he thought there would be any problem. Why don't you just call his room?"

"We're doing that."

"Gene," Dolores says quietly, "I knew something like this would happen. Let's just go."

"It's all right... I'm sure it's just a misunderstanding. Bobby will clear it up." He notices people beginning to stare at them. He tries to explain further, but it does no good; the man just stands there in the sun in his blazer, his hands neutrally at his sides, repeating that the pool is only for hotel guests.

"We do have some very nice municipal swimming pools in Las Vegas—I'm told," the man says. "You might be more comfortable there."

"More comfortable? What are you talking about?"

"Come on, Gene, let's just go," Dolores mutters again. She's now looking down at the cement, no longer vigilant. The thing she was expecting seems to have happened.

"Let me call up to Mr. Blaine's room."

"We've already done that... here," the man says, seeing a man in a suit approach.

"No answer," the second man says, and stands there, glowering at Gene and Dolores.

"I'm afraid I'll have to ask you to leave," the first man says.

Gene looks at the men for a second, realizing there's nothing to be done. Humiliated, he nods, and holds the door of the dressing room open for Dolores. She slips into the room and closes the door with a slam. Gene glares at the two men. "I hope this is not about what I think it's about," Gene says.

"Listen, kid," the second man says, taking a half step closer to Gene. "The only reason we aren't throwing you over the fence into the parking lot is there's a chance you actually are guests of Bobby Blaine. Who should have known better. But just the same, we're not taking any smart-mouthed remarks from you or any race-mixing bastard."

"It's all right," the first man says. His colleague's outburst seems to have freed his arms, and he waves his hands nervously. "We're truly sorry for the inconvenience, sir. In fact," he goes on in a lower voice, "I do not personally agree with this policy. But the majority of our guests are comfortable with it, and we always work to ensure our guests are comfortable."

"I see," Gene says, hearing his voice shake. "We'll just go to the front desk and get a room. Then may we use the facilities?"

"Oh," the man says, his voice rising. "I'm very sorry, but – I happen to know there aren't any vacancies this weekend."

"I didn't think so," Gene says. "Thank you for making that clear."

"I'm only doing my job," the man says.

Dolores emerges, her facial expression completely neutral. Gene ducks into the dressing room and changes as quickly as possible. He doesn't want her out there alone with those two. But when he steps outside again, they're standing in the same positions, Dolores staring stonily into the distance.

Gene offers her his arm, and they march off, followed by the two men. It seems like everyone is the pool is staring at them by now. His heart thumping wildly, he has to resist the impulse to break into a run.

They're marched down a back hallway, and are compelled to exit the hotel by the loading dock and the dumpsters. They walk down the driveway to where it empties onto a back street. Here there are no sidewalks, no tourists, hardly any traffic except for a couple of delivery trucks roaring by. Dolores motions to the left, and he follows.

The sun seems to beat down even harder. The Keds are raising a painful blister on Gene's heels. After a few minutes they get to a corner and turn back toward the Strip. "Where to?" Gene says.

"I don't know about you," she says. "But I'm going swimming."

"Where?"

"Just where he said. The municipal pool. It's in the park where the library is. They close at 6:00 but we've got time."

They catch a bus on the Strip that takes them toward downtown. Dolores sits with her arms folded, clenching her jaw. They watch the hotels pass and then peter off into the less developed area between the big hotels and downtown. For the entire ride, she doesn't move, until she reaches up to signal for the next stop.

They get off just short of Fremont St. A few blocks to the left and they're at the park and an enormous pool, even bigger than the one at the Riviera, and even more crowded with people. Getting in costs fifteen cents.

The concrete area—only a narrow border around the pool itself—is a checkerboard of towels. They pad three-quarters of the way around until they find a place to squeeze in. Next to them is a woman with three toddlers.

Dolores smiles and speaks a few words of Spanish to her. She says to Gene, "They're her grandchildren." She pulls a white rubber swimming cap on her head, a white cap with yellow rubber daisy petals that quiver. She seems a little less angry. Gene's about to speak to her when she stands up and says, "I'm going to swim." She strides forward and dives into the pool.

He sits on the edge of the pool, his legs in the water, and watches her traveling away and then back to him, dodging children playing Marco Polo. The pool is more than a hundred feet wide here and it takes a while for her to go down and come back. She doesn't know the kick-turn that Dana exhibited at Bobby's, but she plows through the water efficiently, her back muscles strengthened by work.

If Dolores has decided to put the Riviera incident behind her, Gene is only working up to a reaction. He really couldn't believe they were treated that way; she seemed to expect it. Details from the confrontation start to stand out: the shifty glance of the towel boy; the way Dolores withdrew as the men questioned them; the weird smile on the face of the second man as he said "they" didn't want any race-mixing bastards; the tawdry smell of the loading dock, a blend of spoiled vegetables and discarded cigarette butts. Most of all, the way Dolores had looked down and muttered, "Come on, let's go." He feels shame, anger, and a fierce wish to defend her from such indignities.

On returning to Gene's side of the pool, she encounters his legs and stops, taking a deep breath while clinging to the edge. "Don't tell me you're not coming in."

He looks down at her. "I don't know if I feel like it. How can you just go swimming after what happened to us?"

She gives him a wry smile and holds out her hand. "Like this," she says, giving him a sudden pull into the water.

The water is lukewarm this late in the afternoon. Without a word, she takes off swimming again. He watches her go for a second, then pushes off and swims underwater, following. She sees him, dives underwater to playfully push him. Amid the sunbeams and stalactites of children's legs, they tussle, come up for breath, dive again.

Later she sits on her towel, takes off her swimming cap, and shakes loose her brown hair. He gets them Cokes in paper cups and they lounge on their stomachs, facing the park through a chain link fence. A radio station is playing pop songs over loudspeakers.

He watches her; she regards the grassy park. "You're always looking at me," she says, still looking away.

"You're nice to look at."

She snorts, squints a little. After awhile she says, "No, really."

"What? I like you."

"What for? All you do is see me cleaning toilets. When we talk I always give you a hard time. But you've been staring at me like that ever since you came out here."

"I dunno," he smiles. He turns over and looks straight up at the sky, so that now she's leaning on her elbows next to him. Some kids run by and a lifeguard blows his whistle, the shrill sound matching the scratchy music. "I'd rather you said nice things to me, but I still think you're beautiful."

She frowns at him. "Don't say that."

He rises on one elbow to face her. Their faces are close, but she pushes him so that he falls onto his back again. "I'm not going to kiss you at the pool," she hisses, a little embarrassed.

He laughs; she snorts again. "And you're so cheerful all the time," she complains. She sits up, rubbing her elbows where they supported her on the concrete. Looking down at his legs, she says, "You're getting sunburned."

"There's no shade here."

"Maybe you'd rather be back at the Riviera, under a big umbrella." She reaches down and picks up her Coke.

"Not after the way they treated you. I can't believe they did that," Gene frets. "I'm so sorry."

"I believe it. Did you see anybody there but white people?"

"But the big resorts are supposed to be integrated now. They made some kind of agreement with the NAACP—I saw it in the paper."

"Maybe they don't read the newspaper at the Riviera."

She sucks up the last of the Coke, then rattles the ice in the soggy cup. Looking out over the pool, she says, "That was one of the places I applied for a job. There, the Sands, the Flamingo, the Desert Inn, some others. Every day I would go down and apply at two of them. I made sure to write really clearly on the application and to speak really good English to the personnel lady. Not a single one wanted me. One of them said, 'Oh, you speak English so good for a Mexican.'"

"She said that?"

"She didn't say 'Mexican,' she stopped herself right before she said it. But she said enough." She turns and leans toward him. "I spoke English too well. I was too smart. That's why they didn't hire me."

"They said that?"

She rolls her eyes. "No, they don't *say* that. But that's why. They didn't want somebody who was smart and well-spoken cleaning rooms for them. You know why not?"

She looks off into the park again. "Because they were afraid somebody who was smart wouldn't be satisfied just cleaning rooms, that I would quit after a week. That's the nice version. The not-nice version is that they were afraid I was so smart I would figure out how to organize the other housemaids—into, like, a union, I don't know.

"A bunch of people fresh off the boat who can't speak English— they can scare them and control them really easy. Put one person in there who can speak English and I might mess up the whole deal." She shakes her head. "It's stupid, really. Can you see me trying to organize a bunch of illiterate Mexican housemaids?"

"Yes," Gene answers. She looks at him to see him looking up into her face. She laughs, to his chagrin.

"I'm sorry," she says, still laughing. "I see you looking at me like that, I can't help it."

He sits up and touches her face. She stops laughing and looks back at him. "Maybe you should get used to it," he says.

"I'm talking about discrimination, man, and that's all you can think about."

"I'm not thinking about *that*," he says. "I'm thinking about you. You had the feeling that was going to happen at the Riviera, didn't you? But you went anyway."

Ignoring this, she shakes her head so her hair falls around her shoulders and neck, and runs her fingers through it, as if shooing something away. With another frown she says, "What do you want, anyway? What do you mean by asking me out to movies and kissing me and telling me I'm beautiful? Are you looking for a girlfriend? Be honest, now."

"I'm honest," he protests.

"No you aren't," she says. "But never mind that for now. Just tell me what you have in mind."

"All right. Yeah. I want you to be my girlfriend. What do you want, a formal proposal?"

She turns and faces the pool again, her arms resting on her raised knees. "This may sound mean, but it's not. I have to think about my future. I can't afford to waste time going out with people who aren't really serious. I've got to think about my future. I'm not going to be a housekeeper for the rest of my life, you can bet on it."

"I know, I know. You're going to be an accountant."

"That's right. A year from now, or two at the most, I'm going to be in college." She turns back to him. "And then I'm going to marry somebody who's getting ahead, too. I don't care if he's Mexican or white. But they have to be serious. That's why I don't have a boyfriend."

"Hey, I'm serious."

"Not just serious about me. Serious about their life. Not somebody who wants to be a beatnik."

It's his turn to be embarrassed. He considers standing up and diving into the pool again, putting an end to the conversation. But he remains still. Finally he says, "That's serious in its own way. I know it doesn't look like it, I know people say beatniks are bums, but it's about reality, and finding what's true."

"I'm going to have to support myself," she says. "That's reality."

He reaches out and touches her shoulder. She looks at his hand as if she's thinking of shaking it off, but lets it remain.

"Let's go," she says. "You have to open the motel in an hour."

He stands up and reaches a hand out to her. "Come on, Dolores."

She takes his hand and he pulls her up; he picks up the beach bag and carries it for her as they walk toward the dressing rooms.

Chapter 14

1

The Cal-Neva sits in a sparse forest of fir trees a hundred yards above Lake Tahoe. It's a cute mixture of western lodge and Vegas motel-casino, with a lot of pinewood paneling and a smattering of cabins down in the woods. It's owned partly by Frank, partly by Sam Giancana, and for all the wholesome family touches, it has a shady reputation. They say secret underground passages connect the casino and some of the cabins, so that a celebrity or a politician can install his girlfriend in a private cabin, sneak down a back hallway and through a tunnel, and never be seen going in and out of doors.

The backstage facilities are cramped. There's a private dressing room for the star, and for everybody else there are two rooms, which tend to get divided between men and women, no matter what act they're with. So I'm sharing a dressing room with Judy Garland's conductor, her piano player, and the male half of the opening act, a magician named Cosmar. He does thirty minutes, while people are arriving, and then I do thirty minutes before Judy comes on. My concern, as I finish my makeup and comb my hair, is that I still haven't talked to anybody yet about what kind of introduction she wants.

I head out of the dressing room to find Judy's manager, a man named Thompson. Asking around backstage—the sounds of the drums and cymbals and occasional applause punctuating Cosmar's act—I'm told her whole party is in her dressing room.

I knock on the door. When it opens, my first impression is that I've stumbled into a funeral: I hear weeping, and the rest of the room is silent. "Bobby Blaine," I say to the guy who opened the door. "I'm on before Miss Garland and I'm introducing her. I just wanted to see Mr. Thompson or someone."

The man on the door jerks his thumb toward a cluster of people arrayed around the makeup chair. Turns out it's the makeup girl who's crying, while trying to finish the job on Judy.

"No, you bitch," Judy is saying. "What are you trying to do to me? I look like the picture of Dorian Gray."

"You're fine, Judy," a man in a tux says quietly.

I still can't see Garland herself, but I can see her reflected in the mirror, surrounded by anxious faces. "I feel like shit and I look like shit," she says, picking up a cigarette and taking a fierce drag. It's hard to disagree. Her chin, sagging despite the plastic surgery, is trembling. Her lips, when they're not sucking on a cigarette, are pressed together, the bright red lipstick already crumbling from the pressure. The makeup can't quite hide the bags under her eyes. It's been barely twenty years since "The Wizard of Oz." She's aged twice that many.

Judy catches sight of me in the mirror.

"Bobby," she says shortly, "How'd you like to take over the whole evening?"

"Wouldn't think of it," I said. "I don't have that much material."

"Hmf. Then how about switching? I could tell jokes and you could sing."

"You haven't heard me sing," I say. "The Cal-Neva probably wouldn't survive the shock."

"Better than nothing," she says vaguely. Then she shouts at the makeup girl, "All right, you graceless twat, get out of here!"

The woman picks up her kit and runs out of the room, still crying. Garland slumps back in her chair, lights a new cigarette off her old one and glowers at her image in the mirror.

I catch Thompson's eye and he draws me over to a corner and we talk about how Judy wants to be introduced. Just as I'm getting ready to leave, I hear her voice again. "Bobby, come back here."

She's still in the makeup chair. In the few moments since she's been left alone, drawing from some inner source that hasn't quite been exhausted, she has managed to pull herself together. Her face composed, her makeup complete, she sits calmly, though a cigarette is never more than a few inches from her mouth. Still wearing a smock to protect her dress from the makeup, she's perfect from the neck up.

"How's it been for you, Bobby?" she asks. "What are you doing these days?"

She means my routines, I know. "Pretty good. I've got some more topical stuff lately—some gags about beatniks."

"I might watch a little from the wings."

"I hope you do." Do I ever. This is the unspoken aspect of the gig that's like an audition—the prospect of becoming a regular opening act for her.

"Listen," she says. "That Frank—he's putting together quite a lineup for the convention this summer. He wants me to headline a hundred-dollar-a-plate fundraising dinner."

"Can't go wrong there," I say blandly.

She nods. "Old Chinese saying," she says. "When the wind is blowing from the east, it carries the emperor's laughter. When the wind blows from the west, it carries the emperor's tears."

"Yeah? What's that mean, exactly?"

"It means I know which way the wind is blowing. You do too, I'm sure."

"Oh, I'm like a weatherman when it comes to that. Or a weather vane, even."

A man sticks his head in the door and tells me three minutes.

"That's your train, Bobby. Break a leg."

"Same to you."

The show goes well. I don't have time to look at the wings to see if Judy Garland is watching my act. I only glance over when I'm ready to wrap it up and introduce her. Thompson is there to give me a thumbs-up, so I launch into her introduction.

Afterwards I rest in my dressing room. Cosmar can't shut up about how successfully he warmed up the crowd for me. I keep saying "Yeah, thanks," and he keeps giggling about it, while finishing packing up his stuff. Then he asks me if I can put in a good word for him to the management. Finally he leaves me in peace.

In the sudden quiet, I hear Judy's voice coming dimly from a speaker mounted above the mirrors. Lucy and I heard her sing at Radio City Music Hall in 1947 or so, just as things were getting bad between us. I had enough pull to get us prime seats. Judy's voice was still a wonder then, and we were so close we could hear her over the amplification. I put my arm over Lucy's shoulder for a few moments, then withdrew it, realizing for the first time we were past that.

After Garland's show I go out into the house to find Peter. He's standing at a table with some excited men—Democrats again, no doubt—and their wives. The men are just helping the women into their mink stoles, and Peter catches my eye as he's shaking all their hands. He motions with his head toward the lounge, and I meet him a few minutes later.

We sit in a booth where Peter can sit hidden from the hoi polloi, who keep wanting his autograph. People seem to treat him as quite a star now, though he hasn't had a leading role in five years. It's not his work people are reacting to, of course, but the Kennedy connection. First Brother-In-Law—or "Brother-in-Lawford," as Frank keeps saying—is turning out to be the role of a lifetime.

"I bring news, Bobby," he says, after finishing most of his first drink, "from the Grand Poobah."

"Your mother?"

"Very funny. I mean Frank. He's giving out assignments for the convention and I've got yours." He pauses, sips his drink. "It's a little odd, Bobby. Apparently certain people found you less than cooperative."

"What the hell does that mean?"

"Apparently the FBI failed to clear you."

"Clear me? Clear me for what?"

"Floor access. At the convention. You know, the politicking and all that sort of thing. One needs a pass to go to and fro, the convention floor, the back rooms and so forth. And apparently you aren't getting one. But that's all right, old chap, you still get to go backstage, and there'll be plenty of work to do there."

"Wait a minute. You're saying the FBI checked into me?"

"Bobby, they checked into all of us."

"So that's what those S.O.B.'s wanted!" He smiles slightly. "You know, those bastards showed up in my dressing room at the Riv weeks ago. They didn't say a thing about Kennedy. They talked like they were doing some kind of anti-Communist investigation—like it was the blacklist days or something. And I played along for a while, but then I told them to go fuck themselves. If only someone had warned me."

"Well, apparently you didn't play along quite far enough."

"Will you stop saying 'apparently'?"

"Sorry, old boy. But never mind—You'll play an important role, I assure you. There are all sorts of events planned. Frank wants Jack to come to Palm Springs beforehand, just to rest before all the events get underway."

"Judy was just telling me about a hundred dollar-a-plate affair."

"Right, and there will be private affairs as well."

"I'll bet."

"Perhaps 'affairs' is not a good choice of words; I'll have to watch that. But since I put my foot in it, I'll tell you something: Jackie's not coming to the convention. She's expecting, you know, and the doctor has ordered her to rest. She had a miscarriage a few years ago, so they don't want her to take any chances."

"That ought to make the atmosphere a tad less formal."

"Indeed. Bit of a stag party, I think you call it. But Jack's mother is coming out to lend a feminine presence." He puffs on his cigarette. "These conventions are partly ceremonial, I'm told, and appearances are important. For example, we might call upon you to accompany some lass to an event."

"Be a beard, in other words."

"You understand perfectly. Look, I'm going to ask them to reserve a room in your name at the Beverly Hilton. If you could plan on keeping close by..."

"All right—anything for the cause."

"Thanks so much, Bobby. I knew we could count on you. And by the way—Frank asked me to tell you to check with Jack Entratter. They have an opening at the Sands and Frank recommended you to Jack."

"No kidding. Well, that's great, Peter. You tell Frank how grateful I am for that." It's a good thing there isn't any blacklist anymore, I think to myself, or I might end up like Maltz.

"Frank thinks the world of you, Bobby. He wants to do everything he can for your career. And the same goes for me. Well, what do you say we congratulate Judy? Think we can get through the crush?"

* * *

2

On Monday, a few days after their swimming date, Gene's working in one of the rooms when Dolores comes in. It's late morning and he's been replacing a medicine cabinet; someone had torn the door off its hinges. "My work's done for the day," she says, "and I wanted to look at the books. You want to look with me? I brought you something for lunch."

They go to the office and he gets out the dusty ledger from inside the counter, where it sits underneath a three-year-old telephone book and a cereal bowl full of paper clips and rubber bands. They open the book together, like two children about to read a fairy story.

It seems Gustafson kept good records for the first couple of years, perfunctory records for a year or two after that, and nothing for the last couple of years. The fascinating thing about the ledger is that, for a while in 1957, Gustafson had created separate columns for "Good" and "Bad" guests—the latter presumably the prostitutes and their cohort, with many more entries in the second column than the first. Perhaps depressed by this accounting, Gustafson stopped keeping records at all late that year.

"Goodness knows how much money he's making now," Dolores says. "I think there's more guests since you started working the desk, actually."

"I don't know why, I don't treat them any better than he did."

"I don't believe that," she says cheerfully.

Gene had found some bank statements in a closet in Gustafson's apartment, packed inside a shoebox on an upper shelf. Gene fetches them and they find a few recent ones. Dolores examines them while he surreptitiously watches her. Now that she has numbers to work with, she becomes attentive as she begins figuring on a sheet of paper. After a while he tires of standing there and says, "Did you say something about lunch?" She holds up a finger and he waits for another couple of minutes.

When she stops calculating, she says, "There's a lot to look at, but just from his deposits in the last few months I'm guessing he wasn't starving. Did you say you were charging more for the rooms you've redone? Then I don't see why somebody couldn't make money off this place."

They sit down to lunch together at Gustafson's kitchen table. She has brought him a chicken sandwich, with plenty of tomatoes and mayonnaise.

He tells her about his progress on the rooms. He counts off the rooms he's done, the ones he doesn't think need work, and the rooms remaining. They talk it over like business partners; she estimates how much the motel can afford to spend a month on maintenance, and he says they can raise the rates on improved rooms.

Gene feels happy anytime somebody gives him a meal, and this one makes him doubly so: when he tells her the sandwich is good, he gets to see her smile.

"Beats eating at the bus stop," she says. "I never dared ask him before if I could eat my lunch at his kitchen table. Not that I really wanted to, it was so smoky in here."

"Now your boyfriend's the boss," he says. "We've got the whole place to ourselves."

"Well, don't get any ideas," she says, but more humorously than she might have before.

He sits back, chewing, and disobediently gets ideas. Could they live together like this? It would have to be in another apartment, not at the motel—or why not? Maybe Gustafson will never come back; he's been gone more than a month.

The days are getting longer. That evening, sitting at the front desk and looking across the street, Gene watches the owner of the auto shop close the rolling doors as his mechanics drive off. That used to happen in twilight; now the sun sets when he's far into the evening shift.

Soon his guests start arriving. It seems odd that they show up in daylight. Gene half-expected them to time their arrivals to that of the night, like vampires. But they show up at the same time, 5:30 or 6:00.

He decides to ask one of them, Moira, one of the "rooms 5 and 6" hookers who shows up with her unnamed colleague at the same time every Wednesday through Saturday. She's never been friendly, but at least she's not a drunk or otherwise messed up.

"Hey, can I ask you a question?"

"What?" she asks shortly, lighting a cigarette as he is making change for her.

"I've noticed you and your... fellow... uh, worker, show up at the exact same time every night. But I thought that because it's staying light later, you would be starting later."

She squints at him. "Whatta you want to know for? Who are you, anyway? What happened to the old man?"

"I'm his grandson. He's in the hospital."

"He never bothered me." She holds the cigarette between her lips, stuffing her billfold back into an oversized bag hanging from her shoulder.

"I'm not trying to bother you. So why do you start the same time every night?"

She plucks the cigarette from her lips, leans on the counter and counts off on her fingers as she says, "Me and my honey get off work at 5:00 every day. We meet up, take a taxi here, and so we get here the same time. We don't care what time the sun sets, because it never sets inside the casinos, and that's where we work. You writing a school paper or something?"

"No, just... curious. Really."

"Curiosity killed the cat." She turns and walks out. After that, when the two women arrive, anytime it looks like Gene is going to say more than two words, she hisses: "Remember what happened to the cat!"

What happened to the cat? Gene keeps on the counter the book the Buddhist priest gave him, and from time to time he reads a couple of paragraphs. There are little stories about ancient Buddhist monks; they're the only parts of the book that make any sense at all. They remind Gene of the stories he used to hear in high school, when one of the brothers, bored with teaching World History, would tell them stories about the Desert Fathers. These Buddhist stories are very similar, except that there's no devil.

There's one Buddhist story that really gets him. In a monastery, the monks are arguing over a cat. To settle the dispute, the abbot cuts the cat in half—which reminds Gene of the Bible story about Solomon. When the head monk, the number two guy, comes back in the evening, the abbot tells him what happened. And in response, the head monk puts his sandals on his head and walks out. The abbot calls after him, "If you had been here, the cat need not have died."

End of story. That drives Gene crazy. The "explanatory" text of the book is no help at all.

He remembers not every Bible story made total sense either. Maybe he's just supposed to read the stories, be kind to people, and unlike Kerouac—who didn't understand Buddhism, according to the Buddhist priest—stay put. Maybe he's done all the traveling he needs to for a while. Perhaps he should stay there with Dolores, run the motel, get married, maybe put in a pool some day. There's plenty of room for it, behind the big green, yellow and white sign with its saguaro's needles flashing green. The worn-out trucker and the hookers could relax in the warm evening air and smoke cigarettes immersed in cool blue water, while he and Dolores watched television in the apartment and ate chicken sandwiches and tortillas. Late at night after the last room has been filled, he imagines her in bed with him, her dark hair catching a bit of the green neon light. Poised above her, he'd kiss her throat and hold her, spending the night in the motel over and over and over again.

Would that equal growing up and settling down? Is it serious enough for her? Alone in the peaceful office, the evening light persisting, he thinks it doesn't sound so bad.

Chapter 15

1

Gene still goes by the hospital a few times a week to look in on Gustafson. The old man's condition has stabilized, but he's lost weight, his skin is greenish, and he doesn't even seem to feel like complaining to Gene or the nurses. He lies propped up in bed watching soap operas all day.

They can't do any more for him. The staff told Gene earlier this week that Gustafson is ready to be released, but he's asked them to hold off until he finishes redoing the old man's apartment. Since his insurance is perfectly happy to keep him there for several more weeks, and they don't need the bed, the hospital staff obliges.

The fact is, Gene finished working on the apartment a long time ago. He has been holding off taking Gustafson back because he likes the independence, and because he has the feeling that once Gustafson comes back to the motel and discovers what Gene's done to his apartment, he'll kick him out.

Dolores comes into the office at the end of the morning to punch her time card. "Hey boss man," she calls, "I'm through cleaning your filthy motel."

"Find anything good today?" he asks laconically, turning a page of the newspaper. She sometimes brings in peculiar items the guests have left behind—if they aren't too embarrassing. Gene's favorite so far was a giant baby bonnet and baby bottle, like props from a Baby Huey cartoon.

"Just a thousand dollar bill."

He stands up and takes his keys out of his pocket. "I'm coming out too. Gonna visit Gustafson again."

"He's lucky you visit him. Without you nobody would even know who to return him to."

"Yeah, well, he's picking up a little. He might have to come home pretty soon." Gene locks the door and they walk down the street together.

"Then you're back to being the handyman. Maybe I should invite you home for dinner while you're still the General Manager."

"Sure," he says. It's become a running joke between them, that she's going out with the General Manager instead of just the handyman.

"No, seriously." If she goes out with the same guy twice, she says, her family wants to meet him and see if he's acceptable. Sunday dinner is the only way.

When Gene gets to the hospital, there's another surprise. Standing in Gustafson's room and talking to the old man is a stout younger man in a white shirt and gray trousers. He's holding a few papers. A suit jacket is draped over the visitor's chair. Gene walks in the door, stops short, and does a double-take to make sure he's in the right room. The man in the white shirt looks up at him.

"Uh, hello," Gene says uncertainly.

"Can I help you?"

"Uh... I came to visit Mr. Gustafson."

"And you are?"

"Gene Kramer. I'm his... " Gene pauses and looks at the man—in his late 40s, and with enough of a family resemblance that he decides not to go with that grandson story. "I work at his motel," Gene finishes. "I'm the, uh, manager since Mr. Gustafson, uh, got sick."

"I'm Karl Gustafson," the man says, without a smile. "This is my father. Are you the person who checked him in here?"

"Yes, that's right." Gene looks from Karl to the old man and back again.

"It says here you claimed to be his grandson?" Karl asks, gesturing with the sheaf of papers. Gene recognizes them now as the admittance forms.

"Uh... That was... That started off as a mistake. They wrote that down on the form, and I tried to get it cleared up, but..." he shrugs. "Then I realized that maybe it was easier if I let it stay like that—I thought they might not let me visit him otherwise. I didn't know how to contact his relatives," Gene adds, realizing that sounds pretty awkward now that someone obviously has.

"The insurance company let me know he was here." Karl looks down at his father, whose eyes are fixed on the TV, the volume of which has been turned down all the way. "His heart attack took place... six weeks ago?"

"Yeah, something like that. I've been coming to see him every couple of days." Karl looks up at him questioningly. "I was the only person in town who knew him, as far as I knew."

"Why didn't you try to contact us, his family?"

"I looked around the office, and I couldn't find any address or letters or anything. I tried, believe me. All I knew is, he was from Chicago, but when I checked, there are about fifty Gustafsons in Chicago. And I called all fifty, but ..." In fact, he's lying about calling anybody. But he figures, who could call fifty people?

"We live in Aurora. A small town. It's forty miles from Chicago." His aggressive manner softens. "We haven't really been in touch, it's true. Send Christmas cards, that's all. My wife always said something like this might happen."

"They tell me he's better," Gene puts in, hoping to shift the focus from himself.

Karl sighs. "Yes, but... How do you feel, Pa?"

The old man smacks his lips and does not shift his eyes from the television. "Like I need a cigarette."

"That's what got you into this mess!" Karl says, suddenly angry.

"Keep your expert opinion to yourself," says Pa. "A fat lot you care."

"I'm here, aren't I?" he snarls.

"Two months later."

"Six weeks! And it's not my fault!" Karl grits his teeth, and shakes the sheaf of papers he's holding, smacking them against his leg. He then fixes his gaze on Gene. "I'll take things from here, thank you."

"Okay. Well. I'll be at the motel," Gene says. He turns to go, then stops in the doorway. "You know where it is? The Cactus Motel."

"I'll get directions," Karl says, turning away.

Gene opens the office that night and cautiously pokes around, as if the Gustafsons might be lurking somewhere in the apartment. But the place is as empty as he left it after noon.

He had been operating under the assumption that, as long as he visited Gustafson in the hospital and regularly glimpsed the owner in all his vulnerability, he didn't have to be concerned about his own position. Gene figured the old man owed Gene too much: not just his back pay, but recognition that he'd kept the place going. Based on this, Gene supposed he would be able to stay on at the hotel, possibly even hanging onto his desk clerk post, until he decided to go.

But Karl didn't seem as if he was going to take any crap, from his father or anybody else. Clearly he hadn't seen Gene as a young man with initiative, but as a flunky, or even a chiseler.

Then again, he's Gustafson's son, so he's bound to be a grouch.

The office door opens, he looks up and is astonished to see the beaten-up hooker from a couple of weeks ago.

"Hey, sir," she begins in the same ragged voice. "I was here a while back."

"Yeah," Gene says. He can't believe his eyes. The woman seems to have mostly recovered from the beating, but there are still scabs on her face around stitched cuts, and her face is somewhat puffy. She holds onto the counter with both hands as if she might fall. There was no taxi, so she must have walked here, but how, and from where, he can't begin to guess.

"I left some things in my room. My purse and shit."

"That was more than two weeks ago," he answers. "I found your purse, but I gave it to the police when they came."

The woman laughs briefly, or seems to; she looks desperately off to the side, as if there might be someone else present with a different answer. "Are you sure?" she asks. "Oh, no. Oh, no," the woman moans.

Irritation rises in Gene. He looks away, suppressing a mean remark, something like he's been glad she hasn't bothered him with her whining anymore. She has turned to look out the window. Her mouth trembles and she begins crying.

232

"Lady," he protests sharply.

She looks quickly back at him, tears flooding her eyes and mouth open in a silent expression of pain. She doesn't cry out loud, merely stands there with a heaving chest, her breath coming in uneven gasps, in and out.

Perhaps because she looks at Gene with such naked pain and vulnerability, his anger suddenly softens.

"Do you want to sit down for a minute?" he asks.

She doesn't answer, can't answer.

"Come back here," he says. "Just come around here."

He doesn't want to touch her, but does touch her shoulder with the backs of his fingers as she comes around the counter, if only to encourage her to keep moving around and into the apartment. "There's a chair right there. Sit down for a few minutes and rest." He has her sit in Gustafson's leather armchair, and from the kitchen he fetches a few paper napkins and hands them to her.

A taxi has pulled into the driveway, and Gene goes out to the counter again. A man comes in, leaving his companion in the taxi. Adulterers—the motel gets some, although mostly they go for a nicer place. Gene gives the man the best room to encourage him to come back. After Gene hands him the room key, the taxi takes them the final fifty feet to the door of number twelve.

The hooker is sniffling behind him in the apartment. He stands at the counter, alone for a moment, and then goes back and gives her a glass of water. She takes a sip and puts it down on Gustafson's end table—not even a table, really, but a stained wooden shelf that hangs on the pole of a floor lamp. Gene picks the glass up and puts a coaster underneath it.

She dabs her eyes with the paper napkin. Standing to the side, Gene can see the top of her head. Through a tuft of hair that's much shorter than the rest of the hair on her head, he can glimpse a head wound. It looks like the stitches there have recently come out. Maybe she just got out of the hospital.

After a moment he goes back out to the counter. He goes back to watching the movie, leaving her alone until her crying stops. During a commercial he comes back to find her asleep in the armchair, her scrawny legs drawn up and her bare feet tucked into the side of the thick cushion. He looks down at her, then goes over to the couch, where there's a faded green and yellow woolen blanket hanging over the back. He shakes off a layer of dust and puts it over her.

During the evening, the patrons stage the usual minor disturbances—a vocal dispute between a hooker and a taxi driver, over some verbal slight; the pimp yelling at his girlfriend and slamming the door of their unit before walking away down the driveway; a beggar in a beat-up white Chevy asking for gas money, because even the beggars have cars in Las Vegas. None of these disturb his visitor. Gene wonders what Karl Gustafson, or his father, would say if they found the hooker asleep in the old man's armchair.

She sleeps for several hours, during which Gene goes back from time to time to make sure she's still breathing. The thing that Gene dreads most does not happen: the return of the woman's pimp. He hopes that the man, having fought with the policemen as they carried him out, is deep in the jail, perhaps in worse shape than she is.

It is nearly 2:00 a.m. when the woman wakes up. "Can I have some water?" she croaks, rousing Gene from his drowsy watch at the counter. He has already turned on the NO VACANCY sign and is just waiting for Moira and her honey to depart. He gets up and goes to the woman, who is trying to unbend her legs and groaning in pain as she does so. He hands her the mostly-full water glass from the table and she gulps it. Smacking her lips, she thrusts the glass back at him and then says, "Where's the ladies' room?"

He guides her to Gustafson's bathroom and she shuts the door. Moira is banging on the locked door of the office. Gene hurries to open the door, take the room keys and return their key deposits. The two women depart in a waiting taxi, and except for the trucker, the motel is empty.

The hooker takes too long in the bathroom, and when he knocks on the door, she shouts "Stay the hell out!"

"Lady," he says, "It's late. I want to go to bed."

"Who's stopping you?" she asks tartly.

"You can't stay here," he says. "You've got to go."

The door opens. She's standing here with a cigarette in her mouth and her wounded lip bleeding. She must have been trying to wash off the caked blood around the stitches. "I can't stop this fucker bleeding," she says.

"Oh Christ," Gene moans. "You can't try to wash it. Just leave it alone."

"But it's bleeding."

"Come out here. I'll put some ice on it, for God's sake."

She comes out, and as Gene reaches in to switch off the light he sees she's left huge wads of bloody toilet paper all over. They go into the kitchen and he takes some ice and puts it in a thin dishtowel. "Hold this to your mouth for ten minutes and don't move," he says.

"Don't order me around, boy," she says aggressively.

"You want to stop bleeding? Use the ice. Otherwise get out."

She accepts it and sits at the kitchen table. She's still trying to smoke but finally gives up and throws the cigarette on the floor and steps on it.

Arms folded, Gene leans up against the kitchen sink, too tired to snap at her. Having to sit at the table, she turns glum. "Mister," she says.

"Yeah."

"I got nowhere to go."

He takes a breath. "You don't have a home?"

"I live with my boyfriend. But we lost our place. We been living in his car. But I don't even know where his car is."

He sighs, thinking what a mess she is. "Lady," he says, then asks, "Listen, what's your name anyway?"

"Ruth," she says through her swollen lips.

"Well, I don't know what you can do. I really don't."

"Let me stay here, mister. Let me stay in one of the dirty rooms. I'll leave in the morning. Come on. You already got paid for the room. Let me spend the night in it."

Gene is about to say no but stops because he can't really think of a reason to. "Listen," he says. "Ruth. All right. You can stay in number five. In the morning, I'm going to come and get you. I'm going to call a taxi and give him ten dollars and tell him to take you anyplace in town you want to go, except back here. And then I never want you to come back here again."

"I got nowhere to go, mister."

"Stop calling me mister," he snaps.

"I'm sorry, sir."

"Oh Christ," he says.

"Christ helped me," she declares. "I was in the emergency room and an angel came and I got up. The angel took me for a ride all over everything, and then boom, I was back in the emergency room. That was a hell of a thing."

He doesn't know what to say to that.

In the morning, he sleeps until past nine. Once he sees the time, he jumps out of bed. He dresses and hurries down to number five so he can roust the woman before Dolores runs across her.

Without knocking, he opens the door to number five. But the woman is gone. At first he thinks he's in the wrong room, but then he realizes that what's happened is that she has made the bed before leaving.

Gene putters anxiously around Gustafson's apartment all morning, cleaning up all the bloody kleenex from his bathroom floor, replacing the yellow and green blanket on the back of the dusty couch, then deciding the whole kitchen really needs at least a wiping down, and from there deciding to rinse off all the dishes and clean out the refrigerator, so that he's been working all morning on the place as if it's his own parent coming home and not his boss, when a taxi pulls up in the driveway.

Gene comes out into the office in time to see Karl climb out, pay the driver, and come around to the left side to help his father out. Gustafson has come home.

Karl has the old guy on his feet by the time Gene comes around the car. He's hardly touched the old man when Gustafson flinches violently away. "Don't touch me!" he snarls. Gene backs off and watches father and son struggle through the doorway of the office and around the counter, as the taxi backs out of the driveway and pulls away.

Gene follows them. "In here, Pa?" Karl is asking. "You want to sit down here?" He lets him down in the armchair, which seems to envelop his shrunken frame much the way it had swallowed up the scrawny hooker the night before. His son stands over him, watching the old man try to catch his breath. "That's more exercise than you've had in a while, huh?" Karl says with false cheer.

Gene goes back into the kitchen. "I was just straightening up in here," he announces.

Karl hardly glances over. "How ya feel, Pa?" he asks loudly. "Just relax and catch your breath."

Gene is washing out some plastic dishes he had discovered in the fridge holding rotten food. After a minute Karl comes into the kitchen and starts looking through the cupboards. "Got a glass?" he finally asks.

"Sure, in there," Gene motions with his head. Karl just looks at him. Gene gets the glass himself and hands it to Karl, then stands aside as Karl fills it with water and brings it to his father.

"That better?" Gene hears.

Gene puts a plastic bowl into the dish drainer, and a plate settles with a clank. "Whazzat?" he hears the elder Gustafson ask.

"Somebody's doing the dishes," Karl explains.

"What?" Gustafson is turned away from the kitchen and can't see Gene.

Gene turns around. "It's me, Mr. Gustafson. I was just cleaning up a little for your return." He comes into the living room.

"Cleaning up? What's to clean up?"

"I wiped things down, and I just threw out some old food from the refrigerator."

"What food? You got no right... to throw my stuff out." Gustafson has to take a breath halfway through the sentence.

"It's been in there for more than a month, it was no good."

"None of your business, dammit," he wheezes.

Karl looks up. "I don't want him upset. Maybe you'd better leave it to me," he says.

Gene shrugs and goes out. It's late morning, and Dolores has gotten all the way to number 12. He goes in. "Hey Dolores."

"Hi, Gene," she smiles. Since their swimming date, she's started occasionally addressing him by name instead of "Smelly" or "Mr. Big Shot."

"Guess who's home? Mr. Gustafson. I told you I ran into his son at the hospital yesterday? He just brought him home."

"How's he look?"

"Not so hot. But just as grouchy as ever."

"Is he going to keep you on?"

"I dunno, he just got in. His son's fussing over him."

"I'll say hello when I punch my time card. Come here, help."

He helps her make the bed, and when she dusts, lifts the TV up so she can dust underneath it. There she finds a dollar. "Look at that. I'm lucky today—I found a five in number 7."

"Frank Sinatra tipped me a hundred once."

"Yeah, so you've told me, about a hundred times. The toilet's stuck in number 4, Mister Big Shot."

He fetches his tools from the maintenance closet, trying to remember who he rented number 4 to the night before. He finds the toilet full up to the brim with water and feces. Gingerly, he tries to plunge it out without any of it spilling on the floor. When that doesn't unstop it, he inserts a flexible metal rod into the bowl and tries to break up the obstruction by feel. He can feel something mushy down there. After a few minutes, he fishes out the plug: a pair of women's underpants, size extra large. Now he remembers who rented the room—a familiar hooker and her john. The panties are way too large for the hooker, so they must belong to the john. He wore them to his date and then tried to flush them down the toilet.

This isn't the first time this has happened. The first time somebody flushed their extra-large panties down the toilet, he chewed out the hooker next time he saw her, and she protested that she had had no fucking idea the guy would do that, that it wasn't her fault.

And here's the important part: that had been a different hooker and a different john. The fact that people, apparently unknown to each other, share the same perversions has been one of the remarkable things Gene's learned during his stay at the motel. He isn't as repelled as he might have expected; he just wishes they'd dispose of the evidence some other way.

The toilet now flushes freely. He goes to clean up himself and his tools, knowing Dolores will stop in and finish cleaning number 4's bathroom as her last task of the day. Then he hauls out paint and brushes, as he's in the middle of painting the street side of the motel. He's on his way out there as Dolores is coming over, her job done for the day, to clock out. Gene holds the door open for her and follows her in, since it's her first chance to face the Gustafsons.

She goes around the counter and knocks on the doorway of the apartment. "Mr. Gustafson? Oh, hello—are you Mr. Gustafson's son?"

"Who are you?" Karl answers rudely.

Gene has come to stand beside Dolores. "This is Dolores Sanchez, Mr. Gustafson. She's the housekeeping manager."

"Oh, Gene," she says. "I'm the *only* housekeeper, Mr. Gustafson. I finish up around this time every day, and clock out."

Karl nods, looking away.

"How are you doing, Mr. Gustafson?" she addresses the owner. She steps into the apartment and comes around so her can see her. "I'm glad you're better."

"No thanks to anybody," he grunts, clutching a handkerchief close to his mouth. "Do me a favor and get me my cigarettes, will you? They're in the bedroom."

"No, Pa," Karl says. "Sorry, Miss, but I think it's best he doesn't smoke anymore. Bring the cigarettes to me and I'll take them away."

"Dammit!" Gustafson says, slapping his thigh. "You don't order me around like some invalid! If you won't bring them, I'll get them myself." Moving surprisingly quickly, he heaves himself out of the armchair and across the living room to the door of the bedroom. There he stops, and practically rears back in surprise. "What the hell is this!?" he yells.

Gene takes a few steps in that direction. "I repainted your room while you were gone, Mr. Gustafson. And replaced the mattress. And a few things."

The owner turns to him, bracing himself on the doorframe. "What right do you have to tear up my room?" He turns back, open-mouthed, and gestures with both hands. "What ridiculous notion did you get in your mind that you had the right to do that?"

"The paint was peeling," Gene says, "and the mattress was shot. And frankly, the whole place didn't smell so good. I knew you'd be gone for a few weeks and I wanted to make it nicer for you, that's all."

"You threw away my mattress? That was a special mattress! Do you know what that cost me?"

"Special or not, it was a wreck."

Karl has been standing by watching this exchange. Now he comes up to look over his father's shoulder into the bedroom. His mouth forms an expression of distaste, but he says, "It looks all right to me, Pa."

"Well, it doesn't to me. I liked it the way it was."

"Let's stick to business," Karl says flatly. "Where are the cigarettes?"

"Go to hell!"

"Pa, come on," Karl says, gritting his teeth. "I'm trying to help you."

Gustafson whirls away from the bedroom door and comes reeling across the living room. "Everybody's trying to help! Everybody thinks they know what's best. What other bright ideas did you have, boy?"

"Well, I kept the place open for you for nearly two months, if that's what you mean," Gene says.

"Any moron can stand here and collect money from scumbags," Gustafson scoffs. "I mean what—" he breaks off and begins coughing.

"Sit... down, Pa," Karl says wearily, as if his patience is already at an end. He goes to help his father, who stiff-arms him and stalks back to the living room, snarling, "Keep away from me!"

"I have kept this place open," Gene says to Karl. "I've been giving Dolores her pay, and I've been paying for materials and so forth for improvements and repairs, and I've been paying off the cops every week. Other than that, I haven't been paying myself."

"Wait a minute," Karl says. "What did you say? You *pay off* the cops? Pa, what is this?"

Gustafson has hurled himself into his armchair to finish his coughing fit. He takes a breath and says, "A hundred a week."

"A hundred dollars?!" Karl exclaims.

"It's one-twenty-five now," Gene puts in. "They raised it."

"You *pay off* the police?" Karl echoes. "No wonder you never made any money off this place."

"No kidding," his father says. "Why the hell did they raise it? Answer me."

"We had a little problem in front here," Gene explains. "A pimp beat up a hooker and I had to call the cops. Except," he says to Karl, "it's not really the cops..."

"I don't believe this," Karl cries, throwing up his hands. "What kind of place are you running here?"

"A shithole!" Gustafson spits. "What's it look like, the Sands? It's a shithole full of junkies, whores and petty criminals. For the privilege of commanding this piece of crap, I clear about a hundred bucks a week. Or at least I did, before the handyman here started thinking he runs things." Gustafson coughs again, then shakes his fist at Gene. "What else? Is there anything else you haven't told me, before I throw you out on your ear?"

"You mean, besides renovating six rooms and painting about half the exterior? You mean besides working twelve to fourteen hours a day?"

"Don't bullshit me. You stand here and take money and hand out keys. That's no work, I'm not paying you for that."

"Except that if I hadn't done it, the whole place would have closed down."

"At least then you wouldn't have spent all that money on God knows what."

"What about Dolores? What about her job?"

"Who cares? They're a dime a dozen." Gustafson commences another coughing fit.

"Thanks a lot," Dolores says. "I'll clock out now."

"Hey, don't take it out on her," Gene says. "She works hard around here. You wouldn't believe the things she has to clean up sometimes."

Gustafson only coughs in response.

"Pa, are you all right?" Karl asks. His voice is more impatient now than sympathetic. He crouches next to the armchair, watching Gustafson. "Are you all right?" he repeats in the same tone.

Gene brings a glass of water. "Here." He hands it to Karl, but Karl just holds it, his lips pursed. "He usually stops after a few minutes," Gene says.

Karl looks up sharply at Gene. "Are you a doctor now?"

Gene shrugs. "It's just my experience..."

"I've heard enough about your experience," Karl snaps. "Paying off the cops! I've never been more disgusted."

"Hey, look, this is Vegas," Gene says. "It's just the way things are done."

"We're from Aurora—you think I don't know about mobsters?" Karl says. "We steer clear of those people. You don't know how hard it is to do business in that area and stay clean. He worked for decades and never got anywhere because he wouldn't play along. After forty years he comes down here for what we thought was a quiet retirement. Now I find out it's a damn hellhole!—Excuse my language."

"You sent him to Las Vegas to get *away* from the mob?" Gene asks.

"You know, it's really none of your business. Are you all right, Pa?" Gustafson's coughing seems to be subsiding, but the old man just waves his handkerchief angrily in reply. Karl stands up, still holding the glass of water. "Just what is your job here, anyway?"

"Officially? I'm the handyman. But for the past seven weeks, I've done everything, except clean the rooms—Dolores does that."

"So you've been manning the front desk? Making reservations?"

"Reservations! Are you kidding?"

"Well, what *do* you do?"

"Well, I do man the office, but it's more a matter of keeping the peace than anything else. The guests are not that high class, okay? They come around here whining for extra towels or somesuch thing, I tell them no. Somebody comes by begging for money, I tell them no. If things get out of hand, I call the cops—the special number, that is. I've only had to do that once, though."

"This is what I paid for," Karl says bitterly, shaking his head. "I bought a motel for my father and he turns it into some criminal hangout. Next you'll be telling me there's prostitution here."

Gene stares at him. "Well, yeah."

Dolores is punching out. She sputters with laughter, shaking her head.

Karl walks over to the old man. "How could you let this happen, Pa? This was supposed to be your retirement... Your place in the sun. You've turned it into a den of thieves!"

Gustafson is just catching his breath. He looks up resentfully. "No thanks to you," he mutters.

"I'm not so sure it's his fault," Gene tells Karl. "It's just... It's the neighborhood. All the motels along here are like this."

"Oh, so it's all right if everybody does it?"

"We're three blocks off the Strip; tourists don't drive down this street. It's just the locals, and what else do locals need a motel for aside from... well..."

"Adulterous assignations," Karl thunders. "I don't believe that. The real estate agent said it was a nice family joint when we got it." He glares back at his father.

"Yeah, sure," Gustafson sneers.

"He's been doing the best he can," Gene says. "That's all you can do here."

"Gene, how can you defend him?" Dolores asks quietly. "Just keep out of it."

"'The best he can,'" Karl echoes. "I refuse to believe that. You have to fight things like this—prostitution and such. I refuse to agree that all you can do is just give in."

"You refuse! You refuse!" Gustafson says. "That's all you wanted when you sent me down here. You didn't want me around, so you threw me right where you wanted me—on the garbage pile. And that's just what this place is—only it gives garbage a bad name. You're so superior, you— God—" his face turns red and he starts pounding the arm of the chair.

"Uh oh," Gene mumbles.

"Pa? What's the matter?"

Gene is already moving to the phone. He picks it up and quickly dials. "He needs an ambulance," Gene says.

"You let me decide that."

"Now who's the doctor? Hello, we need an ambulance, a man's having a heart attack. Again. Yes, it's his second heart attack."

"God dammit!" Gustafson the elder spits out. "I'm not... having a heart attack... I'm just... fed up with you—you pipsqueaks!"

Karl backs away from his father, a look of disgust on his face. He goes into the kitchen, out of his father's sight, and barks at Gene, "Get the ambulance!"

"No, goddammit, just let me catch my goddamn breath."

Karl stands at the kitchen counter, his hands formed into fists that he taps on the edge of the sink. "Get the ambulance," he says again. "This is it. I'm shutting this place down."

Dolores mutters something in Spanish, shaking her head.

"I don't need any lip from you," Karl spits. "From any of you. This whole operation is closing down."

Dolores motions to Gene and they go out onto the tiny sidewalk slab in front of the office. The midday sun is beating down, and they stand in the bar of shade cast by a steel awning. "I have to go," she says. "I'll call this evening and see if the place is still open, okay?"

"Sure."

She reaches up tentatively and touches his collar, pretends to straighten it. After a moment she says, "It was big of you to stand up for the old man after the way he's treated you."

"Well," Gene says. "I don't like this Karl. He's just as bad."

"Yes, he's a *pendejo*. A, uh, fool. But still, it was big of you. I'll call you tonight," and goes off to her second job.

2

"Bobby, Judy loved your act. She said those audiences at Tahoe were some of the best she's ever had. You went out there and warmed them up just great, and when she came on, they were in the perfect mood."

"Okay, Philly, so what about the regular gig?"

"You didn't get it. Timson's getting it. Ha *haaa*, just kidding."

"You're kidding, I didn't get it, or you're kidding, Timson's getting it?"

"Kidding about Timson. You're still not getting it."

Philly and I are at Chasen's for lunch. It's after 1:00 but the place is still full of people doing business. There's Rock Hudson having lunch with Louella Parsons, and two booths down is Spencer Tracy and a publicist talking to Herb Caen. We're across the room from these Olympians, a little lower in status, but not too bad. We're in a lot better position, for example, than those tourists over there with their maps to the star's houses.

The waiter comes and refills our coffee. "She's going with that new guy—what's his name—he does the telephone thing. Who is it?" Philly wonders, tipping his head way back, looking for the answer on the ceiling. "His shtick is to do one side of a telephone conversation. He does the night watchman in the Empire State Building on the night King Kong shows up. Funny as hell."

"Bob Newhart," I say, despite myself. "Moving right along..." I prompt, spooning in a lump of sugar.

"You know, what do you call that effect?" Philly says. He's still looking at the ceiling. "That bumpy kind of shit they have up there?"

"Flocking."

"Flocking," he repeats in a tone of wonderment. "What do you figure, they just spray it on?"

"I don't know."

He nods seriously, pursing his lips, and sneaking another glance. "Handsome effect."

"Thinking of redoing your office?" I ask in what I hope comes across as sarcasm.

He shrugs, and we both take a sip of coffee.

Finally I can't stand it anymore. "Damn it, Philly, do you have anything else, or were you hinting that I should quit show business and become a flocking sprayer?"

"Bobby, settle down. Sure I have something else. Plenty, in fact. I was just thinking. I'm not getting any younger."

"You're right there, Philly. I'm in total agreement. I can feel myself getting older by the second."

"Bobby, I'm serious. Carol and I, we're talking about Florida."

"What about it?"

"Retiring there."

"That's fine, Philly. But not today, right? Not before you tell me if you're gotten me any other gigs?"

"Look who's so impatient. Okay, sure." He takes a notebook out of his breast pocket along with some reading glasses. "Like I was saying..." he says ironically, holding up the glasses. Putting the glasses on, he flips through the notebook. "Bobby, Bobby, Bobby," he mutters to himself. "Oh Christ, that's right, Carol asked me to get cleanser. That's it." He writes briefly in the notebook and then flips a few more pages. "Here you are. Okay, how'd you like to go to St. Louis?"

"Fine."

"Charity benefit there in June."

"All right. I do it gratis, I suppose. Is it televised?"

"No, but they're having a thousand people there. And they pay for a plane ticket."

"Fine. What else can you get me in St. Louis?"

"St. Louis? What's there? I can get you something in Chicago."

"There's got to be something else in St. Louis. A big hotel downtown—they don't have entertainment?"

"I'll look into it, but I'd rather try Chicago."

"Fine, just don't make me go all the way out there for one thing."

"Or Kansas City," Philly says thoughtfully.

"No, stick with Chicago."

"Sure, sure," he shrugs.

"Philly," I say, "there's a big difference, right? Chicago, the Second City: three million people. Kansas City, hardly even on the map: a hundred thousand people."

"Sure, sure. All right. Another three days in mid-week at the Riv, end of June. Or is that something to complain about?"

"It's fine, Philly."

"And look here. Grossinger's and Kutsher's," he says, naming two Catskills resorts. "Wednesday-Thursday-Saturday at one, then the next week at the other. You do each in July, then in August you go back and do them again."

"Now you're talking—but wait. What about the convention?"

"What convention?"

"The Democratic Convention, Philly. The second week of August. I have to be out here. I told you about this."

"But this is work, Bobby. For you to headline."

"The convention comes first, Philly. I already told Peter."

"Bobby, what are you talking about? I get you real work, it's only a three hour drive from New York, and then, I haven't told you this yet, you're at the Bottom Line there at the end of the month."

"The end of the month is fine, the convention's the second week. It's the 10th through the 15th or something like that. Just get me at Grossinger's the next weekend and Kutsher's the weekend after that and the Bottom Line after that."

"Well, I'll try." He makes scratches in his notebook.

I drink some more coffee as the silence lengthens. We haven't said a word to each other about possible movies for weeks now. It's as if Ocean's 11 had never happened.

Finally, I say, "Nothing in movies?"

Still writing, he just shakes his head. So much for that subject.

3

After Gustafson the elder was taken away for the second time—Karl insisted the old man was headed for a nursing home, whether he'd had another heart attack or not—Gene convinced Karl to let the place stay open until it could be sold. So that night is no different from any in the last month or two.

Dolores calls as the western sky is finally turning a pale yellow, before night descends completely. "What's going on there?"

"The place is open, same as ever. I talked to Karl after he calmed down. I convinced him that it would be easier to attract a buyer if the place stays open. He even gave me my back pay, so I'm rich. More than five hundred dollars."

"Mister Big Shot."

"Yeah, I'm Mister Big Shot."

They are silent for a moment. Gene looks out at the Cactus's sign, faintly buzzing in the evening.

"So," Gene says, "Want to go out this weekend? Or is it this Sunday I'm coming for dinner?"

"Oh, I'm glad you reminded me. Make it next Sunday for dinner, not this one. This weekend, sure, how about later Sunday afternoon?"

After Gene hangs up, he sits unmoving on the stool, watching the light fade, wondering at how things are developing. They've only gone out a few times, and already he's having Sunday dinner with her family. They must be conservative, he thinks, to keep such close tabs on her.

A taxi arrives with a couple. The man comes in and asks for the best room. Gene gives him the key to number 12. "That'll be $12," he says.

"So much?"

"That room was just redone."

"Is that for the hour or the night?" the man asks, amused. Gene can tell he's kidding and also a little drunk.

"The night," Gene says patiently. The guy seems a little higher class than the usual guest. Maybe he's in town for a convention or something. But then why wouldn't he just take this woman back to his hotel room? Because he doesn't want anyone else to see her. Maybe he's even in town with his wife.

The man looks around the office, and his gaze stops at the rack of pamphlets touting tours to Hoover Dam and Lake Mead. "Get a lot of tourists in here, huh?"

"Not really. Mostly local folks."

"No-tell motel, huh?"

"Mm-hmm."

"You the boss?"

Gene chuckles. "One thing I've learned in three months working here," he says. "Nobody's really in charge."

"Oh, a philosopher, huh? I guess you're a beatnik."

"Not really," Gene laughs. "Not yet."

Chapter 16

1

A few weeks go by with the FOR SALE sign posted. Gene concentrates on finishing the exterior painting and making sure everything looks as good as possible. One day a truck shows up to cart off Gustafson's furniture, and later Gene gets a call from Karl asking him to repaint the rest of the owner's apartment.

On a Friday in mid-June, he and Dolores walk from room to room, making a list of any work that remains to be done to make each room at least rentable. "And we need to order some things," she says. "I'm going to write you a list. And I was looking at that catalog the supply company sent. You can have them print up stationery with the motel's name on it."

He shrugs. "Why would we want that?" A brown-and-white pickup truck pulls into the driveway and honks.

"Oh!" Dolores says. "I forgot—my father is picking me up. He wants me to go with him to some city thing."

Sanchez is stepping out of his truck.

"Buenos dias, Papa. We were just looking at some of the maintenance," says Dolores.

"Working together, eh? Good, good."

Dolores introduces them. Sanchez is a middle-aged man with weathered skin and, judging from the lines on his face, a habitual smile. He stands on the asphalt in work boots, looking all around at the motel. "So this is the Cactus Motel," Sanchez says, apparently amused at the name.

"Yes. I guess the sign could use a little paint."

"Yes, and over here, too—but other places I can see you have painted. And I hear you're a good plumber."

"Well, actually..."

"Could you show me?"

"You want to see my plumbing work?"

Sanchez does. Gene leads him across the parking lot and into the unit, showing him the bathroom work he's done. Sanchez smiles and nods the whole time, but something tells Gene he's just being humored. When they go back to the office, Dolores is standing at the sink washing their lunch dishes.

"It doesn't look so hot without any furniture," Gene says. "But whoever buys the place can refurnish it."

Sanchez surveys the room. "Hmm, about fourteen by sixteen here, maybe six more for the kitchen." He cranes his head toward the back of the apartment. "Is that a bedroom back there?" he asks. Before Gene can answer, Sanchez wanders back there. Gene follows, explaining the work he's completed.

"Good enough to sell the place, anyway," Sanchez says, rubbing his hands together. "How much are they asking?"

Gene doesn't know. He watches as Sanchez pokes his head into the closet and the shower, bounces on the new bed, and even raps on the water heater. "Luis replaced this carpet?"

"That's right."

Sanchez kicks violently at the floor as if trying to tear the carpet from its moorings. Gene watches mutely. "Good job," Sanchez concludes.

"It's a good thing I didn't insist he let me do this room," Gene jokes.

"Yes," Sanchez agrees pleasantly. He leads the way back toward the front. "Well, shall we go?"

Dolores is wiping her hands on a dishtowel. "Bye, Gene," she says. "See you tomorrow." She slips out.

"Sure," he says.

He follows her father out and watches him get into the pickup. It pulls into the parking lot, turns around and comes back out. It stops in front of the office again. "Here," Dolores says, scribbling. "Supplies." She hands him a list.

Gene steps back, the list in his hand, as the truck drives off. She waves at him through the back window.

2

Gene goes out to Dolores' house on a hot June Sunday. Summer has fully arrived, but for Sunday dinner he's wearing his suit. He recognizes this neighborhood; he's been here before, on his long walks this spring. Many of the houses in the neighborhood don't look so good, he notices, and there is a multitude of junky cars, some rumbling down the street, some up on blocks. But the Sanchez house has a narrow, well-tended row of flowers beneath the eaves, and there is a fresh coat of paint—the same color he's been using on the exterior of the motel, in fact.

He rings the doorbell, setting off a loud rendition of the chimes of Big Ben. The front door swings open; there's that awkward moment when he has to open the outward-opening screen door himself. Dolores' father stands there grinning, waving him inside.

Gene steps into a living room as Dolores appears in a doorway across the room. "Hello, Gene. I told them you'd be on time. He's never late," she says to the rapidly-gathering family. She introduces them all, but he instantly forgets which brother is Jaime, which is Juan, and whose wife is whose. Dolores' sister Felice is identifiable by her advanced pregnancy.

"Thank you for coming to our home," her father says.

Gene holds out a bouquet. "For your mother," he says, handing them to Dolores.

"That's very nice. Dinner will be ready soon. Have a seat."

The women retreat and Gene takes a seat on a plastic-covered, overstuffed armchair. The two brothers sit down on a matching, plastic-covered couch, and their father sits in another armchair, resting his hands on his knees. Gene notices that plastic covers not only the furniture but also the lampshades and vast sections of the rug. Above the fireplace, and on shelves set into the wall, are a great many dolls, all dressed like tiny brides in white lace. Interspersed between some of the dolls are porcelain figures of youths dressed in 18th century costumes and dancing or playing instruments. A multi-level shelf near the front door holds more of the objects. On the top shelf is a detailed figurine of a shepherd girl cradling a lamb, and hanging on the wall immediately above it is a small painting of exactly the same image.

"What nice... furnishings," he says.

"Thank you," Sanchez says.

There is a heart-stopping moment of silence as Gene realizes he has no idea what to talk about with these folks. Then he manages: "And the flowers outside are the prettiest in the neighborhood."

"I grow them," Sanchez says with satisfaction. "I made them from... what do you say?" He looks at his sons and says a word.

"Seeds?" Gene offers.

"No..." Sanchez makes a scissoring motion with his fingers. "Dolores!" he calls.

They all wait in silence for a moment. Then she appears. "Si, papa." He asks her a question. "Oh, cuttings," she says.

"Thank you, my dear," her father says. She smiles at Gene as she turns and leaves. "Cuttings. I made them from cuttings from the flowers at our family house in Mexico," he tells Gene. "I had to hide them across the border," he adds, grinning. "They don't allow them to immigrate."

"I see," Gene says. "But then... ah..." He was about to ask if Sanchez himself hadn't crossed illegally as well, but stops himself. "Uh, what do you guys do?" he asks the brothers.

"Construction."

"Construction."

"Ah, yes. I've been doing a little of that at the motel. I wish you had been there to help me," he says, sounding to himself like some English-learning record.

"Alvaro was there. And Luis," one of the brothers says, naming Dolores' cousins, the ones who helped with the carpets and carpentry.

"They were a big help. Are you also in construction, Mr. Sanchez?"

"Yes," Sanchez answers, smiling, as his sons roll their eyes. "But I'm in destruction. I operate the wrecking ball," he adds, with a gesture of knocking something over.

"Really?" Gene says. "That sounds like fun."

"No, I was kidding you. I drive trucks. Usually a cement mixer. Lots of construction in Las Vegas now. But you—Dolores says you're pretty good with the toilets. You should join the plumbers' union," Sanchez goes on. "Go to work on some of these big new hotels."

"Maybe after the motel is sold," he says. So that's where Dolores got the idea that he should be a plumber.

"My daughter tells me your Cactus Motel doesn't make much money."

"We've been investing the profits in improvements," Gene says grandly.

One of the brothers leans forward. "How big are the rooms?" he asks.

"How big? Well, there's a queen-sized bed in each one, and little stands on each side... Oh, wait, what am I saying—we replaced the carpet in one. It was ten by thirteen. They're all pretty much the same."

The brother who spoke says something to the other one, who answers briefly.

"And how much do you rent the rooms for?"

"The ones I remodeled, ten dollars. The others, seven dollars—that was the rate for all of them before I started."

Some more Spanish translation.

"And how full is it every night?"

"Pretty full," Gene says, wondering about this line of questioning. He expected a little bit of third degree but he thought it would involve his personal details. Instead, all they seem interested in is the motel. Gene thinks back several days to when Sanchez visited the Cactus, and then it comes to him: the family is interested in buying the motel. Before he can reflect on this, he hears raised voices from the kitchen. There is a shout, a clatter, and more shouts. The eyes of the three men all tilt in the direction of the noise.

A cat suddenly streaks into the room, closely followed by one of the brothers' wives. She is speaking rapidly, whether to the cat or to someone else, Gene can't tell.

The cat bounds up on Sanchez's knee, across to the arm of the couch, and up to the mantelpiece, all in a flash.

"Gato!" Sanchez says, futilely reaching out as it races past dolls and statuettes, rattling them and knocking one baby-bride to the floor. The woman is crying out excitedly and the men have risen to their feet.

A dog shoots into the room and stops in the middle, looking excitedly around and panting. "Now the dog," Sanchez sighs.

More excited voices come down the hallway, and then three children run into the room.

"Niños!" Sanchez moans.

The cat has paused at the edge of the mantelpiece just before colliding with a large porcelain figurine resembling a six-year-old girl dressed as Marie Antoinette. The second brother snatches the object before the cat can knock it down, but the motion startles the cat so that it launches itself across the room. The three children scream in excitement as everyone, from Sanchez to the dog, watches the cat hurtle through the air. A middle-aged woman on crutches arrives in the doorway just as the cat lands on the bottom-most of the shelves by the door. The whole unit shakes and the porcelain shepherdess is propelled into the air. "Ai, mi cositas!" shouts the woman, and the children chorus, "Las cositas!"

Gene, sitting nearest the shelf, lunges and catches the shepherdess just before it strikes the dog, which emits a single bark. The cat takes off from the shelf and bolts from the room, followed by the dog and the children, who rush out past the woman on crutches. She turns surprisingly swiftly and follows them as the men burst out in laughter. Gene realizes this must be Dolores' mother.

Gene is left standing, cradling the figurine. He replaces it as the brother who snatched the statuette from the mantle does the same. There is a final crash from the kitchen, like distant thunder after a storm has passed. They all sit down again, the two brothers talking excitedly, replaying the incident.

"He says you must be a good halfback," the one says. "You ever play football, American football?"

"Er, I was on my high school team," Gene says automatically. "One game I scored four touchdowns."

Dolores returns in time to hear this remark. "Dinner will be a little delayed. Here's some lemonade. Don't believe anything this one says," she adds, smiling at Gene. "When I met him he said he was a writer of jokes for a big comedian."

"I did write jokes!" Gene says. He turns to the men. "You know Bobby Blaine, the comedian? I worked with him."

"You worked *for* him. Driving his car," Dolores says.

Her father and brothers look amused and slightly bewildered. "I thought he worked at your motel," Sanchez says.

"Now that, I've seen with my own eyes."

"At Motel Dolores," says the talkative brother in a teasing tone, raising his glass to her. She replies with a few rapid words in Spanish.

"What other experiences do you have, besides plumber, chauffeur, and comedian?" asks Sanchez. "And football player."

"I do run the office," Gene says, "in the motel at night. I handle the front desk. And I guess I'll do the books now, until the new owners come."

"Miss Accountant can do the books," her brother taunts her.

She compresses her lips. "I'll see how dinner's coming," she says, going out.

"Anyway," her father says to Gene, "it sounds like you have a future as a plumber. Plenty of work in town for a plumber," Sanchez says. "Or maybe you want to manage the front desk."

"You mean in one of the big hotels? I haven't given it much thought."

"You're pretty young, though," Sanchez says, rubbing his chin. "Maybe you're not ready to settle down."

"Settle down?" Gene echoes stupidly. What are they getting at? The room has gotten uncomfortably warm, and he nervously pulls his shirt away from his sweaty torso. The laconic brother laughs and says something in Spanish.

"He says we are asking you questions like a criminal," the elder Sanchez chuckles. Suddenly he thrusts a pudgy index finger under Gene's nose, startling Gene badly. "What were you doing with my daughter the other night?" Sanchez shouts.

For all the fibs, tall stories and outright lies he gets away with, Gene feels the most guilty when accused of something he didn't do. He squeaks, "All we did was go to a movie."

The three men laugh. "I see, I see," Sanchez says, but doesn't explain.

Gene has the sensation of sweating through his clothes; it was insane to wear the wool suit. The men, on the other hand, are wearing white button-down shirts that, on close examination, are work shirts, the kind Gene has seen in the workmen's clothes sections of his father's hardware store. His father and uncle used to wear the shirts themselves, in their various colors; it was a way of both saving money and of identifying with the workmen who came into the store. Gene is surrounded by men who love hardware, whose days are spent crouching with tools, putting a little elbow grease on the problem, getting their hands dirty. They foresee the same for him, whether at the motel or as a union plumber at the latest Vegas resort. A lifetime of backed-up toilets, corroding pipes, dripping walls, sore knees.

As if reading his thoughts, Sanchez says, "A plumber—you should consider it. But you think you've worked hard up to now? My friend, you haven't seen anything. Someday you'll have to work hard from dawn to dusk. You'll have to do the worst jobs. You'll break your back. That's the way you become a man."

"Maybe I'll join the plumber's union after all," Gene jokes weakly. "Don't they only work from nine to five?"

The men all laugh. "That, my friend," Sanchez says jovially, holding his palm out—a gesture meant to stop, or to swear the truth?—"that is only the beginning."

Chapter 17

1

The motel, when Gene returns to it late that afternoon, has been transformed in his absence from a potential love nest to a prison where he has just been sentenced to hard labor. The low-slung building reminds Gene of his elementary school in late February, when the only things to look forward to were two more months of bleak weather followed by Good Friday. In the winter a Midwestern town became a kind of medium-security prison. No recess outside on account of the weather, and even on weekends he was confined to the house. The weeks would stretch on indefinitely, each as gray as the next. Even on a ninety-degree Las Vegas afternoon in June, Gene recalls that feeling.

Until now the work has been challenging but ultimately satisfying. He enjoyed overcoming some of his distaste for maintenance, and seeing the rooms improve one by one gave him a sense of accomplishment.

But that was when the job had a foreseeable end. With the Sanchezes in charge, he might finish work on the motel sometime this summer—the work, after all, is finite—but Sanchez Sr. seems to have a more ongoing task in mind, that of living up to a family standard of endless hard work, union membership, and eventual manhood. Sanchez seems determined to make a man of him regardless of his feelings for his daughter. Gene imagines that Sanchez might use her as a pawn to capture his loyalty, then extract all he can from the motel and from Gene.

Sitting on his stool behind the counter, Gene tries to get hold of himself. Are things really so bad? Sanchez was charming, genial, warm. Not a prick like Gustafson. Even if he does want a lot of work out of me, maybe that's what I need, he thinks. Maybe that's what growing up means.

But that night, his sleep is shallow and disturbed. He doesn't really fall deeply asleep until he hears the first birds, the ones that live in a couple of stunted orange trees at the side of a transmission repair shop next door. He sleeps three hours, then wanders down the block to get breakfast at the diner an hour later than usual.

On his return, he sees Dolores is already at work in the rooms, but he staggers to the bed and tries to go back to sleep. All morning he hides there; at noon she knocks and comes in.

"You *are* in here," she says. "I thought I saw you coming back from breakfast. Are you sick?"

"Maybe so," Gene says. "I haven't felt right since last night."

"I put your sandwich in the fridge in the office. See you tomorrow."

He waits twenty minutes. When he's sure she's gone, he creeps from his room to the office and eats the sandwich. The afternoon still remains, but he can't even think of taking up his next task, that of repainting number 7. He slinks off toward downtown, spending the afternoon seeing movies. It's hard even to go back to the motel for his evening's shift, but he manages it. As Gustafson himself pointed out, there's not much to it.

Tuesday comes, and Gene has to force himself to get out the paint, the dropcloth, his brush, the ladder. Stirring the paint almost makes him sick. Once he gets going, he's a little better, but has no enthusiasm for the job. At least when Dolores sticks her head in to say hello, he can pretend to be working. No, he won't have lunch with her today; he wants to catch up on the work he missed the day before. When she's gone, he almost hurls himself from the ladder. When the morning is over, he's barely done the ceiling.

It goes like this all week. By Thursday he can't avoid Dolores any longer. They eat lunch together and she pesters him with questions about how he's feeling. She also tells him her father has called the real estate office and is trying to find out what it would take to buy the motel. Of course Gustafson wants to charge five times more than it's worth, and Sanchez is debating whether to wait him out or just make an offer. Dolores is caught up in her enthusiasm for the transaction. She shows Gene a page of numbers on which she has forecast how much money the place could make if they were to raise the rate of all the rooms to twelve dollars; to justify such a charge, the whole place would have to undergo a major remodeling, far beyond the patchwork fixes Gene is doing now. She leaves for her other job, and Gene slinks back to his room, his vision of endless labor at the motel made all the more real.

The following week he's in the office when the phone rings—a rare occurrence. It's Bobby Blaine, back in town for a few more nights. "How'd the swimming go, Gino? You and your girl want to come by and do it again?"

Blinking, Gene realizes Bobby has heard nothing of the debacle a month before. "I didn't tell you this before, Mr. Blaine, because I knew you were trying to ... do something nice for me. And I didn't want to raise a fuss."

"Well, what is it?"

"When you were here last month and invited Dolores to come and swim in the pool at the Riviera—they wouldn't let her."

"Wouldn't let her? What happened?"

Gene tells him.

"Those bastards!" Bobby exclaims. "Those rotten bastards. Listen, Gino, they're going to hear about this from me."

Gene puts his hand over his eyes. He doesn't want a confrontation, he doesn't want a fuss to be made. "No, that's not necessary," he says. "It was weeks ago."

"No, they can't treat a guest of mine that way. The idea! I'm going to make sure you get a full apology. Man, that really steams me!"

"Well, thanks for being... Thanks for standing up for her," Gene says. After he hangs up, he sits slumped on his stool, still covering his eyes.

2

"And that's why I'm proud to declare tonight that I will be the first Jewish candidate for President of the United States!" The audience laughs and applauds, caught up in the absurdity of it, as if this were a real campaign event.

The place is full. There's the usual mixed air of relaxed pleasure—as if they're enjoying themselves more than they expected, given that it's just me on stage—and anxious anticipation. I don't have the slightest idea whether the other guys will show up. If they don't, God knows how the crowd will react—and if anybody will come tomorrow night.

"Now as the first Jewish presidential candidate," I go on, and the repetition bring titters—"I'm going to have an open campaign. It will be open everyone regardless of race, color or creed. Just as long as she's female.

"That's right, there are plenty of places in my campaign for women... and in order to accommodate them all, we're adding an extra car to the campaign train. And that's not the only thing I'm going to do to increase housing in this country. Many young couples today, as you know, have their first intimate moments in the back seat of daddy's car. Well, in my administration, the slogan 'A car in every garage' will mean something, and if the cars are in the garage, or in the drive-in, or in a lover's lane, that's your business and not the business of government! That's right, ladies and gentlemen, we're going to get those young people necking down on the park bench out of the park and into their very own American-made automobiles. Now if that doesn't get me the teenage vote, I don't know what will.

"What's that? There is no teenage vote? Well, that's the first thing I'll do in office—lower the voting age to eighteen. Did I say eighteen? Sixteen! Will someone give me fifteen? Going once, going twice—fifteen, thank you very much.

"You don't want the government telling you what to do, do you? In my administration, the government's going to tell you what's bad for you, and then stand back and let you do the dirty work. Smoking? Go right ahead. And in connection with that, I'm announcing that under my administration the U.S. government will take over all the hospitals, with the profits going to subsidize the national debt. You want to smoke, fine—there's a government hospital bed just waiting for you. And let me say there is no truth to the rumor that I own stock in all the leading hospital supply companies. Not true at all. All that is being held in trust by my wife. So go right ahead and smoke, there's nothing in it for me.

"Let's talk now about civil rights. I'm not a radical by any means. Some people say that if you get drafted and you fight and die for this country, you have every legal right no matter what race you are. I wouldn't go that far. First of all, there's no war now, and frankly, we

Jews are tired of waiting to be killed in a war just so we can have our civil rights. No, my position is, if you *watch television* in this country, you're entitled to equal rights. That's right, all you have to do is watch television. And you know, just about everybody can afford a television in this country, no matter how poor they are—and my administration will make sure that if you can't afford a television, one will be appointed for you in a court of law. Where was I?" I ask, stealing Feldman's trademark line. By now the audience hardly knows where one joke starts and the next begins; by the time they've figured out one, they're already too late, so they just keep chuckling and laughing, and the momentum of the whole bit is building without their noticing.

"God knows watching television is tough enough. If I see one more 'Special' I don't know what I'll do. Last week they had a Frank Sinatra special, a Jerry Lewis special, a Bob Hope special, a Judy Garland special, a nature special, a special on Broadway theater, a special on the United Nations, a special on corned beef and a special on men's suits, buy a jacket and get two pairs of pants. If you don't like one pair you bring them back and you still have—"

The audience begins screaming with laughter and applauding, it's too soon in the bit but I think I know what's happening. I turn to one side and the other, blinded by the spotlight, but then another spotlight comes on and swings over to stage left. And here come Dean and Sammy in their shorts, with their trousers slung over their arms.

Dean seizes the microphone and declares, "I want to return these pants!"

"Why?" I ask, once the laughter has died down a little. "What's wrong with 'em?"

"Well, they're too big!" And he tosses them to Sammy, who puts them on—they're Dean's pants, and of course they're about two feet too long.

"I think I want to return them too!" Sammy exclaims.

"That special was last week, fellas," I say. "This week's special is on turkeys."

"Who you callin' a turkey?" Dean asks drunkenly.

"I'm glad you're here," I say to Sammy, who's stumbling around in the too-long trousers. "I'm glad you're here!" I shout again, over laughter. "I want you to be my running mate."

"You want me to run? Man, I can't hardly walk!" Sammy says.

"Can't see, either," Dean mutters.

"No, I want you to be my running mate in the presidential race. I'm running for president and I want you to be my vice president."

"I don't want anything to do with vice!" Sammy says.

"I think I saw them backstage getting a payoff," Dean says. This gets a small laugh, and then Dean gives a huge "worried" take and gets a big laugh. He looks off to the wings. "Just kidding, fellas," he says, taking a second microphone that's being lifted onto the stage from below as smoothly and casually as a second baseman taking a throw from the shortstop. He's facing the wings now. "I mean your donation to the orphan and widow's fund. That's right. Everything's on the up-and-up here." He drunkenly leans back to me. "Where are we?"

"We're at the Riviera."

"I thought this was the Sands! Officer, I was nowhere near the Riviera tonight..."

"What's this about you running for president?" asks Sammy.

"That's it, I'm gonna be the first Jewish presidential candidate," I say, but like a straight line, not a laugh line, supposing he has something on his mind.

"You can top that," urges Dean.

"Yeah, I'm—" Sammy turns to him. "Why am I wearing your pants?!"

Dean looks down, sees he's still wearing nothing but his shorts, and convulses in laughter. This gets the crowd going too, because they can see he genuinely forgot he was standing there half-dressed. "Hey, I may be standing here in my shorts, but you're wearing another guy's pants," he says.

Sammy takes them off and throws them at him and grabs *his* pants—what we suppose are his pants—from Dean. But when he puts them on, they're even longer than the others. "What happened to my pants??" he screams in mock anguish. "Where are my pants?"

Dean extricates himself from the trousers that have wrapped themselves around his head, and points downward. "There," he says vaguely, and when Sammy bends down to look, he sits on him to put his pants on. "What was that you were saying about lowering the voting age?" he asks me, and though this is a complete non-sequitur, it gets a huge laugh. It has nothing to do with *anything*—the physical situation, or the people on stage, or the people in the audience—except the word *lower*. They're mostly laughing at the contrast between the words spoken, which are at least half serious, and the sight of a grown man sitting on another man to put his pants on.

Finally he lets Sammy up, and Sammy takes a comical swing at him. "See, that's why we need equal rights in this country," I venture. "No man should be another man's hassock." That doesn't get much of a laugh because by the time the audience figures out what a hassock is, the timing is off.

"If you'll get me a hassock, I'll vote for you. Say, what is a hassock anyway?"

Sammy is trying to fight with Dean, but he's still hampered by the too-long trousers and Dean easily avoids him. The audience is laughing throughout.

"That's what he's trying to give you," I say. "He's gonna give you a hassock right in the kisser."

"What... what does your campaign offer the Italian vote?" he leers, arching his eyebrows at the ladies.

"A special every week on mozzarella."

"Mozzarella?" Dean mugs, as if he's never heard the word in his life. "Mozzarella? Give me a special on martinis and it's a deal. Hey, where you goin'?"

Sammy has finally pulled the trouser legs up such that his feet are visible, but he's hanging onto the fabric with both hands. He is heading for the wings with a comical gait. "I'm going to find something decent to wear!" he screams, off mike.

"They got a scissors back there, I think," Dean says mildly. "Well, there goes your running mate. Now what are you gonna do?"

"I don't know, maybe I should find somebody who really needs the job. You know any unemployed Jewish comedians?"

Dean gives a comic take to the audience, then a double-take at me. Everyone's laughing at the implication that I've mentioned Jerry Lewis, not by name, of course. Since they broke up their act a few years ago, the joke is that you can't mention Jerry's name in front of Dean. He gets a lot of mileage out of it. Of course, the fact is, you really *can't* mention Jerry to Dean. He'll completely ignore you.

"I know one who might be unemployed very soon," Dean finally says, looking at me. "Hey, is the vice squad still back there?"

"Why call the vice squad on me? You're the one who was running around without any pants on."

"Well at least they were my own pants."

Is this going anywhere? Who cares? Not me, not the audience, not even Dean—who knows I'll be able to get him off the stage gracefully when he's decided he's had enough—and certainly not the management. I know Ed Torres is out there someplace, grinning. Dean and Sammy—not me—have just made his week.

Back in my dressing room after the show, I find Dean and Sammy relaxing. To my surprise, Frank is there too, pacing, in the middle of a story. But he cuts it off when I walk in.

"How am I supposed to know it was this dame's car—hey, Bobby!" He seizes my hand so aggressively that I almost draw back. What is this hand-shaking thing—Frank's never been a glad-hander before, not like this. Then I realize he's been campaigning with Kennedy; he's picked up the candidate's handshake. He must shake everybody's hands now.

"Hey, Frank. Nice you see you." I turn to Dean and Sammy, slumped on the couches smoking cigarettes. "Hey, you guys. Thanks a million for that, that was terrific. Did you see the act?" I ask Frank.

"Yeah, that was tremendous, Bobby, tremendous. You know I've hardly had the chance to actually see you solo. The bit with the beatnik butcher! Hilarious. And you're running as the first Jewish president. That's good. You don't go too far. I like that."

"What about these guys? It was like a barrel of monkeys out there."

"One monkey and one golfer," Dean says. "Hey, what did the monkey say to the golfer?"

"'Where's my pants?'" Frank answers. Sammy waves him off: the heck with you.

"Seriously, you guys, that was unbelievable. That crowd was pissing in their pants. I really appreciate it."

"Don't mention it, daddy-o," Sammy says. "Come by my show sometime."

"Hey Sammy," I say, launching into something I've been dreading. "When I was in New York a couple weeks ago, I met up with David Schlain. You remember him. The producer."

"Oh yeah, sure," Sammy says, raising his head to look at me for the first time—a signal of polite interest.

"He's got an idea for a show and he wants you to be in it."

"A Broadway show? Man, you know, somebody asked me to be in one of those once. I thought, great, I'm really a success now. Then I found out I had to make at least a one year commitment. A whole year doing the same thing? And you can't get any farther from town than Atlantic City? No thanks. Guess what it turned out to be—'West Side Story.'"

"They wanted you for 'West Side Story?'" Frank asks, unbelieving. "What, you were gonna pass for Puerto Rican?

"Yeah, man, I was gonna do the Anita character in drag. 'A boy like dat! will keel your brozzer!'" he sings. "'Forget dat boy! and find anozzer!'"

"Stick to your own kind," Dean says ironically.

"Anyway, a year commitment, there's no way," Sammy finishes.

"Wait til you hear the idea," I say. "A Jewish tap dancer and a Negro tap dancer start out as competitors, but then they team up, and they fight for justice and the American way."

Sammy sputters at this ridiculous idea. "Then what happens?" he laughs.

"Well, it's a little unclear, but there is a tap-dancing battle between a dozen Negro girls and a dozen Jewish girls."

Sammy screams with laughter, Frank joining in. They are convulsed. I chuckle too; it's hard to resist, when two men in the room are laughing like maniacs.

Dean, of course, does resist. He merely smiles through his cigarette smoke.

"A Jewish tap dancer and a Negro tap dancer," Sammy chokes. "Hey, man, I can play both parts!" That kicks them off on another laughing jag.

"All right, all right," I say. "I may as well get it over with. You want to hear the title?"

"Oh, God, yes, the title, Bobby, tell us the title," Frank gasps.

"Fry and Fish."

General hilarity. Even Dean laughs out loud.

Sammy is doubled over like a man who's been shot in the stomach. He points at me. "He's Fish," he giggles, and that really finishes them. Christ, I think. If it's that fucking funny maybe I can work it into my act.

The heck with this. I take a deep breath and say, "Hey, whatta you guys think, we can have a round of golf tomorrow and then come back here for a swim."

"Hey, yeah!" Frank says.

Dean, a little irritated: "I already got a seven-thirty tee time."

"Seven thirty!" Frank replies. "In the *morning?*"

"Whatever," I say, "then we can come back here for a swim."

"Bobby, that's great of you," Sammy says, wiping his eyes. "But I'll have to take a rain check."

"Ah, come on, Sam!" Frank says.

Dean speaks up. "He's being nice, Frank. They won't let him. Maybe golf, but no way they'll let him swim here."

"What are you saying?" Frank says. "Of course he can swim."

Sammy shrugs. "Why do you think I got a pool at home?"

A knock on the door and Ed Torres walks in. "Bobby! What a show! Frank! Was he great? These guys were great!"

"Ed, you got a good one here with Bobby," Frank says. "You keep putting him to work."

"You bet I will," Ed says, completely insincerely.

"Hey Ed," I say. "I was thinking of inviting these guys over tomorrow afternoon."

"Sure, absolutely. Whatever you need, just tell me."

"I was thinking of a setup poolside—you don't have to fence it off. We'll just be like regular patrons."

"Oh, you're not regular patrons! You get VIP treatment."

"No need, no need—you just treat us like everybody. We'll just join in—swim in the pool and everything. Okay?"

"Sure—" Ed says, and then realizes what I'm implying. Despite himself, he looks at Sammy. "Swimming, you say. Sure. I just run the entertainment, you know... Ted Haggin is the hotel guy...."

With Frank in the room, Ed can hardly say Sammy can't come for a swim. I glance over at the guys and they're looking at Ed with new, predatory interest, the way a gang of street corner toughs might regard a lost tourist.

"Ed, that's okay," I say, knowing Frank will press the point now that he's started.

"It's okay with me if it's okay with you, Ed," Frank says, poker-faced.

"Yeah, well..." Ed mumbles.

"Ed, I know you always take great care of me," I say. "The only reason I bother to ask is that I was talking to a friend of mine. He was my guest a few weeks ago. And he brought his girl down to the pool for a

266

swim, and they weren't treated very nicely on account of the girl's a Mexican. Very nice girl, might I say—I met her and she's a very well-brought-up young lady. But she wasn't staying here, and neither are Sammy and Frank and Dean, so I just wanted to make sure it was okay with you."

Ed laughs uncomfortably. "Bobby, I'm sorry, but I never heard about what happened to your friend. You say a friend of yours?" He's wondering what kind of friend.

My stomach is turning somersaults, but I press on. "Ed, I understand, they got a policy to keep up. And I wouldn't want to be treated any different, and I know these gents wouldn't either. So if there's a rule against it, I understand."

"What happened to your friend?" asks Frank, ready to be outraged.

"Just what I said—he invited his girl over. She's a local girl, a good girl. They got to the pool and there was a guy there in ten seconds, kicking them out. Or kicking her out."

"Did he *say* he was a friend of yours?"

"Frank, it's the principle of the thing," I point out gently. "It shouldn't matter whether he's a friend of mine."

"Absolutely!" he exclaims, as if I've just made the world's best argument. "Ed, you don't have to tell us now," he says, giving a big false smile. "We'll show up here tomorrow ready to take a dip. No photographers, no nothing, just us. Give us a cabana and a few lounge chairs and we'll make ourselves at home. I know you'll do the right thing."

Torres is pale. "Frank, you know you're always welcome..."

"Wonderful, wonderful. It's 1960, Ed. Ya gotta change with the times, you know?" He turns to me. "Bobby, your pal isn't in town now, is he? Because he's welcome to come along. With his girl."

I blink. I hadn't expected this. It's one thing to put Ed Torres on the spot, but I'm not sure Gene and his girl want to become this involved. "I'm not sure, Frank. I could find out. But thanks, that's very generous."

Torres retreats, and soon Frank and the boys depart. When the room is empty, I sit down in a chair by the mirror. I'm sweating now more than I was when I came offstage.

As it turns out, we never go golfing or swimming the next day. Frank sleeps until ten and takes me along to lunch with a producer. By the time we get out of that, it's nearly three o'clock. It's not until he's shaking my hand to get into a car that's taking him to the airport that he recalls our discussion. All he says is, "Hey, we were going to come over to your hotel this afternoon. Give me a rain check on that, Bobby?"

So nothing came of it. It was all just a pissing contest with Ed Torres, Frank throwing his weight around under cover of outrage on behalf of colored people.

I say goodbye to Frank with a smile, thinking, It's a good thing I never called Gino up to go swimming again with his girl.

3

"You're still working on this room?"

Gene looks up from his knees. He's on the floor of number 7, painting the baseboards. Dolores comes into the room. "When did you start? More than a week ago. All you had to do was paint."

"Yeah" is all he says. In the last ten days, revulsion at doing the maintenance work has taken root in him, sapping his strength and will. It's a hollow feeling curled just above his stomach, occasionally expanding to enervate his lungs, his arms and legs, his heart. Trying to work means prodding this feeling continuously. But he has to work, no matter at what pace, while Dolores is cleaning rooms. Then when she leaves, he falls on his bed in a stupor. Sleeping or staring at the ceiling in vague terror for the next five hours, he rouses himself to open the motel for the evening.

Lately he's been rereading the parts of *On the Road* and *Dharma Bums* about San Francisco and Berkeley which, as he understands it, is one of San Francisco's neighborhoods. It sounds like a rainy place and a place with a lot of trees and wharves and poets and professors. None of which are present, in any quantity, locally. Nowhere is San Francisco described as hot.

He takes a few half-hearted swipes with his paintbrush, then sighs and sits back on his heels, regarding the painted area. "Tsk," Dolores says. "Come and have lunch."

He and Dolores go into the office. The hollow feeling doesn't stop, but gets worse when he's facing her.

"Is there something wrong with you? You act like you're sick all the time." She feels his forehead. "If you're sick, just stop working for a few days until it goes away."

"It doesn't go away," he moans before he can stop himself.

She looks at him sharply.

"I mean, it's not that I'm sick," he amends. "Maybe I'm sort of tired of the heat."

"Better get used to it, it's like this til at least October. One year it was ninety on Thanksgiving." She puts the sandwich on the table before him—ham and American cheese, lettuce and tomato, plenty of mayonnaise. "I know it's hot in those rooms. Why don't you get a fan, and start early? Start as soon as it gets light, and be done by ten or so. Then you can do other things in the day that aren't as stinky. I'd feel sick if I were in there with that smell."

He just nods, looking at the sandwich. She leans forward over the table and takes his hand. "Is it something about me? Is it something I said?"

He looks up. "No, of course not. You're fine. You're wonderful." But as he says that, the hollow feeling makes the words echo in his chest.

"You've been like this since you came over for Sunday dinner. But it can't be that—nobody else got sick."

The dinner was fine, he says. But then he can't think of anything else to say. There's only one safe topic, that of arranging a date together. As cheerfully as possible, he proposes they go to another movie. Her acceptance seems to dampen his empty feeling. If it's just a matter of making her happy, he thinks to himself, maybe I should concentrate on that and not pay so much attention to what I feel.

"I've been thinking," he says. "Have you ever thought about us being together... for a long time?"

She looks up at him, wiping her mouth with a napkin.

"Maybe," he says, "if your family buys the motel, we could get married and live here and run it together. We'll get somebody else to clean the rooms, you'd just be in charge of all the finances. We could get some more furniture in here..."

"Slow down," she says. "Go back to the first part. You want to get married?"

He gives her his most hopeful face. "Isn't that where all this is going?"

"Oh, Gene. I thought so, yes, but I wasn't sure if you were seeing it that way at all. We weren't really sure—I mean, I wasn't really sure if you were ready to settle down yet."

He shrugs. "We stay here for a few years... it's not forever. We could go anyplace. Say, San Francisco. The important thing," he says, reaching now for her hand, and thinking to himself, this is going pretty well, "is being together."

Before she can say anything, they hear a truck pulling into the driveway and honking. Gene jumps up. Walking into the office, he sees it's the brown and white Sanchez pickup, with Dolores' father and brothers climbing out.

"Hello Gene!" says the elder Sanchez, grinning. "I have come to see the motel."

Gene shakes their hands. "I hear you're thinking of buying it."

"We were just having lunch," Dolores says.

"Oh, finish, finish. Just give us the keys, we'll look around."

Gene gets the passkey and comes back around the counter. "I'll show you around," Gene says.

"No, no, finish lunch," Sanchez says, holding up a hand so insistently that Gene has to stop in his tracks. "Dolores makes a lunch for you every day, you must eat it, so you'll be strong for working."

"Right." He watches the three men go down the walkway.

4

Gene meets Dolores downtown a few days later for their movie date. Since her family inspected the motel and went away without saying anything definite, Gene's malaise has continued. He tries to act more chipper around Dolores, though.

They see a western. He tries kissing her a few times, but she seems reserved, unresponsive. They haven't truly kissed in almost two weeks.

Afterward they walk down Fremont St. together. "In a week I'll be 21," he says. "Then I can take you for a drink after a movie. Hey, I never asked you, how old are you?"

"I'm already 21," she says. Despite the comedy of the movie, she seems a little drained. They stroll slowly through the heat, dodging people in the crowd. "I'll be 22 in December. Take me for a soda." They spot a soda fountain and go in; it's crowded, but there's room at the counter. He sees her in the mirror and thinks how pretty she is; he rarely has the courage these days to look her in the eye.

"Have you thought any more about what you were talking about the other day?" she asks, her brows furrowed.

"Sure, what do you think?" he says.

She shakes her head, staring distractedly off to the side. "What I want to know is what you think. We got interrupted before. I want you to sort of start over and tell it to me again. Because there's something strange going on. I want you to tell me how you really feel."

He takes a gulp of his milk shake. "It seems like events are happening to push us together," he says. "Your family wants to buy the motel. At the same time you're getting crowded at home. It just seems like the obvious solution is for us to live at the motel together and run it. So, to get married."

She looks at him dubiously. "That's about the least romantic proposal I've ever heard of. 'It seems like things are happening' ... 'It seems like the obvious solution'... I don't know what you're talking about."

"Look, we enjoy being together, right? This is a way for us to be together."

"But you're going about it all wrong," she frets. "You're talking about what my family wants, what's happening with the motel, me getting crowded at home. What do you want, what do you feel? This isn't some kind of business deal or job we're talking about. We're talking about getting married."

"I know... But I thought you'd see it that way too. You're the one who's so practical about everything."

"There's a difference." She rests her forehead on the palm of her hand. Looking at the table, she says, "You have to love me. Never mind what else is happening. That's not the point."

"All you talk about is becoming an accountant. That's all I mean by practical."

"I'm doing that because I can do it on my own. It's something I can do instead of cleaning hotel rooms like every other Mexican girl in town. And I'm going to do it, whether or not my family buys the motel, whether or not you stay with me. I'm going to stay here and accomplish it."

They're silent for a while. Then he says, "How come you're so sure about that? Where'd you get that idea?"

"Why shouldn't I be an accountant?" she asks, instantly defensive.

"No, no, that's not what I mean," he says. "I mean, how did you make that decision?"

"I've always been good at math," she shrugs. "They had an AP calculus class at my high school, and I aced it. That's the job for somebody who's great at math."

"Good, but..." he says. "What made you *able* to decide what you wanted to be? I mean, I'm not as good in math, but I could have decided I wanted to be an architect or a lawyer or something."

"Or something."

"I'm saying, I *could* have decided to be something, but it never occurred to me. I didn't know I had to decide already. You've got this idea, like a vision in your mind. Even though you have to go to school and it'll take years, you've got it all planned out. It's like you're an adult already. But I don't have the slightest idea. This whole thing about being a plumber is a joke—I mean, no offense to your father, but I don't want to be a plumber."

"Why not, it's the only thing you're good at."

"Well, I just can't see it. But I can't see anything—that's the problem. You see accounting. I see..."

"What?" she asks, leaning forward, suddenly intent.

"To tell you the truth..." He makes stabs in his milkshake with his straw. "All I see is me driving across the country. Like in *On the Road.*"

She tries to keep her face neutral. "That's not what you said before," she observes.

He sucks through the straw and swallows. "That doesn't mean I can't stay here for a while."

"'For a while,'" she echoes, shaking her head. She picks up her purse and stands up. "Sure, as long as you can drive across the country!"

"Dolores—"

"No. I'll tell my father you're not that interested in staying. Come on, let's go."

"No, wait," Gene says with alarm. He throws a few dollars on the counter and follows her out.

"I did plan to stay," he says, dogging her steps. "Before I knew your father was interested, I planned to ask the new owners to hire me as the manager so I could stay here—til the end of the summer anyway. That's all the work that needed to be done. I didn't know your family was interested in buying it but I planned to stay to finish the work."

"Work? You should hear my father talking about it, all his plans to remodel the place. They want to put in a swimming pool. You'd have to work twice as hard as before," she says, adding, "and ten times as hard as you are now."

He shrugs helplessly, but she's not looking at him trailing her down the sidewalk. "I guess I can do it..."

"You guess?" She shakes her head. "If you'd come up with this idea last month, I might have believed it, but not the way you've been acting lately. I'm sorry, but I don't really believe anything you say now." She dodges a family of six coming down the sidewalk the other way; Gene is forced to stop while they bumble around him. By the time he gets free of them, Dolores has disappeared in the crowd.

5

Sometime early the next evening, the phone rings.

"Hello, is this Mr. Gene Kramer? This is Mrs. Wilson from Preston Properties. You're the caretaker of the Cactus Motel, am I right? I'm calling to inform you that the hotel has been sold. The new owners are prepared to take possession first thing Monday morning."

"Um..." Gene mumbles, trying to clear his head. "Okay. I'll be here. What's the owner's name?"

"A Mr. Eduardo Sanchez.."

"All right."

"Please hand the keys over to him, and he should pay you, and you can be on your way."

"I thought they wanted me to stay on."

"Well, that's between you and them."

"All right, thank you."

"Thank you, Mr. Kramer. Goodbye."

Chapter 18

A few days before the convention, Frank hosts a private dinner for JFK and, yes, his mother, at Frank's Palm Springs mansion. I get a call the day before the event from Hank. As Peter indicated, I am to accompany a young lady, picking her up at a hotel in Palm Springs and escorting her to the dinner. What happens to her after the dinner is not my responsibility.

I drive out to Palm Springs, grinding out three and a half hours of congested freeway driving, and pull into the driveway of the Willows Hotel. My date emerges, a Miss Ciccetti, a leggy lass with a dark mane swept up into a complicated formal hair-do.

The first thing she says after hello is "So, have you met the Senator?"

"Just briefly, this winter, at the Sands," I say. "Didn't spend any time talking to him."

"I always try to find out something about a fellow before I meet him," she confides.

"I hear he enjoys sailing," I offer.

"Oh, that's nice. Does he have a boat?"

"I guess he does."

"That must be nice. And he's from Massachusetts."

"Yes, he is. So he's got a bay to sail that thing. Look, not that I expect anything, but we are supposed to be dinner companions. Do you even remember what my name is?"

"Of course I do. Bobby Bane."

"It's *Blaine* with an *L!* Maybe you should just stick to Bobby."

We get to Frank's gate and are greeted by a foursome of guards—some Frank's, some the government's. Must be that Secret Service contingent Frank mentioned. They check us off three different lists. Up at the house, where a valet takes the car away, there are more guards, the same spook-thug mix.

Inside the house—part of a compound made up of several low buildings, plus an Olympic-sized pool and the new helipad—we're ushered out onto a patio where a number of guests are standing with drinks. A bartender makes our drinks, and Miss Ciccetti immediately takes off to speak to a statuesque blond. I look around for her date and discover Sammy smoking at a patio table, inscrutable behind shades. "Hey, Sammy, how's it going?"

He looks up, and at first I think he doesn't even recognize me. His mouth is set in a grimace; his sunglasses reflect the bright golden sky to the west. Finally he says in a subdued voice, "Hi, Bobby. Glad to see you. Sit down."

"What's up, kid? You okay?"

Before he can answer, Miss Ciccetti is back with the blond in tow. "Sammy darling," the blond says, "I'd like you to meet Miss Carla Ciccetti." She speaks with a cute accent and I realize it's May Britt, Sammy's fiancé. Sammy stands and introduces me to May.

"I haven't yet congratulated you on your engagement," I say. "You're getting a great guy here. He's crazy about you, you know." This evokes a choking sound from Sammy. "Hey, you all right, Sammy?"

"Yeah, man." He kisses May on the cheek and tells her, "I'll see you at dinner, *cheri.*"

She plants a big kiss on his cheek and whispers—loudly enough for us all to hear—"*Je t'aime.*" The two girls go off. In the house I can see more guests arriving.

Sammy and I sit down again. "What's the matter with you?" I ask quietly.

"I just talked to Frank," he says. "You know May and I were planning to get married in Sweden at the end of the month, right after the convention. Now... Frank says we can't. We have to wait."

"What? What the hell for?"

"He says it wouldn't be good for Kennedy," Sammy whispers. "It would... 'force the racial issue.' And Kennedy's got enough problems appealing to the southern vote, being a Catholic."

"My God, Sammy, that's terrible!"

"Frank wants us to wait until after the election. Then he'll give us his blessing."

"For crying out loud! But that's just... Does May know?"

"No, man," he hisses. "I'm not going to tell her now."

"What are you gonna do?"

"I don't know. I have to think, but..." he trails off.

There's a commotion inside the house, and a couple of Secret Service guys come out onto the patio.

I stand up, looking toward the house, then reach down and squeeze Sammy's shoulder. "Sammy, don't you worry. There's got to be a way."

He doesn't answer. People start applauding, Frank and Peter step onto the patio, and between them out steps Kennedy. They stand together and smile and wave, as if they're all three running for something. Then Frank begins applauding JFK and Peter follows suit. Then Kennedy's mother emerges from the house, accompanied by Judy Garland and Shirley MacLaine.

Quite the affair, all right. Kennedy's brought along a few staffers, and I wind up chatting before dinner with a Harvard type whose entire career has been spent working for Jack; he even knew him in the Navy. And his father worked for JFK's father. He invariably refers to JFK as "the senator." All he can talk about is the campaign, despite my best efforts.

"How's Mrs. Kennedy?" I ask. "She doing well?"

"She's a wonderful campaigner. I think she really impresses the female voters, and quite a few men, as well."

"I meant the fact that she's expecting. I heard she's staying home during the convention under doctor's orders."

"That shouldn't hurt us. We've won every primary we've entered. With 90 percent of the delegates needed for nomination, we're pretty confident of a first ballot nomination."

"Well... he's certainly more colorful than Stevenson."

"The senator was a war hero. He saved his men's lives."

"Yeah," I nod. I don't say that he also managed to get his boat rammed by a Japanese ship first. "You know, there's a film script going around about that. They say Frank is a pick to play the senator. Can you see it?"

"I haven't seen it. But Mr. Sinatra's done a lot for the campaign. He's a great supporter."

Do I detect a certain dry tone in that remark—as if the guy isn't that keen on Frank doing a lot for the campaign? "Nixon was in the Navy too, though, wasn't he?"

"He commanded a desk," the aide says dismissively. "We can't wait to take him on. You're in television, Mr. Blaine; tell me what you think about this. We're thinking of staging a presidential debate on television, a month before the election. Both candidates, side by side, offering their views. It'll be the greatest political event since the Lincoln-Douglas debates."

"Very interesting. Let me know if you need an M.C."

I was kidding, but the guy isn't laughing. "That's a possibility," he says evenly. "We're still working out the format."

"No, I was joking," I say. "I don't know anything about holding a political debate. All I could do is introduce them, you know, maybe like a prize fight. *In this corner...*"

"Err, we'd probably want to make it more dignified than that," he says.

"Oh," I say. I'm amazed at this guy, I cannot get through to him. Those two FBI agents were balls of fire compared to him. "Well, if you want to capture the real Lincoln-Douglas feel, just make sure Nixon holds Kennedy's hat while Kennedy talks."

He purses his lips, looking dismayed. "That's all anybody remembers about that."

Eventually we get to dinner. Perhaps to balance Kennedy's three aides, Frank has invited three "aides" as well. There's Hank, at his right hand as usual; Jimmy Van Heusen, a songwriter and general pal; and Ed, the driver-bodyguard. Between them they maybe have one high school diploma, so I'm thinking JFK's men better know plenty about baseball, otherwise that end of the table is going to be pretty quiet.

But instead of sports, the aides spend the dinner giving lessons in American politics to May Britt. May's not as dumb as she looks, but she's leading them on, letting them fall all over each other explaining the presidential nominating system. Then Pat Shriver speaks up.

"Frank," she says, "I hear you're going to repeat your performance of the national anthem. Frank sang it at the '56 convention," she adds, for May's benefit.

"Not just me," Frank says, "but Judy here, Sam, Peter, Shirley — the whole bunch of us."

"It's wonderful to have so many *industry people* involved," she gushes, throwing out the term so we know she knows it.

"The Republicans are holding their convention in Chicago," I offer. "I hear they're having the anthem sung by a bunch of dead guys who voted in the last election."

"I thought those dead guys were Democrats," Kennedy quips.

"They vote for whoever is more of a stiff," Sammy says. He seems to have recovered some of his *savoir faire*. "They loved Stevenson."

"I may have to factor that into my choice for Vice President," Kennedy says.

"I thought we might see Marilyn Monroe here tonight," Pat says. "Jack, you've promised you'll introduce me one of these days."

I think Kennedy's going to choke on a piece of pasta. "I believe she's making a picture," he gets out. "It may seem like they closed down Hollywood for our sake, but apparently there's a few people still working."

"That's the western with Gable and Monty," Peter says. "They're shooting out in Nevada somewhere." He makes a vague motion with his head in the approximate direction of Nevada.

"Marilyn on a horse?" Sammy asks. "That I'd love to see."

"I hear Bobby wanted to be in it so bad he volunteered to be one of the horses," Frank says.

Jimmy and Hank and Ed collapse in laughter. Hank is sitting right across the table from me; he has just shoveled some pasta into his mouth, but that doesn't stop him from seizing the moment. His fork still in midair, he points it at me and exclaims, "But the horses' union said no!"

I catch JFK's mother looking at Hank in shock. Frank catches her reaction too, and clears his throat. Ed and Hank stop snickering, just like that, and Hank swallows and gently lowers his fork to where it belongs.

"I was hoping," Frank says, in his most elevated tone, "that this dinner would be just the first in a long collaboration between the best that Hollywood has to offer, and the Democratic nominee for president. Now I've asked Jimmy here to write a campaign song for Jack. And I'm going to record it, and we'll put it on every jukebox in the country—right, Jimmy?"

"You bet, Frank, "Jimmy says, turning as red as a schoolboy caught chewing gum.

"You take care of that for me, Hank."

"Yes, Frank."

Frank turns to the candidate. "I've got an army, too," he cracks. "They do what I tell 'em. But you're the commander-in-chief."

"Glad I can call on you, Frank," Kennedy says archly.

After the dinner, I find myself back with the speechwriters, standing in a hallway while the main part of the party has coffee out on the patio. One of the aides is from the Philadelphia area and we're comparing notes when Hank comes up to me.

"That dame who came with you," he says. "She won't be needing a ride back. One of the boys will take her back later."

The aide doesn't even raise an eyebrow, as if he's seen it a million times.

Chapter 19

1

"It was a great event, a great event. You shoulda been there."

"So you've said."

"Frank M.C.'d the event, but you want to know the truth? I think he should leave the M.C. work to you. Don't tell him I said that, though."

"Okay, Hank. That's the third time you said it and the third time you asked me not to tell Frank you said it. So okay, I won't tell him."

"Okay," Hank says, in a voice that's finally satisfied. I've been on the phone with him for five minutes and he's about to get to the point. "So tonight. A limo will pick you up there at the Hilton at quarter to four. You'll go to the Ambassador Hotel and pick up a Miss Rolens. Then the car will take you to Puccini, and you'll be having the early dinner with Frank and some friends. The convention starts at five," he adds by way of explanation.

"Who else is going to be there?" I ask, knowing he won't tell me.

"You'll know him when you see him."

"Anything else? Do I need a secret password? Should I wear a red rose?"

"Ha, listen to this guy. You definitely shoulda been there last night."

Yes, I should have been at the big pre-convention Democratic Party fundraiser, held downstairs at my own hotel no less, with all the candidates and Frank, Peter and Judy sitting right up on the dais.

I thought M.C.-ing is what Frank brought me here for, if anything. But after I checked in I managed to get through to Frank's suite and found that he was going to do it. Somehow I didn't even get a ticket. So I sat in my room watching "Gunsmoke" and trying to keep from getting drunk just in case I did get a call.

Finally, after midnight, I heard people in the hallway, and I looked out and saw a few guys in tuxes with their dates, or hookers, definitely not their wives. Figuring the event was finally over, I took off my tux and went to bed, only to be awakened by Hank's call at 8:00 a.m.

I spend the day mostly in the hotel room, doing a little work on some material for those Summit record albums, the ones where I'm going to "introduce" Frank and Peter and Sammy and Dean. I write five minutes of material for each, which is probably four minutes too much. They can cut. They will cut.

By 3:45 I'm in a limo, on my way to pick up another dame for Kennedy. I wonder what happened with Miss Ciccetti from a couple nights ago. No, I *know* what happened; but I wonder just how these assignations take place—after Hank tells me I can leave, *sans* dame, who has already found herself deep in flirtatious conversation with the candidate. At some point most of the people in the room fade away, and he asks her to join him for a little more private conversation in his room.

Fine. But what happens after? Does she spend the whole night? At what point does she get up and put her clothes back on—when Kennedy falls into blissful senatorial slumber? And then she emerges from the room—is an aide there, holding her wrap out, ready to escort her to a waiting car? Or does she stumble down a dark hallway looking for somebody, maybe blundering into the poker game Frank and his buddies are holding in a back room? I can see Frank, half drunk, squinting at her through the thick smoke, then becoming solicitous, saying, "Hello, baby, wasn't Ed out there? We've got a car to take you back. Would you like a drink? No? You're my guest, *mi casa es su casa*, so anything you want..."

At that point one of the guys says, "Come on, Frank, we're playing cards here," and Frank turns on the guy and says, "Can't you see I'm talking to a lady here?" Then turning back to her: "We'll have a car for you in just a minute, sweetheart. Hey Hank, go see where Ed is. Tell him to take the Lincoln. You're at the Willows, is that right? Okay, honey, you just go with Ed, here he is, hey Ed, take this lady to the Willows, if you please. And pick up some more Scotch there while you're at it, put it on my tab. And—anybody else?—some gin."

And in the morning the candidate wakes up fit as a fiddle, ready for another day. Frank's caught maybe ninety minutes of sleep, says, "How about some golf?" And they get in Frank's own cart, followed by two carts carrying all their bodyguards, and buzz down to the first tee. Frank's heavy clears the tee of whoever happens to be there as he and Kennedy make a few off-color jokes about last night's event and the girl whose name neither one can remember, and Kennedy confides an anatomical detail that makes Frank break up in laughter. Then Frank says, "You first, Senator, you can lead our modest foursome" or some unctuous bullshit like that, and Kennedy grimaces as he tees off, on account of that bad back of his, the drive not even going a hundred fifty yards...

"We're here, Mr. Blaine," says the driver of the limo. The doorman is already standing there holding the door open. I give myself a little shake and go into the lobby. I ask for this Miss Rolens and say I'll be in the bar.

"Aren't you Mr. Blaine? I believe she's already there, waiting for you."

I walk into the bar but the only people sitting at it are two men. "What'll it be?" the bartender asks.

"I'm supposed to meet a lady here—a Miss Rolens."

He nods toward the back of the place. I catch sight of a bare shoulder and a scrap of yellow dress in one of the booths, she's sitting with her back toward me. "Gin and tonic," I say, "and this'll be for hers too," putting a ten on the bar and turning to walk back there.

A few steps brings me to the booth; the woman is leaning forward on the table, eyes cast down at her drink. "Miss Rolens?" I say.

She looks up, and I see. It's Lucy. Not a look-alike this time, or a hallucination, not one of the thousands of women I've seen out of the corner of my eye for the last twelve years thinking I've spotted her, but the real thing.

"Lucy?" I say slowly.

She looks up with a tight smile, more embarrassed than surprised. "Hello, Bobby," she says. "They told me you were coming."

"You're not... you're not the lady I'm supposed to meet." I say it more as a statement, daring to be proved wrong.

"Yes, I am," she says.

"Your name is Rolens?"

"Wrolinsky, actually. Rolens is my... the name I use sometimes. Sit down, all right?"

I ease myself into the black vinyl seat across from her.

"Wrolinsky being the name of my ex-husband. We were divorced six years ago." She takes a sip of her drink. "Well, why don't you say something?"

I'm stunned. The most I can get out is, "Whatcha been doing lately?"

"Oh... You mean for the last ten years or so?"

"Twelve."

"Let's see. After Wrolinsky I took up with a composer—nearly got married to him, but he turned out to be queer; he was kind enough to tell me the week before the wedding. Then I met a fellow who had just gotten elected to Congress... And I started living in Washington. Stop looking at me like that, will you?"

The bartender brings my drink, I toss back half of it, call "Another!" This amuses her.

"You can still put it away, I see."

"Not really," I rasp. "But I'm in a little bit of shock here. Jesus. Lucy. I can't believe it."

"I'd ask what you've been doing, but you've done quite well enough that I don't have to."

I purse my lips, ignoring this conversational opening. "I was just talking to a pal... a month or two ago... in New York. Feldman... a comic. He told me you'd gotten divorced."

"I don't know a Feldman."

"No." I've been looking off to the side, steeling myself, and I knock back the rest of the first drink and face her directly.

She's looking good. Hair straighter, still a deep, deep brunette. Her face is showing a few of her years but not all of them, no way. She could be twenty-nine, thirty. I feel helpless, stopped up, like all those years' worth of words and confidences and sighs are stored up behind a dam but I can't find a way to let them flow out.

"Lucy," I say.

"Bobby," she says quietly, not unkindly. "Get hold of yourself."

She takes out a cigarette. I light it for her, and she blows smoke off to the side.

"Bobby," she finally says, "Let me tell you something. First of all, I'm glad to see you. I really am. I bear you no ill will. You're a nice guy and I'm sorry to see some girl hasn't grabbed you, because you're a hell of a guy.

"Second of all, when they told me you were going to be the one to pick me up—having no idea we were once involved, of course—I was a little shocked at first, sure. I've thought about you over the years, don't think I haven't. So I thought, well, it's finally time to say hello again.

"But I thought you'd have your head screwed on a little tighter. You're acting like Humphrey Bogart in *Casablanca* when Ingrid Bergman walks into his gin joint."

That makes me chuckle a little. I rub the back of my head, smiling. "Okay, you're right. Enough with the melodrama. I am glad to see you."

"Glad to hear it," she says, in her smooth, smooth way.

The bartender brings my second drink. She shakes her head at him, saying she doesn't want another. "Drink that up and then we ought to go," she says.

The smile vanishes from my face "My god," I say. "I just remembered what I'm picking you up for." I look up at her. "I haven't seen you in twelve years. Now I see you only to..."

She sits, legs crossed, holding her cigarette in the air. "Well, Bobby, go ahead and say it."

"I mean, it's one thing to..." I can't say any more.

She gives a snort of impatience. "Really, Bobby." She picks up her purse and finds a compact and a lipstick and redoes her lips, then shuts it back up in her purse and looks at me. Not a nice look. A flat stare.

I scramble to my feet. "I have to get change," I say, going over to the bar. I rub my face while I wait for the bartender to give me some ones and fives. The dam is still holding; I still can't think. I go back to the booth. "Shall we go?" I ask, trying to make it sound like just an ordinary thing to say.

"Well, all right," she says, now with a condescending smile, as if to say, the sooner I get away from this lunatic the better.

The limo ride should take only ten minutes, but there's a ton of traffic, on account of the convention. I'm happy to have the additional time. Lucy smokes in silence; I force myself not to stare at her. I grope for something to say. "Lucy, I'm sorry I'm so flummoxed. We've got a lot to catch up on. Why don't you meet me for dinner next week?"

She exhales smoke. "Next week I'll be back in Washington."

"You work there?"

"You might say that," she says, deadpan.

I swallow. "Fine, I'll come see you in Washington. Just tell me where you're living."

"An apartment," she says. "It wouldn't do to meet there, though. I'm not sure it's a good idea at all, in fact."

"Look, you're seeing me at my worst. I'm thunderstruck here. You've got to give me a chance to talk to you once I've picked my jaw up off the ground."

She stubs out her cigarette. "Bobby, I don't think so. I'd better be brutally honest with you, because I can tell it's the only way to bring you back to earth.

"I'm not the same person you knew—that's something you've got to get through your head. I've become what is politely known in the newspapers as a socialite. Translated that means a professional Other Woman. I'm kept, basically, by two or three important men. Each thinks he's the only one—or pretends to think so. Tonight you are conducting me to an event being attended by one of those men, who happens to be running for president. We'll sit near each other at dinner and I'll keep him entertained with clever conversation and subtle but smoldering glances. After dinner you and I will go to the Biltmore Hotel, and I will go into a certain suite and you'll go home, and if you behave yourself, I'll very much appreciate it."

After a minute or two she breaks the silence and says, "I have good memories of you and me, Bobby. Don't think that I don't."

We're approaching Puccini, but there's still a long line of taxis and cars and limousines. Either it's the nearness of the end of our time with each other, or her grudging statement, but my capacity to think and speak suddenly comes unplugged.

"Lucy!" I say. "Listen to me. I've changed over the years too—God knows I have. But down deep you're still in my heart. I know it's been a long time, but give me a chance. Don't get out of this car. Don't let's go to this. I'll tell the driver to take us someplace. I've got to talk to you."

She turns to me and says, with perhaps more gentleness than I deserve, "Bobby, it's out of the question. I don't break my appointments." She says *appointments* with so much gravity she might as well be referring to a U.N. treaty. "If you're thinking we can pick up where we left off, your head's still in the clouds. I'll say it one last time— we can't go back to the way we were before." And then, in the one time I hear a slight waver in her voice, a tremor so slight that if I didn't know her voice so well, even after all these years, I would doubt that I really hear it. But I do hear it, a slight waver as she repeats herself: "We can't go back at all."

The car stops in front of the restaurant and the doors open on both sides. I walk around the car and offer her my arm, tipping right and left, and with my ears ringing guide her into Frank's restaurant.

The place is packed with excited Democrats, smoking and shouting and dropping ashes on each other's shoes. The maitre d' runs interference, conducting us to a back room where the private dinner will be held. When the door closes, the sound from the main room vanishes to a faint hum.

Most of the dinner guests are already there—Peter and Pat, Dean and his wife Jeanne, Sammy minus May this time, and Hank. It's supposed to be a small party but there are a few waiters and bus boys buzzing around, as well as Secret Service men. I've barely introduced Lucy—managing to use the name "Rolens"—when Frank and Kennedy come walking in. We all put down our drinks and applaud.

"Now, now, the convention hasn't even started yet," Kennedy protests, laughing.

"We know you're the nominee!" Frank says. "You're going to beat that piker Johnson."

"First things first. How about a drink?" Kennedy says, and everyone laughs on cue.

The senator manages to shake Frank and begins talking with Dean and Jeanne, so Frank comes over to me and my date.

"Lucy, meet Frank Sinatra. Frank, Miss Lucy Rolens," I say, as evenly as I can.

"I believe I've had the pleasure," Frank grins, and I instantly understand that Frank has made it with Lucy already. How else did she get here? He takes her in his arms as if to dance with her, while I stand there with my mouth open. "It had to be you, it had to be you," he sings.

"Frank, man, what have you been drinking?" Sammy exclaims, across the room.

"I believe he's been into the Irish whiskey already," Peter says in a very poor attempt at an Irish accent.

"Ev - 'ry - thing's com - ing up ro - ses," Frank replies, changing tunes if not moods. He's dancing Lucy away from me.

"It's good to see a happy man," Kennedy remarks.

"It's only because his restaurant's full," Dean says. "The IRS told him if he didn't start actually making some money on it, they'd conclude it was just a front."

"Jack Ken - ne - dy is going to the White House," Frank sings, now improvising. "I won't have to wor - ry anymore about the I - R - S."

"That's what he thinks," Kennedy says.

"Don't waste your vocal cords, Frank, we still have the anthem to sing."

"That's right, that's right," Frank says merrily. "What time is that?"

"Twelve minutes after five," Hank answers instantly. "You leave here in forty-five minutes."

"Good God, let's eat," Frank says. "Sit down, everybody. Hank, tell them we're ready. Senator, you know Miss Rolens," he adds, holding out a chair for her.

"I certainly do," Kennedy says, a few breaths behind Frank. He sits down in the place of honor, just across from Lucy. "And there's Bobby Blaine. Hello, Bobby, how are you?"

"Fine, Senator," I say. "Glad to see you made it out of Palm Springs okay. Usually Frank doesn't let his golf partners escape with the shirts on their backs."

"Fortunately I have the Secret Service," Kennedy says. "I had them ready to give their shirts to Frank just in case it was necessary."

"But Jack won," Frank says. "He scored an 89."

"On that course of Frank's?" Dean says. He turns to Frank. "You didn't pull the phantom sand trap joke on him? No wonder he did so well."

"Phantom sand trap, what's that?" Lucy says cheerfully, and she's so good, she really does sound interested.

"Whenever Frank's losing, when he gets to the 16th hole—it's a par 5 and it's hard to see the green through some trees—he tells the guys in his foursome that they ought to hit their drives way to the left, that there's an enormous sand trap in the center of the fairway, just out of sight beneath a rise. So everyone believes him and they hit their balls to the left where there's horrible rough, it's the edge of the course and they're basically hitting their balls into a gully at the edge of the property."

"It's the desert!" Frank says with glee. "It's the biggest sand trap in the world!"

"Oh, you big meany," Lucy says.

"I see Frank as diplomat material," Kennedy deadpans. "If he can lie like that, he'll make a great ambassador."

"To Sicily," Sammy suggests. Jeanne and Lucy think that's hysterical.

"Are you going to be singing with Frank and the rest tonight, Bobby?" Kennedy asks.

"I think I'm on the bench," I say, "just in case somebody sprains an ankle."

"Nonsense, you get up there too. Sing the national anthem with everyone else. You look a little down in the mouth. Do you good to get up there. I want you to know I'm glad to have your support, Bobby."

"Thank you, Senator."

Kennedy finds himself glancing at Lucy, and I see him stifle a chuckle. My support, indeed. He picks up his drink. "To our host," he says, turning to Frank.

"To the next President of the United States," Frank replies.

"Hooray," Lucy says.

I hate her. We all drink.

2

When the dinner ends, Hank calls for the cars to be brought around. Frank and Peter and Sammy are smoking cigars with Kennedy, and they go out together. Just before they leave the room, Frank mutters to me, "Come on Bobby, offer your arm to your lady friend."

Lucy comes up to me. I'll give her credit for this at least: she looks me in the eye. There I see a mixture of fondness and an impenetrable distance and determination. Before either of us say anything, a waiter brings the shawl she had spread over her shoulders, and she turns her back to me as I take it and drape it over her. My hands don't have a chance to rest on her shoulders for even an instant; she takes a small step forward, saying, "Thank you."

We go through the restaurant together and emerge onto the sidewalk. The boys have already climbed into a big black limo, and the rear door is still hanging open. I help Lucy in but then find the car is full.

"Hey boys," I call weakly, trying to make light of the situation. "You're stealing my date."

"Oh—Bobby," Frank calls, "Sorry, but the Secret Service is taking up your place. Ride with Dean, will you?"

"Make sure Pat gets there," Peter adds. She's been kicked out, too—Jack's own sister. The doorman slams the door and the limo pulls away. Then the guy looks at me for a tip.

Hank comes out with Dean and Jeanne and Pat. Tony Curtis, who was sitting in the main part of the restaurant, is behind them. "Gents, can I hitch a ride with you?"

I say, "Take my place, I think I'll call it a night."

"Are you kidding? You're not coming to the convention?"

"Don't be silly, Bobby," Pat says, and Dean chimes in, "Absolutely, you're coming with us. You heard Jack, he wants you singing that national anthem. You're part of his broad-based coalition."

I catch Hank giggling a little at this. I'd like to wipe that smirk off his face, but instead I just go along with everybody and pile into the next limo. Despite myself, I'm grateful just to be able to sing the anthem with the others. Then I'll clear out and get drunk.

We poke through the crazy traffic, and despite myself, along with the others I become anxious about the time. Now I'm worried we won't make it in time to sing with everybody else. But they wouldn't start without... uh, without Dean. Of course he's the only one who's not worried. Sitting back, his right ankle crossed over his left knee, he looks around at the rest of us with a twinkle in his eye. "What's the matter with you guys?" he asks. "You'd think you'd never seen a traffic jam before."

The limo finally stops dead a quarter mile from the Sports Arena, and the driver turns around and tells us we may as well hoof it from here. So out we go, along with the madding crowd, across the street and through the parking lot, past spotlights and giant TV trailers sprouting cables as thick as your leg. Instead of racing ahead, Dean and Tony gallantly stay with the ladies, handing them off to Hank only at the last moment, and I get in on their coattails.

Now we're running through fluorescent-lit corridors where the dim sound of a band playing marches echoes off yellowish tile walls. There are men in red blazers who seem to be ushers or officials of some kind, and Dean is yelling, "Where's the green room? Where does the talent go?" and the redcoats have no idea what he's talking about. Finally Dean demands, "WHERE IS FRANK SINATRA?" and they understand that, they point forward, and we race on.

Finally we find a room with Sammy and Peter, and in addition to our contingent there is Judy Garland, Janet Leigh, Betty Bacall and Shirley MacLaine. There's a great deal of shouting and joking at Peter's expense: "Hey Peter, was 'The Star Spangled Banner' on your citizenship test? Sure you know the words?"

Frank's nowhere around, but presently he appears with Hank and screams out that the band will play a four-bar intro so we have the key.

"Make sure it's not too high, man!" Shirley MacLaine shouts.

"She should worry," mutters Betty Bacall in her deep voice.

It's nearly six o'clock, we're running late and people are getting antsy—there's no bar. Then we get the call and all plunge back out into the endless hallway. It seems to go in a circular route deep in the bowels of the building. Then we're shunted off to the left, blinded by darkness, and people are cursing that they can't see a thing. "Everybody follow Sammy," Dean says from somewhere in the dark.

"Steps up," warns Tony, who's in front of me. The noise of the crowd is getting loud, and now we step out onto a stage fifteen feet above a vast arena floor, with people off to the back and sides rising up to the rafters. I've never worked a house this big in my life. Later I read they had fifty thousand people here on the convention's opening night.

The band crashes to a halt and an announcer asks the crowd to rise for the anthem. Thousands of JFK boaters, LBJ cowboy hats and other candidate-associated headgear are doffed. Seventy-eight of the brightest spotlights in the United States hit us. "I haven't been lit up like this since I flew bombing missions over Germany," Tony cracks.

As the band plays the intro, the dozen of us are still jockeying for position to be near a microphone. I can't get near a mic, but I do manage to get in the front row. Frank, Sammy and Dean are on the center mic, and I stand next to Dean, across from Frank. I place a hand on Dean's back so he doesn't totally turn his back on me.

We start singing "The Star Spangled Banner."

Around the time we get to "twilight's last gleaming," my eyes adjust to the spotlights, and I become aware of a certain roiling motion in the crowd at the foot of the stage, just over to the left a little. The people down there are yelling something.

We go on singing, "through the per - i - lous fight," and I catch sight of one of the big state signs: MISSISSIPPI. It's the Mississippi delegation — they're yelling something at us.

We get to the bridge and a couple people drop out on the high notes and I'm now able to hear what they're shouting at us: "Get that fucking nigger off the stage! Fucking race-mixing nigger, you're dead! God damn you nigger!"

Still singing, I turn in astonishment toward Sammy. He's still singing, but there are big tears rolling out of his eyes. The glass one included.

Frank puts his hand over the mic and says to Sammy, "Those dirty sons of bitches! Don't let them get to you, Charlie! Sing your fucking heart out!"

And we all swing into the ending, "O'er the la - and of the freeeeee," and as we pause for breath, I hear the Mississippi rednecks chanting, "Die nigger die! Die nigger die!"

If only Feldman were here. He'd tell 'em: We freed the slaves a long time ago, boys.

The anthem ends and the auditorium fills with an ovation. The band starts playing "Stars and Stripes Forever," and Frank has his arm tightly around Sammy, and he's waving to the crowd. Some of the singers are waving, too; others, the ones who have noticed Mississippi's impromptu exercise of First Amendment rights, are just standing there staring at the rednecks, who are still screaming under cover of the cheers.

Sammy moves off in my direction and I steer him upstage of me and put my arm over his shoulder, protecting him with my body. We follow Tony and Judy and Janet off the stage the way we came, through the disorienting darkness, and out to the safety of the corridor where we are suddenly alone.

I know Frank and the others were going to take seats on the floor. Sammy stands with me, head down.

"Sammy, come on, let's get out of here," I say. "Let's get a drink."

"Yeah, sure, man," he mumbles.

"I heard that out there. God almighty, those fucking crackers. To think those goddamn rednecks are wearing suits and ties and sitting on the floor of the Democratic Convention instead of standing up to their knees in a stinking swamp. Who the fuck let them in?"

Sammy doesn't answer, but I go on cursing the state of Mississippi and the former states of the Confederacy in general. Finally I realize I'm not doing Sammy any good, and I clam up.

We find a red-jacketed man. "Excuse me, but where can we get a taxi out of here?"

"You want to leave?" he asks in a jolly manner. "Show's just starting. I mean, the convention." I convince him we're serious, and he points us toward an exit. But when we find a taxi, Sammy turns to me and says, "Thanks, man, but I think I'll just go home. I don't want Frank busting into my hotel room tonight. Tell him I appreciate him standing by me."

"Sure, Sammy. You sure you don't want me to come with you?"

"Somebody's got to go back and tell Frank I wasn't lynched," he says, calm enough now to joke a little. "Good night, Bobby." He gets into the cab and it takes off.

I turn and go back into the Sports Arena. Nobody has given me a badge or anything and it takes a little doing to talk my way back into the door I just came out of, but finally I'm back in the vast yellow concourse. Then it takes some doing to find my way back to the room where we waited to go on. It's deserted, with the few chairs pushed every which way and ashtrays full of cigarette butts.

I sit down, tired. The evening began several hours and four or five drinks ago, and I'm beat. I figure Frank will come looking for Sammy here if anywhere, but God knows when; I have the feeling he's anxious to spend as much time as possible showing his face out there on the convention floor. Peter told me a week ago that Frank has some idea they're going to work the crowd like precinct captains, buttonholing wavering delegates and trying to push Kennedy over the top on nomination night. But tonight is just the opening ceremonies, and Frank and Peter and everyone are soaking up the limelight.

I proceed to fall asleep, lulled by the muddled echoes of men making speeches far, far away. After who knows how long, the door springs open and Frank and a couple of his henchmen—where'd they come from?—bust in.

"Bobby!" Frank yells, jarring me awake and to my feet in one motion. "Where's Sammy?"

"He went home," I say, wiping my mouth. "I put him in a cab."

"How was he?—those sons of bitches!"

"How do you think?" I reply. "I heard 'em too. How do you like that treatment?"

"If they weren't delegates to a national convention, I'd break their fucking legs!" Frank says. "Those sons of ..." He shakes his fist, then punches it into his left palm. "I'll call Sammy. He should come back here tomorrow night. Show those goddamn rednecks he won't back down. Show them what America really stands for—Christ, I feel like killing them! God knows I still might, but I think Jack needs the votes."

"Well, don't kill them if we need the votes."

Frank shakes his head. Though he's been sitting on the convention floor smiling and applauding for more than an hour, he's now white with rage. It's never that far from the surface. "Well, Bobby, thanks for taking care of Sammy. I appreciate it. And thanks for that other little favor tonight."

He means Lucy. I hadn't forgotten, but by focusing on Sammy I had managed to block out the humiliation a little.

"Come back with Peter and me, we're heading back to Puccini as soon as the plenary session ends."

I'm not sure what a plenary session is, but I swallow and say, "I think I'll head back to the hotel, Frank. I'm done in. And I need to save a little for the rest of the week. But call me if you need me."

He claps me on the shoulder. "I will, Bobby. I will call you. And I will need you."

"Okay, Frank. 'Night." And I make my escape down the long yellow hallway.

Chapter 20

1

Gene sits on his stool watching TV—the Democratic Convention is being broadcast. It's on both stations, so he doesn't have any choice.

It took the purchase of the motel to break Gene out of his stupor. He finished number 7 in one day and started in on number 6, figuring it's better for him to be in the middle of a project so that Sanchez can't fire him right away. Every day now he's in there, cleaning and painting— cooled, as Dolores suggested, by a fan.

Moira's honey has been moved to number 4 for the duration. It's all right with Moira as long as they share a wall.

Watching the convention with Gene, and sitting on a kitchen chair pulled up in sight of both the TV and the front counter, is Jaime. Gene's supposed to be training him. The Sanchezes showed up the day after the motel sale went through and dropped him off, along with Dolores and a young woman named Marta, the new housekeeper. Dolores spent the morning training her, and when they left at noon, Dolores punched out, then took her time card with her. She didn't speak to Gene.

While the women were at the housekeeping, Sanchez Sr. came to Gene and said, "So, Señor Gene, I would like to know what your plans are."

"I've decided to stay, Mr. Sanchez."

"Very good," Sanchez said.

"For the time being."

Sanchez looked pained. "For the time being," he echoed, as if weighing the words. "For the time being, I have some plans for this motel. It needs a big remodeling, not just the spot work you have been doing. I want to remodel from top to bottom, and I need help for this job. Jaime and Luis will do a lot of the work but I would like you to work too. So tell me, how long is this 'time being' of yours?"

Gene swallowed. "I planned on staying for the rest of the summer. Anyway I'm in the middle of the bathroom of number 6."

"Never mind number 6. What about Dolores? Are you perhaps planning to get married?"

Gene nervously pursed his lips. "I really like Dolores," he said. "But I'm not sure we're at that point yet. We haven't known each other that long."

Sanchez was unfazed. "I knew Dolores's mother for a long time before we got married. Since we were children. She was the cousin of one of my friends. But once we decided we were in love with each other, we got married. No hesitation."

"Okay. Well, I didn't grow up with Dolores."

"Here the apartment is for the owner, no? What better solution than for you and Dolores to get married and live here and run the place?"

Despite the air conditioning in the office, Gene can feel sweat running down from his armpits. He swallows. "You mean you bought the motel because you thought we were getting married?"

"No. It's just an opportunity for a family business. But I thought you love each other, you get married, you live in the little apartment. Actually not so little. I have lived in many smaller apartments."

Gene scratched his head, wiped the back of his neck. "Yes, but... It's a big decision to make. I may need a few more weeks to figure it all out."

"A few more weeks. Well, it will take us a little time to finish our plans. But tell me soon, no?"

* * *

2

Jaime and Gene stare at the screen. After Gene glimpsed Bobby Blaine during the singing of the national anthem, it's been all downhill. Speaker after speaker is holding forth as the network cuts away from the platform once in a while to show Huntley and Brinkley sitting above the floor in a sky box, commenting ironically on the proceedings. Gene is too wrapped up in his own thoughts to follow the speeches or the commentary. But he enjoys the silly hats worn by the convention delegates and the rest of the spectacle.

All he really wanted to do was work at the motel long enough to save a little money and, if possible, talk Dolores into bed. As for actually getting married, he thinks it's nice that they took him seriously enough to think it was likely. And it's nice that, at one point anyway, she seemed to expect it and was apparently willing to accept. But it gives him a queasy feeling when he thinks about the prospect of working behind this counter his whole life, raising little black-haired Kramers in the desert heat. He's just turned 21, and he'd always expected this event to accord him more freedom, not less. They're measuring him for a harness that Kerouac would never accept for a moment. He shakes his head.

"What?" Jaime asks, thinking Gene is reacting to the television.

"Oh, nothing, I was just thinking." Gene has learned why Jaime's English is so much worse than that of Dolores or her father: Jaime was left behind when the family came north, and was raised by Dolores' uncle. He's been in the country only a couple of years.

A taxi pulls up and a john comes in to get a room. Jaime watches the man aggressively. He learned the details of desk clerking in about twenty minutes on the first night, but he hasn't really learned what Gene feels is the essence of the job, the people part.

The john glances at Jaime sitting in his chair behind the counter and then ignores him. Gene hands him his change and the key, and the guy turns and goes out.

Gene turns back to the tube as David Brinkley names whoever is speaking at the rostrum and says, "Let's listen in." The shot changes to a close-up of a spectacled, crewcut man in a dark suit and thick glasses complaining about the Republicans' tenure in the White House. Every few sentences the man repeats, "It's time for a change!" whereupon there is a thirty-second long outburst from the convention delegates.

"Who's he?" Jaime asks.

"I don't know, some politician," Gene yawns.

"What's he say?"

"Republicans are bad, Democrats are good." They watch for a few more minutes, and then in the middle of the man's speech, the network runs commercials.

Another taxi pulls up and this time a woman gets out and asks for a room. She is laboriously filling out the registration card when she seems to notice Jaime for the first time, sitting a few feet from her. "Oh crimeny, I didn't see you there, fella. What are you, the bellboy?"

Jaime looks at her with contempt and doesn't answer.

"Well, what's eating you?"

"Don't mind him," Gene says. "Here's your change and your key."

The woman sets the key down on the counter and opens her purse to put away the money, clearly in not much of a hurry. "Doesn't say much, huh?"

"He's a management trainee," Gene replies. "An exchange student."

"Oh, he's a Mexican, ain't he. Well, Paco, learn some English and maybe you'll get some pussy someday."

Jaime growls several words in Spanish including *chingar* and *puta* and a few other curse words Gene has caught on to.

"Yeah, same to you, fella, and your mama too," the woman says, going out the door.

Jaime rises and makes to go out the door, but Gene stops him. "Jaime," he says, "leave her alone." Jaime returns to his place, muttering. "Don't just glare at people, Jaime. Naturally they'll take offense. You can't be like that to everybody who comes in," Gene says.

"That one," sneers Jaime, and lets loose a few curses of which *puta* forms the core.

"Yes, *of course* she's a whore. That's the main business here. I explained that. You can't be so antagonistic."

Jaime gnashes his teeth. Finally he says, "Whores—we have no more here. We have families."

Gene raises his eyebrows. "Well, you can try."

"We should have a pool," Jaime goes on, with effort.

"What?"

"A swimming pool," Jaime says, making a swimming motion. "Then more families. Not so much whores."

Sander Vanocur interviews a politician. Gene climbs off his stool and says, "I'm just going outside for a second." He pushes open the office door and steps into the heat. Though it's after 9:00, the temperature must still be over a hundred degrees. The sky in the west is still glowing. He takes a few steps down the driveway and stares at the yellow sky above the indigo mountains and thinks some more about poets and coffee houses and cool, gray San Francisco.

3

On the convention's second day, I wait in my room at the Beverly Hilton until I get a call. It's directly from Frank this time.

"Bobby," he says, "I want to tell you again how much I appreciate the help you're giving me and Senator Kennedy."

I say he's welcome, wondering what humiliations he has in store today. Perhaps he'll have me wait tables at Puccini, or escort Lady Bird Johnson while she visits the Beverly Hills shops. Whatever it is, it must be bad, if he's calling personally.

"Boy, that dame we fixed Jack up with last night—she's quite a dish, isn't she?"

I swallow. "Lucy? Yes, she's, uh, she's dynamite."

"You gotta hear this. I screwed her before, you know? And man, she may look like an angel, but in the sack she's something else. What is it the French say? Yves Montand told me—A woman should act like a queen on the street—how's it go?—and a whore in bed? That's her in spades."

I sit there on the bed in the hotel room, gripping the phone tightly.

"I did everything with this broad. And I mean everything. You still there?"

"Sure," I mutter.

"And she was so uninhibited, I thought, wow, I bet she'd go for a three-way. You know, *ménage a trois.* But she wouldn't go for it; she slapped me! Can you believe it?

"In any case, I thought, this babe is perfect for Jack Kennedy. He likes the wild ones, you know? So I set them up. And you know what he says to me this morning?"

"What?" I manage to say in a strangled voice.

"He tried the same thing! He had his other girlfriend in town... what's her name... Judy Campbell. And he calls her up to the suite and says, 'Girls, how about it? *Ménage a trois.'* And they gave him what for!" Frank brays with laughter.

I start sobbing and choking. Frank thinks I'm choking with laughter.

"That's a gas, isn't it? Okay, Bobby, listen. You need to meet me and Peter at Puccini at four. Got that?"

4

At quarter to four, I'm sitting at the bar at Puccini. More than two miles from the convention hall, its remoteness must be its appeal. Frank or JFK can come and go without running into the other candidates or delegates from the convention. And the fact that Frank co-owns the place means JFK can have all the privacy he wants.

The staff begins to kowtow, and a moment later Frank appears. "There's my boy. Bobby, you're being a real trouper through all this. You won't regret it, believe me."

"Anything for the cause, Frank," I say bitterly, but Frank misses the sentiment. I'm being a real trouper, all right. Deadpan is my shtick—I'm never supposed to crack a smile, especially when giving the straight lines. Little did I know a lifetime of practicing deadpan comedy would come in handy for this.

"Well, I feel the same way, Bobby. And that's why I have to ask you to do one more thing, even though it sticks in my craw."

"What is it?" I ask with dread.

"Wait til Peter gets here. Hey Johnny, how you doing?" Frank greets a pal. "Where's Moe? Isn't he in town?"

I nod at Frank's thug-like buddy, then look into space so it seems like I'm minding my own business. Some of the palookas Frank befriends are just tough-guy extras in pictures, some are simple thugs; this one looks like the real thing. He's too well-fed, and with that diamond ring he could signal ships at sea.

Presently Peter comes in and we retire to a secluded booth.

"Okay, men, here's the plan," says Frank like a platoon sergeant. "I'll lay it straight out for ya. You know those goddamn crackers from Mississippi who gave Sammy hell during the national anthem? Well, Jack needs their votes. And he wants you guys to go and make the play."

Peter is in the middle of lighting a cigarette—a patent delaying tactic I see him use all the time. It gives him at least ten seconds before he says anything. So I say something.

"Frank, you've got to be kidding. Last night you wanted to kill them. Now you want us to go over there and make nice to them?"

"I can't help it, Bobby. Jack needs the votes, and they're on the fence. So here's the plan. They're having a smoker tonight at this strip club over on Sunset, and I want you guys to go over there and just say a few words. Be charming. What do you say, Peter?"

Peter removes a tobacco speck from his tongue, looks at it as he flicks it away, and says, "Forgive me, but this is new territory for me. I haven't seen a display like the one they put on since England lost, at home, to Ireland and the crowd beat up all the Irish fans."

"It's worse than that, Peter. These guys hate everybody, but they're so stupid they don't even know what England is. I figure sending a Brit in there will confuse them long enough for you to get a word in edgewise."

"You could remind them Britain was on the South's side in the Civil War," I suggest.

Peter looks at me. "They can't be that stupid."

"Maybe not, but it happens to be true!" I laugh, and I laugh harder when I see the look of sheepish annoyance on his face. I guess that wasn't on his citizenship test.

Frank says, "Bobby, you warm them up. Tell them a few spade jokes if it'll help."

"No, no, Frank. This is getting ridiculous now. How is that going to help Kennedy?"

"It'll convince them that Kennedy is more like them than they think."

"Kennedy just got through speaking to the NAACP, for God's sake. And he's in favor of the civil rights plank the Southern states are fighting."

"Well, then tell them Jewish jokes. It doesn't matter, to them everybody north of Richmond is probably a nigger-loving Jew anyway— you'll pardon my language but I'm being blunt. We all have to make sacrifices, men."

"Sacrifices!" I blurt out. He looks sore, but just then the maitre d' comes over and whispers in his ear. Frank gets up abruptly and goes off with him.

"What bloody sacrifice is *he* making, anyway?" I ask Peter.

"You're about to find out, Bobby." He stands up, and I wiggle out of the booth and stand up too. Coming through the restaurant, to applause, is Frank and JFK, trailed by the aide I met in Palm Springs, O'Donnell. Between them is Marilyn Monroe.

"My God," I mutter as she approaches. She's resplendent in a dark pink dress she must have been sewn into. That's what hits you right away—her figure, how it suggests a kind of bountiful excess without really going overboard the way Jayne Mansfield's figure does. And unlike others' shapes, it's not just the size of her tits, but the proportions of her breasts and her ass and her waist. Then all that blond hair, tonight swept up in a formal do.

"Miss Monroe, you know Peter, of course," Frank says.

"My dear, you look ravishing."

"And this is Bobby Blaine, another of my close associates. Bobby, Miss Monroe."

"Oh yes, Mr. Blaine. I remember seeing you in Las Vegas. I'm so sorry we haven't been introduced until now."

I'm not sure I'm invited to dinner, but I am herded along with everyone else through the narrow restaurant and wind up in the private dining room. But the table's set only for six. "Unfortunately," Frank announces, "Peter and Bobby won't be able to stay for dinner, but I hope they'll have a cocktail with us."

"With pleasure," Peter says.

"Are you attending the convention, Miss Monroe?" I ask, ever the straight man.

"Oh Bobby, please, call me Marilyn. Well, I have to be getting back to Nevada to work on a film. But I wanted to stop by and meet the senator." She turns to Kennedy, whose smirk is a mile wide. "We just spent some time together discussing... policy," she adds.

"Miss Monroe is very up on current affairs," Kennedy grins. "We spent some time discussing my positions."

I notice both Peter and Frank are sitting with fixed grins, no doubt imagining some of the positions. Kennedy's aide also has a fixed smile, but he looks more like I feel, like we're watching some ghastly play.

"I found the senator very... penetrating," Marilyn says ingenuously.

I don't know how much more I can stand, but it would be rude to leave so soon. I try to change the subject. "The picture you're doing, it's with Clark Gable, isn't that right?"

"Yes, it's going to be wonderful," she says, but a shadow crosses her face as she goes on, "with such a wonderful script, and John Huston is the director. I think it's going to be fantastic."

"This is the cowboy picture?" Peter asks.

"Yes, well, it's not a traditional western. Arthur said it was 'an Eastern Western.'"

"What's it called?" Kennedy asks.

"The Misfits."

"Now that's what I call appropriate," Kennedy says, and everybody laughs as if he's said something really funny, Marilyn especially.

"Senator, Peter and Bobby are going to speak to the Mississippians tonight," Frank says.

"Men, you have my deep appreciation," Kennedy says, raising his glass. "Also, I wouldn't be caught dead doing it."

"Any advice on what to tell them?"

"Don't make any promises you can't keep," Frank exclaims, thinking he's being clever. "Right, Senator?"

"That's always good advice," says Kennedy smoothly.

"A first-ballot victory is in their interest, it's in all our interests," says O'Donnell. "Plus Lyndon Johnson can do more for them in the Senate under a Democratic president."

Kennedy raises his hand. "I doubt they'll be in the mood for political talk. Just be your charming selves, and as you're going out, mention my name. It's not that big a group anyway—twenty men or so. But every little bit helps."

5

Peter spends the evening at the convention, working the crowd on behalf of his brother-in-law, and picks me up at my hotel in a taxi.

"How goes the fight?" I ask him.

"I suppose we're winning, but I'll be damned if I do this again." he replies. "I must have shaken the hands of half the people in the arena. My right hand is absolutely killing me."

"The TV says Johnson is still slugging away."

"Maybe so, it all looks the same from the floor. So tell me, what's this about Mississippi? Is it really a state? I thought it was a river."

"It's a state, too. Definitely one of the minor ones. Like Jack said, there's only about twenty delegates."

"Can I confide in you, Bobby?" he asks, putting out a cigarette.

"Sure, Peter."

"I shouldn't be saying this, but I feel it's only fair for you to be on the same footing as I. You might not realize it but we're on a bit of a wild goose chase. This whole convention fight between Jack and Lyndon Johnson and the others is really something of a sham."

"It is? You mean Kennedy's got it in the bag?"

"Precisely the way that fellow O'Donnell put it earlier today."

"Really. Well then what the hell are we doing?"

"You saw those statements last week by the former President Truman, saying he wasn't coming to the convention at all because it was a pre-arranged affair? Embarrassing as hell. They have to make it look good. So they'll have a convention fight."

We reach a lot of traffic on Sunset right around where all the bars and clubs start. The sidewalks are crowded with people, many of them recognizable from their buttons and hats as conventioneers. We're still some distance from the strip club where the Mississippians are gathered. "Do we really need to do this? Mississippi's not voting for Kennedy anyway."

"It's just a way to keep us busy. Frank thinks he's a kingmaker. Actually, he embarrasses them. I hear they're not even going to let him campaign after the convention, because they don't want people to get the idea that the Mafia is involved. What they did in the West Virginia preliminary was bad enough."

"You mean primary. I heard a lot of money was spread around."

"That's just the sort of thing they don't want bandied about."

"So what the hell are we doing, going to talk to these bastards? Did you hear them last night during the anthem?"

"I did indeed. 'Die, nigger, die.' Like bloody Rhodesia."

"Well, I say we tell the cab driver to take us to a bar and then call in an hour from now and tell Frank we did our best."

"I say we go there and do our best anyway," Peter insisted. "As you so rightly pointed out, they're probably voting for Johnson in any case. But they've got twenty votes, and between you and me, if Jack falls nineteen votes short I may not be an American citizen much longer."

The traffic is grinding along at a snail's pace, but finally I see the club up ahead. I hand the driver a bill and Peter and I make our way along the sidewalk. The place is so full, we have to squeeze through the door. There's no room to walk through the place, much less find a seat. The tobacco smoke is thick enough to choke a fireman, and the noise level – the excited babble of the crowd, plus the recorded music for the strippers—is punishing in such a small room.

I find myself next to a bouncer. "We're looking for some guys from the convention—the guys from Mississippi!" I shout in his ear.

"I think there's some conventioneers down there," he says, waving vaguely toward the lip of the stage, where bodies are packed like pigs at a trough. I do see a couple of cowboy hats, the sign of Johnson delegates.

"They're down there, Peter," I shout, pointing.

"Christ, that's no good," he says. "Ask for the manager. Maybe we can get a moment on the stage."

"Are you sure?"

"Come on, Bobby. Don't forget you're a movie star. We're the most important people these twits have met since they put a foot in Hitler's ass. Give it a try. And you go on first."

I ask for the manager. It takes Peter and I a few minutes just to worm our way through the jostling mob. Then the bar itself is packed three and four deep with cocktail-slurping, sweating, smoking, shouting, suit-clad men, either cheering the girl on stage or shouting and gesticulating to each other, not necessarily about politics. I spend about a minute within earshot of a man in a brown suit shouting "I swear he's the greatest quarterback Oklahoma has ever had! In the last three games last year he scored at least two touchdowns each game! I tell you he's gonna win the Heisman Trophy!"

I fight my way down to the end of the bar, and I actually recognize the guy sitting there. He used to run a bar on Beverly where Philly took me several times when I first came to town. "Hey Tommy! It's Bobby Blaine!"

"Bobby, what the hell are you doing in my dive?"

"Your dive? This is your place?"

"Sure it is. I bought it four years ago. Don't you remember? I told you."

"Yeah, that's right. Hey, look who's with me—Peter Lawford."

"My God, so it is. Tommy Fishman. This is my place."

"Quite a success you've got here."

"Tonight it is."

Peter quickly explains to him that we want to welcome the conventioneers to town and give them greetings from our candidate. Tommy agrees and a few minutes later he's on the stage.

"Ladies and gentlemen, we have some special guests here tonight. Well, you're all special... In particular we want to welcome the honored delegates..." and blah blah blah. Finally he gets to me and I squeeze myself up onto the stage.

"Hello, ladies and gentlemen."

Mixed cries of "Hello" and "Get off the stage" and "Bring the girls back."

"You may not know me, but I'm Bobby Blaine. I'm an entertainer here in Hollywood, and on behalf of the Music and Arts Committee of the Democratic National Convention, I want to add my sincere welcome to the city of Los Angeles."

Cheering. There actually is such a "committee." It's all so official.

"Now I don't want to offend any locals by pretending everybody here is from out of town, but the fact is, this is the best-dressed crowd I've seen around here in a long time, so I *know* you're from out of town."

More cheers, laughter.

"After all, this is the town where restaurants actually have to insist you're wearing a shirt and shoes for you to come in. If they didn't do that they'd be overrun by surfers. I know none of you have a problem like that where you come from—Hey, where is everybody from? I heard there were some guys here from Mississippi. Where are you?"

Three tables of men wearing brown suits and gray ones, some of them wearing LBJ stetsons and all of them fat, raise a ruckus.

"There you are. Well, that's exactly what I mean, ladies and gentlemen. Look at 'em. These guys are wearing more buttons than they have on the control board at Cape Canaveral. What's that one say? 'Mississippi, the state with plenty of *s* and lots of *p*.'"

Laughter. They seem to take that well. I try another.

"Well gentlemen, rest assured that your habit of wearing shoes has not gone unnoticed here in our town. The mayor of Los Angeles today signed a proclamation..." This is a sentence I start without knowing how in the hell I'm going to finish it. I find myself saying, "... praising the delegates from the former states of the Confederacy for their fashion sense and general style."

There's no joke there, nothing at all. But everybody breaks up. Hell, I'll go with it.

"In fact, guess who was invited to a garden party tomorrow to teach the Pasadena Ladies Society a thing or two about manners? Well, the delegates from Alabama."

Laughter, some good-natured booing.

"And who's been invited to go downtown and talk to our civic leaders about how to run a city efficiently and on budget? The guys from South Carolina."

Same reaction, and cries of "No, no."

"But the very best assignment, the plum assignment, fell to these very men here. These men came down here to the Sunset Strip to meet some ladies from southern California and show them a thing or two about southern gallantry and, and manhood."

Cheering.

"Yes, these very guys from Mississippi. That's right."

I have no fucking idea where I'm going with this. I should have told Eskimo jokes. I better wrap it up and introduce Peter.

"Well, ladies and gentlemen, I won't keep you much longer. I only want you to know that Los Angeles welcomes you with open *arms,* and maybe if you're lucky tonight..." I trail off and simply smirk. The crowd goes wild. The fact is that I scarcely stopped myself from making a joke about open arms and open legs. God, what have I fallen to? And how bad does it have to get before I actually complete the joke and say the words "open legs" instead of just leer suggestively? Even Feldman has some respect.

"And now, without further ado, I want you all to welcome one of Hollywood's brightest stars. He's English, ladies and gentlemen, but don't hold that against him, because he's also the brother-in-law of one of the men who's running for President this week. Now we're not here to politick, only to entertain you. So without further ado, please welcome Peter Lawford."

And I get the hell off the stage which, given the crush of people I mentioned before, is not easy. It occurs to me that I have even less idea what Peter is going to do up there than I had about what I was going to do.

And what happens next demonstrates that I never could have guessed.

The stage curtain has been closed all this time and I've been doing my bit in front of it. Now I reach a piece of floor and a waitress hands me a drink as the curtain parts. And there—on stage, carrying, I swear to God, a cane and a JFK straw boater he's swiped from someone in the crowd—as a piano starts beating out an intro—is Peter.

In blackface.

And as the piano, heard somehow over the frantic cheers of the Mississippians and others, reaches the end of the introduction, Peter gets down on one knee, flings his arms wide, and begins to sing—yes— "Mammy."

I take a very large mouthful of my drink.

The crowd goes bonkers. They practically drown him out while he's singing. It outdoes even the reception I saw a crowd give Judy Garland when she sang "Over the Rainbow." It is only by virtue of the fact that I am right next to the stage that I hear Peter's singing at all. In fact, I only catch snatches:

> Oh Maaaa - meeeeee, how I love ya, how I love ya,
> My dear old Mammy.
> Before they strung... you... up on that tree,
> You were the very... very... best Mammy to me,
> Oh Maaaa - meeeeee, how I love ya, how I love ya...

What the fuck? I watch in mixed shock and horror as Peter struts up and down the stage, riding on the audience's cheers, making up words as he goes along. No doubt he means to mock the rednecks, but even if they could hear what he was really singing, would they get it? Would they care? Do they think he's singing the real words, do *they* even know the words to "Mammy"? Where the hell did he get that blackface—could it be shoe polish, like in a Three Stooges short? Are we going to get out of here alive?

The song concludes to thunderous applause, an earthquake of applause, and cheers loud enough to wake the dead. The audience screams for Peter to sing it again. Dripping with sweat after his song and dance, he approaches the microphone and makes a short speech about how can they blame him for supporting Jack Kennedy, he is his brother-in-law after all, and would they do him the very great courtesy of at least considering his beloved brother-in-law's candidacy, because whether or not they know it, Jack *understands* them more than they know. He *understands their concerns.*

I'm shitting, crying inside, praying for Peter to get off the stage. Finally he wraps it up and the piano player starts playing "Mammy" again but this time a chorus line comes on and starts high-kicking and after joining it for a few seconds, he waves and disappears backstage.

I want to slip away, of course, but the spot I've chosen to stand and watch Peter's act is unfortunately close to the Mississippians and they drag me over and, ignoring my protests, make me sit down. Then they clap me on the back and buy me drinks and assure me many times that they have never seen a blackface act quite that good, it just goes to show—one ridiculous man assures me solemnly—that Hollywood really does have the best entertainers. "But I never figured any Limey to do blackface and sing 'Mammy'!" he marveled. "I said to Merle here, 'Don't that beat all!' But listen here, did you know that England"—he pronounces it *"Ang*-lunn"—"Did you know that England was on the South's side in the Civil War?"

"I did hear that someplace."

"Not many people know that! They was on the South's side, all right. It just goes to show you, doesn't it?"

"Yeah—uh... show me what?"

"It just goes to show you that there's good old boys all over. Just like you. Take you. What are you?"

"Well, I'm a Democrat."

"Haw haw! Yeah, sure you are! But I mean, what are you— Eye-talian, or Portugese, or what?"

"I'm from Philadelphia. I guess I'm a Philadelphian."

"Come on! Stop shittin' me! I won't take no offense."

"All right. As long as you don't hold it against me. I'm a Jew."

"No shit! Is that right? Hey Merle—this feller says he's a *Jew!* Didja ever meet one o' them before? No, me neither! Well I'll be damned."

He's drunk, they're all drunk as hell, and I'm rapidly getting drunk.

"We're really quite harmless," I say, trying to make a joke, but then I realize what I'm saying.

But he laughs. "Yeah, sure! That's right! As long as you don't lend no money to me."

"Well, I'll be sure not to." I struggle to my feet, not an easy task when I can hardly even move my chair in the crush. "Listen, it's been terrific meeting you, but I've got to go to a Ku Klux Klan rally next and I don't want to be late, or those hoods might beat me up."

He looks confused and offended at first, but then he shouts, "Those hoods might beat you up! Hey, that's rich! Merle, listen to this—say that again, feller..."

But I'm making my way through the crowd, shaking hands, smiling and saying hello, trying to get outside before I puke my guts up. At the door I run into Tommy, the owner, and he shakes my hand and says, "Leaving so soon?"

"Yeah, I was just telling one of those crackers... Well, the hell with it. You ask him."

"What about your friend Lawford? Aren't you going to wait for him?"

"Tell him I'll get a cab and meet him at the back entrance about the time it takes him to figure out how to get that shit off his face. So long, Tommy."

"So long, Bobby. Come back anytime."

The next night, the third night of the convention, Kennedy wins the nomination on the first ballot with 806 votes—45 more than needed. Frank is ecstatic. He goes around backstage slapping people on the back and saying, "We're going to the White House! We're going to the White House!" I notice that the only people who don't avoid him are so low-level and star-struck that they're grateful to have a moment with the great Frank Sinatra, or otherwise they're his show business pals like me. But the others—Kennedy's aides and the high muckety-mucks of the Democratic Party—settle for each other's congratulations. It's like Peter said: Frank's a kingmaker in his own mind, but for the party as a whole, we're all just a flashy embarrassment.

As for Peter, I eventually left the previous night without seeing him again, and when I meet up with him backstage at the convention, he doesn't mention his performance and neither do I. It's a little dim in the backstage shadows, as in the arena thousands of Democrats go crazy chanting "J-F-K! All the way!" and the band plays "Anchors Aweigh," but as far as I can see, all traces of his blackface makeup are gone.

Chapter 21

1

July moves on, and summer reruns return to Las Vegas television. The heat settles in for good. Now the relative coolness of the early morning doesn't last past 7:00 a.m., and by 9:00 the asphalt parking lot of the motel is a soft, sticky griddle. The solution to this is to dig up the parking lot, or part of it, for a swimming pool. For two days the backhoe works, shoveling orange dirt and sand into dump trucks, and then carpenters come to make a form for the cement.

Gene watches the construction from the office. As Jaime had suggested, the plan is to turn the Cactus Motel into a place for families. In addition to the pool, a new sign has been ordered that will say MOTEL DOLORES with a cartoon of a smiling Mexican lady. There's even talk of putting in some kind of shuffleboard court behind the joint. Gene asks who would want to play outside in this heat, and Dolores says the children will play out there in the evenings while the sun sets.

During the morning, Gene and Jaime work at repainting the whole exterior with a color scheme to match the new sign. In the evening, they run the office together. Sanchez gives them the afternoon off; he's not such a slavedriver as to work them all day and all evening. Gene's seeing much more of Jaime than his sister; they haven't gone out on a date since the movie at the beginning of the month. He tries to see Dolores at midday when she arrives to see to the motel's business, but he doesn't know how to act with her. Her stance is pleasant, the way one is with any co-worker—especially one you're not sure is going to be around much longer. He knows she's waiting for him to make a choice one way or another. Until then, she's just friendly and efficient.

Dolores is transforming the place. She has set up a reservations system, is ordering new office supplies, and occasionally goes down to inspect Marta's housekeeping. This morning she is set on finding all vestiges of the old order and replacing them. She takes the half-empty box of registration forms from a shelf and plops it down on the counter. "We'll order some with the new name. Are these the only ones?"

"There're some more in the cabinet there."

"Throw out all those, we'll use these until the new ones come." She peels a form off the top of the stack. "We can mark our changes on this and give it to the printer," she says, marking out the old name of the motel and writing in the new one. "Should we ask people something? This just has name and address, make and model of car, license number, and date of checkin and checkout. Should we ask them how many children they have? How about if they have pets?"

"What if they do?" Gene asks.

"Well, we have to decide if they can have the pets in their room."

"What if they do? Do you want to have a special pet room or something?"

She pauses. "Now there's an idea," she says. "A special pet room. We could advertise it. You mean, like a place with cages to put the pets."

"I mean, actually I was kidding."

"See, that's what I like about you. You even have good ideas when you're kidding."

Gene yawns. The incessant sound of hammering comes from the swimming pool pit. A dip would feel good on these hot days, there's no denying that. He picks up the day's newspaper and turns to the weather page. Yesterday it was 104 degrees; the high in San Francisco was 67.

"What else is there that needs replacing? Anything that says 'Cactus Motel' on it."

"There are these business cards."

"Oh good. We can each have business cards."

"Some for you, some for me... better get some for Marta too."

"Silly! She don't need business cards. Who's she gonna give them to?" She goes to the cabinet and begins taking its contents out.

"Just kidding. I have bad ideas when I'm kidding, too."

"What this?" she says, opening a stained cardboard box. "Oh, it's postcards. Look at that. Look at the cars, so old." She hands one to Gene. It's a postcard of the Cactus Motel, from the late 1940s from the looks of it.

"This must be before Gustafson bought the place."

"It did look nicer then. Look, green trim. He shouldn't have let it go to pot like this. Maybe that's why he put the postcards away, he didn't want anybody to know it used to look nice."

"Poor old guy. His son just wanted to get rid of him, so he sent him down here. I guess he never really wanted to be here. He's still in town," Gene adds, "in that nursing home."

She puts the box of postcards in the pile of stuff to be dumped. "When the pool's done and the new sign's up, we'll get new postcards."

Gene stands up. "I thought I'd go to the library. Unless you want me to turn one of the rooms into the special pet room."

"Ha," she says. "Go on, you're not helping anyway."

"Why don't you come to a movie with me?"

"Somebody has to stay here."

"Why? I used to shut the office every afternoon. Nobody comes by."

"Things are different now. We're not playing anymore. We have a business."

He stands and looks at her, a pencil between her lips, stacks of envelopes and paper on the counter before her. She really does have a talent for this stuff. He wants to reach out to touch her, but she's already working studiously at some to-do list.

Gene sets off for downtown, but he doesn't have to walk all the way anymore. The city has started a new bus line that passes half a mile from the motel. Gene hoofs it through the brutal sun until he reaches the bus stop, a tin shack that provides shade but radiates so much heat that it's actually hotter inside than outside it. Gene elects to stand across the street under the eaves of a liquor store until the bus approaches.

He goes downtown, getting off across from a brick structure with a bluish-gray leaping dog fastened above the door. It's the bus station. A few scrawny people with nothing to do squeeze themselves into a narrow bit of shade along the front wall. Gene crosses the street and goes in.

Three people listlessly play a bank of slot machines against a side wall. A girl, no more than a teenager, sits next to a pile of dirty, breaking suitcases while a sunburned man, evidently coked up on something, stands next to her and gesticulates and pleads with her, then walks away, then walks back, then walks over to the candy counter and buys a pack of cigarettes, then walks back to the girl and, with exaggerated gestures, lights a cigarette while explaining to her—Gene catches the drift as he passes—that they have to go to Los Angeles, that his friend there will lend them money, his friend is a good guy, he's never let him down. A skinny white woman with four kids, including a squalling baby, sits among bags filled with her possessions; an elderly couple, whom the sunburned, gesticulating man is making nervous, huddle on a bench; and a guy with a rucksack sits quietly reading a book.

Gene goes over to the ticket counter and asks about buses to San Francisco.

"There's no direct bus; you have to change in Los Angeles, or in Reno. Reno's usually the best, in the summer."

"Why's that?"

"Well, it's shorter to go through Reno; in the winter, you can't get through the mountains a lot of the time."

Gene is intrigued. "There's mountains?"

"Yeah, the Sierra Nevada Mountains. Ever heard of 'em?"

"Oh, yeah!" Gene exclaims. It's where Kerouac and company went hiking in *The Dharma Bums*.

The guy gives Gene a timetable and tells him the fare's four dollars and eighty cents.

Gene turns to go and now notices that the man with the rucksack has among his things a set of bongo drums. He stares at them, riveted. The man looks up.

"You going to San Francisco too?" the man asks.

"Maybe someday," Gene replies nervously.

The man nods slightly and returns to his book, which Gene can see is titled *Sons and Lovers*.

"Are you going through Reno?" Gene asks.

"Yeah, man. Long way through the desert. But shorter overall."

"You play the bongo drums?"

The man guffaws and puts his book down. "Yeah, man. I play the bongo drums." He picks up the drums, places them between his knees, and strikes them a few times, evoking high and low tones. "Everybody plays the bongo drums. But to really *play* them, you know what you need?" He leans closer to Gene and cups his hand beside his mouth. "You need the *secret mystical rhythm.*" He strikes the drums a few more times, then chuckles and puts them aside.

"Can I see?" Gene asks.

The guy looks up curiously. "You never seen bongo drums? I thought everybody had them."

"I never had the chance." The guy hands them over. Gene sits down and puts them between his knees. "Like this, or the other way?"

"Big one on the right, that's the way most cats do it."

Gene strikes the drums with his hands but manages only a flapping sound.

"No, man, like this." The guy squats in front of Gene. "Hit the edge of the drum head with this part of your hand, like you're gonna slap somebody. Keep your hand fairly stiff. Then it'll sing." He demonstrates.

Gene tries again, does a little better, then laughs and returns the drums. "I guess I don't have the secret rhythm yet."

"You got to smoke some tea, really," the guy confides, sitting down again. "Then you get the secret mystical rhythm."

"Oh yeah," Gene says. He knows tea means marijuana and isn't about to let on that he's never actually smoked or even seen any. "So... Are you a beatnik?"

The guy laughs. "Yeah, man, and I got the bongo drums to prove it. No, really, I just brought these along on a little hiking trip. For entertainment. It's not like I drag them around all the time."

"Where'd you go hiking? The Sierra Nevada?"

"No, out in the desert some. Kind of late in the year to do it, but I went up in the mountains where it's cooler. There's an abandoned mine shack up there I know about. I go up there every year or so. Then at night, the stars! Man! And when there's a moon, it's like daylight out there. I go hiking at night sometimes, it's so bright. Only thing you got to watch for is abandoned mineshafts."

"Wow." Gene sits there for a bit and then can't contain himself any longer. "So, did you ever read *The Dharma Bums?*"

The guy laughs. "Now I get it. You read all about beatniks in Jack Kerouac and now you finally meet one."

"Yeah, that's about it," Gene says. "I've been in Las Vegas all summer and you're the first one I met."

"Well, I'm the last one, too, and I'm about to go. This place is good for gambling and getting sunburned and that's it. There's no culture whatsoever, and the girls are squares. I'm going to San Francisco and cool off and relax."

"You have friends there?"

"Yeah. You?"

"No, I don't know anybody there. I just figure it has to be cooler than Las Vegas."

"It's that, man, in more ways than one. Well, here, to keep your spirits up until you go to San Francisco, let me officially bestow on you, as the outgoing holder of the office, the official title of Only Beatnik in Las Vegas. Here are your bongo drums. Play, and discover the secret mystical rhythm." And the guy holds out the drums to Gene, who laughs.

"I'm not kidding," the guy says. "I'm leaving, you're staying. You read *The Dharma Bums*, man. There's some real wisdom there. Now that you got your bongos, you're the coolest guy in Las Vegas."

"Well," Gene says. "Are you really giving these to me?"

"Yeah, man, they're not expensive. I mean, to tell you the truth, these are really cheap. I got them in Juarez. But they make a sound. They're better than nothing. Here, take 'em."

"Gosh, this is really neat of you."

"Don't say 'neat,' man. It makes you sound like Cubby on the Mousketeers."

"Well, anyway, thank you."

"You're welcome. Now go and beatify Las Vegas. That's what beat means, man. It's not beat like beat-up or beaten-down. It's beat as in beatific, as in beatify, as in beatitudes."

"Right," Gene nods, goggle-eyed.

The guy laughs as he waves Gene goodbye. "Be cool, man."

Gene wanders out onto the street holding the bongos under his arm. He knows the guy was laughing at him, but he still gave him the bongo drums, and a sort of blessing.

That night, as the sun sets, Gene sits on a pile of lumber in the pool construction area and gives the bongos a try. The sky is still yellow in the west after 9:00, though a month into summer the days are already beginning to shorten. A taxi pulls into the driveway, but Gene stays put. Jaime can handle the guests, now that Gene has convinced him to reduce his hostility to mere sullenness. Gene watches as Jaime deals with the guest. It never occurred to him while he was working there: at night, anyone can see in, as if it were a fishbowl or a cage at the zoo. Sitting only a few feet away, slapping at the cheap bongos, Gene feels invisible and free.

He really should leave. But there's the matter of telling Dolores and her father. He doesn't want to look bad in their eyes, and he especially doesn't want to hurt Dolores, but the only thing that will stop her from being disappointed in him is for him to become twice the worker and twice the boyfriend they expect him to be. And he knows he just doesn't have it in him.

July staggers to an end. The pool is completed, they add blue-and-white striped poolside furniture, and one blazing day, the new sign is installed. The whole family gathers as workers remove the faded yellow and green CACTUS MOTEL sign with its saguaro. Gene watches this operation sadly. He'd always liked the sign.

Then they hoist into place the new brown and blue MOTEL DOLORES sign, with the smiling image supposedly of Dolores, though it looks more like the lady on the Sunmaid Raisins box.

After a crane lowers the sign into place and the workers bolt it down, Gene takes pictures of the family in front of the sign, using their Brownie. Dolores and her father, then with both her parents, then with her brothers, then with everybody. Finally Sanchez says, in a somewhat grudging tone, as if in an afterthought, "All right, Gene, now you and Dolores." Later, in an impromptu party in the still vacant owner's apartment, Sanchez draws Gene aside.

"Señor Gene, I know you are a nice young man. But we now need to make some decisions. Tonight Jaime will take care of the motel. You and I are going to have a summit meeting. Like Nixon and Khruschev."

2

Sanchez picks him up around 7:00, long before sunset but after the clientele has started arriving. Driving the family's faded red pickup truck, Sanchez stops in the driveway and comes in. "The sign isn't on," he says.

"The sun's still out," Gene explains.

"Turn it on anyway. I want people to know we're open."

Gene flicks the switch and the sign with its dubious likeness of Dolores bursts into life. You can hardly tell it's illuminated in the

317

sunlight, but it will look nice in the dusk. He pauses at the door and turns to Jaime standing stiffly behind the counter. "Good luck, Jaime," he says. "Don't be mean to the guests, all right?"

Jaime grimaces.

They drive to the Sanchez's neighborhood and pull up in the parking lot of a pink stucco restaurant. They sit on a side patio amid men in work shirts and blue jeans. Sanchez orders for them, and the waitress brings two schooners of beer. "To Motel Dolores," Gene says, before his host can say anything.

Sanchez acquiesces. He takes a big sip, then says, "Gene, a month has gone by. You've been working with Jaime, and you do okay for a young man. But as far as I can tell, you're getting nowhere with Dolores."

Gene coughs. "She isn't giving me much chance," he says. As the days have ticked by, she's become ever more friendly and efficient in the office. The sagging chairs have been replaced, and a potted plant now sits hopefully in the corner. A few new, plastic-covered pieces of furniture sit in the owner's apartment, waiting for occupants—either Dolores and Gene, or Jaime and his wife and kid.

"You are the man," Sanchez says gravely. "You must take charge. She has already given you a chance, now you need to finish the job. Like construction. Once you start a job, you finish." Sanchez elaborates on this theme until the food comes. He uses examples from the courtships of Juan and Jaime for their wives; Juan, it seems, had to build a house single-handedly for his fiancée's family before they would consent to let him wed their daughter. "You have it easy," Sanchez smiles, shaking his head. "Or maybe not so easy. I know my daughter, she's hard-headed. You have to capture both her heart and her head, you see?"

Gene sees. Given the encouragement of his host and a quantity of beer, the final conquest of Dolores starts to sound like a valiant deed to be undertaken. Gene must work as hard at wooing Dolores as he does installing copper pipe. Then someday his story will take its place alongside that of Juan and Jaime in Sanchez's store of anecdotes.

"I love Dolores," he assures her father, his right hand wrapped around the handle of the beer glass. "I'll make her love me. Just give me a few more weeks."

"Good," Sanchez says. Then, dropping his pleasant expression, he adds, "But end of August—that's it."

* * *

3

After Kennedy wins the nomination, I head home, and there I hole up for several days. I don't have any gigs until those Catskills engagements. No filming, no TV appearances, no recording dates. Just a lot of time sitting next to the pool, trying not to drink so much, at least before sundown, and brooding, of course. About the way Lucy looked and sounded on that one night during the convention. The way she disappeared with those sharks. About Frank barking at me on the phone the next morning about how wild and uninhibited she was, such that both he and Kennedy thought she would go for a three-way.

One of the things I think is: If this were some romantic movie—if there ever could be a romantic movie in which presidential candidates and top-ten singers exchange girlfriends with mobsters, and the president's brother-in-law prances across a stage in blackface to score points with redneck crackers—then Lucy, finally fed up with being treated like a common whore, would quit the whole thing, fly back to L.A., and wind up on my doorstep in a taxi. We'd have a tearful reunion, and discover how much we regretted not winding up together. Then I'd quit Hollywood, we'd move back to New York, and I'd make a decent living doing Borsht Belt resorts, bar mitzvahs and the occasional TV shot. Both of us free of Frank Sinatra and Jack Kennedy and their machinations.

But when the time comes for me to fly off to Grosinger's, and she still hasn't shown up, I have to quit kidding myself.

I spend much of the next month in New York, mostly in the Catskills. Philly got me the gig at the Bottom Line, as well as a few other nightclubs where comics are the main attraction. With these new guys around like Newhart and Cosby these so-called comedy clubs are getting to be an established thing. This, too, has me thinking more about moving back to New York. In fact, the longer I'm there, the more it seems like the right thing to do.

On the other hand, it's damned hot. When I get back to L.A. in the middle of August, it's about 75 degrees at 1:00 in the afternoon, not 95. I drop my suitcases in the foyer, go upstairs and change out of my clothes, and jump in the pool. Ah—it would be hard to give this up. Let's see, if I lived in New York I guess I could swim in the pool at the 92nd St. Y.

There's also a message from Philly. He says Frank wants to talk to me.

I've a good mind to tell Frank to go to hell. But then, what the heck. My stock in this town can't go much lower. Maybe I can at least have the pleasure of telling him off. Now that would be something.

I find myself in Puccini on a smoggy late morning when the air looks like it's something that's been scraped off the bottom of someone's shoe.

Frank stands up when he sees me approach his table. I know something's up because ordinarily I would never get that kind of treatment. He's all smiles, and he grabs my elbows by way of greeting me, like we were two heads of state posing for the photographers. "Bobby, Bobby! Still alive and kickin', I see."

"Somebody say I'm dead?" I reply, unamused.

"No, of course not. I just meant it's been a while since I've seen you. I've got something for you I think you'll be interested in. Sit down. What ya been up to?"

"Just got back from a few weeks working in the Catskills."

"The Borsht Belt! Boy, sometimes I envy you guys. No matter how old you get, you've got a sure thing, two weeks at Chutzmann's or whatever it is."

"Yeah. The Catskills resorts are our own little social security system. But you got one too. Called Las Vegas."

"Ha! That's right. And now—whatever Mr. Blaine wants, Jimmy, it's on the house. You want to eat lunch?"

"I never turn down a free meal. It's a long time til the next gig at Grosinger's."

"Never mind that. I've got something you're going to love. This is on the Q.T. You know the Cal-Neva?"

"Sure, I opened for Judy Garland there in May, or June maybe it was."

"Right, of course. Well, it's not public knowledge yet, so don't spread it around, but Hank and I and Mickey are buying the joint."

Mickey is his lawyer, I know. This news is no big surprise, since Frank already has a share of the Sands in Vegas. "No kiddin'. You're developing a real empire."

"It's a great property, I tell you, Bobby. Terrific for families—a completely different environment than Vegas. You know, someday you ought to think about investing in a casino resort."

"Maybe a little out of my league, but thanks for the thought."

"Well, anyway, I didn't drag you here just to tell you about my business deal. Here's the thing. Hank is going to be booking the joint and I want you to be a regular attraction."

"Yeah? Thanks, Frank." I remain calm; I know he's going to spring something on me, another favor of some kind.

"And I don't mean just m.c.-ing. Not at all. And I don't even mean just opening. I want you to headline the main room there, several times a year. And you know that's going to raise your stock in Vegas as well, not to mention Reno."

Where you wouldn't be caught dead playing, I add silently.

"Now we're going to announce the sale this week, and I'm going to be playing there for the next ten days," Frank goes on. "Just to kick things off. Dean is going to join me up there, and Peter, and it's going to be like the Summit. I want you there, too.

"We open on Friday. Tomorrow I'm taking out big ads in the L.A. and Frisco and Vegas and Reno papers. I'm betting people will drop what they're doing and beat it up there, just like they did this winter for Vegas."

"Well, you can count on me, Frank. And thank you. As you said, it can only raise my stock. That will be great." Deadpan all the way.

"I'm glad, Bobby. You did a lot for me over the past couple months and I want you to know how much I appreciate it."

"I did it out of friendship, Frank."

"Of course you did. And even though I'm able to show my appreciation in a concrete way, I'm doing it completely out of friendship with you."

"Thank you, Frank." The bullshit is rising over my eyebrows.

The waiter brings our drinks and a plate of canapés. "Try some of these, it's something new we're trying," Frank urges, ever the entrepreneur. "So, let me just ask you, you gonna be driving up to Tahoe?"

"Well, you know, I hate to fly," I say. "But like you say, it's only a couple of days away. I'd have to leave on Thursday just to get up there by Friday night."

"What happened to that kid you had driving you? You know how to get hold of him?"

"Yeah, I guess so. He's in Vegas now. I ran into him up there a couple months ago."

"Call him up. Get him to help you drive. You have to go through Vegas anyway."

"Okay, but... Well, yeah. Sure," I say, a little confused, wondering why he's being so insistent. "You need a car to get up to Tahoe once you fly to Reno anyway, so... sure."

"There's just something I wonder if you could do on the way."

Ah, here it comes. "On the way?" I echo, in as pleasant a tone as I can manage.

"Yeah. It's a little bit of a side trip, but... not that much. You know Marilyn is out there making that cowboy picture with Gable and Monty. *The Misfits.* I don't know what you've heard, but I've been keeping tabs on it. It ain't going that well."

"Is that right?"

"Marilyn's a little... sensitive. A little high strung. This is just between you and me," he cautions me, leaning forward, as if everyone didn't know that Monroe is famously temperamental. "Her marriage to that writer Arthur Miller isn't going so good."

"No?" I say in the same neutral tone.

"She's being treated for... you know. Depression. Neuroses."

"Oh."

"She's a pill popper, you know. And they're probably a little too much for her to handle. So she's started showing up late to the set. Last couple days she hasn't shown up at all. Just sits in her hotel room in Reno talking to her acting coach. Some New York combination acting coach and headshrinker. Poor kid," Frank concludes, shaking his head. He puts his hand around his cocktail glass and regards the liquor there.

"Hmm," I say, to let Frank know I'm still listening. But he just sits there morosely, contemplating the state of Marilyn Monroe.

Finally I break the silence with the only words he wants to hear. "So Frank, is there anything I can do to help?"

He looks up from the glass. "Yes, Bobby. You can. Here's what I'd like you to do. The kid needs a rest. And I'd like to bring her up to the lodge."

"The Cal-Neva," I say, still not getting it.

"Right. But I don't want to attract too much attention. And I've got a million things to do up there to prepare for the opening weekend. So what I want you to do is go to Reno, to the Mapes Hotel. Pick her up and bring her up to the lodge. It's only an hour's drive up the mountain, maybe a little more."

"Okay..." I say. "Is that it?"

"Yeah. We'll take good care of her there."

I'll bet they will. "She's not a load of laundry, Frank. What makes you think she'll go with me?"

"I'll fix it, don't worry about that. I'll arrange it while you're on your way up. Just pick her up, bring her up there, and then for the next ten days you can relax, everything will be taken care of. You'll have a suite, and every night we'll be killing 'em in the main room. How's that sound?" he says, like he's talking to a kid about a fishing trip.

"Um... That sounds great, Frank. Anything I can do to help."

"That's fine."

"I'll have Philly, my agent, call Hank about the other bookings you mentioned."

"Other bookings. Right, of course. Thanks, Bobby. You're a dependable guy."

He glances around the restaurant, ready to move on to the next thing. But something about him saying I'm a dependable guy makes me stop him. I'll be a dependable guy, but if I let this slide, he'll take me for granted for the rest of my life. "Frank," I say.

"Uh, yeah Bobby?"

"Actually there's something I wanted to talk to you about."

"Yeah, sure." I can tell he's a little impatient, but I've just agreed to drive nine hundred miles for him, so he waits to hear what I have to say.

"Last month, during the convention. Things got a little hectic there and something happened that I didn't get a chance to talk to you about. But I thought you ought to know. I consider myself your friend, and I hope you consider me your friend. Because it's the kind of thing that only friends can talk about."

"Yeah, Bobby, what is it?" I've never had a heart-to-heart with him, and he sounds a little surprised.

"You remember that on the first official night of the convention, I think it was, I had dinner with you and Jack Kennedy and a number of others. And I brought a lady along."

"Yeah?"

"I don't want to make a federal case out of it, but I want to make sure it's clear who I mean, because I actually did that twice, once in Palm Springs and once in L.A. And I'm talking about the time in L.A. when I brought along a lady named Lucy Rolens. Yellow dress, black hair, very classy dame. Not like the kid in Palm Springs. A cut above."

"Yeah, Bobby, I remember. Is something wrong?"

"I don't know why I'm telling you this, but I think I have to. Anyway, here goes. That lady turned out to be someone I knew some time ago. I met her at the end of the war when she was about 20 years old, and I was in radio in New York. And we went together. For a few years, actually. It wouldn't be stretching things to say that, for more than a year or two back in the late 40s, she was my fiancé.

"Then, unfortunately, things didn't work out between us, and we broke up, and I didn't see her again until that night last month."

"Is that so?"

"It was quite a shock, let me tell you. Now I know you didn't know this about her—you didn't know that... she was to me like... well, maybe you had someone once whom you carried a torch for. It was like that with me."

I'm acutely aware that I'm on thin ice. I know very well—everybody knows—that Frank sure did have someone he carried a torch for, for years: Ava Gardner. Her memory is so sacrosanct to him that even by making a comparison between her and anyone else, I'm risking offending him seriously. I hold my breath, waiting for some reaction from him.

His face takes on a grave expression. "I see," he says finally. And he says it in a quiet, warm way that tells me he hasn't gotten sore, that he isn't going to tell me to go to hell and cut me off for years, the way he has done at various times with, for example, Sammy and Peter. Instead, he accepts the comparison. Now feeling more confident, I go on.

"So you can imagine what a shock it was to me to have to pick her up and bring her to that dinner, and watch her go off with you and Jack like she was some kind of... of call girl. And even though I got a chance to talk to her, and sure enough I find out she's changed and maybe isn't quite as high on a pedestal as I had put her—still, it was a real shock. You know, I hadn't seen her in something like twelve years, and to me, she was still that sort of... beautiful girl. And to just hand her off to someone like that... it still hurt.

"Anyway, Frank, I don't know why I felt like I had to tell you that. I don't want you to think I'm sore at you. I know you didn't know. But... well, there it is. Now it's off my chest and we can forget about it."

"No, Bobby, you shouldn't forget about it," Frank says. "I know exactly what you mean. Someone like that, who always has a place in your heart—don't forget about it. You should have said something."

"No, no," I say.

"No, really. Because you're right, I didn't know. And there's no way I could have known."

"Absolutely not, Frank."

"But Bobby, I want you to know that I understand. I realize... that you made a sacrifice that night. And you did it for the greater good."

Now this whole time, part of me is watching us have this conversation. That part can't quite believe I'm saying these things, or that Frank is sympathetic rather than enraged. But since Frank has decided to be sympathetic, to permit me even to draw comparisons between Lucy and his sainted Ava, that same part of me wants to press the matter just a little bit. For the advantage. And so I find myself saying:

"I did it because you asked me to, Frank. Your word is as good as... Your word is all I need."

Do I hear my voice tremble a little? Am I playing it that good? He puts a hand on my shoulder. "Bobby... Bobby, if there's anything I can do to show you how much I appreciate that, just name it."

"Frank, I would never presume. I just want you to know that I'll always be available when you need me. Like this thing with Marilyn... No questions asked."

"Thank you, Bobby," he says with heartfelt gravity. "That means a lot to me."

When I walk out of Puccini that afternoon, I've sweated all the way through my suit. Even on stage I don't sweat that much.

Chapter 22

1

Gene and Jaime paint signs reading NEW POOL! REMODELED ROOMS! FAMILIES WELCOME! They attach them to the lower portion of the motel's new sign. To Gene's amazement, tourists begin showing up, one or two families every night, and whether through coincidence, or through the influence of the newly painted exterior, or the presence of kids in the pool, the pimps and whores start behaving themselves. One night Gene and Jaime are treated to the sight of Moira and her honey— the former clad in a dark-blue one-piece, the honey wearing a cheerful yellow bikini—taking a dip in the pool after their last customers have departed. Gene thinks Jaime's going to have a fit, but he tells him that the women aren't bothering anyone and that the one "family" staying there that night has retired long before.

Sanchez Senior stops by every few nights to check on his new acquisition. One night he finds Gene standing quietly at the foot of the driveway watching the last rays of light disappear in the western sky. Parking the pickup by the pool, Sanchez comes walking back down the driveway to join him.

"Beautiful, eh, Señor Gene?" Gene turns and sees that the owner is waving proudly at the flashing MOTEL DOLORES sign, not the sunset. "How's business tonight?"

"Okay for a Monday."

"The cars there, they are 'good' guests? Good, good. Soon the parking lot will be filled. You know what that means? All tourists, all families. No one arriving in taxis with whores. That day we will celebrate."

He tries to think of something positive to tell Sanchez about his campaign for Dolores' heart. He did take Dolores to a movie, but she maintained the same friendly distance she has affected lately in the motel office. Even her kiss was merely polite. He reports the movie date to her father, exaggerating Dolores' emotional response. Gene feels he can't exaggerate too much; Sanchez might have already asked her version of events. And how much can a young man tell a girl's father, anyway? Even if Dolores were to permit it, he can't exactly tell her father he copped a feel, but how else is he supposed to measure his progress?

Sanchez is unimpressed with Gene's account, tells him he must try harder. "You cannot impress a girl by taking her only to a movie," he says. "Now that Jaime can run the front desk, you can see Dolores in the evening, and come back here together. We have furniture now in the apartment, she can spend the night there." But what might they do in the evening? "See a show," Sanchez says patiently. "Dinah Shore, Debbie Reynolds."

They walk up the driveway together. "By the way, I want you and Jaime to remodel number 8. A real remodel this time. Can you move into another room—say, number 4?"

"The shower isn't finished there yet."

Sanchez shrugs. "So finish it. Meanwhile there are many showers here, just find one. It won't be for long, right?"

"Um... right." One way or another, it won't be for long.

They go inside. "How is business, Jaime?" Sanchez asks in English.

"Business is fine," Jaime replies correctly. "We have two rooms with good guests and seven rooms with bad guests." They're using Gustafson's classifications; the "bad" guests are the hookers and their ilk.

"Very well. Listen, Gene and Jaime, I want you to start charging the bad guests three dollars more a night."

Gene can't believe his ears. "Are you sure? That's almost as much as they charge someplace like a Holiday Inn."

Sanchez shrugs. "If they wish, they can go to another motel. If that means we have empty rooms, then we can remodel them. We must raise the reputation of this place, Gene. Having these whores and... so on is bad for business."

"They *are* the business," Gene argues.

"Not anymore. Families are our business. Tourists. Jaime told me the whores are now swimming in the pool. That's not why we have a pool, it's for little children, not these..." Sanchez makes a sour face.

Gene grips the edge of the counter, the way some of the guests used to when they were drunk or simply felt like they were drowning in their circumstances and needed something to hold onto. "Even so, you can't have different rates for different kinds of people. It's the same as charging a different rate for... Well, excuse me for saying this, but suppose you went to a motel and they said, 'We don't want Mexicans here, so you have to pay three dollars more than anybody else?'"

"Gene," Sanchez says patiently, "you don't understand. To charge a Negro or a Mexican extra is discrimination because they have no choice. These ladies have a choice to live a decent life or to be a filthy whore. Besides, it's my business." He looks at Gene appraisingly. "Dolores told me you had developed, *como se dice,* a soft spot for the bad guests. She says you are a kind person, not just to the whores, but even to the old son of a bitch who owned this place. Very well. But now it's time to get down to business, as they say. The good guests are tourists—they have cars. If no car, then three dollars more."

"I don't have a car," Gene points out.

Sanchez laughs. "Ha! That's right. You don't have a car—and you don't pay anything! You're a very bad guest!"

Gene packs up his things and moves up the walkway from number 8 to number 4. He's accumulated a surprisingly wide scattering of books, plastic souvenir drinking cups with the names of casinos, stained work clothes—almost all his clothes have become work clothes. Instead of spreading his possessions around number 4, Gene keeps them packed. As Sanchez said, one way or another he won't be there for long.

Gene still has his suit, and he wears it Friday to pick up Dolores. The taxi driver can't stop talking about the transformation of the motel. "You figure on a change in clientele, huh? A real family place. Real nice, yeah. And ya got a pool an' all. Oh, that's gonna be great for the tourists."

Dolores is costumed in a gown that looks like it was rented from a formal wear shop, and her parents insist on taking pictures of the two of them. Gene smiles gamely until he climbs into the cab with her. It could be worse—Sanchez could have lent them his pickup truck. They hold hands in the warm back seat, the wind whistling in the slightly opened windows. "I feel like it's our high school prom," Gene says.

She isn't interested. "My father says you don't like the idea of charging the bad guests more."

"That's right, I don't think it's fair."

She rests her chin in her palm, looking out the side window. "Fair or not, he always gets his way. I know, it's the principle of the thing, but he doesn't care about that. And I think you're being a little silly too."

"After what happened to us at the Riviera? It's the same thing."

"It is not, and besides, you're stupid to defend the whores and bums. Nobody cares about them. And don't tell me you do."

"Oh, I'm stupid now?"

She just shakes her head and shuts up, as if it's no use talking sense to him. They arrive at the Desert Inn. As they enter the lobby, Gene looks around for Mr. Lee, priest and bellboy, but doesn't see him.

They both get carded at the door of the Painted Desert Room, but the staff doesn't give Dolores a second look. During the summer, the resorts caved in to pressure from the local NAACP, and the accommodations up and down the strip are now wide-open, racially. The agreement was splashed across the front page of the local paper, and the resorts now include in their advertisements some fine print about how *everyone* is welcome. Were they staying at the place, they could even go swimming.

With the scant influence afforded by Gene's tip to the maitre d, they're seated toward a back corner. Doris Day, the trouper, projects so that every senior citizen and half-drunk Kentuckian can hear "Que Sera, Sera." "Hey," Gene whispers. "It's Spanish."

She just arches her eyebrows and regards the show stolidly, seemingly determined to have neither a good nor a bad time.

When the house lights come up, and room empties out, Gene says, "We can stop in the lounge for a drink before we go back."

"We've had drinks," she retorts. She's had one, he's had two.

He turns his palms upward. "I'm just trying to be nice. What is the matter with you?"

"This is just a big act with you," she says. "A big act, you and my father, taking me out on the town. Is it supposed to impress me?"

"What will?" he bursts out. "He buys you a motel and names it after you. I treat you as nicely as I can—nicer than any one else does."

"So I should be grateful. Well, I am grateful, Gene; my family's treated me all right. You, I think I was wrong about you. I thought you were different. But my father's got you wrapped around his finger now. You're just doing what he wants. I've had enough of that." She starts digging furiously in her purse. "And all you can talk about is how nice you are. Fine, but it's not enough. You talking about getting married—I must have been crazy to listen to you."

"What are you doing?"

"I have to find a dollar for the restroom lady. Since you did me the favor of taking me to this palace. You know what, they wouldn't give me a job either." She snaps her purse shut and stands up. "I'll meet you at the restrooms in five minutes. Then I'm going home."

2

Dolores doesn't come to the motel on Saturday, or Sunday, or Monday. Gene puts in as much time as he can completing the job on the shower in number 4. When he needs to use a shower himself, he uses the owner's apartment.

Jaime never mentions Dolores, and their father doesn't show his face either. Gene is left in a suspended state, jockeying with shower plumbing, taking walks under the crushing August sun. In the evening he sits in the office with Jaime and the television, as the sign outside flashes DOLORES, DOLORES, DOLORES.

Though he finishes the last plumbing job, his malaise has returned—not a physical lassitude this time, but an emotional one. Aside from the hollow feeling, he just feels blank. One afternoon he goes downtown. He's not getting anywhere with Dolores, so her father will probably ask him soon to leave. Perhaps it's time for him to buy a bus ticket to San Francisco. He shuffles through the heat, wearing, as sun protection, a souvenir Hoover Dam cowboy hat left behind by a motel guest.

The bus station is not air-conditioned, and with the smells from diesel exhaust, the restrooms, and two stinking winos passed out in the waiting room, it's more uncomfortable in there than outside. He walks around the waiting room once, twice; he can't gather the will to buy a ticket. He walks outside again, the almost vertical sun providing no shadow.

The Buddhist temple where he met Mr. Lee is only a few blocks away. Gene finds himself drawn to walk by almost every time he goes downtown. But the door is always locked. He could call the man on the phone again, but he wouldn't know what to say. What's he going to tell the priest—his girlfriend troubles? That he hasn't really understood anything in the book Mr. Lee gave him?

A city bus passes with Eastern Ave. on its destination sign. The thought strikes him that the nursing home where Karl stowed his old man is on Eastern. He runs after the bus, climbs aboard, and asks the driver if he knows of a nursing home on his route.

Thirty minutes later Gene is walking into the Sunny Days Retirement Home. The first thing that strikes him is the sharp smell of old people. He asks for Gustafson, says he was driving through town and realized his grandfather was here, and he'd like to see him.

"Oh, yes, he arrived about two months ago," the receptionist says. "You know he had a stroke soon after."

"Um, yes," Gene says. "How is he now?"

"He's stable. But, you know, he can't speak anymore."

Gene looks around the reception area. An old man and woman have come up to the counter to listen in. The man is wearing a neatly pressed brown plaid shirt, but she is wearing only a nightgown. They listen to the conversation with quizzical expressions. Behind them on the wall is a bulletin board with the date and the information that "Today's weather is: SUNNY" spelled out in faded pink construction paper, like a kindergarten.

The receptionist gives Gene the room number, and as he turns to go, the old woman touches his shoulder. "You look just like my dead brother Sam," she says. Wide-eyed, Gene can only smile and nod and turn away.

He finds Gustafson propped up in a chair, not in his room, but in an alcove at the end of a long hall. Across from him is a high window through which can be seen the branches of a tree, but the old man looks straight ahead at the opposite wall a few feet away. The only sounds are of a distant television soap opera and an old woman's voice crying out behind a closed door.

Gene sits on the bench across from Gustafson and tries to get his attention. When Gene speaks his name, the old man's eyes focus on his visitor but show no sign of recognition. "How are you, Mr. Gustafson—I mean, granddad?" Gene asks. "Are you feeling all right?" Gustafson appears shrunken in every way. His white hair, now yellowed, hangs limply over the tops of his ears; his shoulders seem no wider than a boy's. He doesn't cough, or curse, or complain. He just sits there.

"The motel was sold," Gene tells him. "You remember Dolores, the housekeeper? The maid?" he says. "Her family bought it, and they named it after her. They changed the name and put up a new sign that says Motel Dolores. You should see it."

No reaction, unless the shift of Gustafson's eyes, from Gene's face to the empty place on the bench beside him, means anything.

"I wanted to see you because, um, I guess I'm leaving town. I should have visited you before, I know. Are you okay? You look all right... I mean, are you in pain?"

Gene realizes he sounds a little silly babbling to the old man who can't respond. But now that he's here it seems like it would be mean of him to just get up and leave. Maybe Gustafson understands and simply can't respond, or maybe he is merely aware of the simple fact of someone spending a few moments with him.

The silence between them is filled with the buzzing television and the muffled cries of distress. The cries are so regular that Gene supposes they don't signify an emergency, but are simply part of the background noise of the place, a fact of life there. This is so unnerving that he begins speaking again simply to drown it out.

"This seems like a pretty nice place," he says, trying to be pleasant. The only response is the faraway call for help. "At least it's air-conditioned," he adds.

Gustafson's attention seems to be drifting downward, toward the floor, if his eyes are any indication.

"I guess you feel like you got a pretty lousy deal," Gene says. "You got sent out to Las Vegas, stuck with a crummy motel in a bad location, with guests you hated, and then things just got worse. Your son came and put you in here."

Gustafson's eyes return to Gene's face.

"Karl, your son?" Gene asks. There is no additional flicker of recognition, but he seems to have the old man's attention. "Maybe you didn't get along very well. I never even saw his address written down on anything, or a Christmas card from him... I'm sorry he stuck you down here," Gene says. "It's not a very nice place—Las Vegas, I mean. It must be a hundred and ten outside. You should have gotten an air conditioner for your apartment!" Gene laughs suddenly. "That's the first thing I got after... after you moved in here," he concludes lamely.

The old man in the brown shirt has found his way down the hall to their alcove. "Hello!" he says brightly, bending over to them. "Are you coming for Thanksgiving?"

Gene looks up at him. "That's a few months away yet," he says.

"Oh, okay, I didn't know. Well, you be sure and come." Gene thanks him. "There's a turkey dinner!" the man adds. He sits down on the bench next to Gene and goes on talking, first on turkey dinners, then other subjects. Gustafson's gaze drops off to the side again. Then the man in the brown shirt, as if he's forgotten why he's there, abruptly stands up and walks off.

Gene looks at Gustafson. "Well, goodbye, Mr. Gustafson. I'm sorry you don't have your motel anymore, but... I guess you didn't really enjoy it anyway. And now you're here. Well..." He reaches forward and gently pats the old man on the shoulder. "At least I finally learned a little about plumbing," Gene says, trying to joke a little. The old man's eyes go up to Gene's face, and he watches as Gene waves and walks away down the hall.

3

Dolores finally comes back to the motel on Wednesday.

"I've got work to do," she says when Gene walks into the office. She's just putting down her purse and sunglasses.

"So I thought," he says. She ignores him and pulls out the registration slips from the last several days, opens the ledger and starts making notes on a pad.

"I finished the work in number 4," he says, passing along the one piece of information she could possibly be interested in.

"So Jaime told me," she says, not looking up. "I told him to start renting it out again."

"But I'm in number 4," Gene says.

"Oh yeah. Well, I don't know then. It's up to you."

Gene stands there for a minute, wondering what this means, watching Dolores scribble. Her pencil scratches across the pad, and the air conditioner labors in the next room.

"Don't just stand there watching me," she says. "Go clean the pool or something."

"I cleaned it this morning."

"Then figure out something else, just go, I don't want you here."

He leaves the office, going out onto the little walkway. Even in the shade, the heat envelops him. He sits down on the single step, crossing his arms on his knees, looking across to the pool with its big umbrella. No one uses the pool until the evening, and then the sun is low enough (though no cooler) as to make the umbrella almost useless. Its blue panels, alternating with white, already seem to be fading. He walks across the driveway and sits down in its shade. It's not yet noon, the day's chlorine is supposedly not yet fully mixed, so he can't even go swimming. He can't go downtown; he just went there Monday and only walked around restlessly before going to see Gustafson—and he doesn't want to see the old man again and have another one-way conversation. Now he can't even sit in the motel office. I must be an idiot to stay for a minute longer, he thinks. There's nothing here. She doesn't want me.

But he can't face going into his hot, stuffy room, or making any kind of movement at all in the blazing sun. He keeps to the shade of the umbrella for more than an hour, brooding.

When he can stand it no longer, he goes back into the office. "I need to use the phone."

She points to it, head down. He calls a cab, gives the address. "The bus station," he says. His bags are already packed; he never unpacked after moving into number 4. After he hangs up, he stands looking at her still scribbling.

"Listen," he says. "I'm going. A taxi's coming in twenty minutes. I'm going to the bus station and leaving town."

She puts down her pencil and looks up at him. To his amazement, tears are in her eyes. "You're leaving," she echoes.

He isn't sure if it's a question or an answer. "It's pretty obvious there's no place for me here if you don't want me," he says. "I tried but I just can't figure out how we can love each other. There's only one little slot for me in the big plan of your life, and if I don't fit that little slot, then it's like you can't even stand the sight of me." He's surprised to hear himself speaking these words, but even more surprised by her reaction. She should be getting angry, but she just sniffles.

"Where you going?"

"San Francisco, I guess. It'll be cooler there, if anything," he says.

She snorts. "I don't understand you," she says. "You leave L.A. and come up here. Now you leave here and go down there again. I don't understand what you're doing."

"Do you care? Maybe I just want to see the country."

"Maybe you're just playing with your life."

Startled by this pronouncement, he doesn't respond.

"You don't understand about real life, Gene. You think you want to be a beatnik or hobo or something—that there's something cool about playing like a poor person. People aren't poor because it's fun; they're poor because they don't have any choice. And if they did have a choice, they'd be glad to have a job like you fixing toilets. To be poor means you don't have any choice at all.

"But you're not poor, you have a choice. You can join the union, help build hotels and houses and stuff. You don't have to see the country. You know when you see the country? When you're forty years old and you have a car and a family, then you go to Disneyland and the Grand Canyon. And it's called a vacation. But you want your whole life to be a vacation." She wipes her eyes with a kleenex. "Damn, that sun's bright," she says, turning away from the front window, which the sun has just begun to strike.

"Maybe I'll want all that someday, but not yet," Gene says. "I'll travel around a month or two, or a year or two, and eventually I'll go back to college and finish up. It's all right to do that when you're twenty or twenty-five or thirty. It doesn't matter."

"Back to Harvard," Dolores says sarcastically.

"Yeah, sure," he says. She just looks at him sharply. "Well, actually, I never went to Harvard. Just, uh, a community college in St. Louis. For a year or so."

"Oh Gene, I know you never went to Harvard. You think I believed all that stuff you told me? Come on."

He swallows. No sense in arguing now. "Well. Maybe I will go to Harvard, some day."

"Maybe I'll marry Rock Hudson," she counters.

"I could," he protests.

"I could too!" she says. "But what you *are* doing is leaving town to be a beatnik. That's not a requirement for Harvard as far as I know. Don't you smile at me. I don't think you're funny. This is not a joke. I think you're stupid. And one more thing: I'm glad you're going. It won't work for you to just hang around here, wishing you were jumping on a freight train or something. Either you're part of the family or you aren't."

"I didn't realize it was a package deal with you."

"Now you know. You better get your stuff."

He gets his stuff and puts it in front of the office, then goes inside for the last time. She's sitting at the counter, staring into the glare on the front window. Before he can say anything, the taxi pulls up.

"Bye Dolores," he says.

She presses her lips together firmly, takes a deep breath, then turns to him and thrusts her hand across the counter. A little startled, he shakes her hand.

"Goodbye, Gene," she says. "Thanks for working here."

He's reluctant to let go of her hand, but she pulls it back.

"Now go," she says.

"I'll send you an address to send my pay for the last few days," he mumbles.

She picks up her pencil and looks down at her notepad again. "Fine, just go," she says, waving blindly at him.

At the station, he buys a bus ticket and joins the motley collection of passengers waiting for their ride out of town. Fingering his ticket, he waits, half sad, half excited. Not as sad as Sal Paradise, in *On the Road*, when he parts with Terry. Maybe he still isn't enough of a Buddhist yet, or maybe Kerouac was just more sensitive.

Because he feels he should, he thinks of Dolores and the ending of their chance together and his chance at a settled life in Las Vegas. When he thinks that tomorrow morning he'll be in San Francisco, walking the same streets as Kerouac, it still seems like a dream.

He's sitting there lost in thought when a pair of feet skid to a stop in front of him and a familiar voice calls out, "There you are!"

Gene looks up and sees a somewhat rumpled Bobby Blaine, his eyes red and his shirt damp with sweat. "Mr. Blaine!"

"I must have just caught you. I went by the motel—they said you were here."

Gene smiles. "Going to San Francisco."

"Well, listen. I'll get you there. But first I need you to help me drive up to Reno. We got an errand to do up there, then I'll make sure you get to San Francisco. A hundred bucks, whattaya say?"

Gene shrugs and stands up. "Okay with me. I'll cash in my ticket."

"No time for that," Bobby says, picking up Gene's suitcase. "We have to get going. Is this all you got? Just that other bag? Where's your suit?"

"In here. What's the big rush?"

"I'll tell you in the car. Come on, it's around the side. Man, I'm glad I caught you. I'm beat. You drive."

Chapter 23

1

We pull out of the bus station parking lot and I point the way to the highway that leads to Reno. "You know, I tried to find you at that motel you were staying at, but at first I couldn't even find the place. They got a new name."

"Right," Gino says. "Dolores' family bought it."

"Who?"

"The girl at the motel just now? She's the one I took swimming at the Riviera, remember? Her family bought it."

"Oh yeah, of course. I had the feeling you were kind of sweet on her. What happened?"

"I was, but... This summer I found myself doing stuff I never expected to—never wanted to. Plumbing, carpentry, running the motel—it was like, nobody ever expected me to *do* anything before, aside from finish school. Plumbing and stuff is the opposite of what I ever wanted to do. But when I had to do it, I did."

I nod. "Sink or swim."

"But it's not like a prison sentence, is it? Just because I figured out how to fix a toilet doesn't mean I have to do it for the rest of my life."

"I guess not. Some people get themselves stuck. But unless you got a girl pregnant, seems to me you're pretty free."

"Free," he echoes. "What I did this summer, working at the motel—even though it wasn't nice all the time, even though it was kind of a... seedy place—that was real life, you know. When I was doing that, I was really in the middle of life. But life's out here too—maybe not out here," he corrects himself, indicating the darkening desert. "But New York, San Francisco, Mexico, Tangiers..."

"Tangiers? What?"

"Oh, it's in The Dharma Bums."

"Still want to be Jack Kerouac, huh? Well, then you definitely don't want to get stuck fixing toilets in Las Vegas."

"That's what I figured."

"You turn 21 yet?" He nods. "Then you did the right thing. You're too young to settle down. Footloose and fancy free, that's what you should be. And now what are you going to do in San Francisco?"

"I don't know. I honestly don't. Maybe work in another motel... I don't know. But how about telling me what we're going to Reno for."

So I tell Gino how the *Make Nice* part turned into my silly gig "interviewing" the people on the set of a different movie entirely; my gigs in New York, and my pal Feldman, and Schlain the ever-optimistic Broadway producer, as well as my gigs in the Catskills.

"I know it sounds like I've got all these things going," I conclude. "But when you put it all together, you know what? There's no movies in there. I'm kind of afraid my movie career is turning out to be a real bust. If Frank ever makes another movie, maybe he'll throw me a little part, you know... But otherwise, bupkis."

I leave out everything about Lucy, and the convention, except that he says he saw me on TV singing the anthem. And I leave out most of what I know about Marilyn Monroe; when I finally get around to the reason we're going to Reno, I say only that she needs a break and we're taking her up to Tahoe for a little vacation.

The bare desert stretches out before us—400 miles of it. "Oh, man," I sigh. "It just hit me how tired I am. I drove all day long from L.A. I've hardly been out of this car for the last twelve hours. I think I'm gonna try to sleep a little. Just keep going on 95. I'll wake up long before we get anywhere near Reno."

And with that, I slump into my seat. I feel my eyes burning behind my closed lids, and hear the hum of the car. I let that drown out my agonies over what's left of my career, and fall into a deep, weary sleep.

I sleep for a few hours, waking up once in the darkness as the frantic lights of a small-town casino flash by. Then I shift my position and fall back to sleep.

The motion of the car wakes me up more than an hour later. I can taste sleep in my mouth. I stretch and say, "What time is it? Where are we?"

"It's almost nine o'clock. I think the next place is Tonapah."

"We can stop there and get something to eat. It's really the only decent-sized town in the whole trip. How's the road? Not too bad, is it?"

"About like the one to Vegas. Even less traffic."

I yawn. "So what do you know about being a beatnik?"

"Not much," he laughs, and tells me how he was given bongo drums by some guy. "But I think I found out something about that Buddhism stuff that Kerouac talks about. Did you know they have all these little stories that are like parables—you know what I mean? Like in the Bible, the story of the Good Samaritan, for example?"

"Sort of. You have to remember I'm a Jew and we don't read all the parts about Christ."

"Oh yeah. Well, it's a story intended to teach a moral. Turns out the Buddhists are full of them. Let me tell you the one about the cat." And he tells me this crazy story about cutting a cat in half and a man who puts his shoes on his head.

"Is that the punch line? I don't get it."

"Me either. They're all like that," he laughs. "But seriously—I think I did get one thing straight. I went to see this Buddhist guy one day. I went to their temple, or whatever it is, and this Chinese guy talked to me a little and gave me the book with all the stories in it. And he said to remember one thing. 'Be kind to people.'"

"That's it? I don't need a Buddhist to tell me that. That's in every religion."

"I guess so. But it came in handy when I was working at the motel. You should have seen the characters who came there. It was a pretty... I don't know, dicey place. Almost all prostitutes, pimps, johns... drug addicts, drunks, you name it. And I was the only one working there all summer. So I had to deal with all these people. And it helped."

"How did it help?"

"Because the reason you should be kind to people is that everyone suffers. Not just the people I dealt with, although it was easy to see with them. I mean these people were so down and out. But it's not just them. You and me, and everybody, everybody suffers. So because everyone suffers, you should be kind to people—that's what it's about, Buddhism, I think."

"Okay. Well, great. There, that's Tonapah—those lights. Let's find someplace to eat."

2

We reach Reno in the middle of the night; it took more than eight hours from Vegas. I have Gino drive to the Mapes Hotel, an impressive twelve-story pile unlike the newer Vegas "resorts" which are kind of spread out, motel-style. It's more like a traditional big hotel—big for Nevada, anyway. Next door there's a parking lot, and I talk the sleepy guy who's working there into washing my car for twenty bucks, while we go inside for a few hours. I don't want to give Marilyn Monroe a ride in a dirty car.

Inside, I slip the night man a twenty and tell him my buddy and I need a shower and does he have a room we can use. He has the bellboy bring us to a room on the second floor where the bed is messed up but just about everything else is intact. I knew they'd have a few of those. I get in the shower first, and when I come out, Gino's asleep in the arm chair. I let him sleep.

A couple hours later we're sitting in the coffee shop having breakfast. We're both wearing our suits, like we're going to a business meeting. I explain more about the movie that's being shot out in the desert, and how for a week filming has virtually stopped because Marilyn hasn't come out of her hotel room, and how we're taking her up to Tahoe for "a break." I don't mention Frank's request and how Frank now owns the Cal-Neva, because it all sounds a little creepy. I can't see explaining to Gino how I'm doing just one more favor for Frank Sinatra, delivering another kind of package for him.

"How do you feel?" I ask.

"I'm okay," he says, with the same serious expression.

"Something bothering you?"

He puts down his fork and rests his elbows on the table. "I guess I'm a little anxious about moving to San Francisco and all," he says.

"Yesterday I was excited about it. But this morning I wonder if I'm doing the right thing."

"Maybe you're just tired from the drive."

"Yeah... While I was asleep upstairs, I had a dream I was back at the motel. I couldn't find the key, or when I found the key I couldn't find the registration pad because we've thrown out the old ones, and then I was in the room—the motel room... then... I forget."

"You know how dreams are. Forget about it. You're gonna have a terrific time in Frisco."

"Sure," he replies, but his expression remains clouded. He takes another sip of coffee. He's become a real coffee drinker.

It's almost 9:00 a.m. "Let's get going. Go get the car and wait in front of the hotel. Give this sawbuck to the head bellman and explain you're waiting for me—don't mention the other party."

He nods and goes off, and I go to the front desk. By now a different clerk is there. I give him my name and a pseudonym for the party I'm picking up. He looks down at a piece of paper on his desk, then back up to me. "Suite 614, Mr. Blaine."

I don't know what I expected—armed guards, frantic bobby soxers, horny cowboys, or what—but the corridors on the sixth floor are as empty and quiet as those in my own house. There's no watchman, no studio publicists running interference, no assistant directors breaking down the door to get the star to come to the set. Just a long hallway with gold-colored carpet and identical orange-painted doors. 614 has a doorbell, so I ring it.

A Negro woman whom I take to be a servant or assistant—I heard somewhere that Monroe has someone who cooks for her and does her ironing and so forth—opens the door. I quietly identify myself, and she silently nods and admits me. She has the weary, defeated expression of a menial employee whose employer is of a mind to prevent her from doing her job properly.

I find myself in a living room. The woman who opened the door goes into an adjacent room and speaks softly. "Mr. Blaine is here."

"Thank you, Hazel," a voice comes—not Marilyn's. The voice goes on, "I'll be back in just a moment, Marilyn darling."

"Who is it?" I can hear Marilyn asking. "It's not someone from the picture, is it? Didn't you tell them I can't work today?"

"Yes, dear. It's someone else. Just a moment and I'll be right back."

A small, pudgy woman comes frowning into the living room. Her severe expression, black dress and ugly shoes make her look like an Italian widow.

"Mr. Blaine," she says with a trace of a Russian accent, "I want you to understand I am against this. I am against this completely."

"Yes ma'am," I say. "And you are..."

"Mrs. Strasberg. I'm Marilyn's coach."

I remember now—the acting coach from New York, the wife of the famous Actors Studio head. They say she makes more on Marilyn's pictures than Marilyn herself does.

She goes on, "I'm responsible for her, you understand. Her work, her whole professional presentation as an actress, is my responsibility."

"Yes, well..." I say. "We're all concerned for her... her well-being. And I was told she has arranged to take a short break from work. She won't be gone long, I don't think."

"Yes, yes," she says, turning away and waving her hand dismissively. "You were told... I was told..." She turns back to me and speaks in a low voice: "I know what's going on here. Things have been taken out of our control. So that no one knows who's pulling the strings. But don't think you're pulling the wool over anyone's eyes."

"No ma'am," I answer.

"The only way, the only way, for Miss Monroe to finish this picture," she says, in a normal voice, "is for me to continue working with her."

"That's... Well, you took the words out of my mouth. I have nothing to do with that."

"No, of course not," she says with sarcasm.

No wonder Frank didn't want to deal with this. "Is Miss Monroe ready?" I venture.

Suddenly Marilyn appears at the doorway. She hardly resembles the glittering celebrity who presented herself at Frank's side on the second night of the convention. Her face is without makeup, and though her hair has been brushed, it lacks any specific form, hanging dully in a ponytail. Her expression is vacantly anxious; her lips parted, as if she has opened her mouth to speak but can't think of what she meant to say. Without the artifice of makeup and character, she looks ordinary, as if she could be any southern California housewife having a nervous breakdown.

She doesn't say anything, so I say, "Miss Monroe, I'm Bobby Blaine. I met you last month in L.A. I'm a friend of Frank."

"Hello," she replies, not really looking at me. I can't be sure whether she remembers me or not. But that's a feeling I'm used to.

"Frank asked me," I go on, "to bring you up to Tahoe for a little rest. He has a place up there where you can get some peace and quiet."

Marilyn is still looking past me, to Strasberg, I realize. "Paula?" she says, her voice sounding small. "I'm sorry. I want to do the work, I do."

"Yes, dear," Strasberg says. Since Marilyn is clearly looking to her for permission, I'm relieved to see she isn't digging in her heels.

"I promise I'll come back all ready," Marilyn says. "And I'll do such a good job and you and Lee will be proud of me."

"Yes, dear," Strasberg says again. "We *are* proud of you."

"You are? Oh, that's so good. Thank you for that, Paula. Thank you."

The maid brings out a small bag. I'm thankful for the interruption, since I can't stand people groveling. That's funny, isn't it?

"If you're ready, then," I say.

"Yes, I guess I am." The maid helps Marilyn don a head scarf and a pair of sunglasses. "Goodbye, Hazel. I'll be back in a few days, I guess. Goodbye, Paula."

"Take care, dear," says Strasberg, with a defeated air.

I pick up the bag and offer my arm to Marilyn. "Oh, thank you," she whispers. The maid opens the door and we go out, padding silently down the corridor. There's a mirror in the elevator lobby. Marilyn avoids looking in it, but catching her reflection I notice she looks more like a movie star with the scarf and sunglasses than without them. I guess she'd feel more vulnerable without them, so I don't say anything. I guide her into the elevator and we go downstairs and cross the lobby. Heads turn, but no one approaches us.

Gino is sitting in the car waiting; the hotel doorman opens the door and helps Marilyn into the car. I get in the back seat with her, and we take off.

So far, so good. The worst must be over—I wasn't sure how it was going to play out with the Strasberg woman, but apparently Frank or somebody talked to her before I got there. She was obviously capable of more fight than that.

We pass through the morning streets of Reno. I give Gino the directions I got back at the hotel, and soon we're on a road leading to the mountains that loom just west of the town.

"This isn't the way to the set," Marilyn says.

"No, hon, we're not taking you to the set," I say. "We're going up to Tahoe, remember?"

"Sure," she says uncertainly.

"We're taking you up to the Cal-Neva. Frank Sinatra owns the place now, and he's invited you up there."

"Up to Frank."

"That's right."

"It's all up to Frank," she says, with a trace of irony. "You can always leave it up to him."

"He'll take good care of you," I say.

She sighs. "Oh, yes. Well, what about the picture? What about Marilyn?"

"You'll spend a few days up there and then you'll go back to Reno and finish the picture."

She falls silent for a few minutes , then says, "Will you take me back?"

"If you want me to," I say. "When you're ready to get back to work."

"But when?" she insists.

That's what everyone wants to know, I think to myself. "Well, today is Friday. Maybe by Monday or so," I say. "If you're not back Monday they can shoot around you, and then you'll be back on Tuesday."

"But who'll be back on Tuesday?" she says. "Will it be *Marilyn Monroe*," she says, lowering her voice, *"in her greatest dramatic role*—or will it be Marilyn Monroe the..." she trails off, then shoots me a complicit look and twirls her finger next to her ear in the comic sign for "crazy."

"You know what I mean?" she laughs. She takes off her sunglasses, and even without makeup, there's a trace of the familiar Marilyn present again. "Marilyn the majestic! Marilyn the magnificent! Marilyn the *mama mia!* Or Marilyn the morose, Marilyn the mope... Marilyn the *meshugeneh!"* She makes the "crazy" sign again, then frames her face with her hands. "What do you see?"

I blurt out the first thing that crosses my mind. "Marilyn the Mesopotamian," I say.

She gives me a comic dumbfounded look. "Mesopotamian! Are you kidding me? I know what that means. That's a Persian! You lie like a rug!" she chortles. "A Persian rug! Oh man, that's rich. Now I know who you are. You're Bobby Blaine the comedian." I notice Gino giving me an ironic glance in the mirror. "You're funny. I saw you once in Reno."

"Oh really?"

"Yeah, a few years ago. When we were shooting *Bus Stop.* I saw you right there at the Mapes."

"Sure, sure," I say.

The car begins swinging up the mountain on a curving road. Gino takes it smooth, but the motion of the car distracts her. "Oh, I shouldn't be going away," she says, fretful again.

"Just for a rest," I say, trying to soothe her.

"I guess so," she says doubtfully. "Oh, I'm sure everyone thinks I'm crazy. Marilyn the Mental Patient. Well, you know what my doctor says?" she asks, suddenly chipper. "Dr. Greenson. 'They must think I'm crazy sometimes,' I told him. You know what he said? 'Everybody's a psychiatrist now.' Wasn't that funny? He's right. Everybody's crazy now, and everybody's a psychiatrist."

Her mood shifts again, like the car turning this way, that way, winding up the mountain. "I trust him," she says. "And that's the most important thing. How many people do you trust, Bobby?" Before I can answer, she goes on, "I trust very few. I trust Dr. Greenson, and Paula, and of course Lee, and ..." she considers. "There's Joe, my ex-husband. He could be very strict, but he always had my best interests at heart. He'd die for me, Bobby. He said that once, and I believe him. So I have to trust him, because he trusts me with his life.

"I used to trust Mr. Huston," she says, referring to the director of *The Misfits.* "He was an artist. He was going to, I don't know what, save my reputation." She laughs bitterly. "All these artists. They're all so serious. Well, Joe was serious, too, but he didn't have any pretensions. I'll take a ballplayer over an artist any day. Wouldn't you?"

"If I had to make the choice," I say, trying to lighten things, "I might pick the ballplayer. But if he's on the Dodgers, forget it."

"Oh, he's not on the Dodgers," she says. "Is it the Yankees? I think that's it."

"Right," I say.

"They've been shooting around me for a week," she says, veering suddenly to another thought. "They must think I'm horrible! A prima donna! And all I want to do is do a good job and be a pro. That's what the cameraman on my last picture said at the wrap party. He said, 'Miss Monroe, it's been a pleasure to work with you, and much to my pleasure you're a pro to work with.' Isn't that a nice compliment? It means a lot to me when somebody in the crew compliments me. That's why the Academy Awards are such an honor. Because you're elected by your peers. The cameramen vote for the cameramen, and the directors vote for the directors, and everybody votes for best picture. And if you win an Oscar, you're in like Flynn. I hope I'll win one someday."

"I'm sure you will," I say in all seriousness. She looks dubious. "Maybe for this picture," I suggest.

"I don't know," she says. "At first I was so excited. But then Mr. Huston started treating me like just some... I don't know what. And he insisted on shooting when I didn't have my motivation interiorized. I trusted him and now I don't trust him anymore.

"That's why I can't bear to go to the set anymore. They've been shooting around me for so long that I know, from now on, every single shot is going to have me in it. And I just won't look right. I prepared and prepared and I hardly have a chance to act. I mean, all he wants is me running here! Me running there! And reaction shots! Supposedly Gable and Monty and Eli Wallach have just done something terrific, and me and Thelma are just supposed to *react*. But by the time I get to the set, they've already done whatever it is I'm supposed to be reacting to. So I just have to go out there and..." She gives a take, staring out into space, open-mouthed with amazement. "Like that. And one of the reasons I was so excited about this picture is that he said they would film it in sequence. Well, I can't figure out the sequence if I'm not there."

"Well..." I say. "You're right, in those cases an actor has no choice but to trust the director."

"Oh, you've got another choice," she says. "You can always *not show up.*"

I really don't know what to say now. We've got at least an hour of driving to go, crawling up this mountain. We enter an evergreen forest and big firs are all around us, but we pass an open spot where the view down to the desert floor is surprising and spectacular. The view lasts a moment, but Marilyn stops talking and takes it in.

"That's the way it is," she says, shaking her head. "You're deep in the woods and then for just a moment you get a clear view. Then it's back into the shadows."

"Tell me something," I say, to try to get her to talk about something else. "You're shooting way out there in the desert, aren't you? What's it like out there?"

"Very empty," she says, "but somehow grand at the same time. Hot, of course. You think it's hot under studio lights, you ought to try being out on the desert in the middle of the day running around pretending to be a cowboy. In a wig." She shakes her head. "That's one thing I won't miss."

She speaks as if the role is a thing of the past. I could try changing the subject again, but I don't want to sound like I'm interviewing her. But then she does it for me.

"Bobby, are you married?"

"Me? No."

"Because I think you'd make someone a wonderful husband. All you've done is listen to me. You're very patient."

"Thank you. But it's no problem for me. It's a pleasure to get to know you."

She chuckles. "You ought to see me on a better day."

"I saw you that night before the convention, last month," I say. "You looked marvelous."

"Oh, yes," she says. "I remember, you and Peter Lawford were there, and then you had to go away and do something political. While the politician stayed for dinner. Maybe you should have been the one to stay, and let him do his own politicking."

"Maybe so, for all the good it did him. We were supposed to talk the Mississippi people into voting for him, but they voted for Johnson anyway. But since you mention him, tell me about Jack Kennedy."

"Oh, Jack." She smiles, but there's something a little off about the smile. "He's very nice. And very smart. I think he'll make a wonderful president."

"I'll bet he listened to you."

She laughs shortly, and not entirely pleasantly. "In a way."

"You know, in a sense, you're kind of like a president or head of state," I say. "All the most famous people want to meet you. You met Khruschev, didn't you?"

"Yes."

"And the Queen of England, when you were over there working with Chaplin?"

"Yes, that's right. It's true, everyone wants to meet me. Cabbages and kings."

"Ha, good one."

"That *was* funny, wasn't it? It just popped out. Oh, sometimes I'm just convinced everybody in the world is all right. And then I could be all right. But other times I'm convinced that everybody is suffering. At least, that's all I see."

I notice Gino glancing back in the mirror.

"But the worst of all is when I'm convinced that everyone *thinks* they're happy, but all I see is how unhappy they are. Then I feel so alone.

"But I shouldn't think about that. I should think positively. I'll tell you my best day. My best day on this picture so far. We were shooting in Reno, before we went out to the desert. I shouldn't have been so hard on them before, because we really *are* shooting in sequence, at least we started out that way... And I don't know what it was about this day. It was about the fifth day of shooting, and everything was going well. I could see the crew and everyone was just working together perfectly, and you know, there's a feeling you get. It's almost like a lucky feeling, like everything's going to go well.

"So the scene was in a bar, and we shot it down the street from the hotel. Arthur and Paula and I would walk down to the set in the morning, and the people were very nice. I mean the regular people of the town. You could see they were very happy to have this film there, we did *Bus Stop* here a few years ago and they seemed happy to have us back, but they were very respectful. Everyone treated me like just another person, but so politely. I was stopped and asked for an autograph only rarely, and once someone said to me, 'Miss Monroe, if someone asks you for an autograph, you can be sure they're not from Reno, because we understand you don't want to be bothered like that.' Just imagine!

"And on this particular morning we were walking down to the set, just a couple of blocks away, and the mountains were so clear, and it was such a beautiful day. People were smiling at me, and then I started noticing something. I saw a man on the sidewalk, wearing a western shirt and a cowboy hat. It was a beautiful white cowboy hat, I think that's why he caught my attention. And he was walking along with such an anxious expression on his face. Then he saw me, and he smiled politely, and tipped his hat, and kept on going. He was twenty feet away. And after he nodded to me, his face took on that look of concern again.

"Well, then I started to notice—I told you a minute ago that sometimes everyone seems to me to be unhappy? It was a little like that. I was walking down the street and it was like I could suddenly see into people's hearts. And some were sad and anxious like that man, and some were carefree, but the most amazing thing is that everyone was smiling and saying good morning, but I could see the real person underneath. It was the most amazing feeling. And I remember thinking, 'This is really good for my craft!'"

I laugh, and she laughs too.

"Yes, it's funny to think that, but just imagine, if you could read people like that, what insight you could have into their characters, and if you could bring that understanding to your work, then think how wonderful your acting would be."

"True, true."

"So this went on, but as I say it was only a couple of blocks, and yet in those couple of blocks I must have seen a hundred people, and if you asked me on the spot, I could have told you the life story of each one. Then I got to the set, and there was the crew, so professional, and as they were putting on my makeup I tried to keep that feeling. Boy, was I on top of the world. But then we got on with the business of shooting, and I got caught up in it, of course, and I forgot about this strange experience.

"But later in the day, it was during the lunch break, and instead of going back to the hotel we stayed and ate lunch with everyone else. And someone had left a paddle ball sitting there. Do you know what I'm talking about? It's like a ping-pong paddle, with a little rubber ball attached on a rubber band. And the object is to hit the ball so that it bounces right back to you and you hit it again. Well, I got going on that thing, and I was just the champ. Once I counted up to seventy-six before I missed.

"Mr. Huston came along and started watching me, and he laughed and said to Arthur, 'Arthur, we've got to get this in the picture!' So Arthur talked to him and me and Clark, and before I knew it, we had this little scene where I make a bet with Clark—I mean my character makes a bet with his character—that I can do fifty. And they shot it all in one take, and in long shot, so that the audience can see that I'm really doing it. And everyone's counting! 'One! Two! Three! Four!' all the way up to fifty. And I make it, and everyone cheers. Then there's a little bit of dialogue, and Mr. Huston yells 'Cut,' and everyone cheered again.

"And Clark took me in his arms and said how wonderful it was, and Mr. Huston said so too, and Arthur, and everyone was so excited, just because of this little paddle ball!

"So while they were setting up the next shot, I wandered out to the street to catch my breath, and I stood just outside with some of the crew.

"While we were chatting, I saw across the street the same man, in the white cowboy hat. And he looked even sadder than ever. He didn't even pay me any attention this time, he just walked up the sidewalk on the other side of the street. There was a casino across the way. And a man came out of that casino, and he must have just won a jackpot. He was so happy and excited. And he saw the man in the cowboy hat, and called 'Hey Jim! Come here and let a little luck rub off on you!' Then the other man shook his hand and smiled and nodded while his friend told him all about his jackpot or whatever had just happened, and I could see he was happy about his friend, *and* still sad, and that he had this happiness and sadness all together at the same time. And they went into the casino together.

"Then I suddenly realized that I'm the same way, that everyone's the same way. We're all happy and sad, all at the same time, and even if we feel all one way, at one time or the other — we still have these feelings inside us all the time. Like it almost doesn't matter if we *think* we're happy or we're sad. We're happy *and* we're sad, all at the same time."

Marilyn leans back and catches her breath. She licks her lips, and I can see her eyes are bright. If I look closely, I can see the brightness is not entirely natural. I figure what just happened is that the benzedrine or whatever finally kicked in. But I'll take it over the way she was when the trip started.

I glance over at Gino and notice that he, on the other hand, looks absolutely thunderstruck. Like he's just heard the deepest piece of wisdom ever.

"How you doing, Gino? Keep your eye on the road, okay?" I say, my tone light.

He swallows. "Yes, Mr. Blaine. It's about fifteen more miles."

"Okay."

Marilyn is looking out the window. "Oh, there's an overlook. Can we stop a minute?"

"Sure." I guess she isn't going to try to jump. "Stop up there a minute, Gino. Let's see the view."

We pull into a wide spot where there are a couple other cars stopped. Retying her scarf and putting her sunglasses back on, Marilyn steps from the car, assisted by Gino. I go around and offer her my arm, noticing that behind her back, he is looking in wonder at his own hand, which briefly had held the hand of Marilyn Monroe. Then he shuts the door and waits by the car.

Marilyn and I stand at a railing above a bare slope that leads down into the trees. Two thousand feet below us, the desert stretches off into the distance. She shields her eyes from the sun and squints. "Somewhere out there is the set," she says, waggling her hand vaguely. "It's a long way from town—takes almost two hours to get there. I'll bet you can see it on a clear day."

"Maybe so."

"What do you think, Bobby?" she says. "Are you happy, or sad, or both at the same time?"

"I guess I've got a little of both, just like you say. Maybe the trick is not to let either one get out of hand."

"Sure," she says. Her voice is completely normal now, neither excited nor morose. "That's what I wanted, with Arthur," she adds. "After this picture, and maybe one more, I was going to quit, and we were going out to Long Island where his place is, and he could write and I would be perfectly happy just walking up and down the beach, going back to have lunch together, then doing whatever around the house needed to be done. Just a normal life."

"Sounds nice."

"Doesn't it? What's the matter with us, Bobby? Why can't we do that? Why do we have to be movie stars?"

"I dunno," I say, thinking, you can talk. "All I know is, once I got a taste of success, I just wanted success more and more. I still want it."

"You said you weren't married. Why not?"

"I had a girl once. A terrific woman. We almost got married. And then... we didn't."

"I'm sorry."

"Like you say, that's the sad part of the story, and it'll always stay with me. But I'm all right."

"Yes, you are. Take my advice, don't become any more successful than you are. It's really not worth it."

I chuckle and shrug. Maybe I'll find that out for myself.

We go back to the car. I let Gino have the pleasure of helping her back into the car. He's never gonna wash that hand.

Half an hour later, we pull up to the Cal-Neva. She waits in the car with Gino while I go in and see where they want to put her. A couple of hoods appear, standing as straight as if they've just been shocked with electricity. One of them goes off and comes back with a higher-up. I recognize him as one of the shady guys I saw at Puccini last month, the guy with the giant diamond ring.

"Bobby Blaine," he says, extending his hand. "Johnny Roselli. I'll take it from here."

"Hello," I say, trying to think of a way to stall for time. "Actually Frank told me he'd meet me himself."

"Frank's busy in a meeting. They sent me out to take care of things. Where's you-know-who?"

"In the car," I say. "Are you sure Frank can't come out himself? I'd feel a lot better just ... having him around when I... when..."

"When you deliver the package. Sure. But he's not available, like I said. So let's go get her." He and his minions push past me to the door. I hurry after them.

The car's right in front, so it's no mystery about which car is mine. Roselli bends over looking in the window. "Hello, sweetheart," he's saying. "Just come with me and everything will be taken care of."

I can see she looks pretty dubious.

"Come on, doll," he says. "You know me. Me and Moe and the boys. We saw you in Vegas a while back. You remember. We had a party together."

She spots me. "Bobby," she says, "Let's go."

I touch the thug's sleeve and say quietly, "C'mere a sec." Leading him a few feet away from the car, I say in a low voice, "She's pretty nervous about the whole thing. Why don't you let me handle getting her into her room? She trusts me."

He squints at me through his frog-like eyelids. "Why should she trust you and not me?"

"It's got nothing to do with you or me," I say. "But she knows me from having dinner and so forth. Just let me take care of it and I guarantee she'll be all right."

"Okay, pal, give it a shot."

"Where's she supposed to stay?"

"Cabin down there."

354

"Let me drive her down there. One of your guys can lead the way."

With a flick of his hand, the other two go over to a driveway on the side of the lodge and remove a chain that has a PRIVATE sign on it.

I get back into the car. "Follow those guys, Gino." I look over at Marilyn. She has a frightened look on her face. What do I tell her? That it's going to be all right?

From the parking lot, we descend fifty yards into the woods toward the lake and stop near a cabin. Gino gets out and opens her door.

She swallows, turns to me, and says, "I sure know how to pick 'em, don't I, Bobby?"

"Frank will be along soon, kid. Don't you worry, all right?"

"Sure, Bobby." She picks up her purse. "Like you said. Happy or sad, don't let either one get out of hand."

"Same to you, Marilyn."

She touches my hand, then climbs out and follows the two men up and into the cabin. Roselli is coming down the driveway, grinning. He doesn't say anything as he passes me, a predatory expression on his face. I get back into the car and Gino turns around carefully and heads back up to the entrance, then we park around the other side in a lot reserved for VIPs. Gino carries my luggage and follows me into the lobby.

I had honestly believed that Frank was trying to give Marilyn a few day's rest. I thought I was bringing her up here so he could hold her hand. I should have known it had something to do with him celebrating with his criminal buddies—who no doubt put up the money to buy the place. A form of payment from him to them.

Disgusting. Some favor I did.

The bellboys take the bags from Gino, and he stands there attentively.

"Well, Gino, your work is done," I say, forcing myself to be pleasant. "I have an engagement here for the next ten days. I'm afraid it would be a stretch to ask them to put you up for that long."

"Don't worry, I want to be going."

"Fine, fine. I appreciate your helping me with this..." I don't know how to finish the sentence—helping me with this what?

"Heck, it was an honor."

"The bus stop's down the road at the highway—we'll get somebody to give you a lift down there. Or you might hitch, like your buddy Kerouac." He looks at me, surprised. That idea never occurred to him, it seems. I guess despite plugging away all summer with the hoi polloi he's still a middle-class kid at heart. Thinks you go everywhere with a ticket. "So, what are you gonna do in Frisco?"

He looks off across the parking lot to the mountains. "You know, I spent plenty of nights at the motel looking out the window at the sunset, thinking that's where San Francisco is, off in that sunset by the ocean. That's where I wanted to be. But to tell you the truth, I really have no idea what it's like."

"Nice town," I say. "Nicer than L.A."

He's still looking at the mountains. "Those are the Sierras, right?"

"Sure. All around us."

"You notice that sign we passed on the highway, a few miles back? The summit. Everything downhill from there, no matter which direction you go. If you happen to run out of gas right at that spot, it doesn't matter—just point downhill one way or the other and you get where you're going." He nods to himself. "San Francisco this way... and on the other side, back to Las Vegas. Maybe, in a way, it doesn't matter."

"If you're starting to tell me there's no difference between Frisco and Vegas, you're nuts."

"In a way, in a way, maybe there isn't. Back there in Vegas I was stuck, sure, but I was also down there in the thick of things. Remember what she said, back there in the car on the way up?"

"Marilyn?"

"Remember her saying how suddenly she could read people, and could see they were happy and sad and suffering, all at the same time? It's like that."

"What is?"

"One moment where everything becomes clear. That's what I've needed."

"Don't we all. I don't want to make you feel bad, but frankly I think she was a little high."

He ignores me. "That's what the summit is. You're at the top and the road is laid out in front of you. But just for a minute, because then you choose."

Even though we're just standing in the parking lot, his eyes are focused elsewhere, like he really does see his future.

"Well, like I said, the road's over there." I notice he's still got his chauffeur suit on. "Look, you probably don't want to travel in your suit, whether you're hitchhiking or not. Why don't you come to my suite and change clothes? Take a shower if you want."

So we go to my room together, and he changes back out of his suit. While he's in the shower, I notice the bongo drums sitting in his suitcase. I go over and pick them up—just cheap tourist crap. Probably came from Mexico. I'll get his address and send him a real pair, in Frisco or wherever he ends up.

When he's all ready to go, I ask, "So, you know where you're going yet?"

He shrugs.

"Tell you what, I'll flip a coin. Heads, Frisco. Tails, back to Vegas." I reach into my pocket and pull out a silver dollar. They must have given it to me in change in Reno. "Call it," I say, flipping it into the air.

Before I have a chance to catch it, he reaches out and snatches it right out of the air. But then just holds it in his hand.

"Well, what's it gonna be?" I ask.

"I'm going to walk back there to the summit," he says. "A few miles back on the highway. Then I'll flip for it." He tucks the silver dollar in his pocket and shakes my hand. "Thanks for everything, Mr. Blaine."

And like that he's out the door.

Chapter 24

1

I try to catch a nap that day, but I'm too keyed up. The long drive and the exhausting morning of dealing with Marilyn have left me tired enough, but I can't stop thinking about what I've done to that woman. I lie on my bed and think, what are they going to do to that girl? That she probably won't even remember who it was that gave her a ride up here doesn't make any difference. I was involved.

The afternoon passes, and I get dressed and go backstage, ask for a light dinner to be brought to me, and wait for the others in the dressing room. Dean comes in first, speaks a few pleasantries, then sits down and reads the newspaper. Peter and Frank come by and say they want to eat. In the months since the Summit in Vegas, I have forgotten the primary rule of Camp Sinatra—to be ready for Frank whenever he is. Dean gets up, but I point to my half-eaten plate and they shrug and leave.

What the hell, I say to myself, sticking my fork in a piece of chicken. I drove all day and most of the night and then again this morning. And I have to go to work again in a little while. I'm resting.

A minute later, Frank sticks his head back in the door. "Bobby, you open," he says. "I want the audience to have a chance to see you on your own."

"Okay, Frank."

"Start at 8:30 and do thirty minutes, then introduce Sammy. Then stay out there, of course. From then on, it'll be like before. We'll be back before you go on, to work out a few things." Maybe so, maybe not. Frank imagines himself to be like a jazz musician who can just show up, unpack his axe, and start to blow. A rehearsal is a waste of time, and a set list is an annoyance, the sooner scrapped, the better. If we do work anything out, it's not worth the paper it's written on.

Sammy misses the family-style dinner, too. He comes in less than an hour before the show is scheduled to start, his tux over one shoulder, a drink in the other hand. He greets me warmly, but he doesn't seem to feel much like talking either. He looks half-sloshed, and chain-smokes faster than ever, but I want him to know I haven't forgotten our last talk.

"Sammy, how's May doing? Are you really going to hold off on your wedding?"

Sticking his sharp chin out in that way he has, as he lights another cigarette, he says, "This is the way it is, man. The election is November the eighth. We get married in New York on the thirteenth and Frank is my best man, puts a hundred people up in the Plaza, and buys every flower in the city for the reception. But if we get married one minute before the polls close, on the other hand, and I have about as much chance of ever working again in the states of Nevada, Illinois and New Jersey as Martin Luther King has of becoming the governor of Mississippi. Now which one would you choose?"

"Who's Martin Luther King?" I ask, just to let him know I'm not feeling sorry for him—though, of course, I am.

"You know who Martin is. He gonna free the slaves."

"Maybe you should get married by him."

"Him and the rabbi," Sammy says, shaking his three-inch Star of David so that it jangles against the rest of the stuff around his neck. "The rabbi can officiate, and Martin can preach. Ain't no rabbi can preach like a Negro, let me tell you that. Speaking as someone who's been on both sides of the fence."

"I'm supposed to open with thirty minutes of solo material, then introduce you. After that I got no idea."

"Maybe I'll sing a protest song. What do you think, Bobby—I should get a guitar and be like some of these folk singers. They get out there and sing union songs from the 30s and the audience mentally transposes everything to the 60s and thinks they're hip. What do you think?"

"I think you're a little stewed."

"Yeah, man, but can you see me? Like Burl Ives, only darker."

"Well, I'd pay to see it."

Frank and Dean and Peter come back and I attempt to impose a little order. On a sheet of paper I write down BOBBY—30. Then SAMMY. "How many songs does Sammy get, before you guys come on?"

"Two."

"One."

"A verse, half a chorus, then Frank comes on with a potted palm."

"Come on, you guys, give him a break. The audience wants to hear him sing."

"Sammy, you sing whatever you want."

"Notice Frank's still not promising to let him sing a full number."

"He can sing an opera for all I care. *Porgy and Bess,* start to finish."

"Jewish music written for Negroes."

"That's perfect for Sammy."

"Bobby's waiting for the opposite to happen, then he'll start his singing career."

"*Julius and Ethel*—an opera in two electrocutions."

Sammy breaks up. "An opera about the Rosenbergs! That's it, man. What'll they do for 'Ol' Man River'?"

"'Cry Me a River'—that's in Russia, right?"

"What?"

"Crimea—get it?"

"Crimea River. Yeah, man, that's in Russia." Sammy is dying. He doubles over in laughter and slides off the couch.

"Dean, pick Sammy up off the floor so we can get on with it."

"You better get out there, Bobby."

"There's no set list yet."

"Do thirty and bring out Sammy. We'll work out the rest."

"We'll write it on Frank's fly so you can read it," Peter says.

Frank stops laughing, shoots him a look, and the room freezes.

"That wasn't nice, Peter," Sammy says in a sing-sing voice.

"Sorry, old man. That didn't come out the way I wanted it to."

"Forget it. I'm going on stage. You guys figure it out."

"Wait, Bobby. Peter!"

"I apologize, Bobby. Sincerely. I don't know what got into me."

"It's all right. I accept, Peter. We're friends. It's all right, Frank."

Frank comes up to me. "There's somebody in the audience tonight who can float your boat, Bobby. So go out there and do the best show you've ever done." He claps me on the shoulder.

"Aye aye, captain." I leave the dressing room, find the stage manager, and give him the high sign.

For the first time in months, I don't do anything new, I don't improvise. Just tried and true material. But a lot of it's new this year, and in any case, the audience is so excited and happy to be here that they'd laugh if I blew my nose.

While I'm spieling, I scan the crowd. There are plenty of celebrities, agents and columnists here, of course. But it's the suits you don't recognize, the Hollywood executives and New York producers, the men who can give the go-ahead to a new project—that's who I'm trying to spot. I do notice Jack Kennedy's big head, two tables from the stage, sitting with Shirley MacLaine, Tony Curtis and a few other anthem singers. On the other side of the room, Roselli and Giancana and their ilk.

Marilyn is nowhere in sight.

The bandleader stands up after twenty-eight minutes, and I head into my home stretch, the fast, two-minute series of laughs, each topping the last, making the audience laugh harder and harder, until when I say "Thank you, ladies and gentlemen" they burst into happy applause.

I've done well. I haven't spotted the VIP, but whoever it is has seen my best. Now all I have to do is organize the next hour of chaos. "And now, ladies and gentlemen, direct from the Sands in Las Vegas, please give a warm welcome to Sammy Davis, Jr."

Okay, so the applause is louder for the beginning of Sammy's act than it was for the end of mine. Sammy's bigger. I can live with it.

I go offstage while Sammy does his opening number. Frank and Dean are nowhere in sight, so that's a sign they intend to let him work, for at least a while. I go back to the dressing room, expecting to see them there—but it's empty. I go back to the stage, and from the wings, in the middle of Sammy's second song, I see Frank, Dean and Peter, all wearing waiters' jackets and aprons and carrying trays of drinks, coming through the audience. They're setting drinks down on people's tables, taking people's drinks away from them and giving them to other people, and generally causing a commotion. Sammy bears it for a while and then breaks up laughing. Sighing, I go on stage and step up to the mic. "You'll have to excuse us, ladies and gentlemen. Frank just wanted to be positive everyone's having a good time."

2

After the show, I relax with a drink in the dressing room while the others mix with their friends. The adrenaline of performing has made me forget, temporarily, about Marilyn. An opera about the Rosenbergs. That's pretty good. I don't think the general public is ready for the joke, though. If I used it at Grosinger's, they'd skin me alive.

The assistant stage manager comes in and says Frank wants to see me out in the house.

Frank's sitting with Hank, Tony Curtis and Shirley MacLaine, and an anonymous man, no doubt the suit I'd been trying to spot earlier. Mister Big stands up and Frank introduces me. "Bobby, I want you to meet Robert Risikoff, the head of programming at ABC."

"Bobby, meet Bobby," Tony says, unnecessarily.

"Pleased to meet you. I hope you enjoyed the show."

"I certainly did, and you're just the man I want to see."

We sit down and Frank motions for a waiter to get me a drink.

"You were wonderful, Bobby," Shirley says.

"Just great," nods Tony.

"Did I see Kennedy out here before?" I ask.

"Yes, he enjoyed the show too. He's off meeting the public."

There's a short pause while everyone fills in mentally what the senator is probably doing at this minute. Frank and I must be the only ones who know who he's doing it with.

My drink arrives. "Well, Mr. Risikoff, what brings you out west?" I ask.

"You ever spent a summer in New York?" he says. "Compared to that, this place is paradise. Seventy-five degrees, ice cold water in the lake—Frank, you got yourself quite a place here."

"Me and Hank," Frank says, nodding at Hank, who smiles without saying anything. Them and certain other parties, I think.

"Congratulations, Frank," Shirley says. She seems to have dubbed herself party hostess for the table, taking it upon herself to say the most appropriate thing. We all raise our glasses to Frank.

"Thank you," he says. "But that's not going to be the big celebration tonight. Bobby, Mr. Risikoff has an idea I think you'll like."

"Bobby," he says. "We at ABC want to have a talk show, late night. It'll start out like the 'Tonight Show,' and then it'll get better. While they're screwing around over at NBC, trying to figure out who they want as their regular host the next time Jack Paar walks off the job, we want our show to be taking viewers away from them. Eventually, it'll be bigger, and people will say the 'Tonight Show' was the 50s, and our show will be the signature show of the 60s."

"Wonderful idea," I say. I figure he has me picked as the sidekick guy. A cold sweat breaks out on my forehead. Talk show sidekick has got to be the kiss of death. But how can I say no in front of Frank, who's obviously set all this up?

Risikoff says, "We want you to be the host."

It's like a thunderclap in my head. "Me?" is all I can say.

"Oh Bobby," Shirley cries. "Your own talk show!"

"That's terrific, Bobby," Tony chimes in.

"We'll call it 'The Bobby Blaine Show.' Or whatever you want. It'll be your show. You design it. You host it. You call the shots. You'll work with our best producers. And you can name your price."

My jaw actually does drop. "I don't know what to say—I'm stunned."

"Just say yes, Bobby," Frank smiles. He gives a signal and waiters appear with bottles of champagne.

"Mr. Risikoff, that's a wonderful, wonderful offer," I say. "You sure you got the right guy here?"

"So modest!" Frank cries. "Say yes." Dean and Peter and Sammy appear.

Someone shoves a glass of champagne into my hand. Frank is grinning like he's just made his son a partner at the family law firm. Certainly this is all his doing. Sometime between Tuesday and today he pulled all these strings, got the network guy to fly out here, and shook him down until he got what he wanted. For me.

"Well, Mr. Risikoff, I'll give it my best shot. My very best shot."

Everyone cheers and toasts me.

"You'll have the best talk show on television," I vow.

"Everyone!" Frank says. "You're looking at the guy who, in a year's time, is going to be the biggest star on TV. Phil Silvers, Steve Allen, Jack Paar, Jackie Gleason—They're all going to be looking up at Bobby. My pal."

Everyone cheers again.

I say thank you to everyone, and we all drink champagne, and the other fellows clap me on the back and say they'll be on my show the first week. Risikoff says he wants me back in New York the day after Labor Day to start planning the show, and it'll premiere in October.

For once, I stay in my seat celebrating with everyone else. Even if I weren't the center of attention, I don't think my legs would carry me three steps.

Hours later, undressing in my room at the lodge, the happy congratulations still ringing in my ears, I think, what did I do to deserve this? In Frank's estimation, that is. Was it the jockeying at the convention? Was it ferrying Marilyn? Was it my sob story about Lucy?

That must have been it. I went for broke with that story, and dared to compare her to Ava Gardner, and Frank bought it, the sentimental fool. And he, at the top of his power, opened his hand and out came riches.

Of course, the show will be a bust. There's only one "Tonight Show," and everyone already watches it. They've got their format down pat, and no matter who the host is, he'd have to be dead for anyone else to shake that audience loose and get them to watch me. I've got about as much chance as the French did in 1940.

What I can do is stretch it out as long as I can. A year and a half. Maybe two or even three years. Long enough, maybe, that people won't think of it as simply a flop. By the time I'm done, at least everybody will know my name.

I'll have to say goodbye to film roles, though. Except maybe in the lightest comedy. I'll always be that guy with the talk show—or the guy who *had* a talk show. The most I'll get after this is TV. A sitcom, maybe.

But what the hell. I'm forty-three. I can't sing, and my acting is hardly there. I have to face it—a TV talk show host is exactly what I should be.

I realize I should call Philly and tell him. The percentage on this will be a nice addition to his retirement fund.

But I'll do it in the morning, I decide as I slide into bed. My big chance won't evaporate overnight. There were too many witnesses.

I gratefully acknowledge Sara Miles, Christy Calame, Chris Carraher, Shannon O'Leary, Kevin Keating, Katia Noyes, Marilyn Jaye Lewis, and everyone who helped and encourage my work on this book. I'm also grateful to Holden Village and Bishop's Ranch, where I retreated to work.

Many of the scenes in this book were based on actual events of the period. Sinatra really did pull out of a film, written by the blacklisted writer Albert Maltz, due to pressure from Catholic officials. Sinatra's influence helped break the color barrier in Las Vegas. The Rat Pack and other Hollywood stars did sing the national anthem at the Democratic Convention, a Southern delegation jeered Sammy Davis Jr. during it, and according to one account, JFK and Sinatra dispatched Peter Lawford to charm the same group shortly after. These and other parallels between the book and accounts of real events are described on my website, www.toobeautiful.org/makenice.html.

www.ingramcontent.com/pod-product-compliance
Lightning Source LLC
Chambersburg PA
CBHW022144010726
47493CB00002B/331